# THAT GOLDEN SHORE

## A NOVEL BY J.D. KLEINKE

*For Laura, on this very special birthday. So glad we are so far family! Yours - JD.*

**BAYAMET BOOKS**

PORTLAND, OREGON
WWW.BAYAMETBOOKS.COM

# ALSO BY
# J.D. KLEINKE

### FICTION
*Catching Babies*
*Dudeville*

### NON-FICTION
*Oxymorons*
*Bleeding Edge*

**BAYAMET BOOKS**
www.bayametbooks.com
Portland, Oregon

Book design by Heidi Roux

ISBN13: 978-0-578-75439-0

First Bayamet Books Edition: February 2021

10  9  8  7  6  5  4  3  2  1

Printed in the United States of America

for Sam,
    *for showing me how to play the guitar*

for Reb Aryeh,
    *for showing me how to pray with the guitar*

and for Tasha,
    *for showing me how to sing without fear*

*Like an angel,*
  *Standing in a shaft of light,*
*Rising up to paradise,*
  *I know I'm gonna shine!*

"ESTIMATED PROPHET"
JOHN BARLOW & ROBERT WEIR

# SIDE **ONE**

# 1 | MYSTERY COVE

A wobble of temporary blacktop weaves across the golden rubble. Last January's storms, which dumped five years' worth of belated rain in two weeks, cleaved off half this mountain and swept whole chunks of this undulating section of Big Sur highway over the cliff and down to the ocean.

Even over the hum of the van's engine at my feet, I can hear the tide crashing on the rocks a hundred yards below as the road shoots out toward the edge for another look. Stripped of the dark green forest usually robing these great folds of mountain, the jagged hillside, caught in what looks like mid-tumble, gleams a garish yellow in the last of the day's sun.

This could be a wilder version of "Sunset Road," that mythic place Johnny made famous back in the '70s and has sung about 10,000 times since, the road *where your old life ends and your life new life bends.*

Johnny sings it every night, the encore of course, because that's what half of the audience came to hear. The stage lights come down, soften to pink and peach, like dusk falling over the small town at the end of the road, even though we're in some casino auditorium or state fair arena. Beers out, towels around our necks, and it's that last night around the campfire, everybody heading down their own sunset road. Even I, up there strapped into my bass and plugged into the boom of the PA, fall for it: there's that tug in my chest, like I'm sixteen again, falling in love with the girl I've never met, and my whole life is ahead of me.

This evening, the road north into Big Sur is my sunset road, the long way home after last night's gig with Johnny and the boys down south. A couple days of surf, sand, and sleep in my own bed, and then off to next week's gig with Amrita, a big yoga retreat up in Sonoma.

The sea-salt air blows through the open van and mixes with an old country blues rock jam, and I look over and there she is: Calafia. Her big blonde hair is a riotous mess in all this wind, whipping around to cover her face as if she were still dancing in front of the stage last night in that tie-dyed tank top. It spills down her shoulders, muscled from the gym and freckled and honeyed from the sun. As she pushes it from her face, the sun gleaming in those sapphire blue eyes, she just smiles at me, like she did through the whole show. And for today at least, that smile will be enough. We'll meander our way north up the coast in silence, far west of the freeway madness, hugging the coast.

The inky tarmac of the temporary roadway crawls up and over another crest in the slide path, a mound of raw yellow dirt like the tailings of a played-out gold mine. Straight down the cliffside to my left, another cove opens, a chaos of waves and scattering of emerald light, wind-carved trees climbing up the opposite cliffside through rainbow mist.

As the road turns back toward the mountain, I lean out to see if anyone is down there surfing, human or marine, looking for skinny black wetsuits or big brown humps. Nothing but a fingernail of empty beach, a waterfall shooting out from the cliff, more mist, more color.

Calafia smiles again, flashing perfect white teeth out of a faceful of sun, not at all the soaring coastal mountains up ahead, but at me, for how drunk I always get on this scenery, no matter how many times I drive through it.

The road slips into the first big fold of forested mountain, into a deep, shadowy crevice where the wind always dies and everything goes forest-quiet, swallowed up by giant trees marching down the mountainside. This is the start of Big Sur from the south; and yes, Calafia, every single time I've driven this road, camping and hiking and surfing my way through this storied, forested ribbon of coastal highway, it still shocks, like the Grand Canyon, or the Tetons, or Yosemite, more dream than landscape, a hallucination with mileage markers. Sometimes, like all those places, it's too much to grasp, hold, believe. For all the gear in the back of this van, and all the places to pull out ahead and set up camp, suit up, and paddle out, sometimes it seems better just to keep moving than to stop and be overwhelmed by it all.

But today, for all this drunken scenery, something is off.

It isn't until I slow down, and kill the music as I'm pulling into the next turnout deep in the shade of a canyon, that I figure out what it is: the sudden press of intense, dry heat. The air is hot, and dry as crinkly old newspaper, and punctuated with odd gusts of even hotter wind, screaming out of a hair dryer. Like all cliffside landscapes west of the coast ranges up and down California, Big Sur is normally sheltered from the dry blasting heat to the east by this wall of mountains cutting it off from the rest of the world. Down here on the darkened

floor of a forest that towers and canopies to block out the sun, it is not supposed
to be this hot, feel this hot, *smell* so oddly hot. It smells like dryness, like an old
barn made from older cedar and full of old hay, like tinder aching for a match.

Calafia says nothing, her smile gone, her face blank. I wonder if she also
thinks something is off, if she might feel it too.

"That's weird," I mutter to myself, let out a long hot breath and shrug it off,
cranking the music and pushing on up the road.

The plan is to beat the sunset to Mystery Cove, my pretend-secret surf spot,
set up camp by sunset, catch a couple waves before dark. It's pretend-secret
because it's hard to get to: an unmarked dirt road dead-ends at an unmarked
trailhead, and then it's a half-mile hike with surfboard and gear down a
crumbling cliff trail. And while I've never had Mystery Cove all to myself, I've
never been down there with more than half a dozen others. By California
standards, that makes it wild and remote compared to the parking lots strung
out along the PCH — the Pacific Coast Highway, or just *PCH* down in SoCal,
where only the Interstates get "*the*'d" — half a mile in both directions from
every other beach trailhead between L.A. and San Francisco.

Calafia would say she remembers how it was long ago, before this road or any
other, when we would have it all to ourselves. There would be a big extended
family of sea otters — a "romp" of otters, as they're called — swimming around
in the cove, feeding on the same shellfish as we were; a bunch of seals barking
on the beach and pair of dolphins playing in the waves; and further offshore, a
pair of humpbacks rising and falling, rising and falling with the surf.

The road swings out of the shadow — out of that strange windy pocket of hot
air pouring down off the mountain — and back into the sun, the ocean spreading
out before us again.

*Are the humpbacks moving at this time of year?* I want to turn and ask Calafia.

But she won't answer, only laugh at me. Because she never answers. Because
she doesn't exist.

*Oh well*, I say to myself, let out a long hot breath, and crank the music even louder.

Calafia does exist, of course, and has for the past 500 years, if only in
everybody's imagination. So why shouldn't I have a turn?

I would be only the latest in a long line of dreamers to cast Calafia in my own
fantasy, and certainly not the first to take her surfing.

She was the warrior goddess in a popular sixteenth-century European
romance — *Las Sergas de Esplandián, The Adventures of Esplandián* — who ruled

over the vast, wild, golden "island" north of Spanish-held Mexico. She was tall, ferocious, curvy, sexy, and lethal, the queen of a tribe of warrior women. There were no men on her golden island; presumably, they killed them after bedding them, which was surely a better way to go out, back in the sixteenth century, than typhus or dysentery. Or maybe it was just the very first documented "girl-on-girl" porn for the lonely, horny Spanish explorers who dreamed of lucking onto the scene.

Calafia was the feral, carnal, indefatigable counterweight not just to the cold, chaste Virgin Mary but, I'd imagine, to the wife or mother or sister dying of pneumonia and *postpartum* infection back in some feudal hovel in Spain. Garci Rodríguez de Montalvo, the guy who made her up back in 1500 — and all those Spaniards who spanked along to his *Adventures of Esplandián* as they slaughtered their way north from Mexico — painted their fantasy black: she had pitch-dark skin and fierce black eyes. But that was way, *way* back, not just before Hollywood turned the fantasy blonde-haired and blue-eyed, but nearly three centuries before America slaughtered its way west from eastern states full of Northern Europeans.

Which is why this century's version would be like that woman in front of the stage last night: blonde-haired and blue-eyed, yes, and tall, thin, and gym-cut, 35 going on 21, the "girl" at the end of Sunset Road — *who's waiting just for me.* Or how Old Freya — lithe, strong, and still out there surfing like a sex goddess in her 60s — must have looked back when she was working as a PT and massage therapist on the pro tour, fixing banged up surfers.

But it's not just me lusting after Calafia, wishing her along on road trips the way sailors used to wish mermaids out of the sea. It's Hollywood, and the Laurel Canyon troubadours, and the Beach Boys, wishing they all could be California "girls." It's Amrita, Sanskrit for "nectar of immortality," and her trailing tribe of yoga devotees and teacher-trainees and "brand-amplifiers" — the Acoladies, as we call them. It's Johnny and his groupies, and all the other dreamers who ever followed their own sunset road out here looking to fall in love, get rich, or just start over. They all yearn for Calafia, even though they've never heard of her. If she has a last name, it's "Promise." Because she's the patron saint of the gold rush, the big ranch with orange groves, your face on the silver screen, lots of room for a big new house in a brand-new town going up in the desert, an aerospace job, your face on TV, Haight-Ashbury, Silicon Valley. Calafia never grows old, not just because she doesn't exist, but because she's never seen a real winter, just rain, if and when it comes, and maybe some fog, and then another eight months of sunshine and happiness. She never gets sick and she never dies, only shapeshifts in the golden light, dancing, smiling, beckoning.

I see two of her most popular, current incarnations all the time, at the two very different kinds of gigs I've been playing for a living for the past couple of years: Amrita's *kirtans* and the yoga festivals; and Johnny's state fair and casino shows. She's always up in front, moving with the music, a swirl of hair and color and sex and *now!* Maybe it's a little pathetic, especially at my age, but it turns out I'm just as prone to the fantasy as anyone else, and maybe I would have liked to figure out who that was last night smiling up at me from the rail for most of the show.

Until the last few months, after Old Freya worked her magic on me and Radhe came and went, I never thought that way about women in the crowd, except in the usual just-browsing way. I've been perfectly fine on my own for years, after the ten-year starter marriage, and then the ten-year midlife crisis, and then the crushing, two-year, here-today-and-gone-tomorrow of finding Leah and losing her to ovarian cancer.

Or mostly fine.

Fine enough to consider running off with Radhe, after the incident with the redneck and the gun finally drove her back out of the country.

She practically begged me to go with her, if in that understated, forceful, presumptive way of a skilled surgeon. And I really thought maybe, maybe it was time to do what so many other people seem able to do: shape my life to fit the contours of another's life. Because I really did think about going with her, about jumping off this burning, sinking museum ship of a country. And I would have — right? — if I weren't having such a damn fine time playing the fiddle while this whole country burned. (Though, technically, it's the bass with Johnny and the guitar with Amrita.) And/or if I hadn't lucked into my little cottage in Angel Rest, an abandoned hamlet now fully off the grid thanks to Brooke, my bed — empty as it is — all of 50 feet from a big empty beach an hour south of San Francisco. But nobody's life is perfect; and after all the crap I've been through to get to here, what's a little loneliness?

Sure, I miss Radhe. And maybe I'll change my mind. Johnny will finally spin out and end up back in rehab. Or maybe one of Amrita's Acoladies — or one of the Man Buns, the young male groupies, as we call them — will turn on her in a classic California cult killing. Or my cottage will fall off the cliff into the ocean, along with the rest of Angel's Rest, finally, and I'll run off to New Zealand and beg Radhe's forgiveness.

I don't know. Maybe there is something about turning 50 — even if you're still surfing and playing music for a living — that sets the heart to yearning for the simple presence of a woman the way it used to yearn for the simpler pleasures of her body . . .

The road swings out of the shadow of the forested mountainside, flooding the van with screaming sunshine.

The engine digs in as I start up the next climb, the road shooting toward cliff edge ahead, an overlook, nothing but blue oblivion beyond.

So maybe I am just holding out for my own version of Calafia; and if Radhe had been her, she wouldn't have fled. Maybe Calafia was that woman on the rail last night, in the purple tie-dyed dress and cowboy boots, half a foot taller than the rest of the crowd, beaming up at us, the warrior-goddess-queen with her sun-splashed arms raised in benediction of the band, the crowd, the music, herself. She sure looked the part, one of Joni Mitchell's ladies of the canyon, or the one Led Zeppelin went to California for, down from her urban mountain cabin to drink beer, smoke weed, and dance.

If I were in my 30s, or maybe even 40s, I could have given in to the fantasy. I could have been that skeevy guy in the band who spots her from the stage, eye-vibes her the whole set, chats her up as she's lingering over the merch table. Then we're off into the hot summer night, up some juniper canyon to the hot tub behind her hippie cabin for howling sex under the stars.

And there I go again. Great. How long has it been since Radhe left?

But no. No sex, no juniper canyon, and no stars, if only because the gig was in that crappy casino down in San Bernardino.

So I'll skip out on that ugly reality, and stick with the part of the Calafia fantasy that doesn't make my loins tingle and chest ache — for Radhe, off to New Zealand? for my sweet Leah, off to oblivion? for somebody, anybody? — that much more. I'll spare myself the clawing industrial light and burnt metallic air of a San Bernardino County morning, and the awkwardness of getting out of her shitty apartment at the crummy end of the wrong valley, and instead slink back to this van to sleep alone in the casino parking lot. And I'll wake up again this morning, pretending last night's Calafia — warrior-goddess-queen of the whole world, riding me all night long under the stars — is just my road buddy today. I'll make it so she can surf like she dances, as powerfully and fluidly and gracefully as Jill and the other Bettys could ski and snowboard back in Colorado.

Because Radhe could never do any of that, and never wanted to. She is a surgeon, and surgeons are serious people, like accountants, corporate lawyers, historians. My Calafia would be none of that. She'd be cool, right to the end, like Old Freya.

Besides, I made my choice about Radhe when she left for that job down in New Zealand. Radhe thought the mountains and surfbreaks and deserts would sell it, knowing that once before I'd happily left behind everything — a wife, a new house, a big job back East — for adventure and adrenaline in my 30s. So why not in my 50s? It's not like I had kids to worry about, then or now.

Sweet Radhe. You tried so hard. The wild new landscapes down there would have been a bonus, and I might have gone there *for* you, not just *with* you.

But for these gigs. I guess.

Radhe was never really dug in here that way. She was just here for residency and the fellowship. After her run-in with that racist piece of shit in San Jose, I knew she was gone and just hadn't left yet. But she told me exactly what was going to happen the night we met, at one of Amrita's *kirtans* over in Palo Alto.

She came in a few minutes late, and worked her way to the front, the crowd parting with smiles and waves. She sat down right in front of me in jeans and a flowing red and orange scarf, and I watched her dissolve almost instantly into the music, like most people who work their way to the rail. But in between songs — when Amrita was telling one of her endless stories about gods and goddesses and universes and whatnot — Radhe stared at my hands the whole time, in a way that felt both odd and good. Which made instant sense when she came up to me, right after we were done, asked me something about my hands, and told me she was an orthopedic surgeon and working on an artificial tissue implant small and strong enough to work in fingers ruined by arthritis.

Over our first drink across the street, after too much nervous talk about my hands, I asked her what she thought about the music. She said it made her nostalgic, whisked her back to her childhood in Bangalore, and made her miss her parents. That's when she told me exactly what would happen: one day she would want to leave, after paying back her med school debt and finishing up work on that implant.

*Maybe somewhere back in Asia,* she said. *Where I do not stick out so much . . .*

Yes, somewhere out *there*, I think, as the van makes the crest of the next cliff.

I look out at the great glassy metallic plate of the Pacific, shimmering in the sun.

At the next turnout, I pull over and jump out of the van, and scramble up the grassy bank to the very edge of the cliff, bracing for the usual blast of onshore wind.

But — nothing. Just an eerie calm this afternoon.

I stand on the edge and let the vastness of it wash over me.

The ocean, the ellipsis at the end of the story . . .

. . . but this isn't the end of the story, not when you're still around to tell it, right?

Radhe is out there — way, way out there — and I'm still here, still trying to figure out what to do with my life at an age when most most people seem to have figured out theirs, or at least surrendered to what theirs became.

Alone in my 50s. No family, no kids, no real home, not much of anything — just this impossible dream coming true. I have this wild dumb luck of not one but two steady paying music gigs, after two decades of an on-again, off-again corporate grind. Making an actual living as a musician is something I'd never dared dream, even back at the age people do dream it, as thousands of musicians are far better than I'll ever be, and burn their whole lives down for it.

Sure, both my gigs are weird. Amrita is a dazzling mess, a 60-year old woman with big blonde hair, big fake boobs, and still, somehow, the body of a college gymnast; and the yoga festival crowd is a freakshow of women who want to look like her and men (and women) who want to sleep with her. And Johnny is an even bigger mess, a fallen rock star, who goes psycho at least once every gig, either onstage or off, for a crowd of aging hippies who mistake his between-song tantrums for political prophecy.

Yes, both scenes get old. And like it did for Radhe, the seemingly sudden emergence of armed rednecks everywhere — though it doesn't surprise me at all, given where I grew up — is maddening and terrifying; and I too would love to blow off this whole raging, idiotic, shit show of a failed nation.

But look over there, at those soaring mountains, blanketed with primeval forest; look down there at those emerald waves, crashing into a sculpture garden of rock; look out at that magnificent mirror of ocean, ageless and timeless, promising everything and nothing but a dissolution into eternal peace.

*Sorry, Radhe,* I say silently to the horizon. *It wasn't you. It was all of this. This is who I am now, and how can I ever leave?*

I climb down the grassy bank and back into the van, and start down the hill.

The road swings back into the sudden shade of the next forested side canyon, one of the dozens hanging like enormous drapes from the mountains over Big Sur.

But it doesn't go cool like it usually does out of the sun, or dank with spicy green. It's dry like sweetgrass, or old wood in a campfire.

Inside the switchback, the road passes a clutch of little cabins sitting in a copse of towering redwoods.

Up the next cliff, there's the turnout, the cliff where I can see down into Mystery Cove.

I pull in, grab my binoculars, jump out of the van and walk over to the edge.

There it is: the little pocket beach, wedged between two jagged rocky points at the bottom of tumbling cliffs. I scope the trail cutting past the little waterfall to hike down there with my board and gear. But where's the waterfall? I scan the cliffs and it's not there. Dry already, even though it's only June. Huh.

Then, another odd thing this time of the year and hour of the day: a big offshore wind, rushing down from the mountain looming up from the other side of the road, blowing the wrong way, toward the setting sun, feathering the waves down in the cove.

I study the surf through the binoculars. Two surfers out on short boards — only two!

The surf rolls in, one quick little peeler after another, throwing iridescent spray into the offshore wind. Organized, for a cove anyway, breaking a little more right than usual, and feathering pretty badly. But it breaks right, and I'm regular, and can stay low.

I climb back into the van and head down into the canyon feeding the cove.

There's a blast of heat from behind as the highway cuts back into the mountain, the wind dying, the heat welling up inside the van. It will be good to camp down on that beach after a session out on those waves, even without an onshore wind to cool things down. The cove is sheltered on all sides by these cliffs, trapping cooler, moister air from the ocean and turning it into an everywhere-rainbow.

The road turns back out of the canyon, and there it is: that little scratch of unmarked dirt road sneaking behind the guard rail.

I make the turn, and ease the van slowly down the two-track, under the highway, down through a canopy of redwoods to the little clearing.

Another van down here, a Westy, and that's it. Utterly deserted by surfbreak standards. And it's not just because of the tough hike down this trail to the beach. I've seen endless conga lines of people, burdened with surfboards and gear bags and coolers, picking their way down tougher trails than this on surfbreaks from San Diego to well north of San Francisco. This place just happens to be far enough away from both, and inaccessible from any direction except straight down.

I pull on my hiking boots, grab my surfboard and backpack full of camping gear, and start down the trail.

It's a tough hike, especially with my board, switchbacking across the face of a tumbling cliff spiked with agave and wind-sculpted tangles of juniper and chaparral. The seaward side of the trail drops straight down onto great piles of rock and the blanched remains of trees washed down from winter storms.

I climb down the last switchback to the narrow beach, and see the camp from the Westy folks set up at the south end, so I head to the north end and drop my gear.

And breathe out.

Finally, fully, ahh.

I turn to look back up that impossible trail, at the sea cliffs soaring to bound it on either side, and breathe out again. It's an almost perfect half-amphitheater down here, the cliffs tumbling down and exploding into rocky ledges that collapse straight down into sea stacks, the air all about me misted with rainbow.

I remember reading a few months back that if not for the utter isolation of this very cove and two or three just north of here, the whole of the Pacific Coast would have no sea otters. None. Gone.

In the early 1700s there were hundreds of thousands of these smart, goofy, playful creatures — who swim on their backs for pleasure and each have their own preferred shellfish — thriving around the Pacific Rim. In 1911, when the US, Russia, Japan, and Great Britain finally got around to signing an agreement to stop killing them, they had been hunted to complete extinction everywhere but right here. By then, an estimated one million had been shot and clubbed, for their exquisitely fine and thick fur, in less than two hundred years: by Russian hunters from the north; Spanish hunters from the south; American hunters from back East. It was the marine version of the wholesale slaughter of the beaver in every mountain river to the east, and a prelude to the fate awaiting the bison on the Great Plains and old growth forests of the Northwest. To those at the leading edge of "civilization," the sea otter's hide was money, swimming around in the ocean waiting to be "harvested."

But down in this wild and rocky cove, too rugged for anybody's ship to navigate, an estimated 40 to 50 sea otters survived, unmolested, and served as the source for restoring the entire population up and down the West Coast. Even after the signing of the 1911 agreement, the sea otters' survival was precarious, as they were easily caught up in the gill and trammel nets used by commercial fisheries along the coast. It wasn't until the 1990s, when Californians finally woke up to the endangerment of this quirky, beautiful keystone species, that gill and trammel nets were banned and the sea otter population began to grow again.

In romps. A romp of otters. Maybe there's one out there now.

I find a good flat spot in the sand past the tide line to set up for the night, spread out my gear, and climb into my wetsuit.

The tide is coming in, pushing each peak higher, illuminated from the inside by the setting sun like moving, flowing, emerald glass.

The two surfers from the Westy are working the north point, so I paddle out the other way, as far from them as I can while staying well clear of the maw of rocks closing off the south end of the cove.

I push furiously through the foam, out into rolling green hills of water, duck-diving the first two and popping out the back side.

I sit on my board, rising and falling and breathing and beholding: the great folds of dark green mountains thrusting straight up into a perfect blue sky, the lift and push and pull of the ocean, the cleansing salt air. And there it is, descending like light after a cloud moves off the sun, everywhere around me, the perfection and the purity of this moment, the palpable presence of this moment, the very Presence itself. Every breath in feels, suddenly, like a gift; and every breath out is a prayer: *thank you thank you thank you.*

Then, the same thought I've always had when the Presence makes itself known like this: I could die right now, and not from drowning or a neck fracture or any of the half dozen other ways you can die while surfing, but from my heart swelling with so much joy that it explodes.

Like the sudden holler of joy, over the roar of the surf, from the other end of the cove.

I have a good laugh at myself for that old, nurturing, morbid, intoxicating feeling, and kick my board around to see what those two are doing.

Looks from here like a skinny dude and a curvy woman, probably in their 20s, both with long hair and short boards. They are struggling a bit, taking turns, cheering each other on.

I watch the ocean swell up behind them with a good one, the same wave rising up behind me, so I turn and paddle but I'm late.

The next ones are all mush, so I drop to my board and paddle a little closer toward them, into the center of the cove, where the waves are setting up, and here comes one.

I paddle like mad, but I'm late.

Then another, bulging and swelling right behind me, and here we go!

I paddle and kick even harder, my board lifting beneath me, desperate to run, pushing and pulling and urging me on as I pop to my feet.

And time stops.

I unfurl myself, and I'm ten feet tall and weightless, moving fast and steady as a freight train straight at the beach and the light becomes water and I'm no feet tall, just liquid and water and wind and speed and everything and nothing.

Then the wave collapses, all foam, and I fall back into the drink, and spit out a mouthful of ocean, and with it lungfuls of southern California traffic, Johnny's tantrums and armed rednecks, and missing Radhe, all noise and nonsense . . .

I paddle back out, beaming like the happiest fool in the world with no one around to see, except of course the Presence.

When I spin back around to catch the next one, there *is* someone to see, 20 feet away, his big gray head popping out of the water, all whiskers and curiosity, a big seal or small sea lion.

"Hey there, buddy!"

But he just stares at me, not sure if he wants to say *Hey there* back to me.

Then his face finally says *Yeah, whatever*, and he plunges forward and steals my wave.

"So be that way then," I laugh, and set up for the next one.

They keep coming, and I catch two dozen more waves like the first, until my arms are so beat from the furious paddling, and all the paddling back out after each one, that I can barely lift them and it's time to call it.

Back on the beach, I'm so tired and thirsty I can't climb out of my wetsuit for a good ten minutes.

Instead, I sprawl out next to my gear, gulp water, and watch a red-tailed hawk work the cliffs.

Something metallic flashes off one of the high points, then a couple flecks of moving color, and more flecks out on the edge of the cliff.

I dig out my binoculars and see people staring down here and pointing, maybe at me or the other surfers, maybe at the seal out there.

It's good to feel like wildlife, like I did earlier today when I was scouting the break north of Pismo. Or some kind of zoo animal, who doesn't know the tourists in the rental car in the turnout are staring at him and talking about him.

Though I can't blame them for that: I was standing there barefoot — how I like to drive — and shirtless in the heat, just a pair of beat up old surf shorts hanging off me like a hula skirt.

*Lotta surfers out there, huh?* they'll finally say.

*Yep.*

Then, seeing how I'm half-dressed, and the open van, *Do you surf?* or maybe, *Are you from around here?* and always, finally, *Where's the best place to eat around here?*

The farther back East they're from, the more the question *Do you surf?* becomes *Do YOU surf. . . ?* without ever finishing with . . . *at your age?* Or . . . *really??* Or . . . *Cool!*

And when I answer the question the same way — *Every day I can* — I morph from zoo animal to creature in his natural habitat, into that exotic species glorified and ridiculed, often in the same movie, from a person who surfs into a Surfer: edgy, inarticulate, unemployed, oversexed, stoned, free.

Right.

Little do they know that I'm a Surfer because of a chance encounter two years ago on a ski mountain with Gordon, Johnny and Amrita's manager, that brought me to California. Or that I'm a Surfer because I'm still chasing after the same thing I always found above treeline when I was a Snowboard Mountaineer back in Colorado during my rager of a mid-life crisis between corporate jobs: what I call the Presence — or what others might call *God.*

So, no, I may be lanky, and tawny, and standing there half-naked next to the ocean, but I'm not a blond (and wasn't before I went bald), and I'm not stupid. But I have fallen into the cliché anyway: surfing isn't a sport for me anymore than climbing up and skiing off all those mountains was a sport. It's a ritual, a gateway, a quest every bit as profound as what other people do in monasteries or ashrams. It's a way to glimpse eternity, just a glimpse, but in a way so powerful and profound it never leaves you.

I was laughed at every time I tried to explain that to people, so now I don't bother. But if they're curious, or at least willing, I take whoever is visiting out on the big foamie Ike keeps around Angel's Rest for just such an occasion, and try to help them catch a wave, and maybe get just a glimpse of the glimpse. Because watching others on their first wave light up like they probably never have before, from the inside — to connect with the best of who they are — is another chance for me to experience my own first wave again.

That's exactly what happened when Aaron — my old friend from mountain rescue in Colorado — was out visiting with his eight-year old son, Jimmy. I hadn't seen him in nearly eleven years, and suddenly he's a Dad, and more serious than ever. And just like on mountain rescue, he was furrowed-brow focused on surfing as another *task* — as a thing to figure out. But after a few hours of mad paddling and thrashing around on the soupy beach break, when he and Jimmy each caught that first real wave, they both lit up, from the inside, and Aaron's brow let go, and they were both as giddy as eight-year-olds for the rest of the afternoon.

But surfing isn't a task, a thing to figure out, at least not once you figure out how to find your feet on the here-and-gone of a wave. I've seen plenty of attempts at instruction manuals, and not a single one can convey what you do once you find your feet because it is all *feel*.

Maybe this is why surfers are so famously inarticulate. How to describe what it feels like when your body slips from *terra firma* to stand on moving water? To be lifted from the muck of the self into the purest ephemera of space and time, your spirit released from deep within your body to soar — for just a moment that your body will remember forever — toward eternity?

Beats me. Because there's really no good way to explain what that feels like without falling back on the usual surfer *bon mots* — *Sick! Radical! Gnarly!* — no language to describe what it feels like to dissolve into the amniotic, to join the ocean within to the ocean without, to the great ocean, tugged by the moon, that encircles this entire planet.

Or maybe it really is just a God thing, and what the devoutly religious feel in their bodies as they melt into divine consciousness. What the bhakti yoga tribe feels as they dance and sway and sing and cry and writhe on the floor at Amrita's feet when the music is really cranking. Maybe it's that same experience of ecstasy — of dissolution and transcendence the mystics have always craved, sought, blown up their lives pursuing, and tried to describe — because that's what happens when you find your feet on a swelling of the ocean that seems to arise out of nowhere, severs your body from everything you've ever experienced on the earth, and sweeps you away. Just try explaining that to anyone, and the most honest thing out of your mouth is a grunt. Dude.

If to those tourists up there, a serious surfer seems cool, self-possessed, a little aloof, unimpressed with the goings-on back here on dry land, it's because — like me right now — they're exhausted from the thrashings of a good session. And because a part of them is always still out there, on the edge, unafraid. It may look like cool, like a pose, or some studied Buddha calm, but it's the physical residue of what just happened to me out there: the confrontation with all that moving water; the fight to paddle out, stay afloat, and read the swelling of the ocean; the thrill of mounting it, and riding it into the beach.

Maybe that's what has always made surfers look *cool* — to the tourists and magazine readers and armchair dreamers, to everybody back there in landlocked, arrested-adolescent America. Maybe it's why all the kids in the middle of Nebraska and Ohio — and the "still cool" parents among them — wear surf shorts, and checkerboard Vans, and t-shirts and hoodies and hats with Billabong, Quiksilver and Rip Curl logos.

The greatest generation of rock 'n' rollers may look like rich old ladies after yoga class; but even the most aging and broken-down surfers, like Ike, never really seem to age. And in a society that worships youth, fitness, and physical courage, surfing is a ritual of purification requiring all three, rendering surfers — *not* the rock stars — as the ones who are still eternally young, eternally cool. Like Old Freya, pushing 70 years old now, out on those waves every day, as lithe and strong and sexy as any woman of any age, dancing up and down her board in that black wetsuit. Even Ike, hobbling around on his broken hip, has that rugged charisma, the swimmer's bronzed and muscled shoulders, the faraway stare.

I look up at the turnout and there are more flecks, flashes of metal with the sinking sun, tourists lining up for their sunset selfies. To post for their friends back in Nebraska and Ohio, who have no idea why how they came to be wearing t-shirts with Billabong, Quiksilver and Rip Curl logos. I know why; Ike told me one night. In the early 1990s, the founders of California-based Quiksilver traveled to high schools all over America and asked kids who were the most popular jocks in each school. Then they gave those kids their branded clothes to wear. Ten years later, they and half a dozen other brands were selling half a billion dollars worth of t-shirts, hoodies, sneakers, caps, and "board shorts" to kids all across the country. It was a different kind of gold rush story, like the one planted in the 1840s by land speculators in California, except for this version of the dream, nobody had to pick up and move; they just had to go to the mall.

But many did leave, because they wanted a whole more than a cool t-shirt. Maybe it was all the songs, or the movies; maybe it was somebody's big brother — just like in the gold rush — spinning tales for the folks back home about how well he was making out in California. He hadn't sold his screenplay or landed that big tech job, but he was surfing. And to the folks back East, there was nothing cooler than that.

Because he really was changed, and when he went home, everybody could see it.

After a session out on the waves, like just now down here in cove, when I wash ashore after an hour of adrenaline-fueled transcendence, I'm flushed with nothing but peace and quiet. This may be what they see, what has become mythologized: the self-containment of the Surfer in a society of anxious people crawling around in their own imperfect bodies. Maybe this is the thing people sense: the Surfer really has been elsewhere. And while he or she may have come back, they're still out there somewhere, in a place so much more rarefied than the one the rest of us occupy, a place melded with the eternity of the ocean, a place touching the holy.

I hear laughter and look up to see the other two surfers crawling on to the beach exhausted, elated, emptied.

The sun is working its way to the horizon, so I drag myself to my feet, wrestle myself out of my wetsuit into the sudden chill, and set up camp.

I'm making beans and rice for dinner when they come over for the usual check-in — happy-looking kids in their early 20s — to make sure they won't be spending the night down on this remote beach with a psycho, then skitter back to their own camp.

I sit against the drift log I've pulled over, eat, and watch the sun go down. It is not setting so much as dissolving into a rising marine layer — a long, thin, milky streak for a horizon — dropping blood-orange into the blur of ocean and sky.

I slide further down on the log, and watch the cliffs rising all around me turn rose, then magenta, then fade into shadow. The fingernail of a new moon rises out of the inky silhouette of redwoods spiking the mountain ridge to the south. Behind me, I can hear the tide going back out, the roar slowly turning to a gentle rumble.

I have no idea what time it is but don't care to look. I'm ready to pass out and don't want to. I want only for this moment to last forever.

I try to stay awake by remembering the first time I'd been to Big Sur. It was on a work trip, way back in my first corporate job, and the first of what would become an almost weekly ritual to keep my marriage from falling apart by staying away from my wife. We'd gotten married way too young, during the first of our several attempts to fund and finish a college degree; I was 23 and tending bar, and she was 24 and waiting on tables, at a steak and seafood place next to the Baltimore Beltway. We finished those degrees, eventually, and found corporate jobs; and suddenly I'm on an airplane for the first time in my life, flying all the way to the West Coast.

I had a work meeting in L.A. on a Friday. And rather than fly back to a marriage that was dying a long, slow, inevitable death, I kept the rental car and headed north, to this place I'd heard about in the English class I had to take to finish my engineering degree. Stories about the poets and novelists and seekers who came out here to listen to this ocean, run around naked, do a bunch of drugs, have lots of sex, and write about it for the folks back East.

I suppose all that proto-hippie lore was the American Century's version of the Spaniards and Calafia. And it may have been Calafia herself who beckoned to me from that first rental car, down a well-worn tourist trail to this very ocean. If so, she would have been the adventurous, rugged, sexy counterpoint to my always worried, always working wife back East, the reward I imagined I had coming to me after our long struggle to escape our crazy families, grind our way through school, finally get on our feet.

But it wasn't Calafia I found here where the mountains tumble down to the sea. It was the Presence, the same exact thing I'd felt years earlier in the woods outside that small town back East where I would run and hide when my father was on a drunken rampage. It was that sense of being seen, looked after, kept safe. If there was any other presence in those woods besides what one would call "God," it was the presence of the Iroquois, the Indians who'd lived there for centuries — a small multitude of them in longhouses like the one anthropologists had excavated half a mile from our house.

Back then, I tried to imagine it was them, or at least their ancestors from way back, because they were all living in trailers over on the reservation west of town. Like the big kid I worked with in the grocery store. What was his name? But the woods of my childhood had been emptied of them, except in spirit of course, the way that longhouse was reduced to a nub in the woods.

No, it wasn't them I'd grown up with out in those woods. It was still alive, still present, still the Presence, like what I found in the mountains of Colorado, what was out there in those waves an hour ago.

I remember on that first trip out here how alive Big Sur was with that sensation, with the thing I'd lost touch with when I fled to the nearest city for work and school, a place full of crime, and filth, and racial hatreds, and way too many people. Big Sur was and is filled with the Presence, with what is here right now — with the crowd gone, the phone off, and nothing but the sensations of the earth turning beneath us.

I look over at my tent, sitting there in its bag, and I'm too tired to set it up. But that doesn't matter: it's not really cooling off, even down here 50 feet from the ocean.

Which is weird. Because it's almost always chilly in Big Sur, always a little damp from the fog coming in, the heavy mist that waters the redwoods and clouds that usually wreath those hills and inspired all those poets and writers and seekers.

Tonight, it's actually still hot, so I throw a tarp down on the sand and a light blanket over me just because, and stare up into a sky suddenly awakening with stars.

A wave crashes in the distance, and I turn and there it is, the ocean, and I burrow down through the tarp into the coolness of the sand.

Radhe is out there somewhere, at an angle I can approximate from here: New Zealand, the last place left, one of the last English-speaking countries that hasn't completely lost its mind. Right about now, she's going to work, maybe scrubbing into a surgery to fix somebody's ruined hands. Radhe. All those brains and all that dark beauty. I can see her sitting there perfectly still at one of Amrita's *kirtans*, her curves wrapped up in a big flowing red and orange scarf as the music swirled all around her.

I hope she's happy over there, maybe even recovered enough from the incident to think about coming back.

But who comes back from the West? And there's no place more west than that. I never did. And I'd never want to.

Because this is it, right? The end of the trail? When you paddle out around here, you face west, into the sun for most of the day; and when you turn to paddle back with the surge of the ocean, and rise to your feet to ride something that wasn't there and then is there but soon won't be, you can't see the wave, only feel it in your body. It's the same way you can't see that halo all around you, but you know it's there, like the last of the golden light on those cliffs when the sun goes down.

I fight off sleep, try to hang on to the last of the golden light. But the lifting and dropping of the waves a hundred feet away reverberate through the sand, like they do anywhere near the beach, except here they don't just echo through the ground. Here, you can feel the ground lifting and falling with them, down into the crust of the earth as the ocean slips back and forth on that crust, and the crusts slips back and forth on the earth, in waves that come like a great body breathing.

The harder I fight off sleep, the sleepier I get, so I try to remember bright sunshine, Radhe and me walking along the beach, the first time she came out to Angel's Rest.

She said the ocean has the exact same salinity as amniotic fluid, and wasn't that interesting?

And it might be, but I'm too tired to stay awake amidst all the gentle, ceaseless crashing of all that water, the great whoosh of the womb, rising up and carrying me away.

# 2 | LONG WAY HOME

*Siren!* The sound is blood-red, piercing and electric, slicing through the caress of that soft, sweet emerald dream of sleep on the beach.

I'd slipped off with the crashing of the surf, out to sea, like any other warm night up at Angel's Rest with all the windows open, soaked in a dreamless sleep until called back by the gulls or the bark of a sea lion and the scratchings of light in the mist over the mountains.

But not this morning, because that is the blood-red rage of a siren, somewhere up on the PCH.

I roll over in my sleeping bag on the sand, following the siren as it rounds the bend on the still darkened cliffs, then another, looping and angry, slicing through the dark hush of redwoods, then another, stopping, a hundred feet straight overhead.

The squawk of a bullhorn: "Wildfires in the southern section of Big Sur. Evacuate this area immediately. For your safety and the safety of our crews, evacuate this area now."

"Fire, dude!" a voice calls at me from halfway across the cove.

I look over to see one of the surfers from last night crawling out of their tent and scrambling over to help the other one.

I roll onto my back and look up at what should be a mist of sunrise light down through the trees on the cliffs over this empty beach. But there is a strange orange cast over everything, sunset colors at the wrong end of the day.

"Dude!" he calls over to me again. "There's a FIRE!"

"Yeah, I heard, thanks."

This is exactly when I don't panic, when time slows and I go weirdly calm. It's not something I learned so much as honed during mountain rescue training back in Colorado: how *not* to react. It's my eye-of-the-shitstorm mode, the iron calm at my core that was always there, during those dozen mountain rescues, through a hundred existential work crises before Colorado, all the way back to growing up with a crazy drunk for a father.

I wake up instantly, the sleep and dream dashed away, my senses alert to everything: the air acrid with woodsmoke; the strange silence between breakers where gulls should be screeching at each other over breakfast; a steady morning offshore breeze pulsing out to sea, grungy orange where it should be a pale and misty yellow.

"Attention, down on the beach," the bullhorn pierces down through the trees. "We are evacuating this section of the Big Sur coastline. Evacuate the coast, and depart to the north immediately."

The siren again, wailing and insistent, but not moving.

I toss off my blanket, fish my keys and wallet and headlamp out of my hiking boot, and roll everything into my tarp.

The siren gives one last scream as it tears away from the cliff — heading north or south on the PCH? — I can't tell for the forest of giant redwoods up there, which swallow sound in the same way they do time.

Boots on, gear and board under my arms, I check to see that the other two are good to go, then march over and up the sketchy cliff trail.

As I make the ridge, the forest is all bad TV reception: a hazy blue thing fading into empty light. I feel a pull toward the road and flight, a cable pulling at my solar plexus the rest of the way to the trailhead, even with this load, the urge to ditch my board and gear and run.

I breathe it out, march the rest of the way to the top, and toss my gear in the van, my throat suddenly tight, like I'm choking back tears.

A few minutes up the rutted canyon road, as the van tops out on the highway, I'm expecting to see a circus of firetrucks and cops and scrambling tourists. But the road is empty, but for a blue-white haze of wood smoke drifting down out of the trees, crossing the road, bumping into the cool ocean air and dancing up into the darkening sky.

I head up the PCH, the van finds its rhythm, and I start thinking about where to pull over — after I get north of the smoke and smell — to make coffee and breakfast. I was looking forward to all that on the beach, then a morning session out on the waves. But the morning light, breaking through the dank stands of redwoods and cedars on both sides of the highway, isn't giving way to shafts of sunlight and mist: it's coughing out more smoke, flecked with what looks like cottonwood dander, or pollen, or maybe even snowflakes. The ash swirls over the road before rising, darkening the sky at the wrong end of day with that sickly orange, and the smell goes sour, like a campfire with wet wood. Even with the windows up, it urges me on, to push the vans into the curves, rocking with the mantra: *I will outdrive this, I will stop when I get north of this mess.*

Up around the bend, the smoke thickens to a haze, and everything goes darker, flashes red and blue, dark, red and blue, dark. A firetruck is parked halfway across the road, a firefighter in a big smudged yellow coat standing in front of it talking into a radio.

I pull up, catch his eye, and point north.

He shakes his head, and points me south, hard and insistent. It is the exact opposite direction of Angel's Rest and home, a wait until they put this out or a 150-mile detour.

I know the answer, and know better than to argue, but still shrug, *Really?*

"No," he says. "The PCH is closed up ahead."

"But I heard evacuate to the north?"

"Fifteen minutes ago. Fire just jumped the canyon and about to cross the road. Canyon to the south is bad, and may jump too, but north is gone."

He reminds me of the full-timers I met in mountain rescue, with the cinderblock tone of people who have seen terrible things, have heard about even more terrible things, and spend most of their field hours trying to keep idiots from killing themselves.

"I was mountain rescue, Colorado not here. Can I help?"

"Certified?"

"Was. Till five years ago."

"Sorry. But thanks."

"Yeah, and thank *you*." I pull around to head south. "Hang tough."

A hundred feet down the road, and more sirens coming. I pull over as a big ambulance and small firetruck scream past the other way, another blur of red and blue and wailing. Then, empty road, an eerie quiet, and the last traces of smoke on the air.

After a few more miles of weaving in and out of forested mountains washed in burnt orange sunlight, I pull into a narrow little turnout that juts high out over the ocean, framed by cypress carved into the shape of the onshore wind. To the south, it's any other day: bright morning sun pulsing in a perfect blue sky. But as I park, and jump out, I turn and behold the destruction of heaven: Big Sur on fire, its great mountainous shoulders, one after another draped in deep green and dropping to the sea, slashed with a jagged line of orange and red. It is an earth-sized, bleeding gash, blue smoke pouring from it like steam from an open wound, as if a swarm of fighter jets had just flown the length of the range and strafed it with a line of fire.

Another firetruck flashes by, and another. I know I should get out of here, get a jump on all the extra highway miles up the 101 and the traffic I'll have to face now. But the shitstorm has passed out of my body, and I'm suddenly hungry and could use some coffee — though what I really want to do is watch, study, understand. It's like being out on a rescue when something horrible is happening and you can't look away, or reading and re-reading every word of the report for somebody else's rescue. Besides, there is a steady breeze of cool, clean ocean air coming up the cliff, the wind shifted to onshore already, many hours earlier than normal for a warm, sunny day.

I pull my kitchen gear out of the back, set up my little stove, make coffee and oatmeal like I have at hundreds of camps, stops, turnouts. But never at one like this, sitting, eating, and watching, through my binoculars, an earth-scale nightmare unfold, an unspeakable agony of terrestrial transformation, the color of the inside of a raging furnace. All along the zigzag fire line, in and out of the canyons and up and over mountains, there is a sudden flare of color, then another, then a flash as a great redwood or cedar or spruce or fir explodes, throwing a rocket burst of spark-filled smoke into the sky.

My eyes finally bug out, and when I lower the binoculars, I see tiny flecks of white all over my lap, catching in the hair on my arms, falling down into my quickly fading shadow on the gravel in front of me. I turn just in time to see a high, thin scrim of gray-blue pulling across the sun. I walk over toward the cliff for a better view back at the southern end of the range, where I'll turn east and drive out of here.

There is no fire to the south, but from here I can see that the high thin cloud of smoke is the top of what looks like a thunderhead, pouring up out of the mountains and pushed flat like the top of an anvil, high up as a cruising airliner. It is starting to blot out the sun, turning its light from a sickly gauze to a cancerous ochre. All around the van, what looks like first snow is falling, drifting into swirls of the last of the ocean air, never falling to the ground, picked up again by another gust.

I should go.

I stow my breakfast stuff and gear, and head south.

I suppose I could feel sorry for myself for my missed session, ruined day, shitty drive — I do live in California after all, where it is all about me — but Big Sur is on fire. People have homes tucked away through these mountains, funky little houses cut from the redwood and cedar and fir stands spilling down each canyon and draw to this road, all the way back to when it was a wagon trail bringing in the first homesteaders back in the 1800s. There is a Zen monastery up there somewhere, and the Henry Miller library, and some rehab where Johnny dried out in the late '80s. There's the Esalen Institute with its hot springs on the cliffs, where Aldous Huxley figured out that East was West and everything really is connected, and where I've played a couple gigs with Amrita. There are poets and painters and writers and welding sculptors; and hippies so old they really did hang with Allen Ginsburg and Alan Watts when they drifted through; and two generations since of kids raised way off the grid, whose parents were growing vegetables and pot and hybrid varieties of every world religion. Maybe those were the kids I was surfing with last night, whose grandparents were looking over first drafts of Robinson Jeffers' poetry of heaven on earth; who were listening to the auto-didact anthropologist and linguist, Jaime de Angulo, as he spun tales from California Natives, in languages he was the first to write down; who were partying at Ferlinghetti's cabin down on Bixby Creek when Jack Kerouac was rolling around in the bushes outside going through alcohol-withdrawal psychosis. And how many other ghosts, two generations removed, are running around up in these mountains, the lost spirits of dozens of poets and musicians and freaks none of us have ever heard of, who came here for a glimpse of the Infinite and found that or just madness? And today, it's all on fire.

I drive all the way south to Cambria, then east over juniper and golden hills knitted with vineyards to the 101. As the road starts up the steepest pass, two helicopters hauling massive Bambi Buckets scream overhead, weighted with whatever they drop on wildfires.

I push the van up the mountain as hard as it will go, and catch up to a long line of cars and trucks. They're all pushing hard too, harder than tourists do over this same road — pushing harder than most drivers everywhere in California. The road going the other way is completely, eerily empty, except for the flash of a firetruck or cop car every few minutes.

I don't know about the rest of them, but I'm not driving fast because I'm worried about the fire catching me. I just hate driving backward. Especially when backward means forward again for a hundred numbing miles of oil wells, then a hundred numbing miles of agri-factories, then a hundred miles of crushing traffic when I hit the edge of the vortex north into Silicon Valley. It will take most of the day, and I'll have one less day to unpack and repack in Angel's Rest, before I'm back on the road north for a gig with Amrita.

But at least my house isn't on fire, although I am reminded — like after every fire, or earthquake, or landslide — that it could be. My cottage and the rest of Angel's Rest could go up just as easily, with all that tinder-dry oak and cypress and eucalyptus to the north and east; or it could break off and fall into the ocean, with not much of an earthquake not that far up the coast in the Bay Area; or during another winter of furious days of rain, what's left of it could wash right out with a big king tide. Not that I care: we are all just renting the little houses and storefronts left behind, after the houses on one side of the Beach Road collapsed into encroaching ocean, along with the state park beach parking lot and picnic area. We all know every day in Angel's Rest could be our last; Amrita likes to tell me how lucky I am to be truly living non-permanence and practicing non-attachment. And yay, how lucky am I.

But it's still my home, still my stuff, still my "kit" as the mountain men had it. And the part of me pushing the gas pedal, as the van rocks into the curves and the tailgater ahead of me is on and off his brakes too, wants only to get back to Angel's Rest in time to grab my other guitar and my old photo albums, and then let it burn, or crumble, or fall off the cliff and drown. Over the years I have found and lost many great places — to what? live? sleep? call "my own?" — where, as Amrita would have it, I could just *be*. Places in the mountains, the desert, and now the ocean. Places where I can wake up in the morning fully and truly awake, where the Presence — who was there before any of us arrived and will remain long after we leave — is as palpable and real as the sun and moon and stars.

Does this make it easier not to care about the sooner-or-later of what I have now? Especially here on the crumbling edge of the continent, where nothing lasts? Where everything will sooner or later catch fire, or fall apart, or wash into the ocean? If so, I could probably back off the gas pedal a little, but no . . .

The hill climbs to a summit pass, old oaks spiraling out along the ridge and gold grass whipping back and forth. At the top — wham! — that blast of wind, right on the nose of the van.

The road opens to two lanes and half the cars scramble left. I come off the gas because yeah, what if this were really it? How exactly would I say fuck it? Would I fight to the death, when the ATMs and credit cards all go down, in a convenience store food riot? Or go Jonestown with the crew out at Angel's Rest? (I'm sure Brooke, as clever as she is with the chemistry — along with metalworking, engines, plumbing and electricity — could cook up something that tasted good, didn't cause any pain, and did the job.) Or maybe, as was my fantasy during the darkest days back in Colorado, just some proud old Indian death on the mountain, blissed out on hypothermia? Or would I go out *New* Old West style, me and my dying pony, my bones blanching in the sun next to a van at the end of some trail with no gas and no water?

Too funny, me and my metal pony, who is running way too fast.

Down another switchback, and it's chaparral and fences, fields of dead grass, and another switchback, as the last hill spills into long brown flatlands in a cloud of brown dust. The van bangs around in the wind, and through the brown dust I can just make out giant robot armatures, oil derricks, half of them pumping, half idle, no discernible pattern.

Another few miles, and the wind finally breaks as the highway drops into a long, low draw, down alongside an oil field stretching to the horizon. The landscape has been carved into a maze, subdivided for big, rusty-black oil derricks out on their burnt brown berms. There are no humans or trucks or cars anywhere in sight, just squat cinderblock buildings, piles of rusted metal, pipes, wires. In no discernible pattern, half of them sit idle, the other half pumping — round and round and round in a mindless, senseless circle — hundreds of them all running north into a horizon of dust.

This would be the perfect place for an apocalyptic grand finale: out of gas, next to oil derricks on auto-pump. Everyone out here likes to talk about their go-bag: it's a thing they like to share at dinner parties or on dates, like the real estate thing, or the workout thing, or the how-long-is-your-commute thing. So, yeah, I have the biggest go-bag of all — a go-van, full of camping gear — so I could weather a solid week of the apocalypse. But why would I?

Their reasons always involve their kids. Like big-haired, pointy-nosed Diane from L.A., one of Amrita's Acoladies who told me all about her plan for Armageddon when I was stuck across from her at dinner one night. It was a yoga and meditation retreat in a fancy new place in the redwoods outside Santa Cruz, and we were all supposed to be talking about dharma paths, the divine, eternal bliss, etc. But the where-do-you-live icebreaker segued into the usual Cali-chatter about real estate and traffic; and as she lives smack in the middle of Los Angeles, part of which was also on fire at the time, we went straight to our what-would-you-do-if and go-bags.

"Oh don't you worry," she said, picking through her salad with her fork, then pointing the fork in my face. "My kids and I will be fine. My Suburban will go anywhere. And in the back, I always keep ten gallons of water, ten grand in cash, and a handgun. All we have to do is get out of L.A., and stay out till the fires are out and the looting is over."

While Diane went on about her kids, and her job, and herself, I kept wandering back to how she thought the Suburban, cash, water, and handgun would help her and her kids get out of the L.A. basin. Backed into the ocean by mountains from three directions, the only way out for ten million frantic people would be a dozen little canyon roads and a couple freeways threading through chokepoint passes. And curving 50 feet somewhere over each one was a long, thin stretch of concrete, bleached white in the sun, vibrating with the passage of ten thousand other Suburbans, waiting for a little wink from the earth to collapse.

Diane was hilarious, if only because she was so deadly serious. She was smart and wily and tough, like she needed to impress nobody; and yet made sure that I knew she was a partner in some big corporate law firm whose name I'd once been unfortunate to know. And like most of the Acoladies who filled the great halls of Amrita's events around the country, Diane had the sculpted workout body, pricey glow, and confident half-smile you see on the covers of yoga, fitness and health magazines marketed at women exactly like her.

I wasn't about to argue with her that day. But I knew none of that would matter in the desperate scramble of ten million less enlightened people trapped in the frozen rivers of metal and glass of the 5, the 405, and the 10, bracing for the next aftershock and wondering if the freeway up ahead hasn't come down yet.

This was the moment they all pretended they knew was coming someday, just not any day soon, *Because the weather! Because it's always so sunny and beautiful out here!* . . .

Not so up north, not today. The wind is blowing out here so hard that everything sits behind a scrim of dust. Where the road flattens and straightens, I can barely make out the march of oil derricks through the brown haze, even on this ghoulish stretch of two-lane road, empty going back toward the coast and bumper-to-bumper fleeing it, as if we'd be safer when we got to the 101.

Today, an air-conditioned Suburban full of water and cash would do just fine. So maybe Diane — with the perfect nails, and Botox gloss, and boob hoist, exquisitely adapted to survive and thrive in her natural environment — was onto something. Right after that interminable dinner conversation, when Amrita was on an extended version of her welcoming spiel and I was just sitting there between songs with my guitar, I did a hard mental inventory of my go-bag on wheels, this go-van, upping my water stash to ten gallons and putting a few grand at the bottom of the toolbox.

But I couldn't muster up the handgun. I'm too data-driven, and just paranoid enough to know this hard truth about myself, who has been trained to de-escalate: faster than I could use the gun to defend myself, someone would snatch it and use it against me. Or maybe I'm not data-driven at all, but superstitious; and I imagine that, when I am down in L.A. for a gig and the Big One comes, and all those freeways twist and splinter and finally collapse into their canyons, I'd try to use the gun on myself and screw up the job. I'd end up staggering around in the rubble of the 5, or the 405, or the 101, half my face and one ear shot off, and some guy would run up and steal the gun out of my hand, then dash off without doing me the mercy of the finish. The gun story, like the road trip romance story, never ends well, any more than the real apocalypse won't have the family reunion happy endings of all those movie apocalypses. Real guns work only for people willing to shoot them. Not that I doubt for a moment someone like Diane would be willing to shoot one, if it meant her kids, or her Suburban, water, or cash. Me? I have no-one but myself to defend.

I should have asked her how she'd explain that handgun to Amrita, a vegan who has a whole long riff on "practicing non-harming." But this was the part of Diane that spent more time in her law firm than on her yoga mat, and would no doubt argue that Amrita wouldn't begrudge anyone their own self-defense. And maybe she has a gun of her own that I don't know about? She'd probably be right, so it's better not to know one more thing about Amrita. Because no doubt Amrita would look the other way, and not get in her face about the gun: Diane was one of her regulars, one of the Acoladies she liked to keep close.

That was exactly how I came to be sitting across from Diane that first night, at the table with the rest of the band and Amrita's two teaching assistants: I'm the single straight guy in her band, and she was clearly single too. And it was obvious that she, despite the big job and military-grade readiness for the L.A. apocalypse, still fancied herself some kind of Bohemian, at least every other weekend when she didn't have her kids. Amrita knew that even though I ended up playing music for a living, I'd had a corporate job through most of my 30s and 40s, and could also talk about all that. So of course she'd try to pimp me, although I had no interest, even if Diane had no strategic value to her. Because while it is easy to write off so much of what Amrita does at a retreat to marketing guile, the larger, looming public part of her persona is all *bhakti*, the yoga of devotion, all flowing yoga movement to long musical lines, tears and hugs and heart signs with fingers, and always another chance for puppy love for old dogs like Diane and me.

Amrita falls in and out of it herself, every few months, near as I can tell, with an increasingly younger and more smitten young guy — though it's really in and out of bed with them, because I've caught her actually mixing up their names. But despite that — or maybe because of the oxytocin rush of all that? — she still has the matchmaker's vicarious yearning to fall in love over and over through others, to witness, over and over, *the conscious invocation of the feminine and masculine divine.*

So I'll be charitable and say Amrita sat me down across from Diane at that retreat because Radhe had just left — had left not just me, but the entire continent — and I'd been even quieter than usual on that swing of gigs. I'm good at not letting anything show; I've been yelled at for it, by more than one woman. But I know my sullenness was creeping into my guitar lines, and I was dragging the beat on the wildest *bhakti* stuff. Amrita just wanted to make me happy, like she wants to make everybody happy. That is, after all, what they buy; and it works, because she really does mean it.

Up ahead, the 101 emerges, finally, from the wall of dust: two long smears of cars and trucks, glittering through the brown cloud as far as I can see north and south.

The van rocks back and forth, straining against that hard wind on its nose. The traffic finally slows, splitting into lanes at a stoplight, and branching into a sudden sprawl of gas stations and fast food.

I notice for the first time a dull throb in the back of my head, and my gut hurts from clenching and unclenching the whole ride over here from the coast.

My cell kicks in. The light turns red, so I scroll through my messages: Gordon about next week's gig; a couple spams; a text message marked urgent from Brooke.

*Kenny made me put new lock on gate. Fucker. Got key for you. ETA tomorrow?*

The light turns green, so I pull over under the freeway to text her back. The van bobs and shakes with the thunder of traffic overhead.

*Today. 4 hrs. Big fire in Big Sur, bailed.*

*Saw that. Major bummer. Txt me when ur 10 out. Meet you out at PCH.*

I pull up onto the 101 and slip into the river of traffic flowing north. The van is jolted by a blast of sand from the east, the opposite direction the wind normally blows around here. The fire in the coastal mountains 50 miles west of here is sucking wind from across the vast agri-desert that is the heartland of California.

I jam it with everyone else, stuck in the left lane past the trucks, trying to outrun the wind and my own dread, and not just about the apocalypse.


Why would Kenny go ahead and lock up the gate again? Is he finally getting ready to throw all of us out?

He's been selling off the farmland out by the PCH in pieces. And the last piece is the best: it runs through a break in the cliffs, down to the ocean and a half-mile-long beach, and Angel's Rest, or what's left it: the living remains of the little hamlet with the five cottages that still work and the 25 that don't.

Protected in the other three directions by the Santa Cruz Mountains, Angel's Rest is another unmarked turnoff between San Francisco and Santa Cruz, where the coast roads go country. It was built into a long bluff stretching from the pastured cliffs down to a long rocky cove, when the ocean was another hundred feet west. The five buildings where we live, painted five funky colors (mine's orange), sit along the little road carved highest up the brown sandstone cliff. The other 25, blasted by the sand, wind, and rain, are the grays and white of bones set out in the sun.

Beach Road, the pitted lane fronting the beach, cowers behind the riprap, crisscrossed with sand drifts, maybe remembering the ten buildings on its one side that fell into the ocean in the '70s. The only thing still working on Beach Road is the weathered shell of Neptune's, the old general store and café that isn't a store and café anymore, just a place with a room big enough for everybody to hang out in the open air, share food, weed, and drink, and watch the sun go down. The ocean jumps Beach Road every winter, eating away at it, as if to let everybody know that all of Angel's Rest will soon go the way of the state park beach down at the other end, now odd humps of sand dune over what used to be fire pits and picnic tables, bathrooms and a little parking lot.

Not that we don't all know that all of it will eventually fall into the ocean. Or the well that Brooke somehow keeps going will run dry. Or the power system she has jerry-rigged will crash. Or the state or county or feds will catch up, and kick all of us out.

But for me, that impermanence is the attraction of Angel's Rest. I've had my share of mortgages, lost a good house to a divorce, made money on one in Colorado because it was in the devouring path of a ski resort developer. Nice to have a home; but there's always some little heartbreak in every one of them, and the heartbreak lives there forever. And there's always another place.

Because it's just Angel's *Rest*, right? I can just leave when I feel like it. Even though the place does exist — unlike Calafia over there, riding shotgun with me — the place exists out of time, like a funky town in an old song, sepia-toned in the movie based on that old song, an escape to nowhere. Kenny — whom I've never met but who sounds like one of those big, round guys with salt-and-pepper maws and tie-dyed t-shirts who hang around back stage at Johnny's shows — owns the place, or what's left of it anyway. He inherited it from his grandparents, they say, whose grandparents homesteaded it in the 1870s.

They eventually got it on the grid, and ran a cattle ranch that spread north and south across the pastures atop the sea cliffs. They even tried to talk the railroad, the one that was going to run south from San Francisco to Half Moon Bay in the '20s, to come all the way down — before the Model T shifted everything over the mountains to the highways suddenly running south along the Bay, into what would become Silicon Valley. The ranch thrived, along with the vegetable farms and fishing boats out of Half Moon Bay, through decades of sun and fog and rain and sun, because the highway north would slide out and all the big booms were over the hill, rolling south along the Bay.

But Kenny didn't grow up there. His father had fled the farm for the suburbs when he was 18. And so Kenny fled the suburbs for the farm, after following the Dead, then some guru, then the Dead again, before ending up back on the farm in the '70s. The love of his life moved in, or so the story goes, a *kundalini* yogini and *reiki* healer who was living out of her truck, because she couldn't stand the vibrations of electricity in walls. So when she moved in, she had Kenny turn all the power back off. She eventually left Kenny for a woman, but not until after he'd found a guy to move in to one of the houses and set the whole place up with solar power. He was some roadie, or so the story goes, who worked for the Jefferson

Airplane until he overdosed; then he went out on the road with Johnny, whom he'd met in what was Johnny's first rehab.

So, thanks to the that long ago rehab, even Angel's Rest is another thing Gordon set up for me, after those first few nervous gigs when no one knew how it would go. But I'd said I wanted to live near the ocean and off the beaten path, those gigs went well, and Gordon made it happen. I'd said *off the beaten path*, not *off the grid*. But thanks to Brooke — all of five feet tall and wire thin, but armed always with some ferocious looking tool — the lights turn on and off and the water runs out of a system jerry-rigged into the old ranch well. And for the oddity of living in a ghost town at the end of a dirt road, I get to live a seashell's throw from the ocean, in a cottage made mostly of windows, in a hamlet with four other people, a couple hundred seagulls, and the occasional sea lion who washes up onto Beach Road and starts yelling . . .

. . . which is all still four hours north of here, through a cloud of brown dust blowing sideways through maniacal traffic running north and south.

The van kicks in going up another mountain, and blasts through the gap where the wind rushes through to the sea. The cars all hit their brakes, so I hit my brakes, and we start the long way down the back side, toward the dust curtaining across the horizon, a flat brown void suspended in howling wind.

The fields go from gold to brown, chaparral to stubble, then down into a long valley spiked with vineyards dry and brown and dead as the husks of dead locusts. Even at the blur of 70 mph, the contour lines of grapevine are withered, a march of dead leaves after an early, killing frost, twitching furiously in the wind.

Wind. It's what powers the well and half the electricity out at Angel's Rest now, along with the sun. Brooke fixed up one of the old windmills on the cliff that used to power the farm's water with new blades and a turbine she built out of god-knows-what.

But Brooke won't want to run the place forever. She's an engineer, had a good run with one startup before it blew up, then another before it was sued out of existence by a "strategic partner." She's keeping the wheel turning for us as much for kicks as for her way of living at Angel's Rest for free, while driving for Uber and Lyft for her cash, until one of her deals with one of those startups comes through, which could be sooner, later, tomorrow or never.

I don't know why Brooke doesn't just go get a job at one of them, ops or product manager or back-end systems, or whatever, until they get their second or third round of financing, then come on back here to catch up on sleep. She's in her mid-30s and can still take the beating. Sure, it wouldn't be full CTO pay, or even corporate manager pay, but it would be more cash than Uber or Lyft, and a huge backend of equity.

"You'd do that?" she asked just last week, as we watched the sun go down from her porch.

"I would have, back when. I did, with the first one."

"And it worked out?"

"Mostly."

"So why wouldn't you again?"

I wasn't sure what to tell her: that it was something you do at her age, not mine? Because of how hard you have to work, for far more years than anyone tells you, and maybe for nothing but paying your bills and collecting war stories, no matter how hard you work and for no matter how many years?

Sure, I did all that in my 30s, nearly killed myself working; but I also got lucky, which was confirmed when the next thing, for as much work and as many years, blew up, and spectacularly. I didn't tell her that every start-up is a one-horse bet in an ultra-marathon distance race — and your horse may win, place, or show, but it's more likely to die somewhere on the track, and you're five years older and exhausted.

"Why not?" she asked again.

"Because I'm too old for the grind of it."

"Ouch. And I'm too . . ."

And she could have said too gay, or queer, or whatever she is. Or too short, or intense, or weird looking, even for Silicon Valley, with her Rosie the Riveter gone goth look, the big black engineer boots, red bandanna over butch black hair, the flame tats on her forearms. None of that should stand out at any company over in Silicon Valley, where everybody (except the brown shoe 'n' fleece vest 'n' Tesla venture capital dudes) looks like they're still in college. Nor would her being lesbian, or bi, or none-of-the-above. The Valley employs the full acronym, along with immigrants from everywhere — people in hajibs and turbans, lots of people named Mohammed, people named Radhe, yes, Radhe — every kind of person that half our fellow Americans loves to hate. So why not Brooke?

Maybe it's the paradox of her bulldog vibe. She's barely five feet tall but forceful, electrified, filling a space when she enters it, twitching to jump right to whatever needs fixing. Maybe that's the problem: she's smart as the rest of them, but also *manually* competent — something too blue collar, a little dirty, in a flattened-org, open-work-space sea of coders, gamers, and geeks all high on whiteboard marker fumes, squatting in gleaming breakout conference rooms until they get that big cube over there. Maybe Brooke just tries too hard, which is how she can make something like Angel's Rest run; but it threatens people, especially all those "engineers" who wouldn't know how to change a flat tire.

Or maybe she's just cursed.

I wish I could believe in easy explanations like that, however simple or stupid they are. Then I could say that Brooke is cursed by the Gods to live next to the sea but never sail it, only serve us mere mortals who sail in and out; that she will be the last one left at Angel's Rest, jerry-rigging the pump one more time to get the last of the water out of the ground before the whole thing collapses, under another winter of pounding rain, into the ocean.

But until that happens and the world does end, I'll keep paying Brooke a few hundred bucks a month for the water and electricity and I'll get to live right on the beach, *the* California Dream, a thing that normally costs millions of dollars and is way too good to last.

Though it wasn't Radhe's California Dream. Hers was the original American version: house, mortgage, kids. She was off to the perfect start when I met her: a beige apartment in a beige building next to the freeway. She knows calculus, but she never understood that I was living the second-order American Dream, the one that blows everything off and runs west. And when that one plays out, you keep running until you get to California, the apotheosis of the second-order American Dream — one simple, inverted coefficient that sums not to a mortgaged future but to an eternal present. To never growing up.

And the best way to pull that off is never having kids.

I tried saying exactly that to Ike a few weeks back. But he's too lost in the California version of the first-order American Dream: the cool Betty surfer mom, the plucky little grom, the perfect little house by the beach. And we do know guys like that, guys who surfed on the tour with him, who are still hustling to make a living off surfing: retail shops, surf camps, the luckiest still sponsored and making movies or calling events on TV, hawking surf brands or protein shakes. But they set all that up ten and twenty years ago, when Ike was still recovering from the injury and meds. Now he's my age, and he still thinks he can chase around after a kid?

He's only kidding himself. But why hurt his feelings? Why say, *Come on, man . . . you're 52 and you can barely walk, and kids are a decathlon for the first 5 years,. Let it go, dude!*

But he won't. We were sitting around Neptune's, the hollowed out old store and café at Angel's Rest, just last week, three of our four knobby bare feet up on the big table watching the marine layer come in and the sun drop behind it. (Ike can't lift his right leg high enough to get it up on the table, so he plants it in the sand pitted of the floor, his foot sliding and un-sliding on the grit.)

I was talking to him, but he was talking more to the ocean than to me, his eyes always out there searching the surface, or the horizon, or the sky, for I'm not sure what.

His leg finally goes quiet and he shakes his head, like he's trying to get water out of his ears, or sand out his big mess of dirty blonde hair, a catch of wind-blown dune grass down over his sun-splotched neck.

After a few minutes of us sitting in the silence and gathering dusk, his eyes come to rest on something way out there, and his perma-bronzed face — with its wide, muscular, shaving model jaw, and nose peeled forever to pink — finally lets go.

"You just gotta keep looking," he said.

But that's all he ever really does: just look, at the ocean, like some answer is coming from out there somewhere. Like the eternity of it will lend him some time, give him back the last ten or twenty years, make his hip and pelvis whole again, make him as big and strong as he was when he placed in the top ten on the tour, getting top tens on all the bigger wave events, and even grabbing a podium at Pipeline. Like if he stares at the ocean long enough, it will pull him back out on an old longboard — or even better, back in the kitesurfing rig he helped invent and perfect, but pushing way out in front of where they could go, hence the ruined hip and pelvis.

And so I laid off, because he's just a sad guy. He's still waiting to find the woman of his dreams, the one he will marry and settle down with; and because he's too old and has trouble getting around, he wouldn't want to have his own kids with her which would be fine, because she'd already have one.

"I was looking today," he told me.

"Where?"

"On the beach. Up at Pacifica, on the big beach break, where all the moms hang out."

"You were cruising the beach? For married women?"

"Jesus, Jack! Not the married ones. Come on! But a lot of those cool surfer moms are single, like Jen and Rachel. Meet one of them, and that's how you end up being a Dad. Especially if you can't exactly run around after a three-year old."

That's kinda weird, I thought.

"I know it sounds weird. But when you're our age. And it could happen. It *has* happened. I mean — look at Laird."

By which he meant Laird Hamilton, the surfer turned surfing conglomerate, the inventor of tow-in surfing, stand-up paddling, the surf foil. He's one of the world's most famous surfers: sponsored for decades and no doubt forever, with his own protein powder franchise, and what looks — in all the magazines anyway — like a perfect life. He's married to Gabrielle Reece, the Über Betty from the '90s, and they live on the North Shore, because where else would you live if you were them?

"So what about Laird? He's married and has a bunch of kids. You're not going after Gabby Reece, are you?"

I tried my best to sound like I was kidding because I really did not know if he was or not.

"Dude," he gestured, not at me but at the ocean, and said, "Please! I would never do that. I'm talking about when Laird was a kid himself. How he hooked up his mom. You ever heard that story?"

"Not really."

"Laird's mom was a single mom. And he was this ripped little grom."

"Of course he was."

"Seriously. Can you imagine? Him as a grom? He's out shredding huge waves, and he meets some dude out there one day who's ripping it with him. And they take a shine, I guess. So little Laird says 'Dude, you gotta come meet my mom!' and drags him home. And his Mom ended up marrying the guy."

*Wow*, was all I had to say to all of that, so I said nothing.

Ike looked away from the ocean for the first time, his dark blue eyes backfilled with its light, the color of moving water. "Can you imagine?"

"It's a hell of a story," was all I could think to say. I was stuck on how a guy my age could be cruising a popular beach, trying to reverse-engineer Laird Hamilton's stepdad's great fortune. I couldn't decide if it was funny, or touching, or weird, probably because it was all three. Definitely too much to put into a song, except maybe by John Prine or Tom Waits, or maybe even Frank Zappa.

He turned back to the ocean. "Even though it sounds a little weird."

Best to make light of it, I thought. "Hanging around on the beach looking to bump into little kids so you can meet their moms? Yeah, just a little."

"Yeah," he closes his eyes and hangs his head. "I know it is."

The van's engine kicks in, trying furiously to keep pace with the flow of cars and trucks climbing up the next hill out of the valley of the oil derricks.

Up and through the gap, and there's the strongest blast of wind yet — BOOM! — a body blow to the van.

The wind screams a high-pitched whine through the closed windows, and I fight the wheel to stay in line. The valley below is browned out in a giant cloud of dust from the ground to 10,000 feet, as high as a great, looming thunderhead.

Down this next hill, and the 101 straightens, all brakelights at the bottom, and disappears into the brown cloud. It's going to be bumper to bumper at 80 mph from here, all the way down into and all along the Salinas River valley, until I can jump back toward the ocean.

Maybe when I get back, Ike will have some good news, that his new and oddest of all beachcombing adventure has turned up the Betty Mom and little grom he's apparently been seeking.

Sure, the whole idea is weird, and all in service to fantasy, to his version of Calafia. But fantasy is what everybody sells out here, right? From Hollywood to Silicon Valley to the ashrams up north? Because fantasy is what people buy. It's medicine, a salve for the physical ache of loneliness, especially when it fills your imagination with sex, or money, or love, or just some cool little kid to take to the beach. I used to snort that drug all the time, the might-have-beens with this one or that one, the kids that never were, kids who'd be half-grown by now.

But the hangover is awful, leaving you more alone than when you started.

And unlike Ike, I know enough at my age to keep my fantasies in the past. Sure, I've seen how Jill turned out, a Betty Mom still killing it in the mountains. I beat myself up about her for a couple of years after all that; but it was about her, not the whole dream. After I blew her off and she left Colorado, and Danny and Aaron were right behind her, and I was all alone in my mountain house, I used to picture all of it unfurling like a tapestry of blue skies, rainbow fleece, and smiling faces: Steamboat Springs and the bike and ski trail along the Yampa River, surrounded by snow-capped mountains; all that fresh air for Jill and the baby; the old house where Julie was living when Danny and I met her, maybe even Danny and Julie right around the corner; and me back to making corporate money by telecommuting or consulting or whatever; and Jill working up at the resort teaching skiing, not like all those miserable soccer moms out in the god-forsaken suburbs, but Jill, the same hot, ripped, young, smart, cool Betty that she ever was, and now a mama bear too, but with a kangaroo pouch, on cross-country skis.

And who am I to laugh at Ike?

But yes, better to keep all that in the past that never was, not a future that can never be, because you can't do a damn thing about it, only savor it like a dark and bitter beer in an empty bar.

Because who knows what can happen? I tried to learn that very lesson — that you can learn from your mistakes — with Leah. A few years after I finally fled Colorado, I was signing up for all of it with her, not out in the mountains but in a synagogue of all unlikely places, because I really was *in love with her,* as they say. And I didn't want to make the same mistake twice. So I was ready, really ready, I thought, to throw down. So yes, it's best to keep the fantasies in the past, where you can unspool each to the perfect happy ending. Because who knows what might have happened with Leah, if she'd beaten the cancer.

But she didn't.

And the darkest part of me wondered: was I actually relieved?

Because, unlike Ike, I was never running around looking for any of that: not with Jill, not with Leah. I never wanted kids, even blew up a nearly ten-year marriage over it, right after turning 30, when my ex-wife's friends started getting pregnant, one after another.

So when the past is too painful, my fantasies reach back further than anything in my actual past, or in anyone else's, all the way back into the mists of history and mythology, to Calafia. She's the one I take along on road trips, bring to the beach with me, imagine I'm playing guitar for in my bedroom late at night. She's the one there with me when I'm trying to fall asleep in a loud campground or cold hotel room.

So, yes: who am I to laugh at Ike? At least he admits it out loud. And at least he's trying to do something about it, with the same reckless courage that put him in that first, homemade, untested kitesurfing rig. And look how that turned out: sent him 50 feet into the air, before landing him in the hospital for a week and wheelchair for a year.

Though it wasn't a lack of courage that kept me from wanting to have kids. It was pure, unalloyed, cold sweat fear: fear that I could fail at being a father by even one of the hundred ways my father failed; and the commensurate fear that my kids would hate me even one one-hundredth as much as I hated my father.

Because my father was crazy. And a drunk, like they say (and I can imagine) Johnny was a drunk.

But unlike Johnny, my father never made it through a single hospitalization or rehab without storming off to the nearest convenience store. And maybe, if only cosmically, that's the reason I ended up in Johnny's band, as playing music for money was someone else's outrageous fantasy and the last thing that would have occurred to me. I wasn't looking to be in anybody's band, let alone one that was touring and making money; I was just happy to have lucked into my little synagogue and *kirtan* gigs, grateful for roomfuls of friendly strangers to play and sing with after bombing out on Jill and Colorado.

And I never once fantasized about it, forward or backward. It just happened.

Some 20-odd years after my wife and I were one rent payment away from homeless, and I'd long since put the guitar away forever, music was the one thing still there, after everything else had fallen to pieces. Music was the one friend who couldn't leave town, or get cancer and die.

The music is all that matters, all that means anything over time, a fantasy that you can actually inhabit, if only for three and a half minutes at a pop. This is something I'll never forget, never take for granted, no matter how crazy Johnny gets on stage, or how shitty he is to everybody backstage, or how dreary or crappy the venues or hotels or hangers-on.

I know how to power right through that shit, and it has nothing to do with knowing how to play the guitar or bass, or play by ear, or pick up the chords to a song the first time through and the melody the second time through. It's my eye-of-the-shitstorm mode, the thing Gordon saw in me when I was getting his girlfriend and her shattered leg off the mountain that day, and even that wasn't something I'd learned in mountain rescue. The same liquid iron calm that fills my core during a rescue goes all the way back to the old man, and the screamings and beatings, and the standing in to defend my sister and mother, just turning to stone and taking the beating until he wore himself out.

So no, I never wanted kids after any of that. I wanted freedom, and money enough never to be someone's whipping boy, and if I got really lucky, a way to flee my own miserable history back East.

But my ex-wife had the exact opposite plan: after that long, grueling struggle to get ourselves away from our crazy families, and out of poverty, and into the middle of the great American nowhere, she wanted kids — *maybe two, maybe even three!* — because that's what people do. Even 52-year old surf pioneers who are so broken down they can barely walk, apparently.

It's what she wanted to do anyway, with the same determination that got her out of hardscrabble Kentucky. Start a family of her own, and *will* it to happiness, give her kids everything we never had, heal her own childhood that way.

Not me. I'd heal mine by lighting out for the territories, to some place wild, edgy, and beautiful, as far from the middle of the great American nowhere and its happy families as I could get.

Not that much of the West hasn't also been plowed up into its own version of a great American nowhere, with its own cruel history and mindless oblivions.

Like this "farm" all around me as I charge up the Salinas Valley at 80 mph in a river of cars and trucks. This "farm" swallows up everything on both sides of the highway, in every direction: an infinity of factory fields, an endless blur of the same dark green, hemmed in by streaking silver gas pipelines and heavy power lines running along the road. This giant griddle of dark green is dotted every mile or so with a small bus or big pickup truck, and a clutch of workers wrapped in what look like dirty white linen, flapping in the wind. They stoop and rise, stoop and rise, but never seem to move. Only the rows move beneath them, like wave after wave on a long straight stretch of poisoned ocean, unfurling off into a blur of brown dust.

This is John Steinbeck country, speaking of cruel history, a once fertile valley raked and plowed and fertilized and raked again only by wind and flood and drought, and finally brought to heel by monster machines that cut these endless rows of industrial-squared lines. This is where others fleeing to the West came, not for jobs in Hollywood or Silicon Valley or some ashram up north, but for whatever they could put in their pockets and mouths at the end of the day. Out here where the fruit drops from the trees, and the water tastes like wine, or so the old song goes. Until they get past the border, where they don't have the *do-re-mi*, and the thugs and the cops and the county keep them that way, stooped to the ground except on Sundays, safe from the communist menace, divided forever against themselves and each other. And they are still coming, from the south now, and there they are, still bent over in the scorching sun and howling wind.

Past them to the east, over the top of the brown cloud, I can just make out the tops of the mountains, Pinnacles National Park, where thousands of condors used to soar, massive dino-birds with 12-foot wingspans, before pesticides had killed off all but the 22 who were saved, bred in captivity, and reintroduced somewhere in the mountains over there. Do they fly over the top of this monotonous green and brown horror? Does anything live down in those razor-cut rows they can hunt? Or do they keep flying west?

I look in that direction, to the west, past the top of the same brown cloud, and can just make out the back side of the mountains crashing down into Big Sur, the Santa Lucia Range and Ventana Wilderness. The upper air is the color of smoke, the sky flattened, gray, dead. No condors, no other birds of prey, nothing. When all of this is over, and nobody's kids or grandkids can save them from all this perfectly organized, industrial-squared devastation, the condors will have the last laugh. In one of our spasms of decency, we saved 22, and five or six generations later, they will have the run of this place again, and it will come back to life. But not until fires like that one just over that mountain range have burned all of us humans out of here forever . . .

HONK!

A horn blasts behind me, and bursts of taillights everywhere, as the highway spills down off a bridge. Up ahead, a cluster of giant silver silos and white cinderblock buildings smudged brown, and a snarl of trucks and buses full of workers and people walking on both shoulders of the highway, through the first of what passes for towns around here.

The hum of traffic that flowed with the highway now buzzes, angry as hornets, crawling through intersections with lights high overhead. The sides of the highway thicken with more cinderblock buildings, trailers, houses, all coated with dust and splotched with mud, bars on all the doors and windows, with a hulking, dusty crew-cab pickup truck parked outside every third or fourth house. It looks like one of those border towns in Mexico, a place built and managed to serve and supply the other side of the border and be hated for its efforts, a sprawl of squalor on the wrong side of the American economic tracks.

I'm stuck in a steady stream of new cars and trucks passing through with their windows up.

Salinas is the town up ahead, and I've heard there is a John Steinbeck museum somewhere around here. I've always wanted to stop and check it out; but this traffic sucks and I'm in a hurry to get back.

I inch along through the next intersection, truckstops on three of the four corners, and a mountain of rusted something on the fourth corner, a quartet of oil tanks behind that, and billboards everywhere: for fast food, Jesus, "adult" books, casinos, and . . . "Ha!" I can't help but blurt out in the empty van.

Because there he is, one of two employers: Johnny the Rock Star, with the aviator shades and cowboy hat, up on the billboard for the Spirit Wind Casino. And our three dates next month, over on the rez.

I wonder if that casino has booze or not. Some will and others won't, based on some elaborate wrangling within the tribe, and between the tribe and whatever county they're technically in but not part of, and the State of California.

I've been doing this just long enough to have figured out that I prefer the ones without booze, because Johnny is more likely to flip out in the ones with it. Not that he's tempted to drink after all the rehabs. But the proximity of the booze, the oozing stink of it on the air, and the constant, mumbling roar of the crowd when there's nothing to cheer at, or all through a quiet song, sets him off on one of his tirades.

As I drive by the billboard, I can't help but laugh out loud again. "Sunset Road Reunion Tour. Yeah, right, Johnny."

Because Johnny is *always* on his "Sunset Road Reunion Tour." Because it's the one song of his that ever broke through on the radio, way back in the late '70s. It's not a bad song, but it's nowhere near his best one. He wrote dozens of others back in the day, at the then busy intersection of rock, pop, folk and country, many of them covered and a couple made famous, one by the Eagles and one by Linda Ronstadt. The biggest thing he ever sold, after the "Sunset Road" single, was a live album about life on the road, all written from his house up in Laurel Canyon.

Johnny made a ton of money, back when you made tons of money from albums. But, unfortunately, he put half of it up his nose or the noses of a succession of wives who left him for rehab and eventually alimony payments. When he finally got his ass kicked by the coke, lost the last wife, and lost the house in Laurel Canyon, he went back out on the road. But everyone from his original band was either dead, off in some cult, or flipping L.A. real estate and not speaking to him. And his bass player, the guy whose parts I now play, died not of the overdose everybody assumed, but at the hands of the last in a long line of jealous boyfriends and husbands, who figured out how to sneak into the band's hotel with a gun.

After all that, and after the rehab that finally stuck — the one in Malibu, where he met my other employer, Amrita, who was there for an addiction to diet pills — Johnny went back out on the road and has been there ever since. And not because he was one of a thousand musicians who made their fame and initial fortune writing and singing all those bittersweet songs about life on the road, but because touring has turned out to be the last way to make a living from music.

They used to tour not to sell tickets so much as to sell their latest album. And they still don't tour to sell tickets, as all that money now goes to everybody else: the venues, the promoters, the liability insurers; and any spinoff "album" sales go to the tech companies who long ago liquefied albums into songs that now stream — after the record companies have siphoned off their fill — for penny royalties.

Minor legends like Johnny are out on tour so their old fans, and their kids, and even a few grandkids, will come out and buy the merch, the swag: the t-shirts, hats, hoodies, baseball jackets, jean jackets, beer coozies, concert films, refrigerator magnets, vintage tour posters, fancy boxed sets of CDs, and vinyl reissues of records half of them still have packed away in their attics. Because guys like Johnny aren't really rock stars these days so much as they're franchises. And the other guys in Johnny's band — only Curtis from the old days, the rest like me from somewhere else, with no personal history to set Johnny off — are hardly living that old rock 'n' roll fantasy. They're middle-aged guys with mortgages and ex's and kids in college, back out on the road because you can no longer make money recording music, publishing music, teaching music, or getting your latest album onto what's left of the local airwaves, but only by selling your own stuff down at the far end of Johnny's merch table.

I just happened to dumb-luck my way into all of it. I was splitting my time between what was left of a once promising tech job outside Salt Lake City and ski patrol duty that kept me sane, healthy, and flush with lift tickets and new gear. And I was playing with a hippie band in a ski resort bar, and one of the weirder, if most reliable unpaid weekend gigs a serious amateur musician could want: leading the band at a garrulous, new-fangled synagogue on the edge of Salt Lake City.

That was barely two years ago now, when I met Gordon. And it was literally, by accident, his girlfriend's, on an icy ski slope no one should have been skiing, least of all the fancy L.A. people in the matching cherry-red ski suits.

At the time, I was lost in a tangle of heartbreak and rage: over Leah's desperate losing fight with ovarian cancer; over the blitzkrieg cannibalization of a decent little tech company I'd moved from Colorado to try and help salvage, right before the tech behemoth channeling most of its revenue had a mood swing and decided to screw it; over the cruelty and capriciousness of sudden loss. All I had left were those mountains, and music, and the bittersweet, ephemeral release of mixing my guitar and voice in with hundreds of other voices on Friday nights.

I was turning 50, hitting a bottom I didn't know existed, and I didn't care. I'd survived the violence of my childhood, the poverty of my 20s, and sadness of my marriage falling apart in my 30s, but this was the first time I'd ever really let go, had stopped believing in a better day, given up hope. I was a zombie, in between rescues on the mountain and Friday nights on the *bima* with my guitar, when at least I was useful to other people.

And there they were, as I was planting the signs and stringing the rope to close the top of another double-black diamond too dangerous for anybody in the washed-out light: a huddle of cherry-red, half way down a headwall bulging with old moguls and glazed with ice from rain earlier in the week.

I heard their yelling before I saw them, his for help and hers from the pain, and traversed my way down the icy headwall as fast I could. She was sprawled out in the blue-glare shadow of a huge mogul, screaming; Gordon was standing next to her in the middle of the empty trail trying to make his cell phone work; and there was blood all over the snow, from a gash in her left pant leg, where the top of her tibia had stabbed through.

I went straight into eye-of-the-shitstorm mode: radioed for help; took off my skis and marked the spot; and then ever so gingerly lifted and untangled her legs. Gordon stood over me, transfixed, his eyes bugging out through the lenses of goofy, red-framed glasses that filled his flat-light goggles, watching me hunched down over her, as I cut away the cherry-red nylon from the blood-red mess of her shin. Sometime during all that, Leese pulled up with the sled and held and comforted her as I exposed the wound and wrapped it with a pressure dressing to stop the bleeding, then splinted it, the whole time talking with her in that practiced, calm, soothing, minimizing, *this-isn't-so-bad*, *I've-seen-worse*, *you'll-be-fine* voice I learned from Aaron and everybody during mountain rescue training back in Colorado.

It was the look of controlled terror in Leese's eyes — those unblinking steel-blue eyes that said to me, *You may have seen worse than this, in the backcountry, Jack, but I haven't around here, not ever, unless you want to count the tree collision fatality last year* — that finally restarted the clock, jumpstarted my heartbeat, sent the bile into my throat.

But I choked it down when I saw that Gordon had caught the look in Leese's eyes too; gave him my best nod of reassurance; and went back to dressing, packing, and splinting her leg.

It was my rescue, so it was my sled to lead, with Leese holding the tail rope and controlling the speed as we eased her down the rest of the headwall. Even though the fully bundled in Chloe didn't weigh much, it took nearly half an hour of side-slipping in and out of those icy moguls — a cry of pain with every bump — for us to get her down the rest of the trail.

Gordon side-slipped alongside the sled the whole way down, attempting to reassure her, checking in with Leese, then checking in with me: *Are you cool? Do you need a break?* then back to reassure Chloe, *Don't worry, honey, this guy is the man, he's got you,* then back to Leese and then to me.

*Are you cool?* until Chloe finally screamed at him, *Please just shut the FUCK up, Gordon, and let them get me the HELL off this goddamned mountain!*

After the clinic and the paperwork and stowing her for the ride to the hospital and surgery, Gordon handed me his phone number and asked for mine, saying that I'd saved her, saved her leg and maybe even her life, and I told him he was being too dramatic.

"It's just a really bad fracture, we see them all the time, train for them all the time," I half-lied.

"Bullshit on that! What can we do for you, my friend?"

I kept trying to say no worries, it's just my job.

But he insisted, as he was climbing into the ambulance for the ride down the hill to the hospital, that they'd call me, take me out to dinner that night, any place I wanted to go. I told him I was busy that night, which as usual I wasn't, and figured that was the last I'd hear of it.

But four hours later, there was an L.A. number on my cell phone. He told me Chloe was out of surgery, and they wanted to take me to dinner the next night, before they left town. I told them thanks, but I had a music thing I did every Friday night, and he said, *Wow? You're a musician? What kind?* And when I told him it was at a synagogue, there was a long pause before he blurted out, *Really? No way! That's cool! I'm Jewish! Sort of. We can take you out to dinner after!*

With all that forced cheeriness and the "sort of Jewish" thing, I was certain I'd never see them again, just get the usual card and bottle of wine or REI gift certificate I got from most of the harder rescues.

And yet there they were, hobbling into Congregation *Shir Hadash* the next night, ten minutes into *Erev Shabbat* service: Chloe on her crutches, hanging her head in what had to be a bombed-out daze from painkillers; and Gordon in those big red glasses and an actual jacket and tie, like he was going to a *bar mitzvah* in a traditional synagogue. Even if he'd been more than "sort of" Jewish, there was no way he could know what he was in for: a freakfest of a congregation of "sort of" hippies; all that ecstatic dancing up and down the aisles to my guitar and the band; and a fire-breathing redhead of a *Kabbalah* scholar of a rabbi with a voice as strong and clear as Natalie Merchant's.

That service was especially ramped up because it was Passover, and the "Song of Miriam" *parasha*, with some of the most joyful, raucous music of the year. I had talked a couple extra folks onto the *bima* with the band and me: Joey and his conga drums; Ezra and his oud; Margie and her tambourines; and Michael and the clarinet he seems able to play only on 10. Rabbi Miriam was leading everyone around the sanctuary in a big singing, dancing circle, banging on her own tambourine, and I'm up there on the *bima*, trying to play loud enough for the rest of the band to hear me, keep time, and pound out the beat, a wild, hemp and rainbow clad circus of sacred music and movement.

And right afterwards, in the electric buzz that always follows an especially rowdy service, with the *matzah* and hugs going all around, there he was, cutting through the crowd, Chloe trying to limp behind on crutches.

"That was terrific, man! Who knew a serious mountain man could also kick ass on the guitar? And keep a nutty band together in a crazy room like this!"

There were ten other people gathered around us, all sweaty and beaming and looking for the usual hug, so I started to say thanks and turn away, but he cut me off, "You gotta come to L.A., man! You gotta meet Johnny! He needs a bass player, someone who can keep his shit together. And *you* are exactly the kinda guy who can do that."

"But —"

"What? You gotta a regular gig? Besides this, I mean?"

I started to say, *Yeah, well, if you want to call it that, I also play and sing for two dozen people and three dozen bucks with a hippie band up the road,* but the crowd closed in tighter, a blur of *Thank yous!* and *Shabbat Shaloms!* and big hugs, so he backed off, and sat Chloe down in a pew, until the sanctuary was emptying. Then he insisted that I let them take me out for dinner. He was a tough guy to say *No* to, and I was hungry, and curious how Chloe was holding up, so I followed them to the restaurant in their hotel, halfway back up the canyon toward the ski resorts.

Before our drinks came, he started in about Johnny who, until that moment, was just another minor rock star from the '70s I'd heard about and assumed was dead or retired.

"You play the bass, right?"

Before I could answer, *Yes, every guitar player can play the bass — it's two-thirds of the guitar — or they're not really a guitar player,* he said, "Of course you can! Every good guitarist can play the bass. Look at Phil Lesh! He was a classical composer, for God's sake, when Jerry threw him on the bass, because he just knew."

Phil Lesh? The bass player for the Grateful Dead? Was this guy out of his mind?

"Same way I knew when I saw you kick ass on the guitar tonight," he went on, "and hold that insane room together, and that's how I know you'd be the perfect guy to anchor Johnny onstage. He can always use a good anchor up there. Especially someone he doesn't have any fucked up history with."

At the time, I had no idea what he was talking about. I thought it was just another elaborate fantasy cooked up by some rich asshat from L.A. with statement eyeglasses, the feathered remains of a big '80s coif, and Botox freeze around the eyes and across the forehead.

"It's not a glam gig," he said. "But it's rock-steady work, man — festivals and state fairs and casinos, and it pays steady."

I just stared at him, as if he were talking through the haze of a dream at me. It was in English, but the words were scrambled.

"What's the matter?" he finally asked.

Still, I had nothing.

"Oh, shit! It's *Shabbat*, right? You can't talk about any of that! It's work, I get it!"

Still, nothing.

"But wait — you drove here, so . . ."

"It's not that," I said, trying to ratchet on my game-face, because he'd mentioned money, so I realized he might actually be serious.

A week later I was calling in sick to the office and flying off to L.A., to a cavernous black rehearsal studio, where I sat in with the band for an hour, then with the band and Johnny for all of three songs before they offered me the gig.

Which made no sense — was the sky falling but in a good way? — so I just steady-walked it like it was a mountain rescue. And that's why, Gordon finally told me, I was really hired. Sure, I could play the bass as well as anyone else who can play anything on the guitar at will, and well enough to keep people singing. But I was hired to handle Johnny.

A month later, with the ski season over and resort shut down and my company looking for people to quit before they had to be laid off, I was playing those first few tentative gigs with Johnny. It was all eye-of-the-shitstorm mode at first: me hunkered down on the beat and song, trying not stand out in any way that would make someone look over at me from backstage, or in the green room, or from over at the soundboard, and say, *Who the hell is THAT guy?*

Three months after that, I tossed what I still owned into my old truck, and moved into a two-room cottage next to the ocean, in a hamlet out of time, off-the-grid, and falling into the Pacific Ocean. Because wasn't that just like life? You chase after one thing for years, and never catch it, and then something else just shows up, at random. It's exactly nothing like what you'd planned, or wanted, or imagined, or even made up in a bar because you're drunk and bored and lonely, and so is the stranger sitting next to you, hoping you'll distract him with some bullshit story . . .

And now, stuck in all this damn traffic crawling across the agri-industrial flatlands of the once great river valley that created and sustained Monterey Bay, all I want is to get back to my cottage at Angel's Rest. Not so much because I care about any of it falling into the ocean, but because I have an odd need to put my hands on my other guitar, my warm, sweet, mahogany acoustic, and my old photo albums, before it does all wash out to sea — an urge made more urgent still by news that the gate is locked, for some reason Brooke doesn't know, because Kenny doesn't want to tell anybody.

North of the grimy clutter of agri-towns running inland from Monterey Bay, I can finally jog west off the 101. The traffic thins, and the wind suddenly dies, as if spent from the fury of the fire down south.

I turn the radio to the news, wondering about the fire. It's all the usual barrage of political outrage and human tragedy from somewhere else, so I switch to music and drive north up through Santa Cruz.

North of Santa Cruz, I finally get back on the PCH, relieved that it's not on fire, not yet anyway — something I think I've been bracing for in the dark part of my mind since this morning in Big Sur. It's the usual two lanes of rolling open road, with the big blue cheer of ocean down the cliffs to my left, and to the right, farms and ranches and hillsides all bleached and blasted gold and gray in the late afternoon sun.

The flags say there is a steady onshore coming in, but as I pass Waddell's, there's no one out kitesurfing, and the surf is blown out. Wind against wind. Weird. Not that I'd stop. The closer I get to Angel's Rest, the more I just want to get back . . .

Half an hour later, I'm a mile short of Angel's Rest, passing the field where the red-tails hunt, and there he is: the Lost Prophet of the PCH!

He's walking the other way, at that slow, steady pace, his head tipped as always halfway between the horizon and the sky.

I see him every few weeks, wandering up or down the PCH, usually somewhere between Half Moon Bay and Santa Cruz. But I've seen him as far north as Pacifica, and one time all the way down in Ventura.

And there he goes again, heading south, in that same mud-brown, woolen-looking thing that just sort of hangs on him, a ratty charcoal-colored blanket around his shoulders. His face is baked with sun, his bare lower legs and feet blackened by I don't want to know how many hundreds of miles. He just drifts along on the shoulder of the road, a walking stick in his right hand, his head turned half skyward, the way Ike stares out at the ocean for hours at a time.

*Bad drugs, lots of them, a long time ago*, is the general assessment around Angel's Rest, when the Lost Prophet of the PCH comes up over beers down in Neptune's, after somebody has sighted him on the way home.

*Maybe*, Brooke always says, *but you'd have to see the eyes.*

Which none of us can do when we're blowing past him at 60 mph, like I just did, itching to get somewhere.

A minute later, I'm pulling up to our turnout. I park in front of the old iron gate, swung across the dirt road, and locked up with a big shiny new chain and padlock.

Five minutes after I text Brooke to let her know I'm here, I hear her before I see her: the high whine of a small engine down the road, then a dust cloud then a tiny figure on a big dirt bike popping over the ridge. She had just started reassembling that thing from a pile of parts when I left three days ago.

"Look at that," I say, as the bike sputters and stalls on the other side of the gate, and she jumps off, her big engineer boots landing in the dirt with two splats. "That thing was a pile of rusted shit when I left."

"It's still a pile of rusted shit," she says. Her grease and work-stained fingers grab for the jumble of keys hanging from a chain on her belt loop.

"Got her running though."

"Barely," she snorts, as she searches the keys. "Finicky engine."

"I knew you'd get it going," I say, remembering how she wrestled the frame out of a pile of old grills, ruined lawn furniture, and beer cans, in the breezeway between two of the abandoned houses.

"Glad one of us has so much faith in me," she says, working the key off the ring.

"So what's up with that?" I say, pointing at the lock on the gate.

"Yeah," she mutters, straightens her cap, and kicks at the lock. "What the *fuck* is up with that, is what I said."

"Kenny didn't tell you?"

"Nope."

"Maybe it's just to keep the surf poachers and tourists out."

"Poachers will just park out here, like the last time."

"What did he say last time?"

"That too many people were driving down and parking wherever, poking around the houses, messing up the wildflowers."

"Thought by law we had to keep it unlocked? Coastal access and all that."

"We do. But so far, nobody's complaining," she says, handing me a shiny new key. "This one's yours. Kenny says don't let anybody in. But fuck him. Do whatever you want. I have to get back in the goddamn car and make a few bucks."

I get back in the van and drive through, and stop to watch in my side view as her tiny frame swings the gate closed.

She waves as she buzzes around me on the dirt bike, then jumps the ruts of the road, a cloud of golden dust in the setting sun. There is more dirt bike than Brooke, bouncing over the ruts of the little road, and a cloud of her dust as the road drops through the slot, down to the beach.

I just sit in the idling van a minute, watch the dust settle and the ocean spread out straight ahead like a great, curving, shimmering plate, and finally breathe out.

I start down the road, but before I'm halfway across the long stubbled meadow to where the road threads down through the cliff, lit up in the setting sun, she has swapped the dirt bike and is already coming back up the hill.

We wave as she passes me going the other way in her perfectly restored, shiny black Mustang convertible — "Always good for extra tips from the old guys with car fetishes," she says — classic in every way but for the Uber and Lyft stickers.

I breathe out again, and ease the van down the road, past the golden meadow toward the break in the cliff, past the road turning off through the row of cypress sculpted by the wind into the shapes of outstretched human hands.

I slow to a crawl, trying to see up the side road: who's up at the sprawling ranch house where Johnny lives when he's not living in L.A.? Who's up at the once sprawling but now half-shuttered original house where Kenny has been living, along with the ghost of his ancestors, since he came back from college and however many years he says he toured "with" the Dead? No cars, no vans, no microbus, just two deer staring back at me, and a pair of red-tailed hawks circling overhead.

I drive on, easing the van through the break in the cliff, down the switchbacks of the crumbling road. I pass the first lane of little cottages, where Brooke and Ike live, and ease into the next lane, and my cottage. Home, for now . . .

By the time I've unloaded the van and grabbed a bite, I think about walking out to find Ike, see if he wants to hang out down in Neptune's, and watch the sun go down.

I go out onto my little porch — over a breezeway between boarded up cottages down on Beach Road, with its piles of old tires and tangle of salt-scoured beach bikes — just in time to see Ike limping up to his usual spot: a flat boulder on the first shoulder of the cliff at the north end of the beach.

From up there, you can take in all of Angel's Rest; watch the waves coming in from half a mile out; see around the cliff to the north and past the cliffs to the south. On a clear day, you can take in the whole curve of the ocean.

I think I see Ike look this way, so I wave a big wave, for a long time, hoping to catch his eye.

But he doesn't see me, just sits with difficulty, and stares out at the ocean, like he does at the end of most days.

I sit on my porch, throw my feet up on the rail, watch the sun sink toward the horizon, and breathe out the last of this odd day. A wave of exhaustion from the drive washes over me like the waves coming in down there.

Home, for now.

But only for now, as Radhe used to say.

She always felt weird out here, and never wanted to stay over. She loved our little beach, wind-battered as it usually is; and the music jams we have down in Neptune's. But she always wanted to go back to that beige apartment over the hill in San Jose. It was like I was one of the bad kids in school, and she was one of the good girls, the one who would ace everything and end up in med school. She made me feel like a hippie for living here, which shouldn't feel like a bad thing, but it did. Maybe that's the real reason I didn't follow her to New Zealand: I grew up decades ago and didn't like it; now my work is called "playing;" and I don't really feel like growing up again. If I went all the way down there to be with her, there would be no one else but her, and I'd have no other choice but to grow up.

There would be no Amrita and her wild yoga tribe; no Brooke with her tools who can fix anything and who fascinates me in a way I don't understand; no Johnny, who may have made a hash of his life, but is still singing about it; no Ike over there with his binoculars, enraptured as always by whatever the ocean has to say tonight.

The sun is almost down, sinking into the marine layer, a long thin strip of cloud along the horizon, turning the red-orange of a melting popsicle.

I hear my name, muffled by the waves, and look up to see Ike waving at me and shouting, and pointing straight out.

"Dolphins!" he shouts again. "Surf lessons!"

I lean inside the door and grab my binoculars off the windowsill, and stand to study the waves where Ike was pointing.

The waves are all in shadow now, the color of pewter with the sun mostly down. But I can see, maybe fifty or sixty feet out, two large shadows and one small shadow bulging up into the crest of the incoming wave.

The wave finally breaks and crashes, and two fins poke out of the foam and turn in unison, slipping back out for another. It is two dolphins, teaching their baby how to surf.

I stand and watch them catch a few more waves, until the ocean goes dark as ink, then head back into the house and fall into bed.

I have the same exact thought I had 24 hours ago, falling asleep next to this same ocean. It has the salinity of amniotic fluid, she once told me, and don't those dolphins know that too. I hope you're OK down there, Radhe. Because I'm staying here, as long as I can.

# 3 | QUARTER MOON RISING

It's not bad enough that I have to plow through the middle of San Francisco during the middle of the day — through the heart of its twelve-hour long rush hour — to get to Amrita's gig up in Sonoma. But I have to burrow all the way into Pacific Heights to pick up Amy. Or is it Amie, or maybe Aimée? Or is Aimée the one who now calls herself "Parvati?"

Traffic was hell coming up and over from the coast, and there's more of the same all the way in. There's nowhere to park on her steep little side street, of course; but before I can pull up in front and put on my flashers, she's an explosion of blonde hair and mala beads on the sidewalk in front of her gingerbread townhouse, a saffron hempy thing over a tight muscle shirt that says *Spiritual Gangsta*, and white yoga pants that look spray-painted on. She dumps a bundle of rolled yoga mats next to the van, which start rolling down the sidewalk in all directions.

I come around to help her load in, and she gives me the classic, crushing TLH — the Too Long Hug — and a "thank you SO SO SO much for coming to get me!" as she runs back into her townhouse.

In two trips, I help her pile in the rest: rolling suitcase, two more yoga mats in an orange canvas carry, a harmonium, some weird looking lamp, a big canvas bag covered with elephants and *OMs* and little mirrors, and a hemp purse exhorting us to "Live Simply, Dance Madly, Love Boldly."

She climbs up into the passenger seat, looks in the back at the guitar and duffels and camping gear, and says, "Look at you, cowboy."

"Wagons ho," I mumble, as we pull away, and I say a little prayer for the traffic through Marin.

I put my music back on, jam band, then switch it to bluegrass, just to mess with her. But she doesn't seem to notice: she's tousling and re-tousling her hair in the mirror over the visor, which is messing up my view of the Bay, the bridge ahead, and a scatter of sailboats on a bluebird day.

She finally settles into her seat, kicks off her "yoga-toes" flip-flops — *specially designed for toe separation and foot stability!* says the ad in the *Journal of Mindfulness* — and puts her perfect little feet, with their sparkled cotton candy pink polish, up on the dashboard. She pulls out an enormous water bottle, encased in fuchsia, die-cut with lotus flowers and suspended in a knitted rainbow sling.

Finally, she turns to me, pushing her sunglasses down on her nose, and gives me a little pout. "Tell me, Jack," she says. "Who *is* the mystery man behind my soul-sister's music?"

And as if on cue: traffic ahead, a dead stop, brake lights all the way up the ramp to the bridge.

"I'm serious, Jack. We've never really gotten to know each other, all these *kirtans* and retreats." She gestures out at the traffic. "And now here we are!"

"Yep. Here we are."

"So. Who *are* you?"

"I'm just a guy who plays the guitar, or the bass, and keeps the music going when all hell's breaking loose."

"Oh no," she says. "I see you! I see you back there carrying it, carrying her. You *go* there, my friend."

Actually, I do *go* there, all the time, but only half of me, the half listening to the music and feeling the room, not the half still playing the music and watching the people *in* the room. I figured out how to do both back at *Shir Hadash* and some of those first *kirtans*, with Judy and Talia. But not with Amrita or Johnny. I don't go *there* at all in any of those gigs. I have too much to keep track of — most critically, where Amrita or Johnny might be going next — so I just play, and watch.

"I mean it must be *so* amazing," she goes on, "vibing on all that energy all the time."

"It's pretty cool."

"Cool? It must be *amazing*! When Amrita goes *anahata*, and the room is all transformed. My God! So much heart, so much intention. How do you even stay grounded?"

"I just stay focused on the music."

Which isn't true at all. The song structures are simple and the music is easy, especially on those long ecstatic jams. It's as easy as breathing in and out through my guitar, my right hand moving up and down with no more thought or effort than drumming on a knee. After a year of these gigs, I can tell where we're headed, faster or slower, by the turn and angle of Amrita's head, the shifting shape of her outstretched hands, the lift of her brow. So what I focus on, much of the time, is the show: the dancing and singing, the drama on the faces of hundreds of women and dozens of men; and not all of them look like you, Amy/Amie/Aimée, not all of them blonde, yoga-lean, gym-cut, sparkly-toed.

"*So* amazing," she says again, tousling her hair and looking out at the view. Her feet are still up on the dashboard, her toes scrunching and un-scrunching like she's having sex and about to come, which makes me mildly aroused and, simultaneously, mildly nauseated.

I don't know if she's still talking about the music when Amrita really cranks it up, or the sudden view, but there it is: the kaleidoscopic unfurling of the whole of the Bay, drenched in sunshine, dotted with boats, and lined with cityscape as we slip over the Golden Gate.

She could be Calafia sitting over there, with her big blonde hair and big white teeth, and just enough sun splashed all over her face and muscled shoulders,

But no, not with the white yoga tights. And definitely not with the perfect pink toes. Calafia wears surf shorts, her feet are stained with beach tar, and around her neck is a shark's tooth, not some other continent's version of rosary beads. Calafia could kick this one's ass. And Radhe too. And she would if she were still around and saw Amy/Amie/Aimée flirting with me like this.

I suppose there was a time when I'd fall for it: the shimmering hair, the perfect body, the whole show. And I'm sure someone will this weekend, some guy my age up at the yoga retreat to cope with his divorce, or some younger guy coping with his mommy issues, and chase her around the dance floor or dining hall. Amy[3] looks more than enough like Calafia for the older dudes who come to Amrita's gigs, but don't live out here, the ones who still have to go back to their regular grind on Monday. Amy[3] is not really young, which would be especially tacky for those gentlemen seekers — unlike the Old Hempy Dudes in the same crowd, who prefer to chase after the Lost Girls of Yoga. But she never really ages either. She just works out harder; eats healthier and healthier food, and less of it; gets smidges of surgery around the edges; and moves through space like someone who believes that she glows. She is drenched in the honey that catches men, luscious and beautiful from across the room. But I've watched most of those same men buzz away, sugar-drunk, when they realize she's not Amrita, just another Acolady, an Amrita groupie. Because what they really want is the real thing — the Goddess herself — robed in light and music and *eros*, not one of her teaching assistants with the perfect body and perfect little feet and desperate smile.

The van kicks in going up the hill into Marin, and when she realizes I'm not listening to whatever she's saying, she pulls out her phone.

I turn up the music.

Luckily, not all of them look like Amy[3], or sound anything like her. Some have big curves, and brown skin, and long, inky-black or salt-and-pepper or black-and-platinum hair; and they grew up with *kirtan* as their church not their disco.

The threshing floor of a good *kirtan* may fill up with the gyrations of the Acoladies and the Lost Girls of Yoga, and a smattering of the Man Buns and Old Hempy Dudes who chase after them. But the original, actual believers come too; because, like Radhe, they keep coming to California, and all of America, with their food and all those colors. At least unlike in much of California and the rest of America, at a *kirtan* they're the honored guests, the white people happily parting to let them through, to make room for them along the sides and in the back to dance, on the cushions on the floor upfront.

Just like Radhe.

The first time I saw her, she was cutting through the crowd of hugs and *hey-there's* at my first *kirtan* with Amrita in the yoga studio in San Jose. She plopped right down right in front of me, and gathered herself on her cushion, her curves wrapped in a swirl of red and orange, hips forward, hands on her knees. And when the music started, her eyes closed and her mahogany face went as still as a mountain lake at sunrise. She was transfixed by the music, except at the beginning and end of each piece, when I'd ramp it up or down with a guitar sketch or re-sketch of the melody. Her body would stay perfectly still, but her eyes would pop open, and she'd stare at my hands, study them — and not like other guitarists do, trying to memorize what I was doing — but as if she were trying to solve a puzzle.

I hear Amy[3] say something, and look up from the blaze of traffic all around us, radiating heat as we rush north past a blur of restaurants, stores and houses built to the chain-link-fenced edge of the freeway.

"Huh?"

"What are you thinking about? You were smiling! But then you got all serious and sad."

"Nothing."

"Oh, I don't believe that, Jack!"

"Just somebody I used to know."

"Uh, huh," she says. "I'll bet I know who," she teases, her face suddenly, deadly serious. She reaches over and touches my arm. "But I understand if you're not ready to process it."

"Thanks," I say.

"But I'm here. If you need to."

"I'm good. But thanks."

She squeezes my arm, pouts again, and goes back to her phone . . .

Another hour of traffic, and we're finally free of the freeway. Amy[3] doesn't look up from her phone, and I don't turn the music down, as we thread through the retail sprawl of the freeway exit.

The road opens up soon enough, rolling over hills contoured with grapevines and spiked with great oaks, past meadows burnt golden brown in the sun.

The yoga retreat center, spread along a high ridge looking west, is a mile down a dirt road. It is yet another place that looks like a fantasy, a place too picturesque to exist anywhere except in a magazine, shrouded in trees and surrounded on three sides by golden mountains. It's the wine country version of Zen, long, flowing lines of simple, sun-blanched wood, brushed stone, and enormous plate glass; walking paths, meditation gardens, and wildflowers, all of it simple, graceful, and manicured and spontaneous at the same time. Settings like these are half the medicine — Amrita, and the yoga, and the music and dance are the other half — along with the hot tubs, massages, groovy food, and enveloping hush a hundred feet in every direction.

I load my guitar and duffels into my room in the lodge, then wander out the back, avoiding the inevitable as long as I can.

A string of cabins follows along a little creek lined with slender, waving grasses. Each is built from the same simple wood and brushed stone as the lodge, a clutch of still blooming wildflowers around its little front porch. Past the last cabin, I walk out onto the ridge and a little meditation garden, ringed with madrones with long ruddy branches like human arms and red squiggles of manzanita. The ridge spills down into a rolling meadow, fenced in by oaks with limbs waving on an invisible wind. The afternoon sun sinks through the grass, lighting it up like golden hair.

My phone buzzes with a text. Amrita. *Where are you? I want you to meet somebody before soundcheck!*

Great. Time to go to work.

I head back into the lodge, grab my guitar and gear duffel out of my room, and thread through the blur of people loading in, registering — "Where's my cabin? Where do we eat?" — and look for the event space. I'll tune up and wait for the rest of them, and if Amrita still wants me to meet that somebody, they'll find me.

Turns out the event space isn't in the lodge: it's out back in a big open-air tent — a red and white circus tent, not a wedding tent, a vast soaring vertical space — pitched next to the lodge.

Jenna and David are already in there setting up gear, sprawled out on the 8-by-10-foot riser a foot and a half above the great expanse of the room, its dance floor pebbled with sitting cushions, backjacks, folded blankets.

We exchange "Heys," hugs, and "How was the traffics?" then pull our gear out and put the sound system together, in silent efficiency. David gets the PA going first, filling the enormous empty space with a Krishna Das chant.

I pull out my guitar and tune it to the music, and look out across the dance floor. The whole space will be filled soon enough, and for the rest of the weekend, with yoga mats, more cushions, piles of blankets, and people up and dancing, or sprawled out and journaling, or sitting perfectly still like Radhe used to in the middle of all that holy cacophony.

"Ha-ay!"

I hear her before I see her, and look up to see Amrita rushing in, all in white as usual, a string of big mala beads dancing around on a tank top bulging with big, sun-freckled breasts.

She bounces up onto the stage, big hugs and side-swipe kisses for all of us.

"Did you get my text, Jack?" she asks as she plops down on her cushion and stares at her phone. "There's somebody I want you to meet!"

"OK," I say, pretending to be absorbed with the microphone and cables and boxes I'd already set up and tested.

And sure enough, she's on her phone and back off the stage and out the door.

I start playing the first line of our first song into the mike, and David cuts the Krishna Das.

Jenna walks over into the circle of drums and percussion next to me, and straddles her weathered wooden djembe, closing her eyes, rocking back and forth with my right hand. When the first line comes around again, she is right there with her own right hand on the djembe, *thump-thump, thump-thump*.

Nodding along with us, David sets up on the cushion behind his harmonium, a little pump-organ with a keyboard, like an accordion that sits on the floor and is used to lead yoga chants. He picks up the line as I go to the chords, quiet at first, then swelling with the *thump-thump* of Jenna's djembe.

The three of us push the volume in perfect synch, until we've filled the tent with that lush, pulsing sound — the sound of the collective human heart — opening, rising, and lifting to fill the tent, as if the canvas were ballooning outward with an invisible wind.

I hear David slowing, and Jenna taper the beat, and bring it down with them.

We all look over at the entryway to the tent: no Amrita.

David leans over to the board, and fires up the long, aching lines of a tamboura track through the PA. It's in D major, so I know which song he means, and pick up the line, and the three of us play on, each taking a turn to lead the chant on our vocal mikes.

Jenna and I play on, David walking to the back to check our levels, Jenna singing through Amrita's headset. When we have it all just so, we keep playing, just for us and the great empty spaciousness of the place, because it feels so good — and because we need Amrita to come back to check the sound of her own voice in the space and get comfortable with the levels, before we can knock off and go eat.

We are well into a third song when she finally rushes in, "I am *so* sorry, dear ones! You know how it is with everybody showing up!" She steps up on the stage and plops down on the huge cushion in the center of us.

Amrita, the yoga rock star — an explosion of energy and noise and *Wow!* — even without all the Acoladies swirling around her, or the Hempy Old Dudes and Lost Girls of Yoga in the back, or the Man Buns always at her feet. She's another near-perfect incarnation of Calafia: long, flowing, blonde hair and fierce ice-blue eyes; lithe, muscled, sun-dappled; a bronze serpent wrapped around each cut little bicep, and dangle of bracelets and mala beads around both wrists. Her skin-tight yoga whites show off the contours of her sculpted body, and the clink of the *OM* and lotus flower and heart necklaces draw attention down onto her chest, pressurized by her workout bra or whatever is under there holding all that boobiness at who knows what PSI so they're always beaming straight at whoever's in front of her.

"We're good," David says, handing her the headset. "Let's just check your volume."

Amrita picks up the headset, taking care to work it through her hair. She adjusts and re-adjusts her legs on the cushion, then pulls her hands into prayer position at her heart center, over the splay of beads and the heave under her tank top.

She takes in a big audible breath, waits a beat, then pushes it out; takes in another breath in, and lets out a long, slow, low moaning *OM*.

Two more *OMs*, and I find the low rumbling notes to the first line of the first song, then the first chords, and Jenna and David fall in with the drum and harmonium, and Amrita starts to sing, *Hare OM –"*

She stops suddenly, opens her eyes, and while the three of us play on, she crawls over on all fours to the board behind David.

"*Hare OM*," she sings into her headset while we play on, "*Hare OM*," while pushing her volume, and messing with all the levels.

She does this every time.

But no eyeroll from David this time. He's usually bothered by her messing with his setup. Maybe that's because he and Jenna hadn't seen each other in two weeks, until about two hours ago, and they're still glowing with the reunion.

I don't care either way, because it's just more time to play with these three — who are every bit as musically talented as the crowd thinks they are — without having to think about anything, at least not yet. Just play. And for all the silliness about to unfurl out on that dance floor, I love this music, melt into it, feel it pulsing through my body, like warm milk on a cold day, like the glow after sweet, easy sex in a sunny room.

For all that silliness, this weekend's retreat will be the perfect antidote to the gig last week with Johnny. That one was way too loud, all boom-echo off the back wall of the place, with cigarette stench leaking in through all the doors of the casino theater.

Amrita pushes her voice to the point of feedback, then gestures to David to fix the levels to there, pulling it just back from the edge of too much. Then we test the edge, launching into what will be the most raucous song of the evening, one that slow-builds over a ten-minute journey from the quiet hum of David's harmonium into the wild frenzy of an ecstatic dance.

David pumps out the lead melody, note-for-note with Amrita's wordless, throaty mezzo-soprano chanting; Jenna drums out another heartbeat, *thump-thump*, faster and faster; and I paint it all in with bright-orange rhythms, burnt-orange counter-rhythms, and bits of melody like magenta streaks across the front of the whole mural of sound.

"*Jaya Hanuman!*," Amrita finally shapes the melody into words, singing her version of the ancient prayer to Hanuman, the god of selfless service to others, the monkey-god who straddles the universe. "*Jaya Hanuman gyana guna sagara!*"

She sings another verse, pushing the pace and volume, and the levels hold. My hands finally loosen up and start to play on their own, as everything around me melts into color and sound.

The soundcheck and warmup is my favorite part of every gig: no one is performing and no one is really listening and we are just *playing*. A few minutes in, I shake off whatever stupid little thing was bothering me when I walked in, and start my whole day over, like paddling out onto that first wave. And my guitar sounds great in here, clear and crisp out of the monitors.

"Beautiful!" Amrita blurts out, as we are coming off the top again. "Perfect!"

David and Jenna stop playing as she pops off her cushion, and I finish the phrase and stop.

"See you guys ten minutes before," Amrita says as she bounces off the stage toward the door.

I want to sit here and keep playing, but David puts the PA on standby and he and Jenna are up and out the door, hand-in-hand a minute later, and it's just me and my guitar in this big empty tent.

I switch from my semi-acoustic and amp to my acoustic guitar, and play for myself and Hanuman and whoever else might be listening . . .

An hour later, the big doors at the back of the tent are opened from outside, the main lights are down and I'm sitting alone in a bath of soft purple, pink, and even softer white stage lights. The room is half-dark, and half-lit with thousands of moving pinpricks from the galaxy lamp: pink, purple, white, blue, green, yellow and red. Students start to wander in with their own cushions and blankets, water bottles, journals. Some move to the front of the room, trying to seem not in a hurry but in an obvious hurry as they make for spots right down in front of the stage, pretending not to see me. Then they scamper back to linger with the suddenly swelling crowd, all Too Long Hugs and side-swipe kisses, laughter and chatter about the traffic getting here, how *amazing* the food is, how *amazing* the view from their cabin, "how *amazing* it is to see you again!"

I wander out the back door to the bathroom, for my usual pre-gig ritual of quiet, deep breathing, and one last pee.

When I come out, Jenna and David are there at the door to the tent, still holding hands, and Amrita is doing something on her phone. She's always doing that, like so many people these days. But she seems even more distracted than usual, not really absorbed in her phone at all, but avoiding something — turning, circling around David and Jenna, then around me, like she's hiding behind us. Then I see why, who she is hiding from: that Man Bun over there, standing and staring. He's her latest, standing on the threshold of this gig like they all do, a wet puppy just in from the rain, sweet, yearning, pathetic.

This one looks like they all do: tall, athletic, bronzed, and seemingly permanently 29ish, with big sad blue eyes, a scraggly beard, and — as per the namesake of his tribe within the Tribe — a grapefruit-sized knot of dirty blonde hair on top of his head. I think this one is named Jared. Or maybe Ananda. Or Kipp. Hard to keep track.

There is always one of him at these gigs, hovering near Amrita, sitting at the end of her table in the dining hall, following her back to her room. Jenna says that Amrita swears she's never sleeping with the guy; but he sure acts like he is, or once and wants to again, with the upturned hands and that wet puppy sulk.

Amrita wedges herself between David and me, and we push past poor Jared/Ananda, and into the roar of animated voices in the tent.

It's jammed front to back and side to side with a new blur of color: yoga mats, flowing purple and hemp clothes, orange scarves, a blue turban here, blonde dreadlocks over there, and an eruption of cheers. And then a sudden near-silence, just the rustling of clothes and clanging of water bottles, as 300 people wiggle and wriggle into position on their cushions, and we do the same up here on this little stage with our instruments and mikes.

As I'm pulling on my guitar, I look out into the glare of the stage lights and what may be closer to 400 people, half with their eyes closed, the other half beaming up at us like we're about to pronounce them all winners of something.

I hear the first soft pull of David's harmonium, a little bittersweet as the melody dances around the A minor chord. I come in at the bottom end, a little bassline on the boomy A string, and Jenna is right there with the heartbeat, *thump-thump.* It's our usual opening, a quiet instrumental, mostly to find our groove and settle everybody into their bodies and breath.

I close my eyes and reach for the rhythm, rocking back and forth with it on my cushion.

When I find it, I open my eyes and the first thing I see is Amy[3], smiling up at me. She sits where she always does, front row stage left, with Amrita's other teaching assistants. The rest of the first row, and the next few rows, are packed tight with a few dozen other Acoladies, women in their 40s and 50s with shining faces and sculpted bodies, dressed in yoga or dance pants and fancy tank tops or fitted t-shirts adorned with hearts, Buddhas, *LOVE*, and *OM*, all finished with a *bindi*, or mala beads, or armful of bracelets. And right behind the Acoladies, the usual Old Hempy Dudes, long straggly silver hair, or no hair at all, in baggy hemp clothes and big mala beads, hunched over on their cushions, or leaning back on backjacks, a few sticking their knobby feet between the Acoladies.

I close my eyes again, push on the beat, and scribble out the melody with my guitar. Just before I finish the last phrase, a roar from the crowd, and I don't have to open my eyes to know that Amrita has just fluttered her way onto the stage. I finish the phrase anyway, and look over to see her waving and blowing kisses as she tiptoes elaborately up onto the stage, changed into a tank top and skin-tight dance pants, with ruffles at the ankles, that shimmer an impossible white in the stage lights.

We slow the pace, and Amrita stands there in her headset over her cushion, right in the center of the stage, hands spread out across her heart and swaying to the last of the music. She finally, slowly, lowers herself as Jenna tapers her drumbeat to nothing, and I taper off into harmonics and silence, and there's only David's harmonium, playing the same lulling, plaintive phrase in A minor.

Amrita's hands come into prayer position, and she sweeps her way across the crowd with *thank you* bows. Then she flips her big blonde hair over her shoulders, works her way into lotus position, and closes her eyes, swaying slightly to what's left of the harmonium's hum, as if it were a breeze gently crossing the stage.

David finally lets out the last note, and the entire room, easily 400 people, goes completely silent.

Amrita says nothing, only sits there, looking like she's gathering herself in meditation. And maybe she really is, doing in front of everybody what I do in the bathroom before every gig — these and Johnny's — though I'd never dare ask her if she really is meditating right here and now like I do in the pisser.

Finally, she opens her hands over her heart, takes in a big, dramatic, purposefully audible breath; waits a beat; and pushes it out, even more audibly, like she's blowing out candles on a birthday cake.

The room — tent? space? room? — and its three or four hundred people are so utterly silent, I can hear my heartbeat clicking deep inside my ears.

Amrita takes in another breath — my cue to start a drone on the low C/G and David's to start weaving out the C chord on his harmonium — and she finally lets her voice out, low at first, barely audible, a slow release of C flat, sliding it steadily upward to C natural in a long, belly-deep, *OM*.

Right in behind her voice, all those other voices rush in, some lifting to land right on the C, others wiggling around to find it — a few songbird sopranos at the top, mostly altos and tenors in the middle, and the lacquered rumble of a few baritones — until it is one great gush of living human sound.

We taper off on the volume and the pulsing, and their voices follow, crumbling back into separate voices.

Amrita pulls in another huge breath, and lets out another *OM*, and everyone lands on it this time, and we are suddenly engulfed in that living human sound, the fixed walls of the tent seeming to vibrate with it.

I look over and see Amrita beaming, her eyes still closed, her hands spreading out across her breasts like a white dove alighting there. She lets this one run a few extra beats, until the collective sound just starts to falter, and we taper off again.

Another long active silence, the whole place buzzing now in the empty space left behind from the collective voice, and Amrita takes in her longest breath yet; holds; holds; then she finally releases the last *OM*, and the voices can hardly wait, jumping in on the note and soaring, harmony notes here and there, more bass, more everything.

I keep the C/G going, and look out at the makeshift choir in its makeshift cathedral, luminous, glowing, the stage seeming to float beneath the four of us up here and the whole tent seeming to loosen from its pegs, and rise upward from the earth, a spaceship off to what some people might call heaven.

Amrita opens her eyes, smiles, and with a "Namaste, dear ones!" she launches into her welcome.

"We love you, Amrita!" someone yells from the back.

"Aww," she says, and pouts, and tips her head to the side. "I love you too!"

Everyone laughs, uproariously, as if it that were funny, which always makes me chuckle, if only because it's funny to me that everyone finds that funny.

She pauses a moment, then starts in on her invocation, the usual one about lovers journeying toward each other, and the joy of arrival and reunion, and being here now, etc.

And I'd love to do exactly that, and feel myself sinking into the joy of being here now, especially as I'm suddenly weary from the drive up here, the load-in, the soundcheck. But I can't leave completely, because coming I don't know exactly when, there will be that tap on my knee, Amrita letting me know she is about to reach the pinnacle of the story, the lovers reunited, their whole world saved, or wherever she is taking them today.

So I sit, and wait, and half-listen, trying not to fidget with my hands or guitar or butt on the cushion, pushing myself up straighter.

I look down at the Acoladies just beyond the edge of the stage lights, their faces sparkly with the colored lights splashed onto the walls and ceiling of the tent. They are all rapt with the story, some in perfect lotus position, some playing with their beads, others playing with their toes. A few rows beyond them, the crowd is the usual archipelago of oddities: a bunch of Man Buns looking way too serious; Crones with their waterfalls of platinum hair and purple robes; a smattering of mostly older South Asian women in red and pink silk, next to South Asian men mostly in sweatpants and t-shirts and glasses; a few gawky, skinny, bored-looking teenage girls with their gawky, almost as skinny mothers, as rapt as the Acoladies. Right in the middle is a classic Old Hempy Dude, a large, chunky, white-haired, white-bearded guy — let me guess, professor of Classics or Comparative Religion somewhere — with the pale, severe woman in tiny wireframe glasses, half his age and no doubt one of his grad students. And surrounding the archipelago, the sea itself, sitting up like breaking waves, straightest of all on their cushions and seeming to strain to hear Amrita's every word, the Lost Girls of Yoga: all white, in their early 20s to early 30s, mostly blonds with their hair pulled back in painful looking ponytails, with tanned, yoga-sculpted shoulders, gaunt faces, and big shiny eyes. Near the back is an especially large bunch, taller and blonder than the rest, looking like a beach volleyball team in the wrong gym. And behind them the usual couple of creepy guys in their 40s, who always stand in the back, staring.

*Who will be that guy this time?* I wonder, studying the three or four who wander back and forth, studying the crowd. At every retreat, there is always that creepy middle-aged guy who, after getting shot down by all the Lost Girls of Yoga, tells everybody he's happily married and so sad his wife had to miss this one.

And there's that firm tap on my knee.

I look down at my guitar and hear the last of Amrita's words, falling like lotus petals onto the surface of the great stillness in the room.

"The great and eternal lovers," she says, "reunited at last. Not because they were apart, but because their fear of being apart had made it seem so. But the divine and the beloved are never separate, because they are, and always have — been — one."

In the sudden aural void left behind by Amrita's voice, the room swells with the strange pulsing silence of 400 people sitting there, waiting, holding their breath, looking up at Amrita and us. I learned years ago never to rush the music to fill this void, hard as that is for a mind as twitchy as mine, to let this intense collective silence have its different say with everyone. Rabbi Miriam could make a room do the exact same thing, after an especially dramatic *d'var Torah*, or a drawn-out chanting of the *Sh'ma*, or an especially sad *Kaddish* for someone we all knew. Like with *Kaddish* for Leah, dear Leah, for that whole, endless, awful year.

Tonight, this silence speaks the name "Leah" to me, and I cannot indulge it because I can't. I'm in the middle of this gig right now. And it's too fucking painful anyway. So I force her out of my mind, and wait for the next tap on my knee.

Sometimes, these 20 or 30 seconds of silence are an eternity, the crowd seeming to hold its collective breath, my heartbeat clicking in my ears — one beat, two beats, three beats, come on! — until finally, the whole room seems to exhale together, and I know the tap will be coming, in three, two, and there it is.

I glance over at Amrita, who is motionless, her face Buddha calm, and I sweep the tops of my fingers, just barely enough to be audible, across the E minor chord, the same three beats as Amrita's last three words, and we are off.

I strum the chord in sets of three, a little louder and faster.

David's harmonium fills in behind me, and Jenna starts in on her two tabla drums, and we are off.

"*Hare Rama! Hari bol!*" Amrita sings into her microphone.

"*Hare Rama! Hari bol!*" David echoes into his microphone, joined by the crowd, which starts to drown him out on the third cycle.

The pace and volume of the song builds, slowly, steadily, until the crowd is drowning all of us out on the response, and I switch to my fingerpick.

The perfect crawl, from quiet back-and-forth chant, to frenzied singing and shouting takes a full ten minutes, conducted by my right hand keeping one–two time on the guitar and Jenna's hands dancing on the tabla.

As we near the top, the beat pulsing faster and more manic than the loudest and hardest *rockin'* thing we play in Johnny's band, several people spring to their feet, clapping, dancing, gyrating. All the Acoladies are up first, and a handful run off to the sides and start dancing around the room in a circle, followed by a few Crones, a dozen of the Lost Girls, and all the Man Buns and Old Hempy Dudes. More and more people get up to dance, moving in a circle around the great rainbow-colored sea of cushions and mats and blankets. Others stand and sway in place, or circle their hips, and tip their heads back and twirl; and every tenth or so person sits on their cushion, still as a stone post, their hands on their laps or knees or at their heart in prayer position, meditating, a few with faces wet with tears.

When we reach the top again, and can't play any faster or louder without blowing to pieces, Amrita pops up from her cushion, clapping and singing, and steps down from the stage. She starts around the room, still singing into her headset, clapping, gingerly hugging back everyone who dances by her for a hug.

The sweat runs down into my eyes, melting the room into a blur of flowing hemp and hair. I try to blink it away, which never works, and only make it sparkle and run faster, the dancers melting one into the other, until they are only color and motion and light — shapeshifting in my embodied imagination into other tribes who dance like this: rastas and dreadlocks, tie-dyeds and pony tails, black hats and *payos*, buckskin shirts and feathered headdresses. The only difference is up here on stage, in our hands: the flavor of the melody, the syncopation in the rhythm, the name we give the drums.

I rock back and forth on my cushion, my left hand playing the same simple pattern, the same bass line, my acoustic guitar now more drum than stringed instrument as I bang away with my right hand. We push the beat faster, the volume as loud as we can go, and out of the wall of singing voices and clapping hands coming back at us there are shouts of wordless joy, screams of released pain, quick sharp cries of aching pleasure, like a woman's orgasm, held off for minutes, hours, years, going on and on and on.

Now would be when I'd start to pull the room back, so I look over to Amrita for the cue, and she's looking straight at me, grinning like the hot morning sun, and nods *Yes*.

I finish the phrase, and let it sustain a full bar, then leave a void for another full bar where my guitar had been.

Jenna and David hear me and look up, and I nod; and as slowly and imperceptibly as we'd ramped the song — from a quiet creeping along the floor to a wild leaping dance through the canvas roof of the tent — we pull it back, the beat, the pace, the volume, and the collective orgasm slows into throbbing echo, heavy breathing, last whimpers.

Amrita has stopped singing, and so has half the crowd. She wanders back toward the stage through a gauntlet of smiles and hugs, and the music is just us now, Jenna's tabla dropping off, my guitar back to just chords, David's harmonium slowing to a long weary moan. Amrita lowers herself to her cushion, and hangs her head with showy reverence, like she's praying, or crying, or both.

I brush the last bass notes in the chord, and drift to harmonics and then nothing, just the wistful, longing in-and-out breath of the harmonium.

And then that oddest of all silences.

That boisterous hush of hundreds of people, sweating, panting, beaming, weeping, like everyone is shouting, but only on the inside, a winded, gleaming, glorious silence, drowned in aural light. An anguished exhale over here, another over there, a muffled sobbing near the back, as everyone gathers themselves on their cushions and closes their eyes.

And more silence, as Amrita studies the crowd, and waits for her own cue, then waits a little more, until I want to scream: *Please! Get on with it! This is too much! My heart is going to explode!*

Which is when she usually, finally does get on with it.

"Wow," she says, placing her open palms over her heart. "Wow," she lets out a long sigh, and launches into it: the Big Story.

It's always about gods and goddesses and universes in flux and whatnot. It's like a setbreak while still on stage: I can space out for a solid ten or fifteen minutes, study the crowd, see who's flipping out, who's checking out whom, who looks like she really did just have an orgasm, or wants to have one, and wonder what that might be like when she did. There is no greater seat for the show than up on stage.

"Oh people," Amrita finally says, spreading her open hands as wide as they'll go. "Such an abundance of joy in the room this evening. How blessed are we?" And with her usual, "But in the higher realms . . . ," she launches into her story.

But there's a tap-tap, on my knee. What? I can't have missed or forgotten anything.

I look over at her, bewildered, anxious — I've never missed a cue with her, or Johnny, or anybody — and ask with my eyes, *Huh?*

She gives me a little pout, tilts her head, looks back at the crowd, then turns back to me, her eyes saying more than asking: *I hope this is OK with you?*

Oh. Radhe. I realize we are long overdue for her Radhe story — the original Radhe, not the one who left for New Zealand three months ago — but her namesake from Hindu mythology.

*Sure, go ahead*, I answer with my eyes and a shrug.

Like it's going to bother me? Like I'm going to burst out sobbing, like the Acolady in the black t-shirt down there in the last song? Or the old guy halfway back, crying into his hands, or super-skinny Lost Girl off to the side, writing in her notebook then bursting into tears?

Amrita launches into the Radhe story, the illicit consort of Krishna, the one he really loved even if he was still running around on her. Radhe, as Amrita tells it, loved Krishna like the God he was, willing to abandon husband, home . . . everything for him. It's just another cosmic soap opera, like those of the Greeks, the Jews, the rest of the world. The lesson from this particular myth, for the gathered yogis and yoginis? *Go ahead and make a damn fool of yourself for love, as long as it's for God.*

The Big Story is the centerpiece story of every event, and Amrita always spins it around herself, even as she rotates from one god and goddess to the next. She likens every one in the wide-eyed crowd — starting and ending with herself — to one or another deity in the story, saying that we could all be Radhe. Or Sarasvati, if she is really emphasizing the music. Or Parvati, if she's stirring a little more sex into the story than usual. Sometimes it's Tara, a warrior goddess, my personal favorite, because she's the one I imagine most like Calafia. Or if she's feeling especially dramatic, it's Kali, the destroyer, the transformer. With Jared/Ananda, the stalker Man Bun in the house tonight, I would have guessed Tara or Kali, to scare him off; but maybe that would excite him in some twisted way, or make him more desperate. So tonight, Radhe has come around in the rotation, and at least she warned me.

The room is rapt, all eyes on Amrita as she tells the story. And I know it will be a long haul, so I do my best to space out, like it's bad TV in the waiting room of some oil change place, droning background noise that will be over soon enough.

I can kill the time in the usual way, by scanning the crowd and making up stories about them: who's the most obvious headcase? Who has the most preposterous looking plastic surgery, like she got punched in the mouth or her gaze is in perma-shock? Who is the weirdest-looking Old Hempy Dude, or dorkiest Lost Girl, or hottest Acolady? And which of the Acoladies, or the Crones — or maybe one of volleyball players in the back sitting up the tallest and straightest and sexiest in her quiet power? — is the Calafia in our midst? Which one looks like she could bed anyone in the room she wanted, male or female, old or young, attached or not, and simply hadn't decided? But every time I'm about to make the Calafia call on one, so I can study her, make up a fun story about her, Amrita says the name "Radhe" — and I wince, lose track of where I am in the room, bow my head and try not to let anything show on my face.

"Then Radhe said . . ."

I can feel Amrita's eyes sweeping over at me before she looks back to them. It's like she wants to out me, drag me into the story for some reason I'll never know. Sure, she tried to fix me up with Diane from L.A., and with Amy[3] on the way up here, and will no doubt keep pimping me to her Acoladies — or is it the other way around? — because she's always trying to fix everybody up. Because she really is a lovesick puppy, believes the whole *bhakti* thing, romantic love as divine love and *vice versa*, at least for everybody else.

But there's something else going on here. It's as if Amrita wants to break me, to see me cry out about how much I miss Radhe, see how it might sound coming out of my guitar. Little does she know how easy it was for me to let her go. Even Radhe herself was shocked and dismayed when I was there to help her pack, spent that last night with her, took her to the airport, and just said goodbye. I was a little shocked myself, like it was just another run through eye-of-the-shitstorm mode.

And yet, and yet — every mention of her name right now is making me wince, to the point where it must be starting to show on my face. So I look down and study my hands. Because I know they're gawking at me every time Amrita looks my way. I bow my head a little deeper, sink a little more into the cushion, feel the warmth from my guitar under my right forearm. Like it's breathing. Like it too is sick of this fucking story, and just wants to get to the next song.

"And so Radhe . . .," Amrita says again.

*And moving right along,* I think, muting my guitar mic with the box near my right foot, and checking the tuning in the box next to that.

Because my anonymity on stage has been the only thing I have to keep me from flipping out, blowing my cues, or messing up my parts, with all those people down there staring not at me but at the lead singer. The practiced invisibility of the instrumental accompanist is how I was able to come back on stage at all — having given up the whole dream/nightmare in my early 20s — when music came and found me at the age of 40, right after I'd given up on everything else.

*I'm just the guitar player* — or with Johnny, *I'm just the bass player* — I like to tell everyone. *Anything else you want to know, talk to Johnny / Amrita / Rabbi Miriam, to whoever has the lead mike, because they're the anointed ones. I'm just over here keeping time, filling in space, and adding color.*

"Because Radhe . . ."

I wince again, and try to think about next week's gig with Johnny — an outdoor festival up in Tahoe, won't that be something — but when I look up, all I see are hundreds of people, most of them with their eyes wide open now, riveted to Amrita's words and looking back and forth between her and me.

I look over the top of the crowd, to the back of the tent where a straggle of dancers is still standing, swaying to her words like they were to our music. And all I see is the empty space right in the middle of them, where Radhe used to stand. When Amrita launched into this story, I tried so hard not to see her that now she's all I see. Among those faces in the back, all gleaming with sweat, hers is not there, and I feel a wave of sadness wash through me, like an actual ocean wave inside my chest, pushing me up onto a beach empty but for wind, broken shells, dried bones, driftwood.

Even though Radhe would always start out in the front row of a *kirtan*, and watch my hands and the hands of anyone else playing an instrument, she would always end up in the back with the dancers. She'd spin around in one of her red or orange scarves gathered like a silky bedsheet around her long black hair and big shoulders; and the scarf would dance along with her, caressing those shoulders and big breasts, and her cutaway waist and sway hips and little belly, her arms always carving the air around her head, like a Hindu classical dancer, etching her own version of the story in the air with her strong, brown, sensitive surgeon's hands.

I wonder if she's dancing now, if she's found any *kirtan* all the way down in New Zealand.

She always said she would be leaving, though I thought it would be to Singapore or maybe even back to India, after all her training, and after that company launched the device she helped invent. And that was fine with me because I was still numb — from everything that had gone down in Utah with the company blowing up, and Leah dying, and everything falling apart at once. I'd just sold off most of what I'd owned, had moved into Angel's Rest, and was suddenly absorbed into figuring out how not to embarrass myself with these two music gigs that had just fallen into my lap.

Radhe used to joke about me marrying her to keep her here. Or going with her, if I really was as disgusted, as I claimed to be, with the country's gleeful collapse into self-destructive stupidity. But maybe she was only ever half-joking, testing me to see what I'd say, especially after the incident with that redneck with the gun.

"So when Radhe and Krishna . . ." Amrita goes on.

The room is silent but for her voice, and the crowd doesn't stir, their faces all running together now.

I have nowhere to go but into the story itself, even though I've heard it a dozen times now, and even though the best version I've ever heard was from Radhe herself, on our first real date. Amrita juices it with her own made-up details, winky-winking about all the eroticism in the story, but Radhe's version was better, because she left all that out and made the whole thing sound tragic, like a sad love story, not divine porn.

Amrita is still a good five minutes or more from done, so I let myself wander about the story on my own, wondering where else I'd heard it before, in what movies, or books, or pop songs. Because they all come from the same place.

If the mythic Radhe had been the perfect devoted wife, willing to give herself over fully to Krishna even for the one moment he'd have her, wasn't she sort of like Ruth, who ran off to be with the Israelites because she was starving, something everyone has turned into a love story? And the model for the first conversion? Or was she more like Rachel from Genesis, because the union was based on passion and love, not honor and duty? Rachel was Jacob's true love, after all, the Radhe in the *Torah*'s cosmic soap opera about the matriarchs and patriarchs. Rachel was the passion-wife to Jacob, just like Radhe was to Krishna. And like Krishna, Jacob was all over the place, I like to imagine, capable of loving them all — even the concubines who bore most of his children, maybe — and not just Rachel, his passion-wife, but her sister, Leah, his duty-wife.

Yes, Leah.

Ugh.

Because I don't feel crappy enough with Radhe's name filling the air right now? Because I want to think about Leah right now?? When is Amrita going to end this goddamn story???

A flare of pain shoots up from my lower back, all the way up into my hunched shoulders, and I realize I've been slipping off the back of the cushion. I swim my hips around, find a better position, and remind myself that at least I know the story will end soon.

I go back to studying the crowd: people still wide-eyed and rapt, but now spread out and splayed around, stretched out in yoga poses, draped over each others' laps. Except for the dancers, and Man Buns, and Old Hempy Dudes wandering around in the back, they are all riveted to the story, hanging off the ragged edge of the universe, watching Radhe's heart break one more time.

"Because Radhe knew," Amrita says again, her words slowing as she wraps up the story. Then, a long heavy pause, her voice a whisper, right into the mike so everyone can still hear her. "Radhe — knew."

She lets it hang in the air, unresolved, like ending a song in mid-yearn, on the "minor fall," as Leonard Cohen called it in "Halleluyah."

Which is why this long, yearning silence.

Then a gasp from everyone at once and no one in particular, and more silence, with dabs of weeping here and there around the room, punctuated by a sudden wail from one of the Acoladies upfront.

She's a skinny woman about my age in one of those hemp turbans, wrapped so tight on her head it looks painful, sobbing openly.

Oh, please, I think, suddenly irritated, thanks to Amrita rubbing Radhe in my face for the last fifteen minutes. *You don't need any more kundalini yoga, sister*, I want to say to her. *You need a good steak, and a good lay.*

I wait for the tap as Amrita scans the room, reads the faces, hands, and twitches, waits, it seems, for the woman in the turban trying to rein in her tears.

Finally, the tap on my knee.

I pick the notes out of a C minor chord, a circle of bittersweet guitar sound, and David's harmonium swells up around me for four beats, and then Jenna on her djembe, *thump-thump, thump-thump.*

"*Hare OM,*" Jenna sings the first line of the song that will explode into high point of the evening, "*hare OM.*"

And then Amrita and everyone else: "*Hare OM, hare OM.*"

A few times around, and we start to ramp up the pace. But it's not fast enough for Amrita — am I the one dragging the beat? — so she jumps up and starts to clap, and we have to speed up to catch her.

She moves to the edge of the stage, clapping and yelling out the response with the crowd, "*Hare OM! Hare OM!*"

Most of them spring to their feet, clapping and dancing, the rest pulling themselves up slowly, a few still propped on their cushions or stretched out on their mats, meditating, or writing something in their notebooks, or watching everyone dancing around them.

"OK, everybody!" Amrita shouts over the music as she steps down from the stage, "let's make some room! Please move all your stuff off to the sides so we can all come together as one big beautiful One!"

While we play on — just the music, no singing — the cushions and blankets are whisked off to the sides, everyone standing and clapping in a tight bunch, moving to gather around Amrita, who has worked herself to the exact center of the dance floor.

We come around to the bottom, and Amrita shouts out the next round, "*Hare OM, hare OM!*"

We play faster and harder and louder, as the crowd forms into concentric circles dancing around her, a mad whirl of color and hair and feathers and beads, Amrita at the exact center of it, just barely dancing, saving her energy for the long weekend of this ahead. Her arms sculpt the air over her head, her body going perfectly still in the middle of the madness, her eyes closed and face calm as a Buddha statue's, but tilted upward, like a beaming spotlight up to the sky, all the dancers moths fluttering toward her to die in her light.

I pound away on the chords, Jenna's voice now a continuous wordless chant, David's harmonium an avalanche of sound.

The dancers scream and shout and spin in an amorphous frenzy all around Amrita, falling out of the pulsing blob of bodies to crumble on the floor, roll around, crawl off to the side in tears. The *kirtan* version of what the Pentecostal Christians' "threshing floor" or the punk rockers' "mosh pit."

Some odd and faraway part of me wishes I could throw down this guitar, jump off the stage and join them, and dance away this unexpected churning in my stomach about Radhe, and about Leah, all mixed together. And I've never really wanted to do that, never even thought about it. And I can't right now, of course, because we are holding all of them up with our music and Amrita is going to turn around any moment and give me the look to start reeling it back in.

But tonight, I'm oddly jealous of them, of their ability to just let go like that. It's like kids at rock concerts, thrashing against the front of the stage; or everybody back at *Shir Hadash*, dancing around in the aisles to the *hora*, or in costumes at *Purim*, or with the scroll at *Simchat Torah*. How can they just let go like that? In front of so many people? Without feeling embarrassed, or self-conscious, or silly? Without feeling exposed, unsafe, ridiculous? And how are some of them able do this, weekend after weekend, going from peak moment to peak moment like some people go from ski resort to ski resort, or surfbreak to surfbreak, living their lives in some kind of perpetual spiritual frenzy? If everything is a peak moment like that, is anything, really, a peak moment?

But from up here, it looks real: singular, momentous, and permanently transformative. They are out on that floor, gyrating, screaming, and sobbing to confront it, exorcize it, and tear it out of their bodies the same way I'm tearing my own sadness and confusion from these guitar strings, the same way I used to tear all that old anger from my body on long climbs up and terrifying rides down mountains. I'm too old now to pound away on myself like that. And yet my body aches for the same release. So I pound away on my guitar, hoping maybe my body will forget that it once had made plans to leave with Radhe, even if the rest of me was joking, and hoping even more desperately that my body forgets all those times it melted so deliciously into Leah's body, and made bigger plans that that, and meant them, even as she was dying.

"Hey!" David's voice yells at me over the roar.

I look up and see Amrita in the middle of the floor, staring back at us and waving her hand around in the circle.

So much for my never missing a cue.

I nod to David and Jenna, and let the next chord hang, then crumble into bass notes slower than the beat, and we slowly, steadily, pull the beat back, the volume down.

Those still dancing crumble to the ground, some crawling up to sit, others in fetal position, a few still rolling around on the floor.

Amrita tip-toes among the sweaty, glowing bodies, back toward the stage, as Jenna's drumbeat slows to a trickle, and David's harmonium swells into one big long sound, like a curtain slowly pulled across the aural stage, and we end like we began, in that sad C minor.

I let my guitar say it one more time, in those last aching, yearning notes: the story of Radhe's great heartbreak, except it really is about the other Radhe this time; and about Leah, my Leah; and all the other Radhes and Leahs whose great love couldn't save them . . .

Half an hour later, the main lights are on and all the way up, turning the sacred space back into a circus tent. But the air still buzzes with clumps of people hugging and laughing over the quiet, sultry, cool-down chant music David left going on the PA. The whole place smells like sweat, the good, fresh, fecund kind of sweat after a yoga class or in a crowded little parking area at a popular surfbreak as the sun is going down.

Amrita is off to one side in a gaggle of Acoladies, a few Old Hempy Dudes, one of the Man Buns. David and Jenna are long gone.

I am in no hurry to leave, because I'm wide awake like I always am after playing a gig, and my mind is racing and I have nowhere to go but back to my empty room. So I futz with my gear, check the tuning on my guitar, wipe it down again, re-arrange the repair tools and spare strings in the stash.

I finally finish packing up my case and stand to leave, just in time to see Amrita slipping out the door behind the stage, with Jared/Ananda slipping out behind her. Oh well.

I shut down the PA and the room is suddenly, oddly, intensely quiet.

No echo, no buzz, just me, and absolute silence.

Rather than follow Amrita and the Man Bun out the back door into the anonymity of the night, I carry my guitar out into the lobby, not because I want to talk to anyone, meet anyone, get chatted up by anyone — but I don't really feel like being alone either.

People are gathered in groups of three and four, and they all nod and smile when I pass and say, "Thanks for the music!" and "you were amazing!"

I should take my guitar back to my room, but I feel like playing a little more to cool down, maybe that and a walk down that long lane.

I head down the long hallway toward the side door out to the cabins, past more people sitting on chairs and sprawled out on couches.

Down near the end, over on one of the couches, I hear open sobbing and see the arms and legs and heads of three women in a strange embrace. I quicken my pace toward the door, and as I walk past, I see that it's Amy[3] and another Acolady, hugging and rocking a woman who is weeping, and sniffling, and mumbling.

"I'm so sorry, I just — I just —" she cries into their arms.

I expect Amy[3] to look up at me and, especially given the hour, throw me those big blue bedroom eyes from the ride up.

But she doesn't notice me. She holds the woman in her arms, like she's a child, and rocks her, and says, "I know, I'm so sorry, it's OK, I know."

As I hurry past, I see that it's the skinny woman from up front, the one in the hemp turban. Her face is a tangle of raw pain: strained, wet with tears, a harsh, unworldly pallor out here in the bright light of the hall. No eyebrows, no eyelashes, her eyes stark, rubbed raw, hollow.

I hear her burst into open sobbing again. "Why couldn't he wait until I was done with the last chemo before telling me . . . telling me . . ." and I tighten the grip on my guitar case and quicken my pace toward the door.

I stumble out into a sudden shock of darkness, and quiet, and realize I'm out of breath, like I'd just been working it too hard at altitude, or held under by a big crashing wave I'd guessed all wrong. Or maybe it's because I feel like an asshole, and I can outrun the feeling, which always works, or always used to. Tonight, not really.

That woman in the turban could have been Leah barely two years ago; and Amrita's traveling medicine show is every bit her sanctuary, her synagogue, as *Shir Hadash* was Leah's, right until the end.

I stop to catch my breath, and look back at the lodge and tent, gleaming and buzzing with lights and drowning out anything in the sky. It takes a moment for my eyes to adjust to the pond down there, the pagoda in shadow, the gravel lane with cabins lit up against the night, swinging out on the ridge.

I put my guitar down, breathe out, and look up at the sky, still blank with this ambient light all around me.

Where are the stars tonight? They used to be my most reliable friends. No matter how crappy I felt, especially like right now — when I deserve to feel crappy for what I thought earlier about that poor woman — all I had to do was walk out under the stars, and be reminded that nothing really mattered, that we're not even really here. The cold fire of their art against the sky was my consolation prize for always ending up alone.

But not anymore. Not since turning 50, and Leah passing, and Radhe leaving. Not since I started playing these wild gigs with Amrita, and seeing what music does to people, and wanting maybe just a little room on the threshing floor for myself.

I've eavesdropped enough at these retreats — over meals, lingering in the emptying halls — to know that while Amrita's world is full of fools, and lost people, and players, there are at least as many others here because something terrible has happened to them recently, some awful, gut-wrenching, life-altering loss. The catharsis looks real, the pain sounds real, and what happens out on that "dance floor" is really an act of somatic rage, not against others, or against the powers that be, but against a cruel and indifferent universe. What happens out there is the most profound "dance" of all: the reclaiming of a body ravaged by cancer, or a home destroyed by a cheating husband, or a family crushed by a child's addiction, a best friend's suicide, a brother's desertion. It's how my own sister back East might feel, if I allowed myself to think about it.

I pick up my guitar and walk slowly down the lane past the cabins, toward the meditation garden.

Just over the distant ridge, blacked out against the charcoal gray of the sky, the moon is coming up, a perfect quarter moon, half of its face gleaming, half still in shadow.

From one cabin, a man's voice and a woman's laughter; the outline of two people lighting a candle in the window of another; the third dark and quiet; the sudden, sharp cry of a woman's orgasm in another; then one more, darkened but for a reading light in the window.

Past the last cabin, the lane swings further out on the ridge, and the dark engulfs me again. I stop, put my guitar down, and take another big breath of the soft, warm evening air.

I can feel / see it more than I could just see it when I was rushing in and getting ready for tonight, what makes this place truly beautiful. It's the same thing I felt / saw all those nights alone in the mountains back in Colorado and Utah. Exactly like in those mountains, I can feel / see that there is something here beyond its obvious beauty: the presence of something beyond time that is here to witness the singularity of this place and moment in time. What I've always called "the Presence."

And I'm not the only one who can feel it, because why else is this retreat center here?

Like so many of these places around the country, someone stumbled into this valley and didn't just see good water and soil and exposure to the sun — that was half of California a hundred years ago. They also discovered a place that someone a century or two before them — maybe a millennium or two before them — had found holy. They figured out how the water flowed, and where the sun rose and set, and how the local berries and acorns and game cycled through the seasons; maybe they burned a field or two to plant a garden or small farm. And then, on some night just like this, with the moon coming up or sun going down, they too felt it, the Presence. So they placed a stone or two, maybe built a whole altar, or a sweat lodge, or a labyrinth. And they listened to the hum of the land all around them, and the beating of their hearts, and whatever sound the voice within them was making, and they learned to sing along.

Then more people came along, and built more shelters. The more they chanted and danced and prayed here, the more they could feel — or imagined they could feel — all those songs and prayers that had come before. And because this is California, which is to say because it's America but even more so, someone turned that into a business. The product is good, it helps people, it sells, and it's still selling. Even today, after the horrendous drive getting here, even with the cabins and lodge and circus tent back there right now, you can look out over this valley in the pale wash of moonlight and see why: this place is holy, and feels as pure and simple and unspoiled as it did to those first people who wandered in here.

Here they will come home, they tell each other and themselves; here they *do* come home. If they doubted that, all they had to do was take a picture on their phones: of the sun going down and turning the meadow golden, and the hills beyond all ruby-red, and post it, and all the *Likes* and *Loves* of their friends back in the city would make it so.

I don't begrudge them any of that, because I can feel it too, rising up through the soles of my feet, into the whole of my body.

I pick up my guitar and turn back toward the lodge. My body has let go and I don't feel like playing anymore.

The moon is halfway up the sky now, as if its face were turned and looking back from where it came, its milky light washing this place, blessing what's left of this land and of me.

# 4 | WESTERN SWING

I hate this drive: going 80 on I-80, bumper-to-bumper, along a four-lane, hundred-mile corridor through a joyless, utilitarian wasteland of big box / fast food / gas station neon-plexes. Sacramento never comes soon enough, and when it finally does, the neon-plexes thin and the traffic drops off, but only enough to squeeze four lanes into three for the bumper-to-bumper grind up the mountain toward Tahoe.

I could conjure Calafia for this ride, imagine her sitting over there in the van riding shotgun, the dirty wind making a mess of her big blonde hair.

*To hell with it, Jack,* she'd laugh over the roar of the engine as she pushed the hair away from a face sun-honey-freckled with the sun, flashed those big white teeth. *Who cares about the traffic? The mountains are coming!*

Because up in the Sierra Nevada Mountains, Calafia the surf goddess — like Old Freya and plenty of younger women I've met out on the breaks — would of course be a snowboarding Betty.

*Big drops up there,* she'd say, *and big freshies. And clean granite all the way to the summit. And don't forget about the hot tub afterwards . . .*

Calafia would be more than happy to chase backcountry powder all winter, and Sierra summits all summer. And only three or four times a year would we have to make this horrible crossing through the Central Valley — with its dust clouds in summer and ice fog in winter, crushing all-day traffic, sudden, menacing construction stops every night — to get back to the ocean.

*Besides,* she would say, *I'm a goddess and this traffic does suck, so let's just fly there.* She reaches across the gap in the van and takes my hand, to whisk us both up through this bumper-to-bumper stink-cloud, to the very crest of the Sierras.

But we can't achieve lift-off because I need my guitar for the gig with Johnny tomorrow, in its bombproof airline case, and it's way too heavy and Calafia isn't strong enough for me and the guitar, so I have to drop it, or let go of her hand . . . so . . . nope.

And just like that, she's gone and here I am, stuck in traffic on I-80.

The van kicks in with the climb and I switch the music from jam band to bluegrass, the fiddle and banjo and mandolin piercing enough to cut through the throaty roar of the engine.

I push the van still harder because, for all my bitching about the traffic and daydreams about running around the mountains with Calafia, I can't wait to get up there for this gig: *California Summerfest!* at the base of Silver Mountain. No casino this time, but an outdoor venue, with views of mountains in every direction, best of all from up on the stage. And nice rooms at the place, Gordon said, if I want one. But I've opted for camping out back, behind the festival, where I've heard there's a great little campground and all the band buses set up.

It will also be good to be back in the Sierras. I haven't camped up there in 13 years, when Jill and I passed through on that long strange trip from my old house in Colorado to her new grad school apartment in Sacramento. After all of her leaving and coming back, working up and down the Rockies and occasionally halfway around the world as a climbing and skiing guide, she was finally leaving — Colorado and me — for good. Though that's not exactly true. Turns out, or so it was explained to me one dark night back in Colorado, that I'd left her. It was just something she never bothered to explain, out loud anyway, because she was a woman and I was supposed to just know. And on that long, odd, bittersweet journey, on all those glorious backroads through the mountains and desert from there to here, it turns out that I blew every chance *not* to let the one who got away, get away.

But how was I supposed to know? As Tom used to say when we'd screw up something with the business, I made the best decision I could with the information I had at the time. I was 40 and Jill was 26. And as adventurous, interesting, and cool as her globe-trekking life was, she was also idealistic, driven to help fix the fucked up world, and it didn't really matter how exactly, because when you're that age, you get to believe shit like that. And, on top of all that, she still dreamed the soccer mom dream. I had more than enough energy to chase her up and down all those mountains; but I'd already blown through a career and marriage, and wanted nothing more out of life than blue skies over fresh snow and the whole fucked up world just to leave me in peace. In the three years we were together / not-together, the emerging scale and scope of Jill's ambitions looked more and more exhausting. I was dropping out and she was dropping in. And in the end, she simply outgrew me.

I realized what a mistake I'd made right after I'd left her and her truck and her dog in Sacramento, and flown back to Colorado alone. But it was my way (and still is, I suppose) to tough it out. Which I did for awhile, until everyone else I was skiing and climbing with started leaving too, and for the exact same reason: time to grow up. Danny, Aaron, Tyler, Scott — all my mountain rescue buddies from back then — all Dads now, living somewhere else.

But back then, before I met Leah and her parents and everybody at *Shir Hadash*, I wanted nothing to do with any of it. Back then, for me, "family" was just an over-elaborated word for "pain." Something that should feel good, which only makes it feels worse. Something that promises you a place in the world, a stake in the future, but it was beyond my imagining for myself. All I'd ever known of it was ugliness, sorrow, regret. Until I met Leah. And turned 50. Ugh . . .

HONK!!!

A muscle car roars past and nearly rear-ends the truck up ahead, then jumps on its brakes, along with the car in front of me, so I have to jump on my brakes. Jackass. The jam ahead slows and spreads the traffic, and the highway starts into the first long curving climb up into the mountains.

The traffic catches up with the grade and itself, and we're back to grinding up the mountain at 70 mph. The van strains with the ascent, the load of all my gear, my push to stay even with the cars and get to this venue as soon as I can. Because I want to see mountains, and indulge in thinking about Jill — or how Jill was before she turned serious on me — and not about Leah, or families, or any of that.

Because Leah's family was the first, really — the first one that didn't freak me out and send me literally running for the hills. Back East and way back before the start of what now appears to be my permanent midlife crisis, I'd dodged that whole horror show. My ex-wife was as estranged from her parents as I was from mine: we were both orphans, we used to say, which is why we got married in our early 20s and why it worked for so long. In all the years since, no matter who I got tangled up with — however young and carefree and fuck-it-all it started out — there would be family showing up for something. And all of it mystified me, wigged me out, drove me away: their secret languages, their jokes, their strange little sitcom jabs that weren't really funny but weren't cruel. I could never recognize any words between a parent and their kid, no matter how launched or ascendant in the world the kid might be, that weren't barbed, cruel, tinged with bitterness and jealousy, or outright annihilating.

Until Leah and her family. Her parents weren't perfect; but they weren't selfish and weird, like Jill's father and stepmother, or mean and awful like my ex-wife's, or vicious and crazy like my own. When they were out in Utah to visit her and meet me, they came to synagogue and carped a bit like all old people carp. But I couldn't help but see it right there at the kitchen table every morning and night: they just flat-out loved her. And the really weird part: they seemed to love me, right away, just because. I had no means to process any of that, but it was the first time I didn't really try. I watched them fuss over her, and beam at me as I played my guitar up on the *bima* and around the table after dinner, taking pictures of every dumb little thing we did to send to their friends back East.

They seemed like the exception to the rule: a family that actually liked each other's company, rooted for each other, hung around after dinner and sang songs they all knew. They seemed like that elusive thing that everybody who dreamed the soccer mom dream was really after: people of your own flesh and blood to love who love you back.

Yes, it's idiotic not to know these things at my age, but they're not things you can learn from books, or while running a bunch of employees who all have their own agendas, or off on some mountain or surfbreak by yourself. So how would I know?

So maybe it wasn't anything specific to Leah. Maybe it was nothing more than my turning 50, and the news from back East that my father had finally drunk himself to death and was buried in some cemetery in western Massachusetts, not that I'd given even a passing thought to going to his funeral. Maybe it was just my luck changing. (Though I'd never been luckier than with Jill and just didn't know it at the time.)

But I did get there, eventually, with Leah. I stayed put after meeting her parents, didn't wig out and disappear on her. And not only did I stay put, but I didn't say *No*, when she casually mentioned how much her parents wanted grandkids, turning to stare hard into my eyes with those big, warm, brown eyes for the slightest hint of *yay* or *nay*.


HONK!!!

I'm so lost in Leah's eyes I nearly rear-end the car up front, and have to jump on the brakes as we make the crest. The mountains spread out to the north, ridges of gray granite skirted with blackened spindles of burnt evergreen forest, and runs of young aspen greening their way up the gaps and folds.

My ears are ringing with the manic jangle of the bluegrass band bouncing around over the roar of the engine, so I switch over to cowpunk, ancient sounding new country, crooning with an edge, a jagged fiddle, a straight razor for a pedal steel. Like that old saying goes: *rock 'n' roll is for your first love, and country music is for your tenth.*

Leah wasn't exactly my tenth love, but she feels like it right now as I scan the ridge north of Donner Pass. There was a gap up through there Jill and I found and set up camp in, on the second to last night. What was I thinking back then? Was I even thinking? Or had I already run away by then?

Because it had nothing to do with her, I figured out soon enough. And maybe what happened a few years after that had nothing to do with Leah either. Maybe it really was just turning 50, and finally being ready to run after the thing I was finally too old to catch and make work.

Which is what I'm always trying to tell Ike, when he's going on and on about the great surf Betty he's going to meet — his Calafia, I suppose — and the amazing little grom he's going to have with her, or at least the grom she already has and he'll help raise.

He always argues back, as if I were the one running reality's clock.

"Kids are ton of work," I try to tell him, when we're sitting there in Neptune's back at Angel's Rest, drinking a beer and looking out at the ocean. (Not that I'm an expert; but I did watch a bunch of parents raise a bunch and a half of kids back at *Shir Hadash*.)

"But it's fun work," he says back.

"Yeah, some of it. But they take a ton of energy," I told him just a few weeks ago, when he wouldn't let it go. "And it doesn't stop, not until they turn 13 and all of sudden they stop just long enough to tell you to fuck off."

He chuckled and said, "That they do. I know I did. Made my old man crazy when I was that age, and quit baseball for surfing."

So I let it go. Because at that point there's only one point left to make, and it's an even bigger ass-kicking from reality than the clock and goes like this: *as hard as it is running after a kid all day, you're in no shape to run around after anybody now, with your ruined hip and that heavy limp.*

But I didn't say that, would never say that, just worked on my beer while we sat in silence and watched the last of the sun turn orange, then magenta, then melt into the silvery flash of the horizon. Because who am I to wreck anyone's fantasy? Ike would have been happy to let me run across Beach Road, jump into the water, and swim off to the sailboat out there anchoring for the night. Because of course it's Calafia out there, sailing solo, just waiting for me to swim up, climb aboard, and ravish her all night out on deck, under the full moon, to a Beach Boys soundtrack.

So why wouldn't I return the favor, and just nod my head and say, *Cool, Ike, yeah you go do that*, when he tells me one more time how it's going to happen?

It'll be a fine day on a fine beach, blue skies and perfect waves and no wind, when he meets his own little Laird Hamilton — that amazing grom killing it out on the waves — with the supercool single surfer mom. And the three of them will live happily ever after, in a little gingerbread cottage by the beach with a yard full of surfboards and wetsuits draped over the white picket fence, the Cali coastal version of the postcard family, all barefoot, ripped, and tanned, two of the American dreams squashed together. (Leaving out one or two details, like where they find the five million bucks for the little cottage next to the beach.)

"My father put up with a lot of shit like that from me," Ike said, long after I thought we were done talking about it, the sun all the way down, leaving us in the darkened hull of Neptune's.

"Sounds like you put up with a lot of shit from him too," I said, remembering the story he'd told me a few months earlier. His father didn't beat him up, like mine would do when he was drunk, always for some imagined wrong. Ike's father beat him in his own way, for what also sounds like an imagined wrong, with day upon day of silence, followed by a random outburst of ridicule and verbal annihilation, and then more silence. Having been beaten both ways by my own father, I know that the bright red welts left behind by cruel words will last far longer, some of them for decades.

"Yeah, well," Ike said. "He was a pretty hard guy. But he was my father, and he always wanted the best for me."

His father had been a baseball player, Ike told me, one good enough to make it to the minor leagues, where he had spent a couple years before he washed out, went to school and got a job as a civil engineer. But his first love was always baseball. So that even after they'd moved from back East to Orange County — where Ike quickly discovered surfing — his father was still playing in some league with a bunch of old pros, and coaching Ike's Little League team. But by high school, Ike said, he was showing up late or skipping out altogether on baseball practice when the waves were going off.

"There would be hell to pay later," he said, "but I didn't care. Huge day out on the waves? Who cares about baseball?"

He said his father wouldn't go too hard on him, just that icy silence, which would break every time Ike made it up at the game: covering half the field from centerfield and knocking in half the team's runs. And if he didn't hit, he'd walk on, or take a hard one and get on first that way, and steal his way around the bases. Looking at the kind of shape he is in now, even with the ruined hip, and knowing what he ended up doing on the pro surf tour, I believe him.

I would never say this to Ike, but for all that, his father still sounds like a prick. But mine, when he was actually around, was a prick on his good days and a monster on all the rest, so who am I to judge?

"He always wanted the best for me," Ike said again, as he found his way to his feet and limped out of the shadow, through the empty doorway and into the moonlight.

The van kicks in again, drowning out the bleary voice and biting twang, and jams up to the actual summit of Donner Pass.

Poor Ike. What was he expecting me to say? That sure, fathers always want what's best for their kids. And it's just a coincidence when it's what they want, or wanted, for themselves.

Tyler left Dudeville and went back to Denver to run the family business. Aaron — after ten years of working in the wilderness, doing rescues in the mountains, running a ski patrol — ended up back East in med school, like his father. And for all his bohemian, mountainfreak excess, all his Fuck the World and levitating at altitude, Danny ended up back in Portland, where he grew up, and where his father grew up, a salmon finally swimming back to and up his river of origin in the Pacific Northwest. Married Julie, got a cool job with a climbing gear start-up, kids, the works. And of course Jill, for all her ideas about fixing the world, ended up in business school, like her investment banker father, even if it was some newfangled "green" MBA program down there in Sacramento.

"Yes, even Jill," I mutter to myself, as the van pulls up and over the crest, and lunges down into the fractured half-cirque surrounding Donner Pass.

I look down at the lake and the campground, remembering that final, anguished drive out of here to the south and west, to the Sacramento airport where she would finally drop me off to fly back to Colorado. I thought I was going back to the same old Dudeville we'd left two weeks earlier, to my life of adventure at 8,000 feet above everything, to my endless winter of perfect days and perfect snow, and always another big mountain to climb up and ride down. I knew that five years later, she would be married and pregnant.

What I didn't know was that Aaron and Danny and Tyler would be right behind her, one after another in the next few months. Or that the same thing would happen to me, almost, in Utah a couple years later, after Dudeville had turned so cold and lonely I was finally willing to chuck it all for a new job with a new company in the next state west.

Then, just like that, scattered to the four winds, they were all parents — I could watch it unfold because the social media thing was just getting started back then — and Leah and I weren't far behind . . .

Shit! There it is!

I almost run by the exit for South Lake Tahoe, pumping the brakes just in time to turn off I-80.

*HONK!!!* comes the horn blast from behind, and of course the middle finger from passenger side window of the black BMW as it flies by.

As I pull up to the stoplight, the van — after four hours of roaring at full speed around the Bay, across the Central Valley, and up the mountain — is a sudden cavern of silence, and my gut is in a strange knot. I would have been happy enough spinning some sexy fantasy about Calafia all the way up here, but instead am left to wonder about a very different kind of fantasy: how might it have gone, if Leah had lived? And I'd managed to defuse whatever bomb always went off when I got too close to the whirlpool of commitment, parenthood, family? Just one kid? Maybe even two? Would they grow up knowing Aaron's or Danny's kids? Would I be in better touch with those guys now, because I was also a parent, and our kids were growing up like cousins?

It makes my chest ache to think about it, so I switch the music to some old country blues from *way* back East: raw, earthy songs about migration, dislocation, longing, and regret, from people who had bigger reasons than mine for their hearts to ache.

The road turns south, and winds in and out of what's been left of the forest to stand like a stage curtain between this steady stream of cars and all those ski areas, golf resorts, houses and condos. High ridges rise behind all of it, spiked with pines and snow-encrusted peaks silhouetted against an electric blue sky.

Half an hour south, and I finally push through the resort sprawl of South Lake Tahoe, and see the first sign for *California Summerfest!*

Around the next bend and a mile up a side canyon, there it is: Silver Mountain, looking more like an old-school ski hill — rustic lodge, old double chairlifts — than the rustic chic of everything north and east of here. And shabby in the way all ski areas look in summer: scrappy, barren, with clumps of rusted metal everywhere, and weeds growing up through everything. Never skied or snowboarded up here before, but I can see just from looking up the slopes where I'd head first: to the big backcountry drops off to the west.

But there will be very different "drops" on this trip, "launches" every bit as huge and scary, I see, as I pull the van up to a narrow break in the snow fence marked "Band Entrance Only." And it isn't just the sudden roar of a crowd I can't see on the other side of this fence. It's through the gate, reaching into the sky higher than the mountain ridge from this angle, a silver-gray lighting rig, flashing purple and white lights, like the I-beam frame of a three-story building over a stage that must be the size of a basketball court. Yikes. And I'm climbing up on *that* tomorrow?

While I wait for the van in front of me to pass through, the lights change colors and the crowd roars again. And this odd feeling: the same sudden upwelling of adrenaline I'd get way up there on one of those mountains, pulling up to the edge of that big drop on skis or a snowboard. It feels terrifying and wonderful at the same time, activating every twitching fiber in my body to do one thing: *leap.*

I show my pass to the guy in the orange vest, and he puts two armbands on my left wrist, and I think he says, "Thanks for being here, break a leg!" but it's starting to run together like a waking dream.

*This is going to be fun.* I try to snap back into my body, and this van, as I inch it down a little dirt lane between the snow fence and porta-potties and a couple big tents, one marked with a red cross.

The van slips out past the other side of the stage, just as an invisible crowd on the other side of the canvas-draped fence explodes, like a huge wave lifting and crashing way up on the rocks during a king tide.

I stop and just listen, and try to steady myself, waiting for the wave to drop. But it doesn't drop, just keeps pouring, more like a sudden hailstorm now, relentless. Then the boom-boom of a kick drum, the crack of a microphone, and a booming, throaty, meaty holler, "Hell-OHH, California!"

The crowd roars even louder, like a drenching rain of sound. Then the crack of a guitar plugging in, a quick run of bass notes, another boom-boom, and the thud-thud of a drummer settling in. Because I'm only a few years into all this, the sound of the stage firing up still electrifies me, and stands what's left of my hair on end. And that's the casinos and bigger county fairs and smaller state fairs. This festival is 7,500 people, Gordon said, double our usual crowd.

I drive the fence line past more and more unseen crowd, still roaring but thinning, before the lane drops down into a large meadow, spread out at the bottom of a wooded side canyon. The canyon isn't cut with more ski trails or chairlifts, but with a towering trio of powerlines that shoots straight up and over the ridge to the east.

The meadow is mostly wide open, golden in the afternoon sun, and I can feel the dried grass scratching at the bottom of the van as I head across it looking for a place to set up camp. Scattered around in no pattern I can make out are four band buses and two big RVs, several big cargo vans, and a couple regular old surfer vans like mine. The band buses — large, hulking, impenetrable — are painted in moody blacks and browns and charcoal, their windows all blacked out, some with generators humming. They look like perfect, plastic-molded spacecraft.

At the far end, down near the treeline, I see a couple of smaller RVs and regular vans — bands and solo acts for the side stages, and for sidemen like me, I'd imagine — and finally Sam's camper van down at the very end, in the first bit of shade where the mountain tumbles into the meadow.

I head down that way, and see Sam sitting out front in a camp chair, his guitar leaning against his van, doing something on his phone.

I pull up alongside him and hang out the window.

"Hey."

"Hey."

He doesn't look up from his phone, just asks, "Easy drive up?"

"Not too bad. Usual traffic, but it kept moving."

"Lucky you," he says, putting his phone down and picking up his guitar. "Sucked ass coming up from Reno. Bumper-to-bumper the whole way."

He strums a G chord and smiles up at me. "When I lit out from Reno, I was trailed by twenty thousand cars," he grin-sings the Dead tune at me.

I chuckle and his face goes to dead pan and hands stop.

Which is my cue to move along, as he clearly wants to be left alone after clawing his way up here. Or maybe it's something to do with his third wife. They're locked in combat round the clock, so I've heard, with his teenagers from his second wife, and with his daughter from his first wife back at home with her baby.

I leave him to his peace and quiet away from the crowd, and that view and up into the trees of the canyon.

I swing the van further along the fence line, and find a nice flat grassy spot.

As I jump out to set up camp, the crowd roars again, like another big ocean wave crashing, though muffled and farther away. An electric guitar pierces the roar, and bursts into a song.

I look back up the mountain opposite the canyon, with its ski slopes tumbling down onto the festival, and spot the last ski trail threading through the woods and disappearing behind the canvas-covered fence into the crowd. Beyond is the big toothy grin of the Sierra Nevada, stretching to the south, spiked with dozens of gray granite peaks.

I sit in the sliding door of the van and stare up at the mountains like I always used to, the way Ike stares out at the ocean every night, waiting for them to say something like they always used to. But all I hear is a guitar, and drums, and muffled singing, a big bluesy finish, and the crack of the last beat, the crowd erupting again.

I can't decide if I want to hang here — pull gear and fire up my little stove for some coffee — or run straight back to the festival, see who's playing, and check them out from backstage, always a huge bonus for dealing with Johnny and his gigs.

The crowd noise dies off suddenly, and in the vacuum of sound left behind, I hear Sam down by his van, singing some old country song. I used to be that guy, happy off by himself, left alone but hardly lonely with all those mountains to talk it over with. I could be that guy right now. But the crowd erupts again, louder than ever over the opening notes of a fast song, and I can actually feel the vibration of the crowd and the music in my feet, and I have to go see.

I lock up the van and practically run back up the hill toward the backstage area, as excited as a kook running out to his first ever surfbreak.

Behind the stage is a canvas tent with the sign "Green Room" next to the opening. I pull myself up short, close my eyes and take a deep breath, and act like I'm just wandering in, ho hum, just another day at the office.

Inside, a dozen or so people, dressed in every kind of outlandish clothing you'd never see anywhere else except on a stage or in a movie — leather and feathers, big hats and boots, garish makeup — are sitting around drinking beers, or tuning up, or futzing with guitars. Some old guy in biker gang regalia is smoking a joint with two women, one chatting at him, the other looking past him to check out whoever has just come in, like she just did with me before frowning and grabbing the joint.

I walk over to the tables full of food and tubs full of ice and fancy beers and grab one. Then the biggest crowd eruption of all, so I make my way over to the back of the tent, where it opens out onto the backstage area.

The band that had been playing since I got here is waving as they shuffle off this way, two of them lighting cigarettes and another hurrying past me and into the porta-potty set up next to the opening.

The crowd keeps cheering, louder and louder for the encore they know is coming, and I drink my beer and wonder if anyone will mind if I walk through to the big backstage area, even though I have no business being here until tomorrow.

I finally get up the nerve and walk out into the wings — nobody seems to notice me — and stand in front of a line of big rolling cases, trying not to gawk at everything. Roadies and techs, all in faded black t-shirts and black jeans, move around seemingly without worry or hurry, like it's just another day at the construction site. A woman with a clipboard and big headset argues with a guy in a ten-gallon cowboy hat and aviator shades. He must be the emcee, because he's standing ramrod straight, like he's on camera, talking down to her.

The crowd noise starts to fray and flag, before someone puffs it back up with a rebel yell and someone else with a "we love you!" then it droops lower.

"Come on, man," I hear behind me, "hurry up! They're losing it!"

I turn to see if someone just said that to me, and the big guy who'd hurried off to the bathroom almost runs into me.

"Sorry, man," he mumbles and rushes to rejoin his bandmates, all fidgeting with their hair and hats and the towels around their necks, clinking beers, kidding each other.

The moment he lines up with them, they wander out on the stage, smiling and nodding and tossing off little hand waves, and the crowd goes back to full roar.

I have no idea who these guys are, and forgot to look at the lineup posted back in the green room.

They strap back in, and with the weeping pick-up notes of a pedal steel guitar and the twangy answer from a Telecaster, the sound comes straight back to me from my first-ever radio, a plastic yellow Panasonic thing from Sears, when I was in middle school back in the '70s: "Rambler's Dream," the classic country rock song.

I stand and watch the band, Route 66, the singer as old and grizzled as Johnny, his voice every bit as distinct. And distinctly historical. It is a voice out of time, forever on the airwaves of my memory from the one summer when it played, over and over and over, for a month and half. (Though it looks like the rest of the band has turned over, all guys except one woman younger than me.) I can't help but tap my feet and smile. Because the song — three-part harmony with that sweet shuffle around the minor before the resolve — is bathed in a soft, rich amber: it's a hot, muggy night back East, I'd just made out with my first girl, and in just a few more years, I'll be blowing out of that crappy little town forever, and heading west.

The crowd loves it too and gives the band a standing ovation when they're done, so they play a reprise, just a couple choruses as the sun is setting and light softening.

"Keep dreamin', ramblers!" the singer yells as they finish a second time.

Another standing ovation, the crowd like a great swelling of the ocean, a deafening roar. As the band walks past me, the light changes, the very last of the sun dripping red orange through the trees on the opposite ridgeline.

The stage lights flash off, and the front of the crowd is suddenly visible: lots of people my age and older; funny hats and salt and pepper hair and beards and every color of t-shirt; and nothing but wide eyes and big smiles on sun-burnished faces. Ten thousand people, all of them happy or at least acting and looking like they are, if only right now.

And all I can think is: this is my *job*? Really? It's another one of those surreal moments when I cannot believe that for all of my bad luck a few years back, I dumb-lucked into all this, like when Johnny's really on and the band is purring and everyone is up and dancing with everyone else. Or when Amrita has the crowd up and undulating as one body, singing and dancing as we push the rhythm and build the tempo, slowly, steadily, until it bursts into a shower of light and sparks.

I linger on the edge of the stage by myself, wondering at the fact that no one is kicking me out, and take one last look out at that buzzing crowd and the mountains beyond, washed now in the rose of alpenglow.

It's moments like these when I wonder about karma versus randomness, order versus chaos, and what could I have possibly done to deserve all this, other than survive a bunch of hardships for enough decades. Might all this be some mistake? Some massive overcorrection by a messy universe? After the soul-crushing in Utah, with the job, and *Shir Hadash*, and Leah? And then, suddenly, all of this just falls into my lap? I end up in California, by complete chance, and get to start over? With a dream that wasn't even my dream, not in decades anyway, coming true without even trying, like so much fruit just hanging from the trees waiting to be picked? What is a person to do when his heart is so full that his chest aches, like it's going to explode?

And yet, and yet, here I am, and this is my job now. And there's no more to it than one of those things Amrita always says, and actually sells on one of those refrigerator magnets at her merch table: *Blessed Be.* Although I thought that was for Wiccans, not Hindus, but OK. I'll take it. Thank you, California.

Because this actually is my job, and I can't help but think someone is finally going to notice me and come over and tell me to get lost, I put on what I imagine to be my game-face: I purse my lips, narrow my gaze, and walk a few feet out onto the stage, almost far enough out to where I'll be tomorrow, stage left, where I always set up.

I put my hands on my hips and look out at the slow retreat of 7,500 people across a sea of lawn chairs and blankets and litter. Some of them smile up at me and wave, and I nod back, as I study the angle and backdrop from way up here. I shuffle my feet on the weathered black plywood of the stage, and let my body memorize the look and feel and smell of everything so it won't be so jarring tomorrow when I'm up here, my bass plugged in and every wiggle of the index and middle fingers on my right hand shaking this whole stage and the very ground below it. The whole thing feels like a weird dream I'm having.

I turn and walk back off the stage, the surreal, out-of-body sensation finally breaking — it's just another stage check, right? — and head back toward the green-room tent, suddenly hungry, and remember seeing all kinds of food in there.

I walk down the steps and into the tent and — *holy shit, is that Neil Young?* And it sure as shit is! The old hat and denim shirt and porkchop sideburns, bursting like dueling beards from both sides of this face: that's Neil Young right over there!

He is surrounded by old hippies who all want handshakes and hugs, autographs and selfies. Slung over his back like a gun is an old acoustic guitar I can tell he wants to be warming up on, as he politely, patiently, silently smiles and lets each of them take their picture.

I had forgotten he was tonight's headliner. My game-face is gone, and everything is surreal all over again, and the only thing I can focus on is: chicken.

Over there on the buffet. I walk around the clutch of people around Neil Young, and grab a plate and some food, if only so I have a reason to hang around, watch him warm up, and listen to his band's set from back here.

I look for a place to sit down as close to the stage as possible, thinking maybe I'll just hang there, because there's no way I'll get to watch his set from the wings, not with all these people around.

Then, a voice even more familiar than Neil Young's, barking over the hum of the crowd in here, fills the tent.

"I know it's a festival, goddammit!"

I look up from my food and see Johnny, walking in and yelling into his phone at what sounds like Gordon. He's wearing his usual cowboy hat, and aviator shades, so no one can see the dark hollows of his eyes; and that old scraggly beard that never seems to grow but he never trims, so no one can see the deep, ropey crevices cutting down both sides of his face.

"Yeah, but we still need some kind of soundcheck, and you shoulda told that prick we did when you saw that we'd be coming in here cold like this."

He stops to look over at Neil Young — who returns the look, and it's not friendly, and who knows how far back that all goes — and I can hear Gordon saying something on the phone, but Johnny's not listening. He's glaring at Neil Young, who shakes his head and turns back to the old hippies and their selfies.

"Well if you'd known that," Johnny goes on, "and your head wasn't up your ass, you woulda booked us into some shit bar last night in Reno, so I could knock the rust off the boys."

I can hear Gordon start to say something, but Johnny just yells, as loud as he can, "Then figure something the fuck out!" and hangs up.

Then, as if cued by what he just said, he turns and sees me, standing there holding a plate in one hand and a piece of chicken in the other.

"Hey there, fanboy" he snipes at me.

"Hey," I mumble through a mouthful.

He wanders over — as if half the tent isn't staring at him and shaking their heads at what an asshole he is — and tries to make small talk with me, like he didn't just cuss out his own manager in front of 20 people and a living, breathing rock 'n' roll icon, as if it really were just another day in the office.

"All settled in?" he asks.

"Yeah," I say, standing there holding the chicken. "Got over here in time to check out Route 66. They sounded pretty good."

"Pretty good for redneck rock," he grumbles, loudly enough for a couple women with press passes a few feet away to stop talking and stare at us.

Johnny's phone rings and he turns away to answer, and storms out of the tent.

They glower at him, then back to me, like I was the one who had just insulted their boyfriends or husbands or whatever.

"Hey," I say, waving at them with the chicken leg.

They frown at me and walk away.

Half an hour later, just as Neil Young sits on a couch across from me with a guitar to warm up, Gordon pops into the tent and gestures for me to follow him out the back.

I follow him around the back of the stage to the other side, to the empty *Kid's Activities Tent!* where the rest of the band is tuning up and Johnny's mood has gone from shitty to sullen. We're three songs into this "soundcheck" — so far, a near full run-through of our entire set for tomorrow — and he's now bitching more than raging. Sam's guitar is too loud, my bass is too muddy, Mike is late on the fills.

I wish I could say it's the altitude making him cranky — it does that to some people — or maybe the pushy, drunken crowd at the big resort hotel over there where he's staying, instead of in the camping area with the rest of us. But I'm nearly 50 gigs in with Johnny and these guys, and I already have my own way of dealing with him: say absolutely nothing, except when I have to say something; and say it as tersely and calmly as possible. I hate to admit the circularity, but it's exactly how I learned, starting at about age seven, to manage my way around a crazy drunk for a father.

The rest of the band won't speak with Johnny at all, even when they need to. Instead, they let him throw his tantrums and do what they're going to do anyway; and part of my job, as the new guy, is to stand tall and run interference with him, the way I ran it when I had to, growing up, for my mother and sister. If they have to tell Johnny something onstage, they do it through me, with nods or glances or quick shouts back by the drums.

Unlike all the new guys in Route 66, this is nearly the same band Johnny's been playing with since the beginning, all original members from his Laurel Canyon days except for Bill and me. After all the years, fights, rehabs and "reunion" tours — and long after the decade-long lawsuit over songwriting credits and royalties that nobody, except all their lawyers, really won — they're all stuck together, like people in jobs everywhere. And this job may be a hell of a lot more fun than anything in an office, but it is still a job with weird office politics. And a crazy boss.

Those politics? Sam, still long-haired and rail-skinny inside his old denim shirt, bent always like a question mark over his guitar, can't say a word to Johnny without him yelling back; and in an instant they're standing in the middle of the stage screaming at each other about nothing. Curtis tips his cowboy hat to cover his eyes, pushes his fiddle further into the great folds where a neck would be, and sinks even lower into his great big middle, busying himself just off the mike with his solo or noodling on something else. Bill sits squat and square as a giant toad behind the keys, in one of his western shirts with all the piping, smoking and grinning at some private joke after a private smoke, and waiting to fall in behind. Ralphie, back there in his headset and tank top and headband and sweatbands, looking more like an aerobics instructor at a senior center than a drummer, does whatever Sam tells him to do because, I've been told, that's what he's always done. And I'm the new guy with no baggage, the sixth bassist in three decades, and so I too follow Sam and push the bassline on Johnny when it's too late for him to do anything.

He gives me that shitty look every time, but it isn't envenomed with the history he has with Sam or the other guys, and by then the train is pulling away, so he mutters something, jumps on, and starts singing. And I just lay back and fatten the sound, and count, and watch.

"Hold on, hold on," Johnny grumbles, cutting off the song and letting his guitar drop to hang from his shoulders.

He grabs the pencil and scribbles on the tattered pages on the music stand in front of him.

So . . . we stand and wait, on this little stage in this little tent, while no more than 60 feet away, Neil Young and his band and 7,500 people are rockin' in the free world. Curtis is off his mic, noodling on something. Sam checks his tuning. Ralphie looks at his phone. And I'm just standing here watching Johnny scribble, grimace, scratch out what he just scribbled, smile — or his tight-mouthed version of a smile, anyway — and scribble again.

In the middle of our ten-song set tomorrow afternoon, he wants to debut this dark new thing he just wrote, an angry dirge about climate change and the whole world catching on fire. I overheard Gordon trying to talk him out of it; but that only made him yell louder that we are doing it, and who gives a shit if it messes up everybody's good time; and so here we are, the night before the gig, learning a brand-new song about the world ending.

He scowls again, scratches it out, scribbles something else.

Luckily, as he messes around with lyrics for a song we are going to test-drive in front of 7,500 people tomorrow afternoon, they aren't anything we have to worry about: there's no harmony in this dark brooding thing, just Johnny's plaintive lead; and the chord progression is settled and simple enough, except for the way it ends on the minor second. That's the melodic hook, and I'll be hearing it in my sleep tonight, for fear of blowing it by going back to the root, even if I can fix it with a muddy slide back to the second. As for Johnny blowing up in front of this huge crowd, I can always go into my eye-of-the-shitstorm mode; it'll be no different than him throwing a fit on a smaller stage, in the middle of a song we do at every gig. Though I am glad I walked out onto the edge of that stage this afternoon. Because it will be a hell of a thing tomorrow, strapping myself — with just these four strings, three little knobs, and two pedals — into that wall of sonic power.

My eye-of-the-shitstorm mode, as Tom used to call it, way back in my corporate days. We were all a bunch of kids back then growing software in a hothouse; and I was the CTO not because I was the best engineer, but because I was the one who kept all the other engineers from blowing up. When a deal went south, or key employee went psycho, or trade press reporter or Wall Street analyst went sour, I was the fixer, the explainer, the guy who stood there and took it and gave it back.

It's exactly what Gordon saw in me on the mountain in Utah two years ago, and why he hired me for this gig: I'm the only one up on this stage who won't react to Johnny. I won't blow up and storm off, or get in his face, or check out. Just like in mountain rescue: I'll hunker down and power through. The louder they scream, the harder I lock down and deal with it.

"OK," Johnny finally says, drops the pencil, and swings his guitar around.

He strums the chord, hums into the mic, then pops his capo onto the neck.

I count three frets.

"What are you doing, man?" Sam yells. "E flat? Are you fucking kidding? Now???"

Johnny gashes out a loud E flat, and starts in the chorus, while Sam stands there, glowering at him.

I jump in on the E flat, Sam turns to glower at me, and I shrug.

He throws his hands up, shakes his head, and I half expect him to switch out his acoustic for his Telecaster, but instead, he digs a capo out of his shirt pocket.

Hardly eye-of-the-shitstorm mode this time around, but I can feel Sam over there, glowering at me while Johnny launches into the first verse, and too bad. If anything, this dysfunctional family ritual we go through before almost every gig is as much a part of the musical rehearsal. Here I am, the new kid, either staring Johnny down while the rest of the band fidgets with their instruments, waiting to see if he is going to fire me or just start singing . . . or, like just now, if I shove off with him and fill the room with big booming bass notes, and drag the rest of them along.

And the beat goes on.

Johnny finally sinks into the song, tipping his head back and singing out, in the half holler and half cry of a weary old man, the tagline in the chorus: "and I won't stop fighting fire, with fire."

By the time we are done with the rehearsal, Neil Young and the crowd are long gone, and the main stage and festival grounds are dark but for the solitary buzzing glare of a row of security lights out over a sea of empty lawn chairs and blankets.

I am way too wired to go back and just crash, so I wander all the way around the back of the field, over by the main camping area. Every color of nylon is lit up with lanterns inside and out. No campfires are allowed for the fire danger, of course, so people are gathered around stark bursts of propane glow, talking, laughing, a few playing guitars and singing.

I walk the whole perimeter, then make my way back to the checkpoint and through to our camping area. After the main campground, it is oddly dark and mostly silent, but for the low hum of generators. Everyone is in bed already, I guess. A work night.

I climb into my van and make a sandwich out of my cooler, and lay on my camping mattress, let the quiet rumble of the generators sing me to sleep . . .

I awaken to the sound of more generators and a bus idling for half an hour — a grumbly, rattling diesel, like a wheezing old man in the morning — before it finally leaves.

I wander over to the festival and the green room tent for coffee and breakfast and to see who is around. But it's all road people at this hour.

I eat and go back to my van and futz with my gear, play some guitar, futz with my surf gear — set it all out in the sun to air out — then play some more guitar.

Eight more hours until our 6:30 call for our 7 P.M. set.

Ugh.

There would have been a time when I would have squeezed every minute of those eight hours out of one of those mountains, hiking up to maybe that summit over there to look down at all of this. But I don't dare risk getting lost, or twisting an ankle, or coming back even close to late. Not an option. So I fidget and futz.

When the music finally starts at noon, I wander the perimeter and listen, watch people carrying on, listen to the next band, wander some more.

And, finally — finally — it's time.

The sun is going down behind the mountains, and we are warming up, unamplified, at the far end of the green room tent.

Every time the crowd roars — for Pelican Wind, the folk-rock band on now — I swear I can see the canvas wall that separates those 7,500 people from us pushing inward by a blast of wind, even though I know it isn't.

And then, it really is time.

I'm strapped into my stage bass, and following the rest of the band through the opening and into the backstage area, and suddenly, everything slows down.

Sound starts to bend in my ears, and every light is a flashbulb going off, and there is a surging in my chest that rushes down my legs into my feet, and down my arms and into the hands and into my fingers, and I realize how alive and awake I feel — really, truly ALIVE! and AWAKE! — and flushed with as much adrenaline as I've been on a big mountain or any wave, and it feels like I am going to live forever.

I stare at the back of Sam's denim shirt, notice the white rime of sweat stain running along the edge of his ancient leather guitar strap, and hear the rumbling howl of the emcee — all words, I'm sure, though I'll never know what they were — because everything really is melting now as the crowd roars over the top of him.

The sweat stain starts moving forward and I follow Sam out into a blast of white light, into the roar of the crowd. It sounds exactly like the ocean when the tide is turning, like big waves standing straight up and dropping to rake through a pile of cobbles lining the beach — no, it's even louder and rougher than that — like a sudden and consuming hailstorm in the mountains, pounding away on the camper of my old truck, a steady, pounding roar I can feel in my entire body.

The stagelights are blinding, even in the middle of the day, so I do what I always do: focus on the roadie handing me the cable, on putting the jack cleanly into my bass, on checking the volume knob and tone knob and pedals at my feet.

Tuner/feed *on*, tuner/feed *off*. Tuner/feed *on*, tuner/feed *off*. Tuner/feed *on*, tuner/feed *off*. *Off*, *on*.

*This will be fine*, I tell myself, close my eyes, force out my breath.

Then I look up, at a sea of smiling faces and nodding heads and swaying bodies, lapping right up to the shore of the stage. Best not to look that way, to focus on the band, and where the hell is Johnny? He was back there with us, and he always comes in last, makes his entrance. But how long have we been out here?

Then it hits me like an electric surge, the PA comes up, and my tuner/feed is *on* and my right hand feels the hum of the whole damn universe in my bass. I hit the tuner/feed *off*, and then another roar from the crowd, the loudest wave yet, crashing into us.

I turn to see Johnny charging out with his guitar slung over his shoulder, right to the front of center stage, pointing straight out into the middle of the crowd with his right hand and index finger, like he sees them and knows them, and they love it.

He whips around to the mike, his shades still on, so we know he's pissed about something, but they don't. They also don't know that the pointed finger doesn't mean he sees them in any way they would find comforting. They just roar louder still, a wave of sound from front to back, then the echo back to front, like a big wave into a small cove, rocketing around in a circle along the sea cliffs.

The roadie cables him in and he shouts to the crowd and my foot pushes tuner/feed *on*, and there's that surge again, the whole of the PA and the stage humming under my fingers again, even with the strings dampened. It's as if I were holding a giant I-beam suspended above the whole world, and if I wanted to, and weren't in military-grade eye-of-the-shitstorm mode right now, I could do something really awful, the thought of which terrifies me and makes me lock down that much harder.

"Hello Sierra Nevada Mountains!" Johnny yells into his mike.

Then another roar from the crowd, while he smiles what they don't know, but we all do, to be his grim, cynical smile, proof that he knows things they never will. Because he's exactly right when he says that with the pointed finger, and that's what makes him so crazy: they don't really care about the world burning down, at least not right now; they just want to sing, dance, and reminisce. Which works for me, because I'm standing up here, my body charged to full wattage, and all I want is to start playing.

And then, finally, with Ralphie's "one, two, three . . ." there's the honeyed guitar chord, and the fiddle fill, and I'm right there on the A.

"When the sun sets," Johnny sings the first line of the song, and the crowd roars like they always do, so we throw in the extra two beats, "over that old town . . ."

I feel the deep, booming sustain of every one of my bass notes through the stage floor; and while my timing sounds fine in the feed in my ears, I still have to watch Sam's head to make sure I'm on it. It's also good to focus on him, because out of my peripheral vision, the crowd looks like confetti in perpetual motion, or a Jackson Pollock painting in moving animated form, a million flecks of vibrating little colors.

After the second verse, Curtis goes into his fiddle break, his long silky lines the voice of the high school girlfriend in the song, singing back to Johnny, *oh yes, I'm still here, come on home . . .* and I can finally close my eyes, and just count, and play.

The song is all sunshine and small towns, one of those folk-country-rock crossovers from Johnny's first album. It's a cherished old postcard from a cousin who moved out West. And while it's not much of anything musically, it sounds like a pair of old blue jeans fits: soft, familiar, just so, like everything is going to be alright. And it feels like these guys sound together, onstage anyway, the melody and rhythm dancing along, slowly opening, rising, and soaring to the chorus. The song ambles along the back road of its own story, headlights out across the desert hills, the fiddle and guitar finally meeting up on the distant ridge to watch the sunset.

And for all their fighting and resentments and bitterness at Johnny the rest of the time, how could it not sound this intimate, breezy, and sweet? These guys have been doing this since 1975, when three of the four of them were living out of a van the size of mine, playing up and down the coast, and Johnny was still a teenage runaway with a pawn shop guitar. Four decades later, the song has aged perfectly, all those sunny days and all that sweet young love no longer lost, but soaked in sepia and pinned to the pages of an old photo album brought out for the 7,500 people hanging out on Johnny's front porch on a Saturday night.

But Johnny's not having it.

Even as we unspool our usual set and sound as tight as ever, I can see him struggle, can see from the fixed jaw and scowl gathered up behind his sunglasses that he's still in a pissy mood, that he's probably going to pop off at some point.

Luckily, the adrenaline has washed through, and I'm back in my head and most of the way back in my body. I can track with the band, and monitor Johnny's mood, all while laying back, and counting four, and soaking in the singular, intense, surreal physical sensation of this elevated, sprawling stage beneath our feet, vibrating with every pull and flick of my right index and middle fingers.

As Sam switches to his semi-acoustic, with its warm, woody, jazzy glow, Johnny grabs the mike and I brace for it, but he just tips his head suddenly, and lets Sam serenade us solo through the intro, our first slow song.

Johnny nods to the beat, and Ralphie comes in, and there's my cue, and the whole thing weaves like the first line of the song, like the convertible open to the night air down the PCH, the glow of moon out over the ocean, the rush of wind, the dance of juniper and cypress.

I'm finally fully back in my body, and start to sway with the song myself. I close my eyes and feel the stage vibrate, and my breath going in and out.

*OK to look now*, so I open my eyes, right at the crowd upfront for the first time.

At all three generations of them: the grizzled boomers and hippie rednecks as old as these guys in the band, a bunch with younger versions of themselves, Cool Moms and Dads, with Cool Sons and Daughters and In-Laws, a few with little kids in their laps or on their shoulders. And the usual freakers are right up front, platinum hair and salt-and-pepper beards, tie-dye and floppy hats, arms raised and swaying to the music.

Every face is turned upward toward Johnny, bright, open, expectant, a field of sunflowers following the sun — except for the ones who catch me looking at them. There's a moment of shock on their faces at my curious gaze; then an explosion of smile and pure delight, wide eyes fixed on mine and a wondrous grin. As if they have any idea who I actually am, other than a guy in the band who sees them — *He sees me! Johnny's bass player! A guy in the band!* — as if we're on some kind of first date they've been dreaming about forever.

The adoration of complete strangers is the weirdest thing of all about this gig, and about the *kirtans* with Amrita. They have no idea who I am, but they know how what I am doing is making them feel, which may be the most stirring and straight-up *happy* thing they feel all year. Sometimes, the upturned faces and half-opened mouths and wide eyes can be too much, like actual heat too close to exposed skin.

I catch another's gaze, straight down in front of me on the rail, an athletic woman in a tank top with a waterfall of dark curly hair, bronzed with the sun.

Her whole body is a blur of motion as she dances her hips around in a circle, like she's belly-dancing or hula hooping, Calafia again, her eyes riveted on me.

I look away quickly, down at my bass, over at the band, then back at her because I can't help but look.

She stops dancing and just stands there staring at me, her smile deepening from flirty fun to what she looks like she thinks is some sort of profound, mystical contact, like the heavens just opened up to consecrate this moment between us.

I turn back to the band — that was like looking into oncoming headlights — and try to shake it off. But we are on an extended jam, and the song won't end for another three and a half minutes. I glance back her way.

She's still standing and gawking and smiling at me, so I smile as politely and meaninglessly as I can at her and look over her head and past the crowd, to what's left of the mountain ridge across the valley.

The sun is all the way down now, the mountains going from alpenglow rose to magenta to dark. When I turn back to the band for the big finish on this song, the stage lights seem more intense than ever, over-illuminating everyone's face like in a hotel bathroom mirror: every wrinkle; the imperfections in their smiles; the shadows around their eyes.

I hear the last words of the last *coda*, and look over to track with Sam as he brings the tempo down. Count four, then four on the root, and sustain — as Johnny serenades us out of the song, his last goodbye wink of a phrase doused with a sudden downpour of applause, clapping like rain, punctuated with whistles and hollers.

As I go to pedal off my bass, I realize my ears are reaching for Johnny's usual barking "thank you very much!" because there is no "thank you very much!" — just a long tail of applause, a few more whistles, a random holler from halfway back.

And then a vast, low-volume, creepy, expectant crowd-hum.

I look over at him, standing behind the mike, bowing his head and shaking it wearily, then looking up at the crowd.

Behind him, Sam shakes his head in disgust as he turns and hurries to swap out the semi for his Rickenbacker 12-string, and nods furiously to me and mouths *GO!*

I pedal my bass back on, and even though Sam and I are supposed to start with his head nod on the same A, I can see Johnny start to say something, so I pull on the open A three times, the first phrase of "Time Won't Heal This" without Sam.

The entire stage hums with the notes, the drums and cymbals rattling and floor shaking; Johnny turns and gives me what I assume under those sunglasses is stink-eye; and Sam nods in half-disgust and half-amusement as he finds his A, nods to me three times, and we launch into the song.

The only problem with this song: it's the one that always sets Johnny off the worst. He wrote it while he was in the middle of a three-month rehab in Aspen, and hiking every day in the mountains. Apparently, he told everyone it was the mountains and nature that cured him, not the meditation, or massages, or vegan purge, or all the *kundalini* yoga. And, as I figured out some of my oldest and darkest shit up in those same mountains not that many years ago, I would have believed him — except he was back on pills and booze within a year.

We don't do "Time Won't Heal This" very often for good reason — even he knows it sets him off — but we're up here in the mountains, at *California Summerfest!*, so how can we not?

Or so I thought, when I saw the set-list. But now, seeing that look on his face while he's singing it, I can see exactly why not. The words are coming out fine, but his face, even with the sunglasses still on, is a tangle of sadness, pain, and rage, like he is so angry and frustrated he wants to burst out crying.

The song winds around, one more time through the chorus, lingering on the resignation and anguish of the minor seventh, and Ralphie finishes it with the brushes on the splash cymbals.

The crowd, lulled into sitting or swaying to the song, slowly comes back, the applause filtering upward toward us as all the lights fade to black for a long moment, echoing the song's bleak message about the unheeded and inevitable destruction of the planet.

A single spotlight comes up on Johnny for the next song, for the long sentimental intro he does while he's swapping out his Guild acoustic for his Stratocaster and Curtis is switching from lap steel back to fiddle. But he doesn't say anything, and the crowd goes suddenly, uncomfortably quiet, like the sound of a great beast splayed out across the whole field, breathing.

As Johnny steps to the mike in his Strat, his hands aren't in position for the intro with Curtis; they're down at his sides. And he's clenching and unclenching his fists. Which means he's not even holding a pick. Uh-oh.

Sam sees that I see it, and we both look over at Curtis, who asks me with his eyes, *you think I should?* and hurries his fiddle into position.

But not in time.

"It's not just a pretty song, people!" Johnny growls into the mike. "All those big beautiful trees living up there?" he waves at the mountains behind them, now a hulking silhouette against the last of the sunset.

The crowd lets out a lukewarm sort of half-cheer, like they don't want to but think they're supposed to.

There's a stab of feedback from some microphone, and the audience goes even more completely and uncomfortably silent.

"We love you, Johnny!" a woman's voice yells from halfway back.

Then more silence as Johnny just stares at them and shakes his head.

I nod to Curtis, who's still tuning his fiddle off the feed.

"'Sunset Road'!!!" another woman screams.

"Yeah! 'Sunset Road'!" come other voices. "Play 'Sunset Road'!"

"Yeah, we'll play it," Johnny mutters. "But before we get on with the *show*," he says, practically spitting out the word, "I just wanted to take a minute and say thank you. To all those trees up there, watching over us, choking on our poisons, waiting for us to get hell out of here."

Another lukewarm, half-cheer.

"To say thanks to this good earth we've all been given," he goes on, "this one earth we're doing our goddamndest to destroy!"

I look over at Sam, who is turned away from me, Johnny, the audience, everybody, playing something off the feed.

"And the bastards want to tear down these trees! The climate change deniers, the oil companies! The politicians they've bought!"

"Boo!" the crowd roars.

"That's right," he says.

I can't help but turn and look over the fence next to the stage at the parking lot, a couple football fields' worth, lined with cars, vans, trucks, and minivans, a vast grid of metal gleaming in the fluorescence of two dozen klieg lights.

I turn back and catch Curtis doing the same thing, and he laughs and shrugs, and asks again with his eyes, *Should I?*

"But it's not too late!" Johnny yells. "We can stop all this madness! Save the planet! Save the planet!" he starts chanting.

The crowd doesn't start chanting, but swells suddenly into the dull roar of 7,500 people chattering.

"Come on, people!" Johnny yells again. "Save the planet! Save the planet!"

A few up front start to chant along, clapping to the three-beat.

But the rest of the crowd sounds like we just went into our set break, so I look over at Curtis and nod *Yes! Now!*

And there's that sweet, silky tone of his bow across the strings, lifting off into the nighttime air.

Johnny turns and scowls at him, but the second spotlight comes up and drowns Curtis in amber light. Johnny just stares at him, like he's going to browbeat him into stopping.

I pedal my bass back on, and as Curtis turns the intro, I start way high up the neck in C, right where Johnny's guitar is supposed to come in, and walk with Curtis' fiddle down through the turnaround, the rhythm guitar part arpeggiated on my four strings instead of strummed on his six.

Johnny whips around and gives me about as shitty a look as he ever has, but then turns to the mike, and growls "save the planet, people, that's all!" and his guitar fills the space between Curtis and me and we are off on the next song.

Fifteen seconds later, the lyrics flow out of Johnny like none of that just happened. It's another song about time passing, more open roads and more girls left behind, and all that lonely freedom.

The crowd roars again into the chorus, singing along and swaying to the sultry tempo.

Johnny keeps playing, but stops singing and pulls off the mike to turn to Curtis, who ignores him, then to me, and points at the crowd, as if to prove some point.

I also ignore him and look up at my left hand, as if I suddenly forgot where the G was. Because I don't care what kind of mood Johnny is in. I know what my real job is, I know how to do it without flinching, and right now, my job kicks ass. He can fire me the minute we walk off stage. This is *fun*.

By the time the song ends, Johnny's mood has broken, the scowl he walked out here with half an hour ago is gone, and he even lifts his hat and gives a little bow with his head to say *thanks* and the crowd erupts.

Then, the new song, the one Johnny is still working out about the planet catching fire. Uh-oh.

Luckily, it's mostly just Johnny on his acoustic, with chords and melody nearly as simple and square as something by Woody Guthrie — except for the way it goes to that minor second after the tagline, "burning up, burning down, goodbye my love, goodbye old town" — just hanging there in the air without words . . . as if the music is holding out one last hope for us to awaken from our carbon-burning madness.

We muscle our way through the song none of us had heard 24 hours ago, and the crowd is mesmerized, the applause coming in a long, slow build, like a summer rain on a tinder-dry forest.

And that's all Johnny needed: to have his new eco-jeremiad be heard before it blew him up from the inside.

He puts his hands together in prayer position and bows his head, exactly like Amrita and the yoga crowd, something I've never seen him do before. Then he launches straight into his old rockabilly cruiser, with a big staged ha-ha-look-at-them laugh at us, for the audience's amusement, as we scramble to catch up.

The rest of the set is flawless and flies by. Johnny sings all his old songs as true to his original recordings, as if we were a slavish tribute-band version of him and his band for *'70s Nite!* at the local American Legion Hall. Or as if we were playing in somebody's backyard, with 7,500 of their closest friends and the world's greatest home stereo rig.

"Thank you California Summerfest!" Johnny yells into the mike after the final song of our regular set.

The crowd explodes from their seats, an instant standing ovation all the way back.

"Thank you, Sierra Nevada Mountains," Johnny yells and tips his hat. "And thank you planet earth!"

He turns to go and we follow, doing the amble-off-and-wave thing to the loudest audience noise I've ever heard in my life. It sounds so loud, I can't help but marvel at how it actually deafens into a kind of muffled silence, or muted roar, like being held under a big wave.

We hang out for a minute just off the stage, in the same space where I watched Route 66 yesterday. And Johnny actually looks, if not happy, then strangely at peace. His face is relaxed, and with his sunglasses finally off, his eyes aren't burning like they always do. Sam and Curtis are opening beers, and laughing at some private joke, Bill and Ralphie a couple sodas, and me just visibly exhaling as I turn back and watch at the crowd.

I just want to stand here forever, and listen to that noise, and feel the electricity of this moment surging through my body. The only thing this sensation compares to is the moment of making a big summit, after a long, dangerous climb, adrenaline flushing through every cell in my body like white-hot liquid light.

The guys keep laughing, so I turn and notice that I'm what's funny.

*What?* I gesture over the roar.

Sam walks over and points to my bass. Which I somehow managed to pedal-mute, unplug, and wear off the stage without realizing it. Ha!

"You sure do know how to accessorize!" he yells through a grin.

"If that's the biggest mistake I made tonight," I yell back, "I'll take it!"

"No mistake, just funny! You nailed it all, same as always!" Then he points at my bass again. "And hey man — it's a great way to pick up groupies at the after-party!"

He starts to say something else, but the roar of the crowd stumbles, a tiny little break in the dull wash of the sound; and as if on a three-count from that precise moment, Johnny ambles back out onto the stage, as casually as he'd walk into a convenience store to buy milk.

Sam and Curtis and Ralphie all laugh, and mock-gesture to each other, *after you, no after you, no I insist* . . . then they all look over at me, standing practically on my toes to run back out there, with my very heavy and elaborate new fashion accessory trailing from my shoulders.

Our encore is "Sunset Road" of course. And we've done it so many times, it's like I'm still back there in the wings, watching us do it, moving with the sultry sway of Johnny's bittersweet old ballad turned radio gold.

This very song — like the other odd few from Neil Young and Jackson Browne and Joni Mitchell that broke through in the '70s — reminds me of that goofy yellow plastic radio, and the sugary A.M. music that would pour out of it every night after dark from distant cities. "Sunset Road" was in heavy rotation the summer between my seventh and eighth grade, and became a side opener of the soundtrack for every fantasy I ever had as a kid. It gave me reason to believe that I could and would one day leave that shitty little town — with its crappy weather and hardscrabble people, schoolyard bullies and town drunks and dirty old men, with my crazy father, and disabled mother, and troubled sister — because there was some place way out West to leave *for,* someplace sunny, sexy, and beautiful.

I want this five minutes to last forever, want it so badly I could burst into tears right up here on stage.

I feel my throat tightening and my bass wobbling, so I shake my head to break the spell, study my hands, breathe out . . . and turn to look down at the crowd along the rail.

There she is again — tonight's Calafia — with her waterfall hair and bronzed gym-body, still dancing with the music but staring straight back up at me, smiling, like she's trying to say something with her eyes.

I look away because it's weird, look over at Johnny to see if he'll be giving Curtis an extended break on the lap steel, even though I can follow it with my ears and it doesn't affect my fingering. But then I can't help but look back.

She has stopped dancing, and is holding up her left hand, a finger from her right hand through her one wristband. She gestures with her head toward stage left, toward the security exit that connects the audience to backstage.

Oh. I give her a half-smile that I hope says, *I would, sure, some other time maybe, but sorry.*

I hear Curtis reach the end of the phrase, and turn back to the band as we slowly bring it home, the sun finally setting over Sunset Road, that happy little town out West falling into peaceful slumber.

The slow build of applause again, until it is thundering down on us like hail.

"Good night, everybody!" Johnny bellows into the mike and waves as he turns to go.

I remember to take my bass off this time, busying myself with the pedals and cable and strap, because I can feel her down there still staring at me.

"Good job, man," Johnny shouts to me, as he walks by. "High-wire up here, and you nailed it."

Because I am all of two years into this gig, I always want to play more after we're done. Lots more. A 45-minute set and 5-minute encore is just a warm-up, a tease, so I'm always looking for a jam with whoever from Johnny's band — or one of the other bands if it's a fair or festival — back in the green room, or at the hotel, or wherever we're all staying. Most of the time, for Sam, Curtis, Bill and Ralphie who've been doing this for decades — and especially if it's just us at the gig, and not some up-and-comer warm-up band itching to show what they got to the old-timers — it's bedtime, and I'm on my own with my guitar.

But tonight, with at least a dozen bands here, there has to be somebody who wants to play a few more songs with a few new people. Because after all of what just happened up there on that stage, I am not going to sleep anytime soon.

Down in the green room tent, Johnny is already gone, and the guys are digging into the buffet, visiting with old friends, calling home.

I grab a quick bite, tell Sam I'm up for a jam later if any of them are, and head back to the camping area.

As I cross through security, I can see a couple people already playing around a couple lanterns — guitar and fiddle — sitting in camp chairs back among the smaller RVs and vans, right near mine.

"Mind if I join you? I play the bass," holding up my case. "And I've got an old pignose I can run on batteries."

"The bass?" the guitar player says, his worn face lifting from the shadow of his big cowboy hat, sunken eyes gleaming in the glow of the lantern. "Hell yeah."

"Yeah, buddy," the string-bean fiddler looks up, his face even more weathered than the guitarist's. "Grab that pignose, and hammer out a floor we can dance on. This old boy here can't keep time for shit."

"Says the kettle to the pot."

"Yeah, yeah, yeah."

I knew the bass would make me instantly welcome: every bass player started out playing something else — guitar, mandolin, piano — and most would rather play anything other than bass when they don't have to. But I'm still the new kid around here, and these guys have forgotten more songs than I'll ever know; and even though I can jump in on the three, four, or five chords of just about anything, the bass is plenty to keep track of with a couple old road warriors.

I drop my bass, go dig my amp out of my van, come back and plug in my bass.

"What? No 'Apple Blossom Girl?'" the fiddler teases the guitarist with some joke I don't get.

"Hell no!"

"Heck, Billy — you put two youngins through college on that song!"

"Yeah, but not me *singin'* it. It's Luke what put sugar all over the damn thing and turned 'er into a Christmas card. Can't stand it anymore. And they're done with college, so I'm done with that damn thing."

"Except for encores, that is."

"Yeah, well," Billy says and blows his nose. "Boys'll never let that one go. Alright, Charley — 'stead of that Nash Vegas, how about some country that works for a living?"

"Something with a little dirt on it?"

"And a little bit o' whiskey in it, itching for a fight."

He pulls a bottleneck slide out of his shirt pocket, looks over at me and studies my face for the 20 seconds it takes to re-tune his guitar to open G, and finally says, "'Streets of Bakersfield,' in G. Kicks right to the four, back and forth twice, then the five. Verse *and* chorus. Easy as pie."

And before I can find my G, he's off, the slide spinning out a dance hall melody, the fiddle right behind with the two-four chop. I stay low, one–

two, one–two, old school doghouse bass, on a song I wasn't sure about until Billy tips his head back and starts singing. But I recognize it right away, and not from the "Golden Era of Country Music" — the classic Buck Owens song from the '70s, which somebody wrote for him about hardscrabble life in the Central Valley in the '40s and '50s — but from the Second Golden Era of Country Music, the spiffed up version revived by Dwight Yoakum in the late '80s.

I close my eyes, breathe in and out, and hold onto my bass like it's a life preserver, trying just to stay out of their way and not splash anybody. This may be the greatest musicianship I've ever witnessed, let alone tried to hang with.

After the second verse, Billy nods at me, *Keep on just like that, you're doing fine,* and here come the fireworks: the slide guitar and fiddle split breaks, trading the melody and the chop, handing it back and forth to each other like a game of hot potato. They scramble it into something that sounds even older, like a dusty, scratchy western swing number from the '20s or '30s.

The next time through the top, Billy starts down low with his slide, rolling his way up the guitar neck through the melody, emulating the Tex-Mex, border radio accordion that rattles around in the chorus of the original. Charley grabs that last note, top of the guitar and bottom of the fiddle, then weaves in and out of the melody, climbing, climbing, pushing us on the tempo, faster and faster, until he's three octaves up, both hands furious under his chin. My mind's eye fills with a blur of dancers, in a sweaty roadhouse in the middle of nowhere, moths fluttering around the neon, everything in black and white and dusty sepia, the same dust settling just outside, on the fruit orchards and oil rigs and cotton fields running into the darkness in every direction from this neon-firefly of a roadhouse.

The fiddle break finally explodes out of the top, and the dancers who have gathered outside our circle hoot and holler, but no one misses a beat and the pace doesn't break and Billy jumps in on one more chorus, lifts his foot to signal the end of the song, and we stop, right where we are supposed to stop.

And instant silence, but for the low rumble from up the hill of whoever's on stage. Because the three of us are "sidemen" and have stage discipline, and know not to make a sound until somebody else — the lead singer or the audience — does.

"That'll do," Billy says, almost to himself, shaking his head in reverence to the song.

Then another rumble from the crowd back at the festival.

"You boys want a little more steel?"

We all turn toward the deep, throaty voice of a woman coming this way, a tall, slender silhouette in the glare of the lights from the festival, carrying a guitar.

"That you, Rhonda?" Charley asks.

"Afraid so. Coming to see who's making all that racket on the fiddle."

She comes around the front of us, a statue of a woman with long platinum hair, draped in a Mexican poncho and silver and turquoise jewelry, carrying a camp chair and a National steel guitar.

I don't recognize her, even though it's clear from the way these guys straighten up that I should.

She sits down and says "give me a second, boys." She pulls out a slide, scratches out a few open notes, tunes a string, then more notes. "I'll be damned. She was in tune when I put her on the airplane this morning."

She tunes another string, then more notes, then digs in from the very bottom with the slide, and scrambles up the neck, bending them with her fingerpicks, making the cold steel moan, wail, snicker, wail again — then holds it, holds it — and the circle of notes spins around to sink into a slow bluesy moan. It takes me a moment to hear it — that she's playing exactly what we just played, in G — but at about one-third the speed, transforming it from giddy, edgy dance number to wistful blues ballad.

"Whose turn?" she says, still playing, looking around at the three of us.

"All yours," Billy says. "If you want it."

"I got better manners than that, my friend. Whose turn?"

"Well," Charley says finally, resting his bow across the strings while his eyes search for something. "Long as we're going old school — how about an old Bob Wills' thing you probably never heard, half swing, half shuffle, in C. Goes to the third in the verse, then all G in the chorus. One, two —"

And he launches into a western swing song with a breezy tempo that sounds faster than it is, because it's swing, with a vamp that pushes hard on the beat without actually moving it, like all swing, and lots of jazz, and the defining rhythmic impulse of classic bluegrass.

I jump in to anchor it to the ground, while the three of them scramble the melody, one carrying it to the top and handing it off to the other.

The third time around, the fiddler stops playing and starts singing, an un-lacquered old crooner of a voice with the slightest drawl, like the singer in a recording of an old radio show.

Billy comes in right behind with a break, all warm clean lines now. I look over and see that he's swapped out his slide for a steel; his break sounds like a pedal steel guitar, the vibrato and sustain of an old cowboy song. When he comes around, Rhonda tags the exact same note halfway up her guitar and winds the melody in a circle around the C. Then she lets it freefall into open strings, scratching and clawing at the steel until it takes flight, back up the neck. She spins the simple bluesy phrase round and round with her fingerpicks, bending it, on and off the C, making it cry and plead, *please release me!* and finally letting it explode upward into a wild chatter of notes at the end of the verse.

"Oh yeah!" Billy says. "Keep talkin'!"

She keeps spinning the phrase, way up high on the neck until the notes come so fast they run together. On the next chord change, she lets the whole roiling bunch flutter to the ground, bounce off the two bottom strings, the slide weaving and wobbling them halfway up, quieting the roll to just the root, all raw vibrato, bending down to the seventh and back up, down again and back up, the heart-sinking-in-your-chest thing that is the blues.

Then Charley matches her, note for note, double-stops where she pulls whole chords, the fiddle moaning and pleading its way up under his chin, crying and laughing when it gets there in a fury of notes so high it sounds like sparks look, flying off a blacksmith's anvil into the night air to join the stars.

Everything melts, and I hang onto my bass because gravity is gone and it's the only thing holding me to the earth. I am engulfed in music so raw, powerful and virtuoso that it makes my chest ache, throat tighten, eyes blur with tears.

Charley's foot comes up, the last phrase coming around, and *bang!* Dead stop ending.

"Damn you two!" Billy shouts. "Whew, doggie! Looks like I showed up at a gunfight with this here knife."

"Her fault," Charley points at Rhonda with his bow. "With that delta blues throwdown on the bottom. Damn, girl!"

"Thank you kindly," she says.

"Even with all that speed, all that dancin'," Charley says, checking his tuning on the fiddle. "Still a blues song."

"They're all blues songs," Billy says, checking his tuning. "Country, swing, gospel, honky-tonk. Don't matter if you're dancin', drinkin', prayin' it away. All the same thing, laughin' at your own pain. Or cryin'."

"Or a little bit of both," Rhonda says.

"Ya'll playing some blues over here?"

We look up and see two guys about my age coming over, banjo and mandolin, and two more lanterns. They put them in the center of the circle — no fires allowed, as one errant spark would set off all those pines so dry they don't smell anymore — and I feel bad for not bringing mine over. Didn't know this was a thing, but it's a cool thing: the lanterns are like a roaring bonfire now, putting off just enough heat against the chill all around us.

Introductions all around, instruments tuning, beers opening.

"You got something?" Billy asks the guy with the banjo.

"To follow that? Heck no! But long as ya'll wanna swing some, how about a little Piedmont blues, where all that got started?"

"That ain't so," Billy says. "All got started with Mr. Johnson, down in Mississippi."

"Some say," the banjo player says. "I heard tell it all got started over in Africa, with one of these right here. And what they could remember of it, out workin' out the fields. Call and response singing to get through the day. All those long blue notes when the sun goes down. Africa's an old dream they can't barely remember. And freedom ain't coming anytime soon."

"Don't think I know that one," Billy tries to muster a laugh out of it.

But the rest of them are staring into the lanterns, nodding — like me, I assume — to whatever scrap of bluesy melody they're hearing, mine so dank and blue it isn't a melody at all, just one sad, weary note, and I don't want to think about any of that right now.

"Well," he finally says, his fingers brushing across the strings of the banjo, "it goes somethin' like this."

He taps on the banjo's drumhead, one, two, three, and launches into a kind of bluegrass tune, except he's playing clawhammer style, bare fingers on the strings with a driving percussive ring, full of blue notes.

"It's all one and four, with the modal," he hollers over the rolling rhythm and wild scatter of blue notes thrown out by the throb of his right hand. "The blues scale before anyone called it that."

He comes around the bottom, and the mandolin jumps in with a straight vamp. I wait to jump in with Rhonda or Billy, and they both go at once. The banjo player responds by plunking his way up the neck, like a big leggy frog chased back toward water. Charley is the last in on his fiddle, long draws of the bow, big, blue notes, wet as tears.

And just like that, we are a three-story house of a string band, with Charley's slow freight train going by.

The banjo player sings out finally, more sounds than words, hollering and moaning like the fiddle and guitar, like all the songs we just did stripped of syncopation and swing.

"Take me home, oh lordy, take me home," are the words, but just barely. They're the primitive, guttural sounds not of going home, but of yearning to go far away, the sound of someone lost and alone, stuck by the side of the road, or in jail, or up the holler or down on some farm, dreaming only of movement, release, flight.

When the break comes around to Rhonda, she opens up with her slide, long bending notes under the whistle of Charley's fiddle, like long steel rails, bending around a curve, except the curve goes and goes until it disappears over the horizon with the shuffle of the fiddle, then comes back around from the top, a great big unbroken circle . . .

And on it goes, song after song like trains coming and going all night — songs that do not end so much as run through switching yards, rails like the steel-on-steel of a slide guitar, bouncing and bumping along with banjo and mandolin, and hollering out the top, a whistle blowing off to the horizon from the moan of a bow across the strings of an old fiddle — until there are streaks of lavender and peach across the mountains to the east.

I say goodbye to my new friends and crawl into my van.

I draw all the curtains and collapse onto my mattress, my shoulders aching and head swimming with music as I pass out in clothes I've been wearing since the festival stage yesterday afternoon.

I feel like I'm hallucinating from elation, fatigue, and pure joy. There are no mountain summits or ocean waves that feel anything like this particular transcendence of my own body, because this one is full of human faces, human fingers, human voices.

I sure wasn't expecting any of that, just a big show up on that stage and maybe a little jam afterwards. I don't how I'll ever explain what that just felt like to anyone. And who could? Maybe this is why so much music is *about* music, I think, as I fall asleep to the sound of my own heartbeat pulsing in my ears.

I wake up to shouts and the roar of a tour bus turning around in a big circle right next to me.

I lay here, my head throbbing, shoulders aching, wondering to do, not wanting to do a damn thing.

I don't want to leave, even though it means horrible traffic later, because so what. Half an hour later, I'm up and out, back up the festival.

Breakfast burrito at a booth, then off to the green room tent, and why not, I think, looking out at the empty stage. When is this going to happen again?

The mainstage is empty but for a roadie working on something, but I can hear music drifting over from somewhere.

I turn to listen. It's coming from where we rehearsed yesterday — no wait, two days ago now — the *Kids' Activities Tent!*

I walk back through the green room tent and around the fence to the kids' tent, packed to the walls and out the back with people.

There's a bluegrass band on the little stage, looks like a family band, in matching white shirts and red ties and tan cowboy hats, playing an ancient gospel song.

I stand with the crowd and listen, and one chorus in, I'm back in that little white church in Kentucky. It was the one time my ex-wife and I ever went back to where she grew up, right after we got married, the only time I ever met her parents in the ten years we were together.

I don't remember much about the trip — her brother made his living growing pot on an old tobacco farm, and I stayed high for most of those weird three days — but I do remember going to that plain little church with her parents, the worn benches, the aching hymns. The band sounded exactly like this one: music as spare and sparse and un-lacquered as this, old and raw as the green rolling hills of that Appalachian valley. Could even have been this exact same song.

> *I'm going 'way — to that fair land*
> *Toil and trouble'll come no more*
> *Where there will be — no more sad parting*
> *When we reach — that golden shore*

They weren't singing about California, right? They were singing about heaven. But from that part of Kentucky, they may as well have been the same: a place they'd never seen but were sure existed, a place where all of their pain would be taken away, *redeemed.* The happy ending, *in the sky Lord, in the sky.*

But I wasn't all that different. Back East, all those cold, rainy Saturdays and Sunday afternoons when I'd be working alone in the office, then hole up by myself for the evening in the dive-bar around the corner? I'd flown to California by then, and seen Big Sur, and thought only about what kind of work thing I could make up to go back. No one to go home to; everyone I worked with off with their spouses and kids in the suburbs; just me and a few beers and that old jukebox, listening to "California Dreamin'" over and over. I was fresh out of a marriage, flush with cash for the first time in my life, and all I wanted was to run West . . .

I head back to the bands' camping area, thinking maybe I'll take the long way out of the back of here, to the south toward Yosemite, the way Jill and I did when we drove through here that summer.

But I don't really want to leave, so I make some coffee and sit in the open door of the van with it, looking south toward those mountains and the last morning of that long sad farewell road trip all those years ago.

I study the ridge, wondering again which of those gaps is the one we drove over on that last ever morning. I suppose I could call it my own "Sunset Road," the one heading toward the ocean and home. Except Jill won't be that girl waiting for me when I get there. Or Radhe. Or Leah. Just the sunset, if I'm lucky, and the ocean either way.

Maybe that's the real reason Johnny is so angry: for all of his talent as a songwriter and a singer and a guy who knows how to stir up a crowd, the best thing that ever happened to him as a musician is a lie — and a lie that sold big, because everyone is desperate to believe it, and he knows it. There is no sunset road. There's just a road, and no one at the end waiting for you, unless you ask them to.

I sit back in the open door of my van, watching the sun blaze toward noon, and the last of the band buses and vans load up and head off to their next gig.

# 5 | THE BLUES SINGER

Amrita always ends one of her concerts, *kirtans*, or yoga workshops with everyone singing three rounds of *OM*, a long, drawn out, deep resonance of a note, not unlike the sustain of a church organ or cathedral bell. She starts down half a step, on the B, then slowly bends it upward to merge into the C chord weaving in and out David's harmonium and the deep humming bottom C on my guitar.

She says that the *OM*, according to ancient Hindu teaching, signifies nothing less than the life force behind the creation of the universe, still pulsing in every cell of our bodies. It's the sound of the Big Bang, as described by astrophysicists, the echo of it pervading the universe yet today. Or the hum of *Ein Sof*, the liquefied presence of "the Creator" embedded in all creation, as the Jewish mystics would call it. Or the heartbeat of the world we can sense between our own heartbeats, as the Sufis would say. Or the "Everywhere Spirit," as the Lakota called it.

I have no idea if any of that is true. But I do know how cleansing and clarifying the sound can feel when conjured and held by a large group of people sitting in stillness on a floor together. All I have to do is stir that bottom C into David's C chord on the harmonium — the sound of the church organ in a small box — for a few moments before they drown us out. And before Amrita's voice can climb to the C, four or five or six hundred voices all rise up in unison to fold in behind her.

She slows down each successive *OM*, pushing out her climb to the C, slowing the note and David and me down. Voices in the crowd drop out to circle their breath and come back in stronger; some find another note in the chord and add a glowing harmony, like smaller bells in the same belfry, ringing out over the congregation; and by the long, languorous end of the third *OM*, we've built a soaring sonic cathedral out of human sound.

If the crowd is really plugged in, Amrita's voice and our instruments will dissolve into their collective voice, into the glowing swell of choral crescendo, and the room will hum for full minutes in the great silence left behind in the echo. I don't go all the way there while playing — too much to keep track of — but I have, at the yoga festivals when other *kirtan* bands were up there.

With my eyes closed, everything liquefies into a pulsing light made of the sound of the collective human voice. My body goes supple and mind goes blank, like those rarest of moments on top of a mountain or down the front of a wave.

"God enough for me," is how Ike describes the surfer's version.

This past weekend down in Joshua Tree was one of those crowds. Not that big, maybe 200 people, many I've never seen before. And no drama, with Amrita, or any of the Acoladies, or any of her Man Buns. Just yoga and music and dance. And outside every night, a quick walk into the shock of the desert: dry, cold, silent, big spindly trees dancing and praying to a sea of stars out over a silhouette of mountain range.

How many miles so far this morning? 150? 200? And I'm still buzzing with all that music and the almost cherubic joy of the crowd — the highlight of the year for many of them — and those final *OMs*. Spreading through the body like the warm glow after sex, they can reverberate for a good couple of hours: through the load-out; back out on the road; back to the world and traffic, four lanes now; and . . .

HONK!!!

There it is, with a brass section to welcome me back, the first traffic jam of the day.

It's Sunday afternoon, and the entire L.A. Basin — like the entire Bay Area, where I'm heading — is traffic in every direction.

It'll be this way, at a crawl or at 80 mph, all the way up the 5. Until the world ends. And in five hours, when it's really starting to grind, the worst part will be the last few miles to Angel's Rest. Nice spring day like this, and every other family in the Bay Area will have driven over to Half Moon Bay to see the Pacific Ocean; looked at the waves for a minute and taken a selfie; then stood in line at the tourist restaurants, and started driving home, inch by inch, back over the mountain.

This is the horde Kenny is keeping out with the lock, I suppose. But who knows? Brooke wasn't around last week, and hasn't texted anything about what's going on with Kenny and that stupid lock. Which is maybe a little bit why I'm a little anxious to get back. I've been down in SoCal since last Wednesday for a casino gig with Johnny and this Amrita workshop. No texts from Ike either, which usually means the ocean hasn't done anything worth telling me about and he still hasn't met the hot single surfer mom of his dreams. Which also means the lock is still up, the power is still on, and the water is still running.

As much as that new lock is a pain in the ass, at least we don't have tourists wandering down the road and parking wherever they want; staring at us on our porches or through the open window of Neptune's like we're paid actors in a theme park; taking their selfies and leaving a few more beer cans.

Sure, we have no business living there either. But no one has any business living in most of the lower half of California, especially not down here in the concrete spaghetti of the L.A. Freeway system. Not this many people anyway, crawling across this paved-over dust bowl next to the ocean.

I can rationalize living in our little hideaway from climate reality because we are putting up with the off-the-grid hassles. Thanks to Brooke's genius with a welding torch, we're generating our own power and not using anybody else's water. The time will come when it all finally falls off the cliff and is swept out to sea. But not today, OK? I've got my STUFF up there!

HONK!

And now I sit here, ticking off the minutes before the hours ahead of me, before I can finally turn left over the last mountain, and head down that last hill, against beach traffic, into Half Moon Bay.

Good old Half Moon Bay, an old farming and fishing town — or stretch of seaside villages actually — with a history as lyrical as its name. The place has endured the boom-and-bust cycles of farming and fishing over the past century thanks to two very odd side-gigs in two very different eras. With a coastline rugged enough, often fog-bound enough, and just far enough away from San Francisco, it was the chief intake valve for the city's whiskey and beer during Prohibition. And at the pointy top of the half moon that gives the bay its name, where that ruggedness turns jagged and lethal, it also happens to host one of the world's biggest, coldest, and scariest waves.

The bootleggers in the '20s and '30s had to drive the old PCH up through a narrow cut in Montara Mountain and around Devil's Slide. And slide it did, every other winter with the rain, cutting off the coast all the way down into the town of Half Moon Bay, forcing everybody to use the old two-lane road west, which also used to slide. But the Bay Area kept bulging outward in every direction until, in the '80s, its horde of commuters finally jumped the hills; a decade later they widened the highways, and blasted tunnels inland from Devil's Slide, right through the middle of Montara Mountain.

Suddenly, Half Moon Bay was a bustling ten-mile long suburb, with a stunning postcard of a commute in and out of coastal mountain switchbacks and hundred-foot drops to rugged beaches. And that big scary wave, "discovered" by local surfer Jeff Clark right before the Bay Area jumped the hills, started drawing surfers from all over the world — pros, groupies, bucket-listers, the works — many of whom would die under its cataclysmic drops and monstrous hold-downs. That moody dragon of a wave, soon known around the adventure sports world as "Mavericks," was packaged into a contest; then licensed and branded by some L.A. guy as "Titans of Mavericks;" then just as quickly bankrupted, litigated, licensed, and branded again.

Today, we know Mavericks is going off if Half Moon Bay's perma-traffic swells with unusually large cargo vans covered with adventure sports logos, and the marina fills up with a small army of sponsored surfers and support teams. You can't miss them for their matching wetsuits, all dotted with the same logos. They gear up in the launch area at El Granada like they're in some war movie, looking gruff, focused, a little bothered that you're watching them unload all their shit in your town: jet skis, radios, cameras, a dozen boards, drybags, and always more cameras.

I found my way to Half Moon Bay 25 years ago, and not for Mavericks or the postcard commute — though I would fantasize about that soon enough, on the first flight back East — but for one simple fact that jumped off the rental car map to my young and never-been-anywhere eyes: it sat at the end of the nearest road running from a work meeting in Silicon Valley over to the Pacific Ocean, which I'd never seen before.

I switched my flight back East to the red-eye and drove over there, so knocked over by the explosion of blue-green that was the Pacific Ocean from the ridge that I had to pull over and pull myself together before I could drive down to see if it was real or not. Twenty-five years ago, before they cut away six or seven hillsides to widen the road — and long before they blasted those tunnels north — it was a simple country road down to what looked impossibly vast and blue-green and sparklingly alive to my smalltown, East Coast eyes. That view still pops and astounds, even after seeing it 500 times; and with any luck, it'll pop for me again in a few hours.

What I found on that first breathless, gaping drive up and down the Half Moon Bay coast before the sunset was a string of small, sleepy fishing villages and farm towns, running down a rugged stretch of the PCH: two lanes of country road cutting through farm fields that spilled down from the mountains to the east, and rolled off to the west, to sudden cliffs dropping to the ocean through cypress trees carved by wind and wreathed in fog.

From the bartender that first night at a roadside cantina, I learned that most of Half Moon Bay's fishing families were of Portuguese descent, like his own, and went back two or three generations. He also told me that most of its farming families were what people now call "Hispanic" or, even less accurately, "Mexican" — families going back even more generations, some all the way back to the *Californios* who were here first, I mean second, between the Natives and all the white people who came from back East.

That first corporate job needed me back out here all the time — or, as Tom was always kidding me, I made it need me — so I made a routine of it: pushed meetings to Fridays and Mondays, found a little hotel by the beach, and fell in love with the ocean.

I had nothing else to love in those days anyway, except a grueling job back East with an office full of problems, and a starter-marriage that was dying, slowly, of natural causes.

I'd eat at the locals' bar along Miramar Beach, at a place with an actual hitching post outside for the *vaqueros* who used to work the farms along the PCH, but now lead tourists on rides along the beach and cliffs. There is still a hitching post outside Miramar Beach Restaurant, a place always crowded with tourists and Bay Area couples on date-night.

After dinner, I'd go out into the sound bath of the ocean crashing onto the riprap, the great bank of boulders protecting the road from the surf. I'd sit on the highest boulder, and listen to the pause-and-*BOOM!* of the waves, and watch the moon rise over the water, how it would shine like stained glass through the waves, turning them into just a moment of blue-yellow-white stained glass.

That old bar in Miramar is gone now. The ocean won. The wall of boulders was sucked out to sea, taking most of what was left of the beach with it, and the road too, pummeled one January by the jackhammering of a week-long storm, then flushed out to sea like gravel. The Miramar Beach Restaurant is still there and thriving, for now, shouldering always into the onshore wind, its parking lot and road eaten by winter winds and storms and repaved every couple years.

With the new tunnels and the widening of road from the east, the PCH is now a two-lane parking lot, inching along, late for something, pissed: tourists, commuters, trucks, and more tourists, in an endless loop that makes trying to get up there from Angel's Rest for groceries and gas an exercise in misanthropy.

But I'm just a cranky old man. And I have been since I watched Colorado get loved to death in the late '90s. By the time Tom sold the business back East and I could light out for the territories forever, that old bar in Miramar was long gone, and California was out of water, again, and on fire, again. So I fled to an even newer love, who lived above treeline and knew nothing of traffic: the mountains.

But I wasn't there three years before the adventure sports horde was finding its way into the Colorado high country, doing to it what every other kind of horde had been doing for a couple decades to every habitable stretch of ground in California — except for places like Half Moon Bay, for as long as they were guarded by mountains and mudslides.

Because everything in California is the same as everywhere else, just a little sooner and a lot more sped up. In Colorado, as they'd done in California a few decades earlier, the first ones flooded into the hills not for love but for gold, destroying nearly everything in their path — the hillsides, the timber, the wildlife, the rivers, all the way down to the water table — in their mad pursuit of "the color." When "the color" stopped running out of the hillsides with the snowmelt, mining conglomerates took over with hydro-pressure technology that blasted away entire mountains with water. And California had shown the way and perfected the process, enslaving the Natives, and pressing the *Californios* and finally the Chinese into wage-slavery, until everything was played out and half of the conscripted workforce was disabled, dispossessed, and/or dead.

That earth-pummeling fight for gold out here, like so many others, wasn't the only war waged with and powered by water. The influx of millions of people into Southern California, starting a century ago, rolled in on invented rivers, on water stolen from the Central Valley and delivered through 419 miles of canal, tunnel, and aqueduct into the L.A. Basin.

This L.A. Basin, with all this damn traffic today, baking in the sun.

I haven't moved more than a mile in the last 20 minutes.

We should all be under 50 feet of sand by now, but for that contraband water, a draining of the interior — the Central Valley, the foothills and Sierra Nevada, the Owens Valley east of the Sierra — for the coast. Because, California, always ahead of the curve, is hollowing out rural America for its cities. Because it does all begin and end out here with some kind of theft, organized or random, grand or small. John Sutter, the settler on whose land that first gold was discovered — on the aptly named "American River" — was overwhelmed by squatters and thieves and eventually tax collectors, and died penniless, in debt to his lawyers.

Even Hollywood was built on theft, on the lam. The first big studios started as rogue businesses, created on the opposite coast from the Nickelodeon houses and Tom Edison and the other inventors who held patents on all the projectors and cameras on the other coast. And the aerospace industry, built out here to face Japan during the war, and pointing at the stars ever since? Tens of billions in manufacturing, all galvanized by well-placed people and well-purchased members of Congress. And now, the biggest tech entrepreneurs out here still want to go to the stars, or off to their own island in the middle of the ocean, after having just raided California in its death throes, along with the rest of the American corpse . . .

HONK!!!

And here we are, in our mindless metallic bugs crawling across that corpse, the noonday sun screaming off our shells. This would be the perfect time and place for The Big One, stuck on an L.A. freeway, desiccating in the sun.

Cars, trucks, vans, trembling along in a flutter of grimy heat. Arms and legs, all colors, hanging out car windows.

HONK!!!

A white guy and brown guy kicking it, *thud-thud*, in the muscle car next to me.

Brown husband yelling at brown wife coming up on the other side.

White wife yelling at black husband, kids in back on their phones.

Little old pickup, windows all up but for a gap on the driver's side, blue smoke pouring out.

HONK!!!

High school girl doing makeup.

"Yeah? Fuck you too!" from two lanes over.

The traffic nudges ahead, and I creak along, and suddenly, like magic, the car ahead zooms off, like a boat from a dock, and — *Yippee! We're going fast!!* — everyone is speeding ahead.

I jump on the gas and we're hauling around this bend, and . . .

HONK!!!

Dead stop, again.

At least I'm easing up under this big new overpass, out of the sun.

I look out the window, nearly straight overhead, at the long graceful arcing of new freeway stone, bone white against the cobalt-blue sky. It's beautiful, the old engineer in me thinks, as florid a word as you're allowed in engineering.

But the old engineering student in me saw those grainy films about oscillation in school, and did the math assignment on the one that took out the bridge up in Tacoma Narrows. I can well imagine that frozen river of concrete up there, when the tremors intensify, twisting and craning and crashing down; and here I am, buried under all of it; and the next face that will see my face won't be a rescue or recovery worker, but an archaeologist. From another planet.

But none of these good people want to think about any of that — *Because the weather! It's always so beautiful out here!* — as we inch along, and the planet bakes and burns. Oh well.

I finally relent and roll up the windows and submit to the A/C.

What apocalypse? It's nice and cool in here now. Who wants to think of that when you can just roll up the windows, do your makeup, eat your lunch, yell at your kid and negotiate a deal, all while sharing your favorite music, *thud-thud*, *thud-thud*, like Godzilla's heartbeat, with a few dozen of your closest friends. *Because it's always so beautiful out here!*

Nobody wants to think about how it all ends, or they'd never move out here. Isn't that why Gordon finally talked Johnny into not singing "Freeway Blues" anymore onstage? Which is a bummer, because it's the one song of his, for as dark as it is, that's actually funny.

He wrote it in rehab — the one in 1987, not 1983 or the last one — and released it on that icky, right-wing thing he recorded in between those rehabs. Seems weird now, but in 1985, Hollywood was in the White House, Communism and poor people were the enemy, and waving the flag was the surest way to climb back onto the charts.

I sing the chorus over the blast of the A/C:

> *Here it comes, crashing down*
> *The American Century in an American town*
> *Kiss your wife and have a good time*
> *You bought the farm and lost your mind . . .*

So maybe it's not so funny. But it is the one song of Johnny's worth a shit from the '80s. But only he and the band seemed to like it, playing it for a crowd suddenly furtive and restless, waiting for "Sunset Road" and his other feel-good songs from the '70s and '90s.

*Because the weather! Because it's always so sunny and beautiful out here!*

Right before it all comes crashing down.

Which is why I don't leave this van in any parking garages at the airport or downtown, so when The Big One does come, I'll have at least a fighting chance of getting the hell out of Dodge.

I remember bringing all of that up when I was having dinner with Tom and his wife, right after they moved to San Francisco. She looked at me like I was crazy and said, *Why worry about it? I can't do anything about it. Why waste my energy on it?*

So maybe it's just me, always bracing for impact. But why I shouldn't I be? By the age of 50, I've lost everything, twice, and started over. And that was after starting out with nothing — other than being white and male and book-smart and able-bodied in America, all of which is, I know, plenty of something. But I'm always bracing for the literal impact of a father who on any random night might come home, drunk, go into a rage, slap my mother around, and give me a beating because he couldn't stand that I was book-smart and able-bodied.

I've always thought, *I will piss on your grave one day for all that*, which would be a fitting tribute. I learned early on that he'd stop beating me when my bladder finally gave out and I was pissing on his lap or all over the floor. He didn't want any on him, or maybe he figured I'd had enough; so I learned that after two or three whacks with the belt, let the piss go, and I'm off the hook. Change my pants, run off to the woods until dark, and some day soon I would run away for good. Huck Finn, motherfucker.

Maybe this is why I always ran back to the mountains — or the ocean, this last time around. I can talk back to them all day long; and if they decide to talk back with hailstones or avalanche or raging river, they aren't talking back to me. They couldn't care less about me. They just are, just like the ocean.

What Psalm is that again? 121? "I lift my eyes to the mountains, from where will my help come —"? Something like that?

Because that's where my help came from one more time, in Utah, when Tom's friend's start-up was sued out from under us, right in the bottom of the "Great Recession," and then after Leah — left us, left everything, left me — six months after her diagnosis. Where else would I go but to the mountains?

It was the same place I'd run off to in my 30s, when my marriage fell apart. The same place I ran off to when Danny and Aaron and Jill all left Colorado, to newer mountains one state west. I moved to Utah, with my oldest and newest friend, an old guitar I'd pulled out of cold storage, and started over, with a new job in a new company in a new town half an hour from a new mountain range. And of all odd things, a brand-new synagogue — for me, anyway — at the edge of those same mountains.

I learned to be useful in the mountains all over again, on the ski patrol this time, because where else would I go, and what else would I do? I could still show up, help somebody having a worse day than me — like Gordon and Chloe on the mountain that day . . .

HONK!!!

I look up and the traffic is easing forward, and then, just like magic — *Yippee! We're going fast!* — everyone is speeding ahead.

I jump on the gas and here we go, finally.

Back to 80 mph, bumper to bumper, in this river of metal and glass, heading north, thinking about Utah.

This time around, I wasn't finding solace only in the mountains, like when I'd fled the East Coast for Colorado five years earlier. In Utah, I was playing my old guitar for hours every night, going from a random open mike night to a regular gig with a bunch of old hippies at a ski resort bar — the most tanned and fit old hippies you ever saw — and from there to the gig at *Shir Hadash*. Which wasn't a gig or traditional synagogue or even an especially clingy spiritual community so much as it was a big, messy, re-assembled family: a hothouse of wide-open people channeling the ancient Jewish drama of redemption through prayer, dance, and song. Just walking in the place that first time, thanks to Rabbi Miriam's email insistence, I had as many aunts, uncles, cousins, nieces and nephews as I could ever want, and could make it official and forever with the simple act of showing up at somebody's house for *Shabbat* dinner with my guitar.

Because if Rome is going to burn, I figured back then, why not play the fiddle? After fleeing a suddenly lonely Colorado, and realizing what a mistake I'd made with Jill back there, I was at the rock bottom of my life and didn't really care at that point what happened to me, as long as it was reasonably painless. But I did have my guitar, my oldest friend; and while it never does exactly what I want it to do, it never fails me either, like a dog who never dies. And we were making up for lost decades.

Long before Colorado, way back in my early 20s, I'd given up on the music fantasy — not that I ever dared really believe in it, poor as my ex-wife and I were back then. It wasn't until 20 years later, with Jill and the rest of my friends gone forever from Dudeville, that the guitar made its way out of cold storage and into my empty, fidgety hands. It turned out that my music, like the mountains, ocean, desert and trees, was still there, growing and changing as I got older and quieter, alive and well and waiting for the sun and water of study and practice.

Then I landed this nutty new gig, in a synagogue of all goddamned places. I immersed myself in a brand-new world of people with ancient music I'd never heard before — at least not consciously — and the weirdest part was how easily all that new music came to me. Every weekend and on half a dozen holidays, I was playing behind the plaintive ache and wail of Rabbi Miriam's voice, following it down into those dark musical caves or out across that storied desert. Most of it, I came to discover — without instruction or even really thinking about it — was in a key so old it wasn't minor or major, but a combination of both, an alchemy of joy and sorrow catalyzed by the flatted second and flatted seventh, where the melody breaks into what sounds like crying. In a few months of just following along, it all came rushing back to me, not from without, from Rabbi Miriam and the band, but from within, from nowhere I thought I'd ever been. It felt like it was coming back to me from another lifetime, as if encoded in my DNA, even though technically my actual DNA may or may not ever have encountered it. (But that's another, even stranger story for another time.)

The hard part of all that — the truly terrifying part, with far scarier exposure than the fiercest mountain I'd ever climbed up and skied or snowboarded down — was all those people, looking right at me on the *bima*, singing and dancing along with everything I was playing. If I screwed something up, I may not have trashed my leg or triggered a avalanche or been caught out above treeline in a thunderstorm to die in the drunken bliss of hypothermia. Far worse than that, everyone in the room would know, everyone would see.

Not that they would care, as Rabbi Miriam tried to convince me when she was talking me up onto the *bima* those first few times. But I quickly figured that out for myself: they loved what we did up on that *bima*, because it sent them *there* — the same exact way that Amrita sends them there, and Johnny, when he's on.

Still, it was such an odd gig, after decades of my being a pagan, a mountain / tree / rock, sun / moon and stars worshipping misanthrope, practicing my earth-based religion of one. And when I tried to explain it to Aaron and Danny, the couple times we ever caught up on the phone, they had almost nothing to say, other than "Cool" and "Huh" and "That's something," then long awkward silences, like I'd lost my mind, like *Judaism? You?? Really???* is what they wanted to say, especially Aaron, who'd been raised in a conservative synagogue back East, where there wasn't a lot of ecstatic dancing going on.

I suppose I can't blame them. I was the guy who had just blown off civilization when they met me; and all of a sudden I've dropped my climbing gear so I could put my shoulder to the bulwark that kept western civilization and its most gruesome repressions and exploitations running: organized religion. *Yuck!* Hard to explain all that — even if "organized religion" found me, not the other way around — at my regular gig one very weird Saturday night.

But that's what happened, with the same dumbass luck of landing the gig with Johnny: two people, set in motion by the iron law of randomness, converging in one discrete place, so that one day far too many people will say to them, with a sigh flush with *verklempt,* "it was just meant to be" . . .

I was playing with the hippie band up at the ski resort bar — though it was Utah, so it was a "club" not a bar, which was good news for the band because "membership" meant there was a cover charge.

Our lead singer was sick that night and had to bail, so we took turns singing his songs, and did a bunch of extended jams. I sang a lot more that night than usual, fueled by more beer and weed than usual, and that's when this intense little woman showed up out of nowhere, still in her ski clothes, and stood right up against the stage, stock still, until the second set ended.

She was short and wiry, but held herself like she was tall, her head cocked back and hands on her hips. She had big flaming red hair and, I noticed right away, burning black eyes — pinpricks of yellow light at their center, fierce as a bird of prey — like they were vibrating so fast they were actually still. They were burrowing right into mine when she asked, "you guys know any Janis Joplin?"

Of course we did, and the place was starting to thin out, so we invited her up to sing one. It took her all of one verse and one chorus to warm up and then let loose with a voice, if not with the full sound and fury of Janis Joplin, then with a different kind of emotional rage, barely contained, a voice pleading and insistent, like it was singing for its own survival.

There was something oddly unsettling about the strange fire of her presence up there next to me, her supreme confidence and self-possession, and the way she could just turn and speak to me with her eyes: *Just a little faster* and *Now slow it down,* and *Quieter, quieter, now bring it down.* She was as good a professional singer as any I'd ever been on any stage with, and she made me nervous, like she could look right through me. I ended up drinking a bunch more beers — figuring I could always sleep out in my truck, like I'd done a few hundred times at trailheads.

The rest of the night turned fuzzy, and I don't remember exactly what happened after that, other than her finishing the entire set with us.

But I do remember waking up the next morning with a crushing headache, on a couch in a living room full of books, still in all my clothes, with my guitar on the floor next to me.

Before I could crawl to my feet, I heard her voice, coming from another room, something about helping myself to coffee and letting myself out.

Surely I hadn't gotten so loaded that I actually slept with that singer, whoever she was, or anyone else hanging around when we closed the place, I remember trying to convince myself as I tried to sit up on that couch. But I wasn't used to getting drunk like that, and couldn't be sure.

"Good morning, maestro," came the voice again, as she came around the corner into the room, in a long black dress, a cup of coffee in one hand and a bulging canvas bag in the other. "Hope you slept all right out here."

"I uh — I did," I said, sitting up and avoiding those burning eyes from the night before by looking for my shoes. "I guess."

"Good," she said. "You were in no shape to drive home. I was out with friends, so I drove us back here in your truck."

"Oh," I said, focusing on getting my shoes on so I could follow her out.

She started for the door, so I scrambled to my feet, but she said, "Oh, you don't need to leave with me. You can just let yourself out whenever. But I have to get to work now."

"It's Sunday," I said, looking at the bag, jammed with books and papers spiked with Post-It notes out the top. "Where do you work?"

"Sunday morning is Hebrew school. I'm a rabbi."

*Wow*, I may have said out loud, or just thought to myself.

And I do remember thinking it was odd that she'd leave me alone, a strange guy in her apartment, so I reached for my guitar, and almost fell over from the wave of nausea and the bile up into my mouth.

"No hurry," she said. "There's coffee if you want some," she nodded back toward the kitchen from the front door.

"Cool, OK, then I'll go. And I'll lock the door behind me."

"Don't worry about that," she said, gesturing with her head toward the darkened hallway behind me. "My girlfriend will be up in a few minutes. She'll let you out."

HONK!!!

And . . . traffic, another wall of it, across eight lanes going to six, the last-suburb-before-we're-out-of-L.A. suburb, which runs uphill through this canyon, two frontage roads of a town, built for on and off.

And just as suddenly, more horns and it's moving again.

HONK!!!

I didn't push the van into the start of the climb, and now I have a posse of drivers behind me, honking and shaking their fists, and that guy racing around my ass to cut back in just past my nose.

The van jams it up the hill, and I'm glad to be leaving the L.A. Basin behind.

The traffic finally spreads out with the extra truck lane right for the long, manic grind up and over Tejon Pass.

Funny story, I remember thinking, for the guys in the band next Friday. *Remember that singer from last week? Turns out she's a rabbi!*

But the story got complicated a few days later, when she called me — I don't remember giving her my number — and asked me to meet out for coffee.

I assumed it was some sort of recruitment: that she mistook me for Jewish, like lots of people always have; she saw what I could do with a guitar; and thought I'd be a good find for congregational picnics, or singing with the kids, or whatever Jews did. None of that would be relevant, of course, but I went anyway; this would be a once-in-a-decade chance to talk about God, something I dared never do with anyone I actually knew, for fear of ridicule. Because talking about God was her actual job, right?

I would run by her what I'd come up with after countless days and nights and weeks in the mountains and out in the desert, alone, thinking not about "God" *per se*, but about what I've come to call the Presence, what I've always sensed all around me when I was alone in the wilderness. I'd tell her how the Presence is nowhere more intensely present than above treeline, at the top of a mountain, with all of creation spread out before me; or at the very bottom of a desert canyon, with all of Time, or at least all earth-time revealed to scale above me; or pouring in off the ocean, in pulsing waves of consciousness beyond my consciousness, crashing in on a big empty beach to match the actual waves at my feet.

I'd tell her about how most anywhere I go where it is wild and beautiful and expansive, where the world dissolves and the planet takes over, I can find the Presence, in about five minutes of sitting still and listening.

Like up here on Tejon Pass, a mile or two north or south up into those desert hills.

If I pulled off this highway, and parked the van far enough around that bend — where I can't hear any of this traffic — then hiked down into the next juniper and chaparral canyon, down to one of those lakes, the Presence would be right there. As if waiting for me, wondering what took me so long.

But recruit me to organized religion? *Pshaw!*

After I tell her about all that time in the wilderness? And share all my other deeply considered paganistic, animistic, American Transcendentalist auto-didactions? If she's got too pat an answer for all that, from some ancient Jewish mystical text or whatnot, I remember thinking, I could just double-back on her, and cop to all the weed and a few go-rounds with Ecstasy and 'shrooms back in Dudeville. And *double-pshaw* on your western God, with the big white beard and the penis. Though I assumed a lesbian rabbi would have a rationalization around that last part.

The meeting didn't go that way.

She showed up with that canvas bag crammed full of books and the strangest little *yarmulke*, a dainty spiral of colors, pinned to the top of all that red hair.

"Guess I could have left my hat on for this one," I said when she came into the coffee place, pointing at my ski hat on the table.

"Why?" she deadpanned. "Is it cold in here?"

I had nothing.

"I'm kidding!" she smacked me on the arm.

She asked me about the bar and the band, and I told her how we were just a bunch of guys with day jobs who met at an open mike a few months ago, right when I was stepping out with my guitar for the first time in 25 years. And that was her real deadpan: she could have listened to me all night, or appeared to be listening, like a good poker player.

So I decided just to put my cards on the table, cards I'd never shown anyone — except for Danny, when we were stuck in a tent way up on Zachary Pass for two days' straight of rain, and except for Jill, during that long, sad, goodbye road trip. I started in on the wilderness and the Presence, and how I wasn't Jewish, or didn't think so anyway, because I wasn't raised that way, even though I'd heard rumors about my father's mother, whom I'd never met.

She stared at me with unblinking eyes, inky black with bursts of yellow, like tiny campfires, so I kept going, stumbling and stammering like a teenage boy delivering a make-up book report to his teacher. And before I could summarize with *Pshaw on your western God!* she leaned toward me and asked, "Is that decaf?"

"Yeah, well. I don't get to talk about this very much."

"But you think about it a lot."

"I've had a lot of time *to* think about it. A lot of time alone up in the mountains, down in the desert, next to the ocean. And on that scale, the whole idea of God — like some pissed-off accountant up in the sky — looks pretty silly."

"Yes, well — I don't know too many practicing Jews who believe in the pissed-off accountant version of God. Half the practicing Jews I know don't believe in God at all."

I had nothing and stared at her.

"Not that kind of God, anyway. More like what you're talking about. A force in creation. No face, no name, no ledger. Just — how did you put it? 'Presence?'"

"In our tradition," she went on, "we have dozens of names for God. Because no single name can begin to capture all the different things God would actually have to be, if God actually existed from beyond the edge of the universe to the interior of the smallest subatomic particle."

She let that sink in a minute, in a way I could tell was she'd been doing for years.

The silence was starting to make me itch, and she wasn't going to scratch it. My turn to say something.

"So what do Jews actually believe in? When they're praying, saying the name of God, doing the dance?"

"They believe in learning," she finally said. "In social justice. In confronting yourself and trying to do better. They believe in being Jewish. In family, community," and she nodded to me, "music. For many Jews — and that's me on bad days — God is just a focal point, the perimeter of the universe, the biggest idea of all in a world where ideas are the only things with lasting power."

It sounded like me, standing on top of a mountain or at the bottom of a canyon, counting the layers against an x-axis scaled in billions of years. Or Amrita, on her cushion before that first *OM*.

"Or it's the latkes."

"It's what?"

"Or it's just being Jewish," she said, "having an identity. A tribe. A thing to call yourself. Friends who are not just friends."

With that, I wondered if she could see how lonely I was, something I'd been my entire life and just lived with, like some people live with a limp. At least until it started eating away at me these past few years, since Jill and everybody else left Colorado.

"Come check it out. We have a great little band every Saturday morning, the music's beautiful, and if you hate it, just turn around and walk out." She swatted me on the arm and waved. "It gets loud in there, and no one will even notice you!"

Which was exactly not true of course.

Because the following Saturday morning, I was the new guy, walking into a roomful of wide-open people who'd been praying and dancing and singing together for the last decade or more.

What was true about what she said: it did get loud in there. A Saturday morning service at *Shir Hadash* was a full-course *Torah* service, bracketed by a Grateful Dead concert, in Hebrew, with lots of sweet little old ladies dancing in the back. It was like nothing I'd seen back East, the few times I went to someone's wedding under the *chuppah*, or *b'nai mitzvah* for work friends' kids, or when I snuck off once as a kid myself to a friend's *bar mitzvah*. It was a spirited, joyful mess of color, and music, and raw emotion. The band played with more heart than skill, three graybeards and two twirly ladies, guitars, violin, oud, and hand percussion. They played with their eyes closed, heads tilted back, in what looked not quite like rapture, but full and peaceful repose. Just like most of the faces in Amrita's crowds. They missed all kinds of cues and chord changes, but no one seemed to notice or care.

After I'd gone a few Saturdays — because it was fun and I had nothing else to do, I told myself — Rabbi Miriam emailed me a couple of their songs she thought "could use a little extra guitar."

I could certainly use a little extra pressure on my chops and some new material, I thought, so I why not?

Within a few weeks, I was learning their whole *Shabbat* service, then the music for the next holiday; and suddenly there was somebody's wedding, and a new baby; and six months later, I'm not only in the band, but I'm helping lead it — if only because I was the one who didn't close his eyes and tilt his head back, because I had to keep one eye on the flow of the music through the *siddur,* the prayer book, and the other eye on Rabbi Miriam's voice and expression.

And there was an odd adrenaline rush to all of it. I had no idea what I was doing, but I did know how to play the guitar, and being up on that *bima* those first few months — with a hundred people singing and dancing and praying, the shatter of hand percussion all over the place, a joyous racket of sound and color and motion around that synagogue — was just another version of my eye-of-the-shitstorm mode. And just like on a mountain rescue, or way back during an old business crisis, being in that deal-with-it-or-else mode felt good, all the way down in my bones. It felt good to be useful.

The hippie bar band was loads of fun; but climbing onto the *bima* with a guitar, to sing in a language I didn't know, and play in an exotic new musical scale, was oddly like climbing back into the mountains, through the hole in my guitar, another terrifying, consuming, captivating adventure. Maybe I was emboldened by the strangest part of all: that exotic music actually wasn't alien to me. The creeping notes of that odd scale — the haunting thing that makes the skin tingle, the spine shiver, and could be conjured in the eighteen notes of a blessing — was as familiar to me as a lullaby from a childhood I never had.

Which was the key to everything. Because everything in Judaism, I was discovering, was music. (With food a close second.) The prayers were "chanted," which really means sung. Visiting rabbis would teach history and theology and ethics with their guitars on. And some, like a rabbi they all called "Reb Aryeh" from Oregon, felt like they were visiting not from the West Coast, but from the hippie makeover of an eighteenth-century European *shtetl*. Even the reading of the *Torah* was sung, in another melody that defied the not-major, not-minor musical scales but mixed both — a melody that lifts to hover in the air, breaks into a cry, crumbles back to earth.

So I spent my weeknights learning the music, half a dozen versions of every song from all over the world, piecing together the one thing that pervaded them all: the "catch" in an otherwise happy melody that made it sound sad, the crack in the vessel that, as Leonard Cohen used to sing, lets the light in. But it wasn't just light into the soul — it was the crack that let the soul run in and out of the music.

I spent my Friday nights and Saturday mornings locked down into eye-of-the-shitstorm mode — watching, listening, playing, nodding cues back and forth with Rabbi Miriam — launching the next song, speeding it up to speed up all of them, slowing it down to bring them back, and then slowing it all way down to bring the room back to stillness.

Within a year, after we'd cycled through all the holidays, I was sitting down with Rabbi Miriam a week or two before the upcoming one, exploring new songs to try, rearranging older ones — and we were coming up with our own melodies. Brand new ones that sounded a thousand years old. From where they sprang, I didn't know, don't know, will never know. Out of the ether?

There was another odd thing about just showing up and being sucked into the center of *Shir Hadash*. Very much *unlike* with every other group of people I've ever stumbled into — in business, on a mountain rescue team, at a local surfbreak — the graybeards and twirly ladies in the band were happy to give way, to let the new kid step up. They could just tip their heads back further, and wait for me to shout the next cue over the crowd.

The sideways glances came not, in public, when I was stepping up as bandleader after only a few months in town, but in private, when one of the graybeards would ask me to show him the chords for a new and tricky song, or something they'd always worked on but never got quite right. He could hear the melody, but couldn't follow the chord changes, couldn't make his fingers go where they had to go. And he'd look over at me like I was playing a dirty trick on him.

He'd practiced this song for hours, riveting himself to the chords in a songbook, thinking he could make the music through blunt force; and when he realized he couldn't — and I could just knock it out at will — he'd stare at me with a mix of bewilderment and bitterness: *how come you can just do that? I've been practicing that for hours, and you can just do that?* But the answer was the last thing any of those guys wanted to hear: *because I just can. Sorry!* Because it had nothing to do with the music itself, or how much I did or didn't practice; it was simply another example of the fundamental truth that life isn't fair.

But all was forgotten by Friday night, back up on that *bima*, when I was pounding out the right chords and they could just throw their heads back and forget all that . . .

HONK!!!

Cars racing along either side, the van churning up the hill toward Tejon Pass, time to move over to the slow lane, with the trucks.

Where was I?

Up on the *bima* at *Shir Hadash*. Now those were good times.

Up there is where I learned everything I now know about the strange and terrifying power of music, in the moment, and how it will take over the seeming entirety of a human being.

Until *Shir Hadash*, I'd never even heard of this thing called "ecstatic dance," with its origins in the Sufi tradition of Islam, or this other thing called "*kirtan*," drawn from the yogic traditions of Hinduism.

*Kirtan.* Sounds like an esoteric religious concept, but it's simply the Sanskrit word for *repeat*, as in *repeat after me.*

And as different as the two musical traditions and practices of Judaism and Hinduism look from the outside, they are, in the ways that matter, the exact same thing. The *kirtan* chanting of Hinduism and the sung prayers of the three major western religions are based on the same simple drivers of physiology on mood. If you sing the same words over and over again, in a roomful of people singing along with you, until you've lost all track of your body and they of their bodies . . . and your voice is drowned into their voices and your breath in their breath . . . everything around and within you will echo and vibrate and shine, until you are no longer separate from anything, until you are no longer even there at all, but halfway to someplace people might call "heaven."

If you were still thinking in the midst of all that, you'd think: *how glad am I that I lived through all that shit, if only so I could feel what I am feeling right now — and maybe, just maybe, what I am feeling right now will give me the strength to keep on living through all the shit yet to come.*

Which is the exact same thing I used to feel and think and say to myself at the top of a mountain, or the bottom of a desert canyon, and how I feel now every time I catch a wave.

The scariest thing of all, which I also saw up on that *bima*, was that music really is raw power. Watching them out there in the pews, singing and swaying, the tears streaming down their faces — just like at a *kirtan* with Amrita — I saw how much emotional evocation there can be in a simple guitar phrase, or in the way a melody twists minor, or how a steady one–two rhythm can send people spinning off into the mist.

I watched, while playing those same prayers over and over, how familiar music can enter the willing body, contort it into an aching mix of ecstasy and pain, and let loose a flood of memory, sorrow, longing, and, finally, peace.

I saw it for what it was not so much because I was on the *bima*, watching and waiting for cues from Rabbi Miriam, but because I'd always felt alone my whole life, and this was the perfect drug for feeling alone. Drumbeats are heartbeats; and when mixed with words, sung over and over in unison, they run like watercolors through the text field of your closed eyes, blur into just sounds,

sounds that may have rocked you to sleep as a baby. In Hebrew, or Sanskrit, or Latin, in Greek, or Arabic, or Lakota, it doesn't really matter. A Sufi dance, reggae rockers, drums at a powwow, it's where they all go — in *Shir Hadash*, or at one of Amrita's gigs, or even along the front of the stage, arms outstretched, when Johnny and the band are really *ON*.

Now, when I watch any of them depart this world, their bodies loosened from their confines, dissolving into rapture, the ears within my ears cannot help but hear the living truth pulsing through all it: we are all one, and this is how we get there, and this might actually be what people mean when they say "heaven" — or *Gan Eden*, the Elysian Fields, Paradise, the World to Come. It was the exact same thing up on the *bima* at *Shir Hadash*: the repetitions, the intonation of the sacred language, the chanting, the way the voices vibrate against the walls, making the room glow and the building seem to lift off its foundation as they danced around in a circle with the *Torah* or just danced around in a circle of light and sound, *Hare Rama* or *Hallelu Yah*, the same exact thing.

On one of those first Shabbat mornings, an even stranger thing connected all that back to my Dudeville days. It happened on maybe the tenth or fifteenth time I was up on the *bima*, when I was just starting to get a handle on all of it. I sat down after a long section of especially rowdy music, Rabbi Miriam stood up for a long stretch of service, and I wouldn't have any cues for a good ten or fifteen minutes. So I plopped down on a pew off to the side and closed my eyes, and was overtaken by the sensation of plopping down on my snowboard on a rock at the top of a mountain empty but for the Presence, before a long descent through pristine powder under a perfect blue sky. My body was infused with electricity and drenched in light, and every cell in my body was breathing out the words *thank you thank you thank you*.

All from one random encounter with a stranger a few months earlier, from the opening line of a bad joke, a rabbi walking into a bar.

*Shir Hadash*, as I'd learn soon enough, was part of the Jewish Renewal movement, founded in Boulder, Colorado — what is it about the Jewish soul at the foot of a big mountain? — back in the '60s. It coalesced around a group of Roundtrippers, Jews who ended up in Colorado, and Utah, and all the cities on the West Coast, after leaving (or fleeing) traditional Jewish upbringings back East for All the Way East: Buddhism, Hinduism, Sikhism, Taoism. Many of those Jews — disaffected by the long shadow of the Holocaust in their families and/or lured onto a caravan of pop culture figures — went to India, found their own voices within those traditions, and came back as leaders, gurus and musicians in the Americanized versions of Eastern traditions.

But many Jews who jumped onto that caravan never found the path, or never found it to be path enough. Instead, they came back and found what they'd been looking for in the old trunks in their attics and basements, and it wasn't in Sanskrit but in Hebrew, after all. It wasn't in the shimmering oranges and pinks and golds of Hinduism, or the cool gray world of Zen, but in the blue and white folds of the old prayer shawl from their *b'nai mitzvah*, in all those old stories in the *Tanakh*, in their ancient music, in the Hebrew letters, black fire on white parchment. They did exactly what the Dalai Lama told a handful of rabbis — in *The Jew in the Lotus*, when he was seeking their counsel on how Tibetan Buddhism could survive in exile, as a diaspora — when they asked for his counsel about all of the Jews looking to the East for a richer, deeper spiritual experience. *Tell them to go look in their own backyard*, he said.

That's exactly what those first Roundtrippers did. They went both global and backwards at the same time, rejecting all the ways Judaism had become watered down and pasteurized in America: assimilated, passive, routinized, like traditional Protestants going to church on Saturday instead of Sunday, for as long as it took to get the kids through the process, and then a couple holidays every year. The Roundtrippers reimagined all the old prayers with eastern practices like meditation, chanting, and *kirtan*; amped up the music and added ecstatic dance; transformed the dull and polite synagogue services they'd grown up with from stuffy performances in East Coast suburbs to participatory *be*-ins on the edges of the American desert. They'd become hippie versions of the old Chasids, dancing, singing, and sweating out their prayers, and it was a blast.

Leah was like the rest of them, after her own roundtrip through Buddhism.

"Coming home," is how she explained it to me, over those long-contemplated, quasi-forbidden first drinks — the date that wasn't a date, because I was on the *bima* and she was new to the congregation — after however many Friday night services since she'd shown up in *Shir Hadash*.

Leah's version of the roundtrip? From childhood *shul* in suburban Philadelphia until her *bat mitzvah*, then only *Yom Kippur*, Passover, and funerals . . . to meditation and intro to Buddhism while at Berkeley, which led to her first job in Southeast Asia with a refugee services organization . . . then back to San Francisco for a management job at its HQ, and immersion in some American Buddhist Thing, which blew up . . . and finally to Utah, to run a refugee health clinic, and immersion in a local meditation circle, which was sprinkled with members of *Shir Hadash* who let drop about the Jewish meditation circle at their funky synagogue.

Which is exactly what Leah would do on all those Friday nights: sit at the end of the second row of pews while they danced and sang and twirled past her, one circle this way, another that way. She'd sit by herself and meditate, with just a hint of a half-smile on her gleaming, freckles-on-alabaster face. Perfectly motionless, the dark-red ringlets that usually played across her forehead, perfectly stilled. The rest of the time, she would follow every word in the *Torah* service in her worn-out *Tanakh*, or sing along quietly, to herself, and tap-tap on her little hand drum, just loud enough for her to hear and for me to see, the weekly telling of our little joke about how she couldn't be a groupie because she was *in* the band.

"Coming back home," she said again, then paused to look me straight in the eye. "Like people do when they're thinking about starting a family."

And I didn't flinch. I blinked once or twice, and thought of Danny back in Portland where he had grown up and gone back to, and his wife Julie pregnant again, but I didn't look away. A first, at 49 years old.

Leah.

I can't believe how much it still hurts, like a slow-motion implosion in the center of my chest, the pressure pulling my head down and shoulders into the vacuum, and beckoning the rest of me into some kind of fetal position . . .

But I can't curl up into fetal position, and let out that whelp gathering in the bottom of my throat, because there's Tejon Pass, Elevation 4,160 feet.

I breathe out, and so does the van, as we make the actual summit of this dragon of a desert mountain, after miles of climbing and weaving in and out of false summits.

And now, the long ride back down, cars flying down the other side.

I switch on some music, but I have to turn it up to beat the road noise, and none of it sounds right banging off inside these vibrating walls, not after running all that old *Shir Hadash* music through my head.

I switch it off, and decide to allow myself to wonder what might have happened, and not just with Leah, but with all of it.

A few years in, and Rabbi Miriam and I became a thing around the broader Jewish community in the Salt Lake City area, and up and down the Wasatch. Meditation retreats, *Erev Shabbat* and *Havdalah* services under the stars, *b'nai mitzvah* up in the mountains, conversion ceremonies, hippie weddings with rainbow *chuppot*, new babies with or without the actual *bris*, funerals with graveside music that went on for hours.

But as funky as this re-constitution of Jewish life was compared to the traditional streams I was learning about only in books and visits to other synagogues in Salt Lake City, some old habits could not be broken.

Often, when Rabbi Miriam and I would show up at a gig with our gear, the old lady organizing it would walk past her and come over to me — and not because I was half a foot taller, but because I was the man — and say, "Thanks for being here, rabbi!" Or "here's where we want you to set up, rabbi."

"Um, she's the rabbi," I'd say, pointing at Rabbi Miriam who, only I could tell from her fixed jaw and the even harder, brighter yellow points in her eyes, would be standing there seething.

"Oh, I'm sorry," the nice old lady would say to me, not to her, and then turn to her, "*You're* the rabbi! That's so neat!"

I laugh to myself and realize I'm driving way too fast as the 5 finally lands on the valley floor, after what feels like the long slow descent of an airplane from 35,000 feet.

Up ahead, the 99 splits off for Bakersfield, and the mountains beyond.

I have a strange urge to go that way, all the way back to Utah even. The simple act of remembering all that conjures this strange sensation that everything is still back there the way it was, because all of that is buried somewhere deep inside my body. Even though I know *Shir Hadash* has a new bandleader. And Rabbi Miriam has moved on to Seattle. And Leah, well.

It hurts to think about it so I switch back to Rabbi Miriam, about how mad that used to make her.

"No, *she's* the rabbi."

Still makes me laugh.

The van settles into the steady stream of bumper-to-bumper cars and vans flowing north in the left lane, past trucks, RVs, and old cars spitting black smoke to keep up in the right lane. The noonday sun floods straight down, blanching the brown run of fields in every direction a flat, sickly yellow.

Me, the rabbi. Hilarious.

It's especially funny for someone with a family history of who-the-hell-knows-what, whose immigrant grandparents, one of whom died before I was born and another I never met because he wasn't speaking to my father, never talked about where in Germany and Italy they'd come from as teenagers. All we were ever told was that it was awful, even worse than their lives in New York and Boston — and don't ask your grandmothers about it! — both of whom died before I was old enough to ask them anyway.

Me, a rabbi, who wasn't raised in any way Jewish and only stumbled into all that, by accident, in the middle of a raging midlife crisis. Though I do remember wondering — back in seventh or eighth grade, as I was starting to learn there was a world out there and contemplate these cruel and unhappy people who were supposed to be my parents — if I weren't an orphan they'd adopted or foster kid they'd been struck with, a convergence of their bad luck and mine. And if so, I could just as easily be Jewish as anything else.

The closest thing I had to a friend back in those days was Jewish. Adam and I ended up in all the same classes; he was smart and funny, and his house was a safe, quiet place to study, work on projects, talk about girls, sex, life, etc. And hanging out there was a sneaky little way of sticking it to my father: Adam's father was a lawyer, and our town's justice of the peace; and he put my father in jail for five days for drunk driving — one day for the DWI, his second in as many years, and four for each of the empty beer cans he threw out the window when the cop was pulling him over. This had unleashed an anti-Semitic rant from both my parents, and threats of a serious beating if they ever caught me hanging around with Adam again. Which of course compelled me to hang around with him even more — including sneaking off to his *bar mitzvah* one Saturday when we were in eighth grade.

Not that they ever knew or cared where I was most of the time. I was usually alone in those days, off in the woods, or riding the back roads on my bicycle, not hanging around in Adam's or anybody else's *shul.*

Because those woods were my *shul.* I spent hours out there, digging around in the creek, fishing and swimming, clearing brush and building a shelter out of salvage lumber, fantasizing about running away and living out there. And I was never really alone. I imagined the Iroquois, who'd lived all through those woods until they'd been driven onto the reservation west of town, out there with me, testing me, teaching me things about the woods, maybe even adopting me. And I would talk to what was emerging in my consciousness as the Presence: give thanks for the hours away from the ugliness back at the house, ask for peace — even ask for peace for my parents — and gather strength to go back and live through another night.

The sacred power of those woods held me and carried me until I could finish high school and get out of that town forever. And they were there two decades later, writ large two decades and two time zones later, when I fled for Colorado after everything back East blew up. In those mountains, I found the same sanctuary, exploded upward and outward a thousand-fold, the Presence everywhere, especially above treeline, as far from everybody as you can get and still make a living with a telephone and a computer.

Which may be why no one was more shocked than me — including all my old Colorado friends when I told them about it on those awkward catch-up calls — that I wasn't spending my Saturdays up in the mountains with skis and an ice axe, but up on the *bima* of a synagogue with my old guitar.

Where they all wanted to know about the new kid: *Where and how did you grow up? Which denomination? Was your family observant? Cultural Jews only? Are you a Roundtripper too?*

I obviously didn't have good answers for that, except the one I assumed they *didn't* want to hear, even if a third of the congregation had chosen to be Jews and gone through the rituals.

So I just changed the subject, and they seemed oddly relieved: they could then imagine the new guy, the one stirring up all this old music in them, to be whatever fit into their own narrative about their journey to, back to, or on through Judaism.

Now, thanks to science, I can find out exactly what I am, if not who. If I want to. But do I?

I still haven't gotten the DNA test, because this far down the road, I think I just want to let the mystery be. The mists of time, *etc.* The only facts I have are a few spots on the map: my grandparents all immigrated when they were teenagers, fleeing fascism of one kind or another in Europe. They came in through New York and Boston, and changed their last names or had them changed for them somewhere between the boat and dry land. My parents grew up in hardscrabble towns out in western Massachusetts and up the Hudson River, and somehow found their way into UMass and Albany State, where they turned into beatniks or hippies or whatever, before dropping out to become hippie farmers, back when they still had a chance to be anything.

By the time I was old enough to wonder about any of that, my grandfathers had long since worked themselves into early graves, and the only time I saw my aging, raging grandmothers was over "the holidays." Which consisted of lots of sniping, at each other and at my parents: about food, candles, the music, the tree, too many presents, too few presents, the neighbors' lights, our lights, America, the cost of everything, going to Mass, not going to Mass, heaven, hell, and *why does your son drink so much*, and *if only your daughter wasn't so crippled, maybe then he wouldn't drink so much* — all to an endless loop of "I'll Be Home for Christmas" and "There's No Place Like Home for the Holidays."

There was a rumor my father's mother was Jewish, and that it had been beaten out of her by his father. Sounds awful but I wouldn't know because I never met my grandfather. Came close as his front door one time when I was a little kid, but that was such a weird day and so long ago I'm not sure if it really happened or if it's just a dream I've been having since.

Bent and broken as they were by life, my parents could have used a little religion, or at least the Jewish version I came to know at *Shir Hadash*, for all the reasons they hated it: religion is a place where you are allowed to be bent and broken, and where some people will actually embrace you for it. But instead, hatred itself became my parents' religion. They believed they were smarter than everybody, The Truly Chosen, and everyone else sucked. As strict devotees of the religion of Everybody Sucks, my parents were avowed anti-Semites, my father especially so after five nights in jail thanks to Adam's father.

So I don't really know what I am. Just an orphan, an American mutt with no childhood pictures and a sister he hasn't spoken to in years. But I have turned out to be deeply religious, in a deeply private way I'd shared with no one until Rabbi Miriam that day. And after those first few months and first few questions at *Shir Hadash* no one seemed to care: they assumed I was born Jewish, or they didn't want to know, or they didn't care.

What they did know about me: I could play the music they all felt in their hearts, could play those songs as readily and forcefully as they came out of Rabbi Miriam's mouth, and I eventually learned to sing them too, as easily as if I'd grown up going to *shul* every Shabbat like two-thirds of them had. Sure, it could have come from somewhere cosmic, somewhere pre-incarnated rather than epigenetic. But the rationalist in me knows it was probably just that cold, hard, iron-clad rule about music: it's a gift randomly given to a lucky few. The notes and chords and techniques can be memorized, learned, willed; but the music comes or it doesn't. Which sure as shit isn't fair. I can just hear something, and figure out where the chords are going next, and remember the melody and the words after two or three times through. And maybe my wandering into

Judaism was just more dumb luck, my ability to channel all that ancient music some sacrilegious parlor trick.

The rest of Jewish life, I learned back then, isn't randomly bestowed at all. It's actually a grind, a ton of hard-headed, repetitive, nuanced work; and if you try to fake something, anything, you *will* be called on it. Such is the tribal discipline of creating and maintaining a text-dense religion with a full calendar, honed by two thousand years of wandering with it, intact, to nearly every country in the world, carrying it around a globe full of people who may welcome you one day and try to wipe you out the next . . .

Yuck! There's that horrible smell, the acrid bite in my nose, the sudden roiling in my gut. The feedlots.

I can smell them before I can see them, the stinkhole in the middle of this great, empty, god-forsaken part of California no one ever sees on TV.

Halfway up the Central Valley, and everything suddenly, literally smells like shit, even with the windows up and A/C on. Like cowshit and urine and a gigantic open gas jet ready to burst into conflagration. Which means one thing: we are coming up on those feedlots over that next ridge.

The landscape in every direction is blank — dead, brown, desiccating out here in all this horrible searing light.

The highway makes the ridge and the car in front of me speeds up for the same reason I do: it's too horrible to look at, that stink-ass feedlot. It goes north and south and east for miles, with its miserable, dozing mass of cows, a blur of black and white and brown, coated in drying mud and swelling in the sunlight into next month's fast food hamburgers.

Ugh. I push the van and try to remember where I was.

Wandering the world, with the tribe and an ark and *Torah* scroll, yes, much better.

Judaism may have wandered through here like it did everywhere else, but it would have kept going, as fast as it could through here, like me and all this traffic today. Because there is no orientation out here, no mountain for reference, only wind and dust from in every direction, and those wretched creatures and this horrible smell.

No mountains at all, even though I know they're back there somewhere. Only that wall of dust.

It wasn't just the Jews lifting their eyes to the mountains for help, direction, orientation. The Christians are all over Psalm 121 too, I assume. Mohammed had his mountain. And Native Americans all over the west look to the mountains, to Devil's Tower, Spider Rock, the Black Hills. The three dozen or so tribes up north of here, as different as their languages were, all located their own Creator up on Mount Shasta, which they called *Úytaahkoo*.

Of course that could just be human brain chemistry: what happens when we look up after a hard day of looking down at our work, and catch the way light and shadow dance across the face of a great mountain, the act of seeing — and feeling seen by the mountain — giving us strength and succor to get through another day.

That's why I went back to the mountains after Leah, even though I could or should or might have gotten strength and succor from all those people at *Shir Hadash* suffering the same loss — or almost the same loss — as I did.

But back to the mountains was what I knew, from Colorado, from all the way back East, to those woods growing up. I could deal with it the way I used to, privately, the mountains my sanctuary, the trees my congregation, the Presence my version of God — Elohim, the creator of earth and water and sky. I wanted the purity and clarity I'd discovered above treeline, or down at the bottom of a canyon: I wanted to dissolve into eternity, to inhabit my body so fully that it melts and the mind goes blank, and in the space left behind, there is nothing but peace.

That time, though, for the first time in my life, the mountains didn't fix it. They didn't make me feel, if not better, than at least whole, a little hopeful, and glad to be breathing if nothing else. Instead, they were cold, and lonely, and reminded me only of Jill, a loss every bit as big as Leah, but that one purely of my own making. And they reminded me how much I missed Danny and Aaron, ten years into their own lives by then on opposite coasts. The mountains would not be "the source of my help" as the Psalmist would have it; they made me feel only more desperately alone. The Presence wasn't up there anymore. It was back in *Shir Hadash*, with those grieving people, and that gaping hole at the end of the second pew.

HONK!!!

Whoa, close call, muscle car versus 18-wheeler for the left lane, trying to get around the smoke-belcher going 40 in the right.

HONK-HONK!!!

And two middle fingers, nice.

No, the Presence was long gone from those mountains after Leah died. And it sure as shit isn't anywhere around here either, out on these two streaks of blistered tar, with their scurry of ants up and down this barren land between their nests and their sugar source. Northbound, southbound, everyone in a mad rush to get across this blanched, scabbed, charred earth and out of this merciless sun.

But everything changed after Leah, not just the mountains. I was forcing myself to play through services at *Shir Hadash* without falling apart, through the worst of the days with that awful black hole where she'd always sit, singing to herself and tapping on that little drum. So I played harder and tried to sing louder, all that ancient plaintive wailing to the crushing patience of eternity. But all I saw was that black hole, and Leah not as she was, but as she was dying. Whenever we would come around to her name in the *Amidah* — the prayer where we recite the names of the Jewish patriarchs and matriarchs, *Abraham, Isaac, Jacob, Sarah, Rebecca, Rachel, and Leah, Leah, Leah.* Or on Friday nights, when we sang the "L'cha Dodi" she really liked, the song welcoming in the feminine presence of God, the bride at the weekly wedding that is *Shabbat,* I'd choke back the tears, and try not to look down at that black hole in the second pew, at her ghost, still sitting there in her scarf, her eyes closed and freckles washed out, gray and hairless, like she was already gone, and then she was gone . . .

HONK!

Give a rest, you guys.

It's too loud to hear music over the roar of the engine in the empty cavern of my van; but I can't stand the song playing in my head right now, so I turn on the music anyway.

Nothing sounds right except the rawest, dirtiest, saddest old kind of blues.

It's the music of displaced men and women who knew suffering far worse than any of mine. The music of hard-pressed people who were old and weary apparitions of themselves before they'd turned 30, out on the road alone, always alone, going nowhere because they had nowhere to go, just going.

And here I am, driving across this god-forsaken wasteland, but I sure as shit don't feel like singing about it. The only thing I see is that black hole, at the end of the second pew. Leah was gone — along with the start-up I moved out to Utah to work for — and so was the rest of the life we'd just started to map out, a life that looked like a belated version of Aaron's and Danny's and Jill's. But what if, what if, what if? What if I'd never been on ski patrol on a weekday to rescue Gordon's girlfriend, and Leah had survived the cancer? Today we would be . . . but thinking about her like that makes my chest tighten, and ache, and the sadness wells up inside me so suddenly I want to vomit it out.

I turn the music up loud enough to hear over the screaming of the road and roaring of the van, and just try to drive it away. Because *poof!* goes life, and your world ends, and *poof!* this is who you are now . . .

An hour north, the highway finally claws its way over ever larger ridges to the turnoff for Hollister and Gilroy, where the northern most agri-factories meet the bottom of Silicon Valley.

Off the 5, the music is deafening, Muddy Waters howling at the moon about some woman, so I turn it down, and start up the hill toward San Luis Reservoir.

I pull over at the top, and jump out of the van to take a pee.

The reservoir sprawls out across a wasteland of hills burnt a sickly brown in the sun, into side canyons, arroyos, and washes, and looks like the hardest three-dimensional calculus problem I ever saw: a perfect, iron-gray, geometric plane slicing through dozens of oddly shaped, oddly sized hillsides. The plane has sunk two-thirds of the way down the vertical axis of the terrain, leaving a layer cake of bathtub rings looping in and out of the maze of hills, and stranding dozens of sickly stumps — the rotting skeletons of massive old oaks — on the ringed banks, looking suddenly exposed, naked, embarrassed.

I climb back in the van with Muddy Waters and head down the hill toward Gilroy, *Garlic Capital of the World!*

A few songs run together, and my mind is blank as I drive past fields stinking of rotten garlic, like the whole earth ate cheap Italian food last night and is sweating it out today. In the sudden silence of a red light, a searing guitar explodes out of the speakers. No voice, just the white-hot scream of a Chicago blues line, right at the edge of distortion, wailing and pleading, then storming off with a snicker into neon blue oblivion.

Yeah, man. There aren't any words for how that feels, just a primal scream that says *I'm not dead yet.*

And that's about where I was, after Leah, alone in the little house we'd been renting.

I was playing my guitar like my life depended on it, because maybe it did, just like that blues guitarist. I was turning 50, with no job, no woman, no family, and a synagogue full of pain. And the lonelier and more desperate I got, the easier the music would flow. I would play my hands numb, until I passed out, the guitar next to our bed, and I'd wake up and start playing again.

That's when the strangest thing of all happened: I could hear voices deep inside the box of my guitar, when I was playing, or in the sustain, a moment or two after I'd stop. The old engineer in me knows there is a rational explanation: it was just the very long sonic "decay" of all those luscious overtones from wood weathered and well-cared for and played for 50,000 hours. Or was it? Because that "weathering" wasn't weather, but voices, all those people who'd been ten feet from that guitar, singing, dancing, shouting.

HONK!!!

And there it is — traffic — right where it always is, five miles outside a town that used to be in the middle of nowhere.

Up ahead, the 101 is already backing up, an hour south of the heart of Silicon Valley, "rush hour" in the middle of a Sunday afternoon.

I work my way into the four-lane lurch of cars, vans, big trucks, little trucks and everything else on earth, going from here to there.

I turn the music back up, John Lee Hooker now, singing in sounds more than words, a song about nothing more, I suppose, than the fact that he's still alive and kicking.

And that's something, so fuck this traffic. I'm still alive and kicking, and I'll be home in another hour, back to the ocean, and a million miles away from this madness . . .

Another hour is all it takes, bobbing and weaving past the cloverleafs and clusterfucks of San Jose, Santa Clara, Cupertino, and Sunnyvale, and up past Mountain View, Palo Alto, Menlo Park and Redwood City.

Finally, there's the northern end of the Santa Cruz Mountains welling up to the west. A long low cloudbank stretches along its wooded ridgeline, fog up from the ocean, fingering its way through the gaps and down to these reservoirs, which run north and south along the San Andreas Fault.

I head west on 92, the road up over the mountain, through that fogbank, down to the ocean, to Half Moon Bay, Angel's Rest, and home.

The traffic is all going the other way, the usual Sunday afternoon rush hour back from a day at the beach.

I push the van up the hill, into the fog, and sneak a glance at the turnout just up Skyline – where I'd first beheld the Pacific Ocean some 25 years ago — and start down the hill in the cool gray air.

There are the usual jam-ups at all the lights in Half Moon Bay, everyone trying to get back up and over the hill, but who cares. I'm almost home.

Ten minutes south on the PCH, the mountains rising to my left and ocean opening to my right, I finally slow down for Angel's Rest.

As I'm pulling off the road, the sportscar running up my ass races around me, and nearly slams into the old farm truck coming north.

I nearly drive into the closed gate — still not used to that lock — and jump out and unlock it.

As I'm coming down the dirt road, through the break in the cliffs, I can see Ike sitting out on his perch at the end of the road, watching the ocean. Then a burst of sparks from the other end, the old stone cottage without windows Brooke has turned into her welding studio.

I park behind my place and start to pull gear when I get a text.

It's Brooke, to me and everybody else living down here: Ike; Chuck, the old hippie mailman; Ryan, the park ranger who works up at Half Moon Bay State Beach; and Brittany, his wife, who works all the way down in Big Basin State Park.

*Jack just got in. Everybody cool to meet in Neptune's in 5?*

That's strange. A formal meeting? And they were waiting for me?

Ryan and Brittany are already sitting in the open air of Neptune's, with their feet up through the empty frame of what used to be the big picture window looking out at the ocean, when I get down there with a beer. Ryan is drinking one of his own, and Brittany — who looks a lot more pregnant than the last time I saw her, only a week or so ago — sips from a water bottle.

"What's up?" I ask, opening my beer and dropping onto the old couch.

"Beats us," Ryan says. "Must be important though. Brooke has been around but keeping to herself the last couple of days."

"Except to ask if we'd be around later today when you got back," Brittany adds.

We sit around, drinking our beers, kicking at the sand piling up on the floor, and bitching about traffic until Chuck comes around the corner with his dog, and Ike limps down the road.

"What's up?" he asks, stumbling in and dropping into the chair next to me, then putting his good leg up into the open window.

"Sounds like nobody knows," I say.

"Hey, kids."

We all turn around to see Brooke's short, wiry frame shoot through the back way, past the old counter-top bar. She's still wearing her welder's apron, and there's a sweaty black streak across one cheek.

She stands behind the old bar, runs the water, and splashes her face, running her blackened fingers through the platinum blonde shock of her crewcut.

"Afraid I have some fucked up news," she says. "And I wanted all of y'all to hear it at the same time."

"We're getting kicked out," Brittany says, bolting upright, her feet dropping out of the window and right hand slipping around her swollen belly.

"Yes," Brooke sighs.

"When?" Brittany asks. "Soon?"

"Why?" Ike asks before Brooke can answer.

"I don't know exactly," Brooke says to Brittany, then turns to Ike. "Because Kenny's selling it."

"Really?" Ryan asks. "For how much? This place would be worth millions — if you could get whatever you want to do with it through the Coastal Commission."

"Actually," Brooke sighs again, and pulls a beer out of the big pocket on the front of the apron. "He already did sell it."

I look from face to face, and they're all looking at her, mouths half open with worried questions.

"That's why the new lock," Brooke says, then takes a long swallow of beer. "Fucker was too chicken to tell me about it. Until last Thursday, when I have to let this fucking survey crew down here."

"Well shit," I say, because what else is there to say.

"Well shit is right," Brooke says.

"The good news is, it'll take whoever a solid year or two to get permits to start in on any of that shit," Ryan says. "The Commission, the county, fish and wildlife. This is the California coast. You can't just fuck it up like everybody used to."

"Yeah, you can," Brooke says, "if you have enough money for enough lawyers."

"And anyone who can buy this place has more than enough money for lawyers," Chuck sighs.

"Who is it?" I ask.

"The guy who founded Synapsys," she says.

Oh, I think. *That* guy, Jamie Armstrong, and Synapsys. One of the earlier Silicon Valley start-ups, founded and run for maybe five years by Armstrong, *the* prototype — fleece vest, silver faux hawk, brown shoes, Tesla, the works — for all the tech bros running round now. He and all his VC buddies who learned to dress like him grew that thing into a billion dollar a year hardware re-packager that went public in 1999, right before its proprietary enterprise software and hardware platform was wiped out by Linux. But none of that mattered to him: he'd cashed out at the top, and has clearly been managing his money well ever since.

"Even though Kenny wouldn't say who he was," Brooke says. "The sale is registered to some bullshit trust managed by a couple partners at a law firm over in Palo Alto."

"But it's Jamie Armstrong," I say.

"Yep," Brooke says. "The original tech bro. I figured out how the law firm was connected to him — they were all on his board when he cashed out — when I Googled them."

"Well shit," Chuck says, the first word he's said since he got here, and stands to go. "Nothing good lasts forever."

"Yeah, but —" Ike starts to say, but Chuck keeps walking, out the door and down the road, his old dog behind him.

Ryan lets out a long sigh then just stares at his beer.

Brittany stares out at the ocean, pursing her lips, still clutching her belly.

Ike finally crawls to his feet, and slowly makes his way toward the door.

Brooke comes over from behind the counter, collapses into the chair next to me, and sticks her big black engineer boots up in the window.

*Squwaaaak!* and we all jump as a seagull wheels past the window, a crab leg in its mouth, and *Squwaaaak!* another wheels right behind it, pecking at it for the piece of dead crab.

Brooke turns to the three of us, and says "sorry."

"You're right, Ryan," I say. "Even with his billion dollars or whatever, it'll take months of permits and hearings and whatnot, a million bucks in legal fees, easy."

It was the first time in my life, after a long and messy business career, I ever took comfort in the idea of a million bucks in legal fees.

"Oh well," Ryan says and stands. "Like Chuck said — nothing lasts forever."

He helps Brittany to her feet, and they head out and down the road.

I don't feel like going anywhere, so I just sit there staring out at the waves.

"Sorry, man," Brooke says, tapping at the loose window frame with the toe of her boot. "Not what you needed to come home to, huh?"

"Yeah, well. Like Chuck said."

Brooke pulls those big boots out of the window, and drops them into the sand on the floor with a dull thud.

"Yeah, well," she says, springing to her feet, then turns to walk back through the bar and the back door. "Welcome home, dude."

I sit alone in Neptune's watching the gulls fight over the crab leg, then look out at the ocean, the late afternoon sun dropping out of the marine layer and shimmering back at us from across the water.

Down at the north end of the beach, Ike climbs awkwardly up the the rocky path to his perch. I watch him settle onto his rock, lean back against another rock, and settle in like he does every night to watch the sun set and the ocean go dark.

# SIDE **TWO**

# 6 | SURF JAM SANTA CRUZ!

And . . . traffic. Because why shouldn't it be rush hour at 3 P.M. on a Sunday, in both directions between Santa Cruz and Silicon Valley? What I get for making a plan involving tides, waves, and a surfboard. And for trying to scramble out of that weird yoga retreat as fast as I can, thanks to the creepy sex buzz all weekend.

The event was weird from the start: Diane the Acolady plopping down across from me, in the dining hall with everybody Friday night, to stare me down with icy silence for betraying and humiliating her for not calling for a second date. And it ended really weird, with that Man Bun — calls himself "Ananda" but his name is really Jared — freaking out on Amrita and us having to perp-walk him out the front door.

Amrita was forced to hide in her room the whole weekend, and David and I finally had to collar him and drag him over to the front desk, while the manager threatened to call the cops. This is the third time he's shown up for one of her events since they broke up — I mean since they *chose separate paths* — and she's tried to keep him away. But each time, he has registered for the program under a different name; and Amrita lets him hang around because, until this weekend, she's been trying to be too cool to have him thrown out.

"Because throwing him out would be horrible for her brand, right?" I asked Jenna and David when we were worrying over it back in Sonoma.

"Not at all," Jenna said, pulling off the saffron-orange headscarf she wears when we play and shaking out her hair. "The Acoladies would be psyched to see that. And they should be. It's empowering."

And it turns out, Jenna was exactly right. The Acoladies were all there like sisterfire, cornering him while Amrita snuck out the back. I was there too, all ready to go into eye-of-the-shitstorm mode, but they didn't need really David and me. I think Diane would have beaten the crap out of Ananda/Jared had we not been there.

Not all the Man Buns Amrita has fooled with have turned psycho-stalker the way Ananda/Jared has, as far as I can tell. But when they do, it's ugly. Some are the wet puppies, whimpering for sympathy at the door; others are that kid in high school who would break up and make up with his girlfriend, every few days, in front of everybody; others are like Jared/Ananda, who just stand in the middle of the doorway of the event space, where everyone can see him, and stare at her.

I can't imagine how broken they must be, because Amrita swears she's never slept with any of them, only ever fooled around with them.

"When I felt like it would help them move forward," she says. "They're emotionally wounded, and so often that shows up as sexually wounded too. Mostly shadow-stuff from their mothers. That's why they're attracted to me. I'm not old enough to be their mothers of course — but when I have the room going, I'm like the divine mother, and they get that all mixed up with their mommy trip."

All of which may be true, except the part about her not being old enough to be their mothers. But a big chunk of the crowd does seem attracted to her, not just the Man Buns, but the Hempy Old Dudes too, and plenty of the women, straight as they may be the rest of the time. Because the whole vibe at these events is sexual, like so much in the yoga world has been sexualized and eroticized, what was a spiritual discipline with a minor physical component has been re-purposed as fitness and "wellness," i.e., weight loss, i.e., attractiveness. Though sexuality does pervade the Hindu mythology that provides decoration, if not devotion, to those rooms. Many of those gods and goddesses were famously horny, just like many of those in Greek and Roman mythology, and they too put a lot of energy into running around the universe getting it on. In Hinduism, they didn't have wives, or lovers, or friends with benefits; they had "consorts." And they consorted till the sacred cows came home.

"She breast-feeds them, you know," Jenna told me while we waited for Amrita to dis-entangle herself at the back of the empty event space from yet her then-current Man Bun, so we could do our soundcheck.

We were sitting up onstage before Friday night's opening *kirtan*. The then-current Man Ban must have seen Ananda/Jared skulking around, when this weekend was supposed to be his turn.

"Huh?" I said. "She does what?"

David shook his big hairy head and tried to hide a gossipy grin.

"She calls it 'breast-feeding.' When they're making out."

"You're serious," I said, and glanced over at David for confirmation, that he has heard this too, if only from Jenna. "She told you that."

"How could I possibly make that up?" Jenna said, as we sat there in the middle of the stage, waving at both of us, then at the Man Bun across the room with Ananda. "You guys are all boob-crazy. And she's got big ones, God knows we can all see that."

"But they're fake," I said.

Jenna searched my face. "How do you know that? *Do* you know that?"

"Of course I don't *know*," I said. "I just assumed. You know . . . from how huge they are. And how skinny she is."

"So you don't know."

David bails me out. "No, he doesn't, Jenna. And how would he?" he smirked at me. "He's way too old for her."

"Thanks, dude."

"The really weird thing," Jenna went on, "is she doesn't actually sleep with any of them. Or so she says. And I believe her."

David pushed harder on the grin, scowling and pursing his lips, his moustache and beard rolling into the gap.

"And isn't that the weirder part," he added.

"I'm not really sure how you parse that," I tried not to burst out laughing, until he caught my eye and his beard blew out and we both burst out laughing. "So . . . they fool around but don't have sex?"

"Nope," Jenna said, sitting up on her cushion on the stage, mimicking the straightening of the spin and hand gestures for descending energy into the body. "She does the *kundalini* thing. *No* intercourse, except with a committed life partner. And that's none of these guys, so far anyway. And it sure backfired with Ananda what's-his-name."

"And with that one," David pointed across the empty event space at Amrita, her hands on the sunken shoulders of the crestfallen Man Bun, trying to console him.

"But she still fools around with them," I said, trying to assimilate new information I was embarrassed to find of sudden interest. "To help them with their mommy issues."

"That's what she told me," Jenna said.

I looked across the room and could not help but think: of course. A guy like that, in his late 20s or early 30s? Single, lonely, horny, and fit enough to be doing yoga all weekend, dancing for two nights in a steamy, sweaty, wide-open room full of mostly fit, mostly attractive women? No, he wouldn't be all that happy with just making out, with spending all night on second base, with the goddess guru half the room wanted, even if she was his divine mother, as weird as that sounds. But when I was that guy's age, I'd been married seven or eight years already, hadn't ever heard of yoga, and sex was something you did with your wife, if and when you weren't both exhausted from working on your feet all day. Who knows what kind of Man Bun I would have made?

But I'll cop to wondering about it. Because, like everybody I suppose, I've had my fantasies about Amrita. No different than my serial fantasies about Calafia — who may right this minute be pulling herself into her wetsuit, down on that surf break in Santa Cruz and wondering why I'm so late. So how could I *not* wonder about Amrita, with the big boobs and sculpted body and ferocious self-confidence? If anybody actually looks, sounds, and moves like Calafia, it would be her.

But for all that, the idea of just sucking on those boobs all night seems like the kind of frustration no amount of self-love, back in your own hotel room, would be able to fix.

"Just boobs," I couldn't help but say out loud. "All night long."

"That sounds awful," David finished my thought. "Talk about —" He cut himself off with a chuckle.

"What?" Jenna asked. "Spill!"

"Kind of reminds me of a yoga teacher down in L.A. Managed one of those teacher training factories down there. She'd been a model, then tried to be an actress. Did some commercials, she said, and a speaking part in a TV show. Almost got a little speaking part in a movie too. Least that's what she said."

He can't help but burst into a grin.

"Oh no," Jenna said. "You can't leave us hanging like that. What?"

"But she did finally find a way to make good money out of yoga. Made videos of herself, doing yoga naked."

Jenna stared at him as wide-eyed as I must have been.

"For real," David went on. "She would do what she called" — he raised his hands to air-quote — 'private lessons' — for a couple hundred bucks an hour. Which was her just doing her regular practice, buck naked. While they jerked off, I guess."

"Eww!" Jenna scrunched up her face, and rolled off her cushion to punch him on the shoulder. She gathered her hair back up into her scarf, then poked him in the chest and kidded him, "So why haven't you ever told me about her?"

"Didn't have to. Back then, I never had the couple hundred bucks."

"Yeah, yeah," she laughed, and put her arms around his neck. "Sounds like a good idea for somebody's birthday maybe."

"Yours or mine?" he kidded her back. "And who's doing the yoga?"

"You make me crazy," she said, and kissed him like I wasn't there, right in the middle of the stage.

HONK!!!

And the traffic slows to a dead stop down at the bottom of the hill, still ten miles from Santa Cruz. Great.

I cannot believe we're bumper-to-bumper, this far from the Valley, on a Sunday. Sure, the beach is that way, but it's late afternoon, and all these people should be going the other way.

Because the other way is even worse: a two-lane parking lot of cars and minivans, family after family heading home from the beach. Dad behind the wheel, looking bored and pissed. Mom on her phone. Two kids in the back in headphones, looking down at their phones.

Where was I? Oh yeah. David and Jenna, and the weird sex buzz all weekend.

They are always doing that around me. But they live at opposite ends of the state, and see each other only for these gigs or every other weekend when their little kids are with their exes, so I can't begrudge them the PDA. Though it can be so sweet and strong and unedited that it stirs me up enough to make me feel not horny so much as lonely.

Sex buzz indeed. Because everybody — except for Amrita and me, as far as I know — was teenager-gooey like David and Jenna all weekend. Maybe it was all the other Man Buns taking it up a notch, when they saw not one but two of their brethren recently cast off by their goddess. Or the Acoladies going all sisterfire for their guru. Or the great big hot tub at that place, looking back into the redwoods.

It certainly wasn't anything Amrita did this time. In her big warm-up story Friday night, she wasn't Lakshmi consorting with Vishnu. Or Rati, the goddess of pleasure, seducing Kama, the god of love, into endless orgasmic bliss. Nor, thank — uh — God, was she Radhe. Though she wouldn't be, because she did Radhe last month at that gig up in Sonoma, and she likes to keep the whole rotation going. This weekend she was Saraswati, the goddess of music and arts and learning, dialing the sexuality way back.

176 | THAT GOLDEN SHORE

But to no effect. Jenna and David were oozing with it, and Diane, behind her icy indignation, and a couple women who were grinding off to the side for last night's big final ecstatic dance.

Maybe it was the spicy, dank quiet of that place, a brand-new yoga retreat center in the Santa Cruz Mountains, tucked up a long, deep ravine filled with towering redwoods. The grounds and some of the buildings of *1440* — named for the number of minutes in the day, a mindfulness thing, get it? — used to be some sort of Bible college before going belly-up. So maybe the whole place is still vibrating with the repressed sexual fury of all those college kids.

Nonetheless . . . I really don't want to know how repressed, or broken, or just plain fucked up a guy has to be about his mother to go for that whole breastfeeding thing. The closest thing I can imagine to all that is what happened with Old Freya last year. But that didn't have anything to do with my mother, or with my endlessly parsed sadness about her own infinite sadness, about her rage at my father and her physical and mental infirmities, about all the ways she couldn't be anyone's mother.

Sure, Old Freya was halfway to how old my mother would be now, but that's not why I went there on that strange evening after we were out surfing at Angel's Rest. Though, now that I think about it, it was her breasts — just out of her wetsuit, sprinkled with drops of water the color of the sunset, nipples perked with the cold air — that got all of that started.

So fine, we all go there.

But from what I've seen while up on stage at these gigs, I know that Amrita gives all of them — the Man Buns, the Old Hempy Dudes, even the straightest of the Acoladies who would gladly switch teams for a night with her — something far more powerful than the promise of a healing suckle. She gives them the three things they want most: to feel alive; to feel good about themselves; and to be seen. She gives their life meaning, the way the truly clever and cunning CEOs do their hapless workers. And when someone can give your life meaning, "their" people will kill for them.

It's not just that she's monetized them; she has hypnotized them. They don't just buy her books and cards and DVDs and bumper stickers; or sit propped up on their cushions, hanging on every word for the solid half hour it takes her to tell one of her stories; or push themselves in yoga postures she's leading them through to near sweaty collapse. After dinner, when we're back in the event space doing a *kirtan* — when the music gets as rowdy and the room as hot as it did last night — they will literally fall down while dancing, and writhe at her feet.

She will seem not even to notice, except to step carefully around them, her arms dancing through the swirling splash of lights from the disco ball. Because there is always that light show to heighten the effect of the music, and drive the dancers, and send people off into the ether.

Which isn't a whole lot different from what happens on the rail at one of Johnny's concerts, I suppose.

Johnny and Amrita aren't just skilled performers who know their craft and how to pump up a crowd: they are *Rock Stars*. They're mythic creatures their fans have imbued with the power to make them feel alive, feel good about themselves, and feel seen. They're *Gurus*, possessed of great wisdom their followers are compelled to worship with ritual. And with their very public, oft-celebrated conquest of their troubles — in Johnny's case, a staple of VH1's *Behind the Music* — they are *Heroes*, mythic creatures who are also human: accessible, flawed, lost for a time, and now redeemed.

And with Gurus, sex is a thing, the world over, a thing that has destroyed ashrams and meditation communities, and brought down entire schools of yoga. Which is especially odd because it looks to me like the bond between Guru and Follower has nothing to do with sex and everything to do with the Guru's hunger for power and the acolyte's hunger for acceptance, or meaning, or whatever else they think is worth handing over all their power.

But the two Gurus I work for seem fine with the power they have — Johnny even seems to have a perverse contempt for it — even as all their followers are still junked out on their end of the bargain. Johnny has two ex-wives, but he hasn't had one in a decade and doesn't have any girlfriends, as far as I can tell; and I've never seen him diddle with any of the women hanging on his every word backstage. And Amrita, for all the eroticism and sensuality in her look, and in the way she floats into and through the room, seems every bit as celibate as Johnny. Or maybe that's just "the *kundalini* thing" Jenna said she practices.

Because there is sex threaded through all those stories she tells: the tales about a Hindu god "consorting" with a goddess, or a god or goddess "dallying" with a human, and always "such divine union you can't imagine, for hours and hours, their moans heard from one end of the universe to the other" — always with that lusty aside, and a wink, always a lusty joke, with everyone tittering on cue.

No matter the story itself — divine betrayal, divine retribution, new universe created, old universes destroyed, at the center of it a great romance, seduction, or whatever polite way she can find to describe rape — at its center, there will be a sex scene. Because, like rape, it isn't about sex, it's about power, the kind that can create and destroy universes, or at least entire schools of yoga.

So how is it any Man Bun's fault if he falls in love with her, especially after she's let him latch on a few times?

Maybe she's actually celibate because that's how she really gets off: in public, with all of them at the same time. She does like to work herself into every story, wrapping it up in the seemingly universal psychological truism that gods and goddesses are all expressions of human impulses. Isn't that the source of their great diversity? And both the the grandeur and perverseness of so many of them? Even the Jews, despite stern prohibitions against attempting to make any craven image of a vast, singular, all-encompassing God , as Rabbi Miriam used to say, still couldn't help but humanize Him/Her/It, the kabbalists conjuring up the *Sefirot* as a hierarchy of the *attributes of God*.

So Amrita will tell the story of Shakti, the primordial source of cosmic energy, because she's feeling expansive and dynamic. Or, if she's feeling the need to cleanse, she'll tell the story of Savitri, personification of purity and avatar of Sarasvati, who builds the universe with Brahma, the Creator. If Amrita's feeling dark and gloomy, then she'll be Kali, the demon-fighting aspect of Parvati, the eternal partner of Shiva, the Destroyer.

"Because," as she always says, "that's who I'm feeling like celebrating right now, and maybe that should be my real name."

And then she'll roar.

And then they roar back.

As if "Amrita" were her actual given name, and she's just now shaking it off. Because that's what so many of them do, when they go through enough yoga teacher trainings, and start wearing white to everything: change their names to Ananda, or Devi, or Shanthi or God Knows What. As if "Amrita" weren't the name she did give herself, starting with her second yoga instructional videocassette tape back in the late '80s — because the first one by "Nancy Smith" didn't do very well.

But thanks to a couple airplane rides back and forth to the East Coast with Amrita, and lots of time waiting around hotels when no one else is around, I know exactly who she is: Nancy Smith, runner-up for *Miss Wisconsin* in 1980, who discovered yoga and meditation and her songbird of a singing voice in a six-month rehab, after nearly starving herself to death during an attempted comeback in 1984. Nancy Smith, who is both wildly charismatic and unreachably lonely; supremely confident in public and insecure and anxious in private; economically and emotionally dependent on the adulation of young men and middle-aged women; and addicted to plastic surgery.

But there is that voice of hers.

She doesn't talk so much as proclaim, with a voice that can melt in three words from story to song, in a deep, glowing alto that can enter your body. She sings with the rooted power of a Joan Baez or Emmy Lou Harris, probably from decades of yogic breathing practice, with just enough grit from the years, like whiskey and smoke in the voice of an old blues singer. It's the same thing Johnny has — and Rabbi Miriam, now that I think about it — a bellowing voice that proclaims, gathers, charms and transports, the thing that roars. It stirs shit up in people, makes them feel things they can't feel any other way, I'd imagine, as I sit next to her onstage and watch them liquefy themselves with it.

Unless it's going to be a long story, and then I just space out . . .

HONK!!!

Ha! Like I'm spaced out right now, in all this goddamn traffic, slowing to a dead stop as lanes converge into Santa Cruz. Great.

I got out of the retreat center as fast as I could, and not just because of the weird sex all over the place all weekend. On my way down there Friday, Brooke had texted me with the latest shitty news about Angel's Rest — the first permit has already been approved, for testing, and somebody dropped off a backhoe out by the gate — and all I wanted to do when I read her text was run back to the ocean and jump in and start screaming, or have a good cry, or both.

Spent this whole weekend checking the tides and swell, and planning this drive down to Santa Cruz because to hell with it: I'll surf while I can, before my borrowed time on the coast runs out.

I haven't gotten out on the waves in a couple weeks, and the sun won't be down for a few hours. Though it looks like I'll be burning a bunch of those waves in this traffic. But at least I'm out of there.

What a weird weekend, with the Ananda/Jared situation, and yet another lovesick Man Bun mooning after Amrita. And with Diane from LA, following me around the whole time while acting like she wasn't: making herself busy with some task in the event space while we were setting up; hanging around at the end, when it was just us and the Acoladies doing actual teaching assistant stuff for Amrita.

I knew I'd run into Diane eventually, after Amrita fixed us on that date last fall, right after Radhe left. And normally, Amrita would have been in full follow-up mode, positioning who sat where at dinner so Diane would be sitting across from me. But with Ananda/Jared and the other Man Bun after her, Amrita wasn't at any of the meals over in the dining hall, just in to grab a banana and muffin and out the back.

It wasn't until the very end — when I was waiting to check out of my room, Amrita talking with the manager of the place about the Ananda/Jared situation, and Diane standing there, appearing to be engrossed in her phone — that Amrita finally turned and swooped back in.

"I am *so* glad the two of you are here!" she said. "Are you two sticking around to unwind, now that the crowd is gone? The hot tub here is big and yummy!"

"Yes, it is," Diane said, looking straight at me. "With beautiful views down into the trees. Very yummy."

"I'd love to," I said to Amrita, "but I'm heading down to Santa Cruz to surf."

"*Surf?*" Diane said, a suddenly sour look on her face, as if I'd said I was heading out to smoke a cigarette. "Really?"

Yes, really.

Just not anytime soon, apparently.

Instead, I'm just sitting on the van's brakes, inching my way down the hill toward the ocean, watching the cars and minivans full of families crawl their way back over to the Valley.

Poor Diane. She sure wasn't expecting that, especially when she broke her icy silence toward me right there at the end.

That reaction reminded me of all the Wall Street guys I used to have to deal with: *did you just actually say no to me?*

I can tell that she is used to getting her way; and if she doesn't, who the fuck do I think I am, telling her no?

But to her credit, the look on her face — when I said *thanks but no thanks* to frolicking around with her in that very yummy hot tub — showed the real power of regular yoga and meditation practice. Seriously. Her eyes flashed and face flushed, ever so slightly, like she wanted to open a can of corporate lawyer on my ass; but after two and half days of yoga and singing and dancing, she looked only mildly hurt and a little confused, her ego disabled by whatever actual inner light she's been cultivating. So she snorted, and managed a smile, and went back to her phone. I'm guessing that's not how she might have reacted back in her other world, had we been lined up by a co-worker or busybody friend for a happy hour or dinner party, and she'd asked me to jump in a tub with her, and I'd said no.

Luckily, Amrita was too pre-occupied with the Man Bun situation to press her cause and make it even weirder for both of us.

I hate to be crass, but I suspect that Amrita — who seems genuinely to want people to fall in love, with each other as well as themselves, and who like a big sister does worry after me and what she perceives as my loneliness — is also intent on pimping me to Diane, if only because she is a great source of referrals. She did all of Amrita's yoga teacher trainings and still goes to her biggest retreats, like the one this weekend. And she always brings a friend or two or three, women new to yoga or meditation, or newly divorced and/or peaked out at work who needs both: women who have money, or at least appear to, and despite the nails and Botox and boob jobs, are suddenly aging out in the brutal, blanching sunshine of the L.A. basin.

But even as women like Diane look like they want to project the same raw feminine power of Amrita, which none of them can by half, they do move around the event space, by the end of a weekend like this, with what looks like renewed grace and power. It's only over the meals in the dining hall, or in hushed conversations in the common areas, that I've gathered up the details of who they really are the rest of the time: lonely, horny, and bored, with more money than friends, teenagers who hate them, and an ex long since remarried and onto his next litter.

With all their money and free time and energy, I suppose they could be doing good things in the world for those in need. But they seem more likely to end up in far worse places — drunk at some country club, fucking their kid's tennis coach, trying to ruin somebody's marriage — so they end up in Amrita's tribe instead, finding somebody else's version of God and/or finding something like rhythm, and mentoring one or two of the Lost Girls of Yoga. Because these practices do work, even if all somebody is doing is going through the motions, because the motions are a portal into all the other practices.

I saw a similar thing dancing in and out of the pews at *Shir Hadash*: the full-throated singing, the ecstatic dance, and my first ever *kirtan*. They had events every few months, usually coinciding with a Jewish holiday, that looked and sounded like a Hindu or *bhakti kirtan* — cushions on the floor, music, candles — but all in Hebrew. And a few weeks after that first Jewish *kirtan*,

Leah and I went to a yoga workshop with a band that played the exact same music, on the exact same instruments, but sang in Sanskrit. It was as confusing as it was compelling, as I toggled between easternized, ecstatic Judaism and westernized bhakti yoga, because it was the same embodied music pulling me in from all directions at the same time.

Was I was traveling backward? Forward? Just spinning around in some weird cosmic circle? That pulsing, chanted music sounded odd not in Hebrew, but in Sanskrit, with a dozen or so names of the most popular Hindu gods and goddesses swapped in for the half-dozen most popular names for God in Hebrew: Krishna for Yah, turning *Hare Krishna* into *Hallelu Yah*; Ram for Elohim; Gurudev for Adonai. What I recognized instantly was the music: the low hum and lulling repetitions, the long slow build of the rhythm and tempo and dramatic tension toward an ecstatic explosion, and then the release, and the enormous peace rushing in to the fill the space opening up in the room, the body, the heart, the whole world.

It wasn't until I got this side gig with Amrita — thanks to Gordon again, and no random accident this time — that I fell into this parallel universe, this wholly other subculture of religious music, with all of its own rites, references, idioms, and dress. Aside from its sobriety and supposed chastity (ha!), it was actually not all that different than the blues festival crowd, or the bluegrass jam scene, or all those folks still trailing after the remnants of the Grateful Dead tribe, now three generations strong. There is a whole world of Hinduism-originated *kirtan* up and down the West Coast, lifted from India and transplanted like everything else in the California sun to bloom in wild new forms.

Because it works. I've seen it work, in two languages and cultures that share no texts or music, no food or dress, scant history of contact, and maybe one or two cognates. In both cultures, I've seen it bring people back from hell, from inconsolable losses, lifelong addictions, crippling depressions. I am as hard-headed as any old engineer, which makes me equal parts skeptic and empiricist, and here, the latter wins out: there *is* something going on out on those threshing floors that I will never understand.

So maybe all that *woo* from both the East and West — all those grandiose metaphysical fantasies about gods and goddesses, the *Sefirot* and *Kabbalah*, the soul and "the subtle body" and whatnot — is actually true. Maybe there really is a place beyond this place that can't be seen or quantified in the physical world, only entered, after enough meditation, chanting, music, trance-dance. Maybe there really is an astral plane where our souls leave our bodies to dissolve into a mythically frenzied cosmos.

Or maybe people just want to lose themselves for a couple hours. Because it is hard, boring, scary, and lonely, being a human being.

Dear sweet Radhe, who grew up in a culture where science and religion aren't hostile to each other, but separate descriptions of human reality? Who has an MD and a PhD in biomechanical engineering, and loves to sing and dance and meditate as much as any of them? She seemed happy enough with the first explanation. "The universal mystery behind the empiricism," she would call it, the thing we will never be able to verify, only witness in its transformative effects on broken people.

"God is everywhere and everything," she once said to me, without irony or self-consciousness on that first date after the *kirtan* where we met. "Everywhere, the same. The language does not matter. It's why we have so many names for God. Because there are so many embodiments. But it's all one. All just God."

But maybe that was just Radhe: rooted and sturdy as a tree on a mountainside, humming in the wind, joyfully awake and alive inside her own skin, dancing in circles by herself in the back of the room at our *kirtan*.

Until the incident anyway, thanks to how dark that skin is / was / is . . .

But I don't want to think about Radhe. What I want is to get out of this goddamned traffic and down to the break on the other side of Santa Cruz, before the tide is going back out and the surfing blown out with it.

Yes, dear sweet Radhe. She could dance as effortlessly as she could breathe. And she loves to marvel at the human machine, especially at human hands, and loved to study my hands while I was playing. She comes from a culture where science was just another manifestation of a cosmos bursting with creative energy.

I come from a very different culture, from the sneering cynicism of my broken parents at war with their neighbors in a small town full of true believers, to the skepticism of a science and engineering education, to the Golden Calf worship of corporate America. Everyone I'd ever known, until I stumbled into *Shir Hadash*, viewed religion as just another cynical swindle of the Poor American Fool by those in power to cow them voting against their own economic interests. A Roman circus, with the bread going the other way, to keep stupid people stupid. All of my own religious feeling, out in the woods of my childhood and eventually up in the mountains, I kept to myself.

I still keep it to myself, and groove on the empiricism, on all the things I witness from the stage, on the *bima*, in a *kirtan* circle when I see them "*go there.*" It all looks like the same God-trip to me, no matter how they're dressed or what the kind of music we are playing to take them there . . .

And just like that, it looks like we are finally going there too.

The traffic is opening up as the highways split, cars and vans and trucks all racing into the void, and I'm pulling into Santa Cruz, and the next backup.

It is all the same God-trip, and the music is the gateway, the portal. Rock 'n' roll is no different from all that, at least not how it appears from up on stage with Johnny. The mystery behind the rock tribe's own musical rituals and bodily transports may not be so audacious as to explain the nature of the cosmos; but when they are down there on the rail in their own ritual garments — tie-dye, fringes, floppy hats — dancing and twirling with their eyes closed and heads tilted back, I can half close my own eyes, and see the same people doing the same thing at one of Amrita's concerts or in the sanctuary at *Shir Hadash*.

"Everywhere, the same —" Amrita would say, just as Radhe did. "The language does not matter. All One. All God."

I suppose this is why I can toggle back and forth between Amrita and Johnny's gigs. And isn't this why they can have the same manager? Because the music business has all the same problems — money, media coverage, groupies, sex — as the yoga business? The yoga world may not have the same drug problem as the music biz; but it makes up for that with sanctimony, passive aggressiveness, and a much lower bar for ambitious people with a smidge of talent and a lot of stage presence to declare themselves gurus.

Because just teaching yoga is no way to try to make a living. Like rock 'n' roll, there is no middle class. A teacher works her ass off for decades for almost no money — or she's one of half a dozen Amritas, a star like Johnny, and they throw money at her. And the more remote she seems, the more they want to be near her, so they can throw more money at her. And everybody else starves.

Amrita got her start in the '80s, when the only gurus — like that nutjob with the Rolls Royces in Oregon — were hidden away in ashrams. As with Johnny, who got his start back in the '70s, she went from Nancy Smith with her first videocassette tape to Amrita by her second, back when people paid real money for records and tapes and CDs — more in actual dollars then than they do now, 30 years later, for the exact same DVD at either of their merch tables.

Which is how I ended up with this very odd job or, really, two odd jobs. Because it's the same job "sidemen" have been doing since the beginning of recorded music, most of which involves lots of driving around and waiting around to play the rock star's music for the rock star's fans. Amrita is out on the road maybe a third of the time, and in ways that work around Johnny's permanent, part-time "Return to Sunset Road Tour," so I get to play both. And as weird as these two gigs seem for one musician, the business side makes perfect sense: two crazy rock stars who need someone next to them on stage to keep them from floating away (Amrita) or flying off (Johnny) into the ether with their dancing, twirling fans.

Gordon introduced me to Amrita a couple months after I moving out here and going to work for Johnny. She had met Johnny when she came to do a special, private meditation and yoga weekend during one of his special, private rehabs in Ojai; and because that was the rehab that finally stuck, so did she as his guru, for a time anyway, until they each realized that the cosmos wasn't big enough for both of them to be running it.

But they are still friends, to the degree Johnny is friends with anyone, which is why she turned to him and his manager when her last guitarist quit. She kept cheating on that guy, or so the story goes, with one of the Man Buns, even though they were supposed to be polyamorous, because he was getting too old for her and making noises about moving into her big fancy house overlooking Pismo Beach.

"*Not* my kind of gig," I tried to tell Gordon when he told me the story and asked if I wanted to audition with her.

"How do you know?"

"Because the first thing you learn as a bartender," I said, "after how the cash drawer works, is 'Don't shit where you eat, or eat where you shit.'"

He burst out laughing at me. "You don't have to worry about that with Amrita," he said.

"Why not?"

"Because you, my friend, are *way* too old for her."

HONK!!!

Up ahead, huge backup on the main drag through Santa Cruz to go left toward the beach.

The tide will be all the way in by now, and turning by the time I'm out on the waves, but it's still worth a try.

I crawl along and finally make the turn down toward the ocean and Steamer's.

The parking lot is still mostly full, and all the parking spots along the seawall. Looks like most everybody is back in — pulling off wetsuits, opening beers, smoking bowls — though there's always plenty of that, waves or no. But it looks like not everybody is back in, which means the outgoing tide hasn't blown up the waves.

And there's a big space opening up right on the curb.

I swing around and pull the van in, look out at the surf, and feel that old burst of adrenaline, the surge of anticipation from my chest all the way down into my legs and feet.

I climb in the back and unhook my board, pull my wetsuit and wax, and jump out the back.

Out on the break, there is a long lineup in both directions, 30 or so surfers in clusters of two, three or four, all in inky-black wetsuits. Most are on short boards, jockeying for position, arms and legs and torsos kicking, paddling, bobbing up and down with each wave.

This is a notoriously tough, territorial wave, a sort of surfer gangland. It's a perfect point break, right in town, and the whole world of surfer tourists — groms from the Valley, bucket-listers from around the world, kooks as old as me on social media suicide missions — knows about it. But guys as old as me will get a pass when the locals see us catch that first wave, paddle out the other direction, and respect the rules.

I pull out my binoculars and study the lineup: lots of big tattoos and long hair out there today, lots of faces bronzed from the sun. There is a group of three spread out right in the center, right where you'd set up if you had the place to yourself, everyone else out there giving them a wide berth.

The smallest of the three, a spidery looking guy with a tangle of long braids, launches on a short board, pumps the crest for speed, and then shreds the wave top to bottom, grabbing his rail at the top and spinning a 360 down to the bottom. Pro surfer shit. I think I'll hang down near the north end, where it thins out.

I thread my arms and legs into my wetsuit, and as I struggle to pull up the back zipper, drifting right by me on the sidewalk, *it's him!* The Lost Prophet of the PCH!

I've seen him how many times, wandering up or down the PCH? Always in that mud-brown, woolen-looking thing that just sort of hangs on him, that ratty charcoal-colored blanket around his shoulders. Sun-baked face and bare lower legs, bare feet blackened by how many hundreds of miles, just drifting along on the shoulder of the road, with that walking stick. Bad drugs, we all assume, though Brooke always says you have to look into the eyes to tell for sure.

Wow! Up close, he looks far younger than any of us say he might be, when we're reporting our latest sighting.

Just now, as he shuffled past me, I saw right into those eyes. They weren't blank, as I've always imagined they'd have to be; or on fire with fury or madness, as Brooke says she imagines they might be; or smiling, giddy almost, with the simple mirth of the truly free, as Ike always says the Lost Prophet must be.

I watch the back of him, with that blanket over his shoulders and those bare feet the color of beach tar move slowly and purposefully down the sidewalk, the surfers and sightseers all stepping well out of his way. None of us are right about what his eyes might say: I just saw them, three feet away, and they're bright, full of light, as curious and inquisitive as a young child's, like he just woke up, or got to town, and started walking down the coast half an hour ago, and all of this is new, fascinating, almost too much to take in.

I turn back to my board, pull out a bar of wax, and laugh to myself: maybe *that's* the guy for Amrita. He's young enough, and lost enough, and definitely looks like he could use some breastfeeding. Or maybe we can fix him up with Diane. She can clean him up, put him through rehab, turn him into her own fawning Man Bun.

I'm still laughing to myself as I head down the stairs to the thin margin of beach, and scout out my launch into the lineup.

The ocean shocks with cold, with that wet slap on the face that always says: *this is real, don't be stupid, I can and will kill you.*

"Fuck you, kook!" somebody shouts from out on the lineup.

And another shout, "My wave, motherfucker!"

Not at me, but it's best to paddle the other way.

Way down near the end, the waves feather out, and the crowd too. Not much to catch down here, but when it breaks further out, I have the tail all to myself. I make three of them in a row, standing up to shine in the simple glory of nothing but now, of walking on water as it rises from the deep to kiss the beach hello and be gone.

Then more yelling from the line-up, so I paddle back out in the other direction after every wave.

Down at this end, it's just me and a couple kids who can't be older than 14, bendy little groms on squirty little boards; a dude with dreadlocks turned to soup in the water; and a ripped, sun-honeyed blonde Betty trying to teach him how to time his launch. He's terrible, and keeps yelling at her like it's her fault.

When I paddle up, we all nod at each other, as if to say, *yeah, there are a bunch of assholes that way, but we're all good down here.*

I drift further down and out, and the whole Santa Cruz waterfront opens up to the south, lit up with the sinking sun behind me.

I don't need to catch another wave. I'm happy just to sit out here on my board, bobbing up and down on the shoulders of waves, letting the weirdness of this weekend's gig and whatever's going down with Angel's Rest run out of my body and out the bottom of my feet into the ocean.

But here comes another wave, not quite big enough, so I let it roll under me. Then another, setting up right behind me.

I turn and paddle like mad and pop to my feet, shoot down the face and cut back off the bottom, riding back up the face and turning along the crest, then unfurling to stand, steady and straight and clean, enshrouded in rainbow iridescence, as the wave carries me on the last of its breath.

Wow, I think, but because what else is there to think? That will be the wave I remember from this session, I think as I paddle back out. There's always that one wave where everything lines up, and time stands still . . . though I will line up again, and try for more like that, until the sun is almost to the horizon and the waterfront turns peach and rose.

But that was the one, and all the tension — from the weird weekend, the worrisome month, the whole last year and my entire life — has been swept out to sea with the dispersed water particles of that one wave. I sit on my board, bobbing on the water, and my whole world is at peace.

When the sun finally melts into the ocean behind me, I paddle back in and head up the stairs to the street.

Before I get up to the top, there's the screeching chug-chug jackhammer of surf punk music, and three angry, snarling voices screaming *fuck you!* and *go home!* and *motherfucker!*

So much for my whole world at peace. There's a showdown in progress, ten feet past my van, on the sidewalk between an open, hulking jeep and the retaining wall down to the beach.

It's that small, wiry guy with the long braids, flanked by two other bronzed guys, one beefy, the other also wiry and covered in tats, the top half of their wetsuits off and down around their waists. They've jacked some pale, terrified looking guy in his mid-30s, still in his wetsuit, up against the retaining wall, like they're about to push him over and down to the sea rock 30 feet below.

The beefy guy cuts in to take the short board from the guy with the braids, and carries it over to the jeep, vibrating with that bone-crushing music, and tricked out with floodlights along the roll bar, big knobby tires, a bunch of surf stickers, and a license plate *SC4EVR3*.

A cluster of people stands just past them, watching in rapt, unmoving silence.

"We don't need your fuckin' kook ass around here!" the little guy with the long braids screams right into his face, his hands now free to grab him by the wetsuit collar and shove him harder into the wall.

"I'm — I'm — sorry," the "kook" stammers, his face pale and eyes bulging with terror as he looks from one guy to the other, thinking maybe he can reason with one of them.

He looks to be about 35 years old, on vacation or a work trip or something, judging from his pale face and pink feet, and obvious cluelessness what to do right now. And what he ought to do is *not* let them back him down; just shove his way through them into the street, where the passing cars will start honking and cut them off and maybe some cop will come by.

"Oh, you're sorry, huh?" yells the beefy guy.

Then the guy with the braids pushes the poor bastard even further up against the wall, until he drops his surfboard with a clatter onto the sidewalk, and his back bows over the edge.

"You're gonna be a fuckload more sorry when we throw your ass down on those rocks!" he spits in the kook's face.

"Yeah, Mikey, throw the fucker overboard!" the other little guy says, then reaches in and slaps the kook's face.

Bullies. I am flooded with rage, can't just stand here and watch, oh crap, here comes my eye-of-the-shitstorm mode . . .

. . . and I'm watching myself drop my board on the sidewalk and charge toward them — *but there are three! Stop, Jack!* I hear some voice far off in my head — but I can't stop, and here we go.

"Hey!" I yell as I keep charging.

They turn to look at me, their mouths hanging open, the smallest one still holding the kook by the neck of his wetsuit.

"Hey yourself, motherfucker!" he yells at me. "What the fuck do you want?"

The other two actually step back just enough for me to move in and square up.

"Picking on some tourist? The three of you? Really?"

"This yuppie dicksucker here snaked our waves," the one hisses at me, and his braids, which I can see now are thin and beaded, jangle from a hairline receded almost to the crown of his sunbaked head. "He don't belong out there!"

The biggest one steps toward me, balling his fists. "And what the fuck you gonna do about it, old man?"

"I already did."

"Oh yeah, motherfucker?" the third one hisses at me. "What'd ya do?"

"I memorized your license plate."

"Yeah?" the little one says. "Well you can go fuck yourself with that!"

"Won't be me getting fucked, Mister Santa Cruz Forever Number 3. If that's how you think it works." I look down at the rocks below the wall. "That drop down there is a good 30 feet. Attempted murder, for all three of you. Serious prison time. But hey — kook snaked your wave. Go for it."

The big one shakes his head, like he's heard enough and ready to make his big move, and clenches his fist and jaw.

I just stand and stare at him, ready with a kick to the balls with my right foot and left knee to the face if he does make a move.

He shakes his head and tightens his fist, and lurches at me, like he's on an invisible leash, his eyes going straight to the sidewalk. The invisible leash tightens, so he shuffles from foot to foot, then looks back at the other two, as if for approval, or to measure their disapproval.

I want to burst out laughing, but that would be the worst thing I could do, so I just put my hands on my hips and stare at him.

"Cool out, braw," the third one grabs him, like the invisible leash isn't there, and he needs to restrain him. "You don't need the cops on your ass again."

"Yeah?" he spits at me, but doesn't look me in the eye. "Fucking cops!" Then he turns to the crowd gathered around us now and pumps his fists in the air. "Fuck the police!"

I can't help but burst out laughing, and my body suddenly rushes back, and there's a ringing in my ears, and a chorus of laughter from all directions.

Wow. Shit. Here I am and there they are and what next?

The kook has slipped out of the short guy's grip, and scrambles to grab his board and back off through the crowd.

The three of them stand there, staring at me, also wondering *what next?*

I can hear my heart beating in my ears, and the quickness of my breath.

The big one doesn't look at me, just stands there clenching and unclenching his jaw and fists.

"Yeah?" he finally says. "Well fuck you, you fucking old piece of shit! You're not from around here either, motherfucker."

The little one steps in front of him, the beaded braids flying, and points up at me. "Yeah, old kook! Who the fuck are you? Get the fuck outta here!"

Which means we're done. None of them are going to hit me, only try to sound like they just had, finishing me off with those deadly f-bombs to impress the crowd, they think.

But most everybody gathered around us in wetsuits and shorts and towels are grinning and nodding at me and rolling their eyes.

"Public sidewalk," I say, standing there, scanning the crowd on the sidewalk to make sure the kook is long gone. "I'll get the *fuck* out of here, when I feel like it."

"Yeah, well fuck you," the little one hisses at me, then turns to kick at nothing and slinks off to join the other two, who've shrugged their way over to their jeep.

I stand and watch them load their boards and shoot me what they think are menacing looks; and when I don't move, the big one starts up the jeep and turns their shitty music up even louder.

Back at the van, I wait until they've screeched away before I pull off my wetsuit.

I sit down in the open side door and feel the last of the adrenaline finally drain out of the bottoms of my burning feet.

When I look up, I notice that most of the crowd is still lingering, staring at me, talking and laughing. Then they start coming by in twos and threes, like some sort of weird receiving line, nodding at me and giving me the thumbs-up.

"Awesome, dude!"

"Fuck those surf Nazis, braw!"

"Goodonya, buddy!"

I just stare back at them, my hand up for their high-fives, like they're talking to somebody else.

After the last of them are gone, I wrestle my way out of the top of my wetsuit, and when I look up, there's the dude with the soupy dreadlocks out on the wave near me. He comes over and high-fives me and clasps my hand. "You the man, man!"

Then the Betty, who was out teaching him how to launch, steps around him and says, "It's about time somebody called those assholes out. They can rip it, especially Bobcat," she says, as she turns to look out at the waves. "He's got mad skills, but —" her voice trails off.

"He the little one, with the funky braids?"

"Do you recognize him?"

"Should I?"

"Only if you're a tour freak. He was ranked for a couple years. Sponsors, all that hooey. But he's a total jackass now. Nobody can stand him around here. But nobody ever stepped to him like that either." She smiles at me, then actually goes to shake my hand. "Thank you."

"Yeah, man," the dude says, and high-fives me again. "That was a serious solid." He puts his arm around her, and they walk down the sidewalk.

I suddenly feel like I want to vomit. My head is hot and woozy, my muscles still clenching and unclenching, and it finally hits me how lucky I am how that went down. I'm wiped out, like I'd just climbed up and skied off a big summit — drained, empty, belly-hungry — and it takes everything I have to climb out of the rest of my wetsuit, until the chill of the coming night finally finds me and prods me awake with full body shivers.

I pull on a big warm hoodie and ski hat, and futz with my gear until I'm finally ready for the drive back up the coast to Angel's Rest . . .

It isn't until I am well north of Santa Cruz on the PCH — the ocean a vast iron-blue spreading out toward a horizon streaked with the last traces of rose and peach — that I finally exhale fully, letting it out with a big nervous belly laugh.

And then this odd thought: I hope someone's out and about when I get to Angel's Rest. Not so I can tell them what just happened, but because I want to tell them about seeing the Lost Prophet up close, about that curious look on his face.

Because after seeing the Prophet, and catching a few waves, I'm not really sure what just happened. I'm not even sure who that was stepping to those three surf punks. I sure as hell don't get into street fights. I'm the sort of guy who cleans up after them, the way I always did at work, or up on some mountain. I've always avoided conflict in all its forms, something that served me well in the old corporate jobs — where it's never wise to say anything to anyone's face, because they will retaliate the other way — even if not saying what I was thinking didn't work very well with my ex-wife. Or with Jill, back in Colorado.

I just snapped back there with those assholes. It felt like the same perfectly controlled fury that would flood into my body when I was out on a mountain rescue, or when Johnny is melting down: I watch it all unfold, feel none of it, only see and hear it from the other end of a tunnel. I watch myself throw down, deal with it, fix it. But a street fight? Next to a surfbreak?? Who was *that* guy???

Maybe it's because I cannot stand bullies, because I grew up taking blows from the biggest bully of them all: my father when he was drunk, until I was as big as him near the end of high school.

The nearly empty PCH shoots out along the top of the sea cliffs, each rise a silhouette against the ocean, now a sprawling, sleepy gray haze except for the shimmer stretching along the horizon.

How pathetic that those surf punks think they can commandeer their own piece of the ocean. We did lots of bitching about the hordes vacationing in Colorado and crapping up the trails and trailheads in the mountains around Dudeville; but we never beat anybody up, or threatened to. We just grumbled to ourselves, and went deeper into the mountains.

I suppose surfers on their local breaks don't have that kind of option, short of lighting out permanently for Baja, or Bali, or God knows where next.

Back in Dudeville, none of us were on any tour, trying to *make it*. We did all of that for love, not for money or sponsorships. Some of the Bettys who toured with Jill won enough ski races or "extreme ski" competitions to get some sponsorship money. But that's not why any of them did it, not how they made their living; they did that teaching and guiding. And I can't see any of those three idiots down at Steamer's, no matter how good they are on their boards, teaching anybody anything except maybe how to be a bitter asshole. Because they're clearly good at that, especially the little one with the "mad skills."

Maybe that's his problem. He was almost good enough to "make it" — but not quite. So welcome to California, buddy, where the people who are almost good enough to make it, for all their mad skills and hard work and passion, don't. Because there are 100,000 others just like you out here — not just surfers, but actors, singers, writers, dancers, and directors down in L.A. — and another 100,000 up in Silicon Valley with their prototypes, PowerPoint decks, and manic optimism.

They may have all been the shiniest stars in their high schools: the prettiest, the funniest, the lead in all the musicals; the most talented, or creative, or charismatic. They may have been the gifted athlete who could pick up any sport he tried within minutes, surfing the very first wave he paddled out to on that family vacation in Mexico, or Hawaii, or San Diego. They were the anointed ones, everyone always told them, and so they came out to California — just like Amrita and Johnny did — to consummate their talent, monetize it, make the dream come true. But what they found were those other 100,000 people and nothing but closed doors, high rents, and traffic, and some guy in the next lane over screaming to get out of his way because he too was the anointed one, and was late to a meeting he finally got with somebody who knows somebody who says he can help him.

Maybe this is the real source of the rage that idiot unleashed on the tourist kook who snaked his waves: the rage of being so damn good, and burning so many years and so much energy becoming even better — but never becoming quite good enough, or lucky enough, or vicious enough to your competitors, or never figuring out how to be fake enough to the gatekeepers standing between you and what is yours.

Or maybe I'm just glorifying all those anonymous little tragedies. Maybe it's nothing more than the plain vanilla rage of every redneck asshole in America. Like the one who went after Radhe last year in downtown San Jose, pulling out an actual gun and waving it at her over a parking space — "go back to your own country!" he screamed at her — the rage of believing that what little you have in your world has been taken away by someone who isn't from around here and therefore doesn't deserve it . . .

The road is dark now, the ocean a looming silence a hundred feet down those cliffs, as the van grinds its way up the next climb.

I've lost count of all the times I've wished I could have been there with Radhe, and not over in Phoenix for a gig with Johnny. Though if I had been, and had gone into eye-of-the-shitstorm mode, I'd probably be dead and buried from a gunshot wound to the chest. So maybe it's just as well. Especially because she was probably going to leave the country anyway, with or without me. Though that redneck did not help.

The roar of the van is starting to wear on me, so I turn on some music, honky-tonk, because as much as I'm trying to calm myself with this mercifully empty road and normally fun drive, I'm still agitated, still *up*, itching for a fight.

I wonder how Radhe is doing now. I wonder how the new job is working out; if she found *kirtan* down there; if she's still dancing. She'd just started looking at jobs in Singapore, Hong Kong, even back in India. And of course they all wanted her. Who wouldn't want a surgeon and bioengineer who had invented a way to make crippled hands work? But would she have gone anyway? Even if the redneck hadn't freaked her out? Or I had been there to step up and defend her?

She used to joke, when the hospital down there was recruiting her, about the two of us running off to New Zealand together, about how we'd have to get married so they'd let me in with her. But she wasn't really joking, now that I think about it. She was testing me. And I failed.

I suppose I failed because I was still messed up about losing Leah. Even if I kept telling myself and insisting to Radhe — and to Amrita, Ike, Brooke, Gordon, the Acoladies, and everybody else who wouldn't stop asking about her — that I was fine. That I was over it. Really.

But I wasn't fine. I was still numb, and the only time I felt anything was up on stage, playing and singing with more power and passion than I'd ever had, wanting the set to go on forever because I couldn't stand the silence rushing into the void after a night of raucous music. Because I couldn't stand the too-short walk back to my empty hotel room or van.

After that run-in with the redneck, Radhe stopped "joking" about us getting married and running away to New Zealand, and just flat-out asked me, three different times, over dinners in the three nicest restaurants between Angel's Rest and her house over by the hospital.

But all I could do was just stare, mumble, change the subject.

I was checked out, exactly liked I'd been with Jill all the way back in Dudeville more than a decade ago.

"Very well, Jack" she finally said during the third dinner, and went into doctor mode, something I saw her do only when she was exhausted, or frustrated, or pissed. "I do not really want to get married either. It must be the lingering effects of the trauma, most certainly. The man with the gun. I am very silly to think somehow marrying a white man will make me safe. It will not. I am still brown, you were not around, and cannot be all the time anyway."

She searched my face, waiting for me to challenge all that.

But I said nothing

Then she burst into tears and hurried off to the restroom.

I still don't have anything to say to that, other than what I managed over that third dinner: "I'm sorry."

And I was sorry. But that was it. Because the great mindfuck of checking out is the certainty that you are *not* checked out: you are fine, and the other person is crazy. Which does make them crazy. Which confirms that you're fine, and they *are* crazy. And the best restaurant with the best view on the coast can't fix any of that, only rub it in harder, because everyone around you is glowing with the spectacular setting for their special date.

The worst part of that mindfuck, thinking about it now, isn't that I didn't want to run off to New Zealand with her. Because maybe I would have, just a few months later. Who knows? Maybe by now, I'd have been the one planning our great escape. Radhe and that wild new country could have turned out to be for me — after wandering from one end of this fucked up, played out, lost cause of a failed nation to the other— the happiest of endings. Marriage to a smart, sexy, interesting woman doing the most important kind of work I can imagine? Maybe even a kid or two, all these years after blowing it with Jill, and losing Leah, and giving up on all that?

But no. The worst part was my dead-eyed cruelty to Radhe. I let her think — absent any other explanation — that there was something wrong with her, that I wouldn't want to throw down and be with her, in New Zealand, or here in California, or anywhere. I'd done the exact same thing with Jill more than ten years ago, and thought I'd learned from the mistake. And yet I had nothing for her but the same chill indifference, spilling from under the locked door of my prison of sadness about Leah.

Maybe that's why they all kept asking, after I moved here and took on these gigs, whenever Leah would come up: *Are you OK? How are you doing? How have you dealt with the grief?*

I always said I was fine, and thanks, and don't worry about me, I've been through lots worse in my life. But I didn't even know what that word was. *Grief?* That was for old widows, or people who've lost children, for refugees who've seen their towns destroyed by war. I'm Jack; I don't grieve. I'm the guy who deals with shit, steps in and fixes things, stands strong while others fall apart. Grief? Me? Please.

I'd cut off all contact with my parents 20 years before they died, and couldn't be bothered going east for their funerals. And I'd abandoned my sister not long after cutting them off because every time I saw her, or heard her on the phone, all I saw or heard was *them*. No, I didn't grieve; I ran away. I kept myself busy, kept inventing and reinventing my life, moving further and further west each time. Where there might have been this thing called "grief," I'd known only anger, bitterness, and cynicism, stoicism on a good day, nihilism on a bad one.

But I was grieving over Leah, and the horrible way she went; I just didn't know it at the time. It was mixed up with everything else that had gone wrong back in Utah with the start-up getting bulldozed under, the whole country losing its mind, the mountains catching fire and the oceans rising.

All I knew was that something was trapped down there, somewhere deep in my body, in my lower gut, my core, and all the way down into the center of my pelvis, in what the yoga teachers call the first chakra. It's the place where sex comes from, they say, the ball of fire that thrusts and thrusts and thrusts and isn't put out until — well, it's put out. All of that was gone, numb, dumb, insensate.

Until Old Freya saved me and set me free.

Or so I'd thought, because I'm a dumbass guy, and had just passed the Muddy Waters test, and had all the proof I needed. I'd gotten my mojo working again, after nearly two years of working only in those few dreams when Leah would visit, her eyes bright again, her eyebrows and hair all grown back in, smelling like she used to, of pinyon pine and lemon and soap, her belly soft and smooth, those angry red gashes gone.

But even after Freya, after she'd set that part of me free, it turns out I was far from over it. I was still in a smoldering rage at the cancer that took Leah. And I was ashamed of how I'd shut down on her, down there, even as she was willing and wanting — in between those last crushing rounds of chemo — even as she was dying from the inside out.

No, I wasn't done, hadn't let the worst of that go. The dumbass guy in me had thought that Freya, riding the ocean at sunset like a shimmering, 70-year-old surf Betty crone of a Calafia, had fixed me; but all she really fixed was me down there.

I wish I'd known all that before breaking Radhe's heart. But I didn't. Because Jack was back! Right?

But now I do know what grief is, thanks also to Freya, the first person to utter the actual word to me, or maybe the first person I remember uttering that word. I know that grief is like a really bad drug: you can't think straight when you're on it, can't think your way through anything; and you don't know what you're really feeling because the grief crowds out everything else. Until it wears off. And it doesn't just wear off one day. It didn't for me anyway. It wriggled itself away, good days and bad days, the classic regression effect, with a long tail. For losing Leah, that tail stretched from the mountains of Utah to the coast of California coast, apparently.

FLASH, FLASH!

Red and white lights pierce the darkness up ahead, well west of the road, about where Pigeon Point Lighthouse would be spinning its signal out to sea.

But that beacon stopped working years ago, and the little white buildings around the historic lighthouse are all boarded up for repairs.

I push the van a little harder, wondering what that might be: emergency vehicles coming? A fishing boat in distress?

The red and white flashes dip and swerve; and as I pass a break in the cliff down toward the ocean, the flashing is fixed in the dark looming down there, red, white, red, white, as I go by. Must be a Coast Guard helicopter. I hope it's just a nighttime training mission and not a rescue this long after sunset, which means it's probably not a rescue but a recovery. Speaking of somebody's grief. Ugh.

I blink away the flashing in my eyes and try to read through the darkness swallowing the empty road ahead. It straightens across the great rolling tabletop of these cliffside ranches, dropping off to the ocean on my left, running off to the Santa Cruz Mountains to the east.

And there's the moon, popping from a big gap in the ridge, three-quarters full and washing everything in a pale blue gray.

There was a moon out that night with Old Freya. I could see it just past her shoulder, through the open window in my place at Angel's Rest, while she brought me — part of me anyway — back to life.

It had been almost a year since Leah died, and nearly a year and half without any sex, something I think she could tell just by looking at me and the way I was looking at her as we were pulling off our wetsuits. And even though she looks exactly like Calafia might, especially for a guy my age, she didn't just throw me down and fuck me silly like Calafia would. She was gentle, sweet, and just there, all of her, stretching out her long, warm, half-loose and half-limber surfer body alongside mine, running her strong, sinewy hands up and down my belly and chest, searching my face with those soft, wrinkled old eyes.

She'd come down to Angel's Rest to hang with Ike and get in a few waves. But Ike wasn't around, just Brooke and Ryan working on some old truck, and a couple kids who were up working the point. I wasn't thinking about surfing that day — I was out on my porch, working on a new Amrita song — when

I saw Old Freya paddle out by herself.

I knew from Ike that she was as solid as anybody out there, had surfed anything and everything while working the pro circuit as a massage therapist and cook, knew she could handle herself out there. Still, I watched, and worried, just in case.

She'd come out to surf at Angel's Rest a few times, paddling out while Ike sat up on his usual perch and scouted waves for her and whooped and hollered when she caught a good one. She used to live out there, Ike told me, before she met her husband and moved over to the Valley, and that was how he had come to land here.

I'd never surfed with her; but I did come home one evening after one of her sessions, when she and Ike and Brooke were all hanging out in Neptune's, drinking beers and watching the sun go down.

That's when the *grief* word came up.

Ike had just blurted out Leah's name, and when he saw whatever sad or ugly look came across my face, said, "Sorry, man," and then hurried to explain that Freya was working on some book about massage therapy for cancer patients.

"It's all good now," I said, brushing it off and changing the subject back to surfing, the waves that day, how her longboard handled the beach drop when the tide was coming in.

But she just stared at me, or rather straight into me.

I looked away, down at my beer or out at the ocean or wherever — anywhere but into those eyes, sharp and unnervingly steady. They were fixed like headlights on me from out of the hollows of her sun-splotched glow of a face, carved by time and weather and a life lived outside, and framed by frizzy, wind-blown silver and platinum hair. Whatever blue or gray or green her eyes had once been was washed out by all those years out on the water under all that sun, leaving them the color of water and sky.

A month or so later, when I saw her paddle out by herself, I stopped playing and just watched — the old mountain rescue guy in me, I suppose — because she looked so tiny out there, just a graceful, curvy fleck of wetsuit and ancient brown longboard in all those big crashing waves. But even from way up on my porch, I could see that she was good: steady in her stance, her body supple and quiet, her head up and shoulders back, her arms out and lifted to the sky.

I put my guitar down, and grabbed my wetsuit off the railing, and ten minutes later I was paddling out.

I'd never been out there with her, never really even watched her out there before, so I hadn't noticed that she surfs exactly like I do: for the ride, not the shred, for the simple joy of standing up on moving water, and riding down the face of the wave, into a long, flowing bottom turn.

When I was out there with her, she didn't look like a curvy fleck at the mercy of the waves. She may have been well into her 60s, maybe even pushing 70. But she was standing perfectly upright, with her shoulders back, lithe but powerful, her arms raised like she was conducting an orchestra, with big strong hands and sturdy brown feet, and all that platinum hair, iron-gray with seawater, dancing down the back of her wetsuit. She looked like any other Betty out on a surfboard, the cut of her waist and flare of her hips and ass, a little more pronounced. But unlike any of them, she surfed with quiet, contained power, the perfection of stillness in motion, while her ancient longboard dropped down the face of a crashing wave, her arms flowing through the air, hands opened to the sky like a ballerina, or Balinese folk dancer, or classical Hindu dancer shaped to emanate some goddess.

As we traded waves and I sat on my board more interested in studying her every move than catching my own, I watched her surf with the grace and power of Amrita dancing in the center of the room on her best days. Or how I imagine a really good *vinyasa* yoga teacher might surf. Or how I know Jill would surf, after watching her ski down all those impossible mountains, if she stayed healthy another 30 years and traded the mountains for the ocean. Old Freya didn't ride waves so much as dance them.

In those moments, with the sun going down behind her, and splashing her face and the cliffs and everything around us with golden light, she *was* Calafia.

And I was mesmerized. All of me.

We paddled back in when the sun was all the way down, lingering by the open back of her old VW bus there at the end of Beach Road.

Nobody ever wants to wrestle out of their wetsuit and into the sudden chill, which is why I thought she was happy to stand there waiting, staring at me as I tried not to stare at her and pull myself back up the road to my house.

She gave me a little smile, then turned and grabbed a big saffron and fuchsia beach towel out of the pile of gear in the back of her bus, shook out her hair.

"Well, that was fun," I said, turning to go.

"Yes, it was," she said, toweling off her hair and studying me.

She had to have been able to tell that I didn't want to go anywhere, that I was suddenly aching for her. Because right then and there, in that moment, my body had just burst awake from that long sad slumber. And why her? Because she was the closest I'd come to seeing Calafia, and if I didn't have her, I'd die? Because she certainly wasn't Calafia in that moment — she was a real, live, human being, a sweet and quietly powerful woman old enough, if not to be my mother, then to be some really cool aunt of mine who had taught me how to surf.

"Lots of fun," I stammered again, and went to futzing with my board or leash or whatever. But every time I'd look up, she was just standing there, her bare feet caked in brown beach tar and golden dirt, looking right at me. Or no, she wasn't looking at me so much as straight into me again.

Then, like any other woman at any other surfbreak, she draped herself in her towel, like a cape, and peeled off the top half of her wetsuit, shimmying it down to her waist.

"Anyway," I gulped, and forced the words out. "I'm sorry. I'll let you change in peace. It's not very gentlemanly of me to stare."

She turned and gave me a mischievous little grin, like a wink that wasn't a wink because she was studying me too hard for that.

"It's not very ladylike of me to enjoy you staring," she said, as the towel started to slip off one of her tiny, powerful, sun-splashed and freckled shoulders. She didn't go to grab it, just let that towel slide down her sinewy brown arm, until there was a breast, and a nipple, and then two breasts and two nipples, staring straight up at me.

Her nipples were large brown ovals, smiling out of the bottom of breasts dangling left and right, like two hopeful eyes, covered in droplets of water, tears from the ocean. She toweled away the droplets, and her nipples hardened, and I wanted her so badly, my chest tightening and stomach leaping, that I thought I was going to throw up.

"After I lost my husband," she finally said, "the thought of sex only made me sadder."

"Yeah, well," I shrugged, and stared at her feet, her long brown toes scrunching and un-scrunching in that golden sand.

"That lasted a long time," she said, re-wrapping the towel around her body. "Then it was awkward. Scary. Not so much like I was cheating on him," she went on, shimmying out of the bottom of her wetsuit, until it was dropping at her feet. "I'd let him go by then, and was done crying. It was more like losing my virginity all over again."

She reached into her gear, pulled out a pair of faded red sweatpants, and like every woman at every surfbreak, started shimmying into them under the towel.

"Yeah, well," I said, because I had no idea what else to say.

I was starting to shiver in my wetsuit, from the coming night air, sure, but also from an overpowering rush of desire, panic, confusion, arousal, then more panic. And what she said then makes sense to me now; but right then, it might as well have been in Sanskrit or Greek or Mandarin. At that moment, my entire being had been reduced to this sudden pressure in my chest, and heat in my belly, and swelling right where it's supposed to swell. I'd been deafened suddenly by a cacophony of desire, pain, and longing, immobilized, my stomach up in the bottom of my throat with an aching, desperate hunger.

"I know what it is to deal with that kind of loss, Jack," she said. "And with how good it feels when you finally start to come back from it."

"Yeah, well," I said again, and tried to shrug off the volcano erupting somewhere down around my first chakra.

A burst of ocean breeze sent another chill through me, and I looked over at her, watched the breeze tickle wisps of her hair, silver, platinum and white, poking up to dry in the last of the light.

"Do you want to come back?" she asked me. "Are you ready? It's OK to say no. Or that I'm too old. Or that you need to be in love, or need it to mean more that."

She moved a step closer to me, those bright, nearly colorless eyes searching mine for the thing so obvious I couldn't figure out how to say it, and finally said, "It's OK to want a woman again, Jack."

Five minutes later, we were up at my house, and while I tried to lunge at her the moment we walked in the door, my wetsuit still on, she laughed at me, and said "you should probably get out of that wet thing first!"

Then, while I was struggling to tear my addled body out of my wetsuit, she gathered up all my blankets and cushions, and arranged them just so on the floor in the main room. She asked if I had any candles and I said just a couple old ones, so she went out to her bus and came back with four or five big ones, and massage oil, and incense.

This would not be sex, I realized. This would be ritual, as electrified as my body was to enter hers and explode, and it would last until dawn.

She turned out the lights, and lit all the incense and candles, placing them on the floor in a circle around us. Out of my wetsuit, I was shivering, so she wrapped me in a blanket, and sat me down on a cushion in the middle of the circle.

With her back to the open window and the last of the deep magenta light out over the ocean, she suddenly went from busy sex-nest builder to softening silhouette, standing before me, all flowing hair, and strong, graceful little shoulders, and those sweet little smiling breasts. Her sweatpants were still on, but just barely, hanging off the bony corners of her pelvis, a hint of abs flexing and unflexing through dark skin dimpled and marbled with sun splotches, freckles, little nicks and scars. Her navel, pouting and pierced with a gold ring, stared straight at me, rising and falling with her breath and little pouch of a belly, hanging down over a ledge that disappeared into the top of the sweatpants. It looked like some kind of scar, but I couldn't make it out in the candlelight.

"What's this?" I asked, running my fingers along the gap.

"My C-section scar."

"They're that small?"

"Yes. And my son is six-three now."

"Wow."

"Yes," she laughed. "That's a word for it."

I just kept looking, my eyes going up to linger on her breasts, and the ghostly shadow of her face against the open window, then back down along that pebbled abdomen and little belly, rising and falling, like the little breezes of ocean air through the room.

"What kind of cancer she did have?" she finally asked, so quietly I wasn't sure I'd heard her right.

"Ovarian."

She let out a little whimper and said, "I'm sorry."

"Yes."

Then her hands were on her waistband of her sweatpants, and the sweatpants were sliding off to reveal the crescent moon of scar, and a thin spray of gray and white pubic hair, and then her vulva, soft shadowy folds of it bulging out, like the bloom of flower from a hanging basket.

I rocked back with the suddenness of the scent: of the ocean, and sand, and sweat, and sex. Before I could think to do anything, she was bending down, but only long enough to find my right hand, with her left hand, which was slick with massage oil. She ran her fingers through mine, then brought my hand up to sweep along her belly, to feel the heat in there, to release more of that intoxicating smell from her skin, back and forth from the hip point to hip point.

"That must have been very painful," she said.

"It was."

"Poor dear," she sighed. "And you couldn't save her."

"No."

"You don't need to save me," she said, taking in a long breath and still running my hand back and forth across her belly. "I'm still whole down here."

She slid my hand down through her pubic hair and over the top of her vulva, my fingers opening to spread through the folds of that blossom. Then took her hand away from mine, and squatted, just enough for her legs to open enough for my finger to slip through, and into her.

She started to breathe harder, and rotate her hips as my finger found its way further in, and then another finger, and then my thumb up through the top of the blossom. Her hips started circling more, a little faster, and her breathing deepened, filling with a low moan; and with each circle, she sank a little closer to the floor, her legs and vulva and all of her opening as she lowered herself, pressing her abs and chest to my face as she slid down onto me, and my penis found its way inside her, and her legs were out from under her, straddling me.

Her face was directly across from mine, the details all in shadow, but I could see that her eyes were closed and mouth open, and then I could feel her legs tighten up around my lower back, and the last thing I remember — before yelling out, and her yelling out, and both of us, still sitting propped up on that cushion and crumpling into each other's arms — was that moon, just out the window, over her shoulder.

It aches still to remember that night, deep down in my body, as in my mind's eye, something like dark matter flew out from the core of my core, every time we'd rise from the blankets, and ride each other again, off and on until dawn . . .


WHOA!

Too fast!

The van is hurtling down this last hill, and I have to pump the brakes over the bridge as the road finally bottoms out to cross San Gregorio Creek.

Just thinking about that night with Freya makes me want to pull the van over and remember it all properly; but the urge fades faster than I can scramble to indulge it. Which is what always happens, even with my mojo now back in full working order, and Radhe come and gone for months now.

I suppose I've never been able to do that because that night with Freya wasn't so much a spontaneous and wild romp with the latest Calafia, with some woman spotted in the crowd, when I'm bored or lonely morning in bed by myself. That night with her was ritual, an ancient thing charged not just with eroticism but with mystery, hovering out of ordinary time like a wedding or religious conversion ceremony, a perfectly unique inculcation of a perfectly replicable thing that might happen to anybody, but only at the exact right moment in their life.

At the bottom of the next hill, fog drifts up the gap from the ocean, twisting in the headlights like a dragon that has just made landfall. The van slices through the dragon, the fog spinning off in either direction, and digs into the big climb up to the last cliff, and Angel's Rest.

No, what happened with Freya that night now seems both inevitable and singular: it happened only that one time, exactly when I needed it; and I do not want to spoil the memory of it in my body with some tawdry recollection in my fevered imagination because things are indeed working again.

Little did I know in the months to follow, when I met Radhe at that *kirtan*, that this would get me only halfway back from the dark place I'd gone after Leah. And Radhe wasn't interested in only half of me. Maybe I should have spared her all of that, and just hung out with Freya herself until the end. Good surfing, great sex, and nothing to worry about except making sure we're together at Angel's Rest when the big one comes, so we can paddle out together into the tsunami for a good ritualized death. She would be my Calafia then, and I her lost explorer, his ending truly mythic.

But that wasn't an option either: some rituals are designed for every week, or every spring or fall; others for once in a life-cycle; and that's what had happened with Freya.

She made that perfectly clear without having to say a word, when she was back out at Angel's Rest a few weeks ago to hang with Ike.

I was pulling in from that great festival gig up in Tahoe, and there she was, sitting up on Ike's perch with him, scouting waves.

Half an hour later, I was down in Neptune's with Brooke and Ryan, telling them about that festival — the huge crowd, the all-night jam afterwards — when Freya and Ike came in.

She just smiled at me and said, "it's good to see you again, Jack." And another sweet, slight wink and smile and goodbye hug when she got up to leave. And that was it . . .

And there's the road down to Angel's Rest right there.

I slow down and turn in, and there's that damn gate, closed and locked like it has been these past few months.

I jump out with my keys, and as I'm walking over to the gate, my eyes adjust to the darkness and I notice, hovering about ten yards into the meadow and ten feet into the air, a tall, ghostly white rectangle.

I go back to the van, grab my flashlight, and walk out into the meadow, through the scratch of waist-high dried grass and wildflowers to the base of the sign.

It is actually two signs, two squares shiny with new white paint, nailed to a single new pole planted in the ground, and rising a good 15 feet over my head.

The smaller one on the bottom, right at eye level, says

*PUBLIC NOTICE OF HEARING*
*RE-ZONING OF ANGEL'S REST PROPERTY*
*A-2 AGRICULTURE TO H-2 / R-3 HOSPITALITY*
*PLANNED HOTEL RESORT FACILITY*
*APPROX 210,300 SQ FT HOTEL & CONVENTION CENTER*
*40 ACRES FOR 2 GOLF COURSES, TENNIS, HORSE RECREATION*

I step back and scan the larger sign, ten feet off the ground, with my flashlight. *Angel's Rest Luxury Resort & Spa Coming Soon! Two Championship Golf Courses, Tennis, Swimming & Riding Stables!* it says, above a drawing of a landscape I recognize.

The drawing is a bird's eye view from the north, a cross-section of the whole place from the meadow, down through the break in the cliffs to the beach. The landscape has been scraped clean of every structure, and covered with the cartoon rendering of a sprawling hotel, all glass and sleek curves, spread along the edge of the cliffs and spilling down toward the beach.

Our houses are all gone; and all along what used to be Beach Road, and Neptune's and all those other empty buildings, there is a long curving seawall, with an infinity pool, restaurant, another pool, what looks like a bar, and then more seawall. And this meadow I'm standing in right now — home to a family of coyotes, half a dozen cows, one old horse, and a pair of red-tailed hawks who hunt these golden grasses for rabbits, mice and snakes — is carpeted with bright green grass and little white dots and kidney-shaped ponds, and spiked with tiny people in tiny golf carts.

Oh well, I mutter as I head back to the van. This really is happening, and I really do need to come up with a plan.

But where do you go when you've reached the end of a long and winding road that began on the opposite coast?

I look out across the meadow, past the cliff edge with its inky silhouettes of wind-carved cypress, at the great looming silence of the ocean, washed a pale gray in the moonlight.

I knew none of this California dream of mine could or would last, but I somehow allowed myself to forget that it wouldn't, allowed myself to pretend that this place could be my angle of repose, the end of the trail for me.

Where do I go from here? Back to Colorado? Everyone I cared about in Dudeville is long gone, so no. Back to Utah, and *Shir Hadash*, and Leah's ghost? Off to New Zealand, to beg Radhe's forgiveness, because it wasn't just about getting my mojo back; it was about getting the rest of me back, and I have, almost, maybe?

I have no idea what to do except promise myself that I'll figure it out tomorrow, or the next day, so I climb back into my van and stare at the shadow of that sign, standing like a solitary tree in the middle of the meadow like a stake through the heart of everything.

# 7 | CEDAR CROSSING

"The mountains are calling, and I must make a reservation."

That's what Danny scoffed when I told him about the new rule up at John Muir National Woods: you have to go online and make a reservation. For a parking spot. To walk into a redwood forest named for the nineteenth-century naturalist whose words awakened the world to the great wonders of the American West. (Who was, I might point out, also an engineer from back East, who blew it all off to go God-crazy out here.)

We were standing in line at the office for climbing permits for Mt. Whitney. Danny had a line on one from a guy at his gear company up in Portland, but we still had to show up and do the paperwork.

We didn't know how lucky we were for that inside track, until all the dirty looks we got from everybody waiting in the big line. Lining the walls of the cramped office and scattered all around the busy parking lot outside were a hundred clumps of people, waiting, pacing, kicking at the curb with their hiking boots, pissed off in a dozen different languages. Half thought they could just show up like this was any other trail in any other park, and start up the side of the highest mountain in the Lower 48. Others had permits, but for only two of their three hikers; or for the wrong day and wanted to switch.

Danny was down here for a gear-testers meeting in Bishop, the ranching town turned climbing town, "Old West to New West in 20 years," he said.

We hadn't seen each other in almost six years, since he and Julie were down visiting her family with the new baby. But climbing Mt. Whitney would be like the *good old days* in Colorado — *if* we could get out ahead of the permitted horde with a midnight start and far-flung tent site, somewhere right along the treeline. The top of the mountain to ourselves, and a crazy big summit at dawn.

We got the permit by noon and wandered back down the hill, through the great buckling folds of shattered rock where the Sierra Nevada Mountains meet the Mojave Desert, to Lone Pine, another ranching town turned climbing town.

Big meal, food for the trip, and a quick-camp for the afternoon. Hang around, snooze as much as we could, then head up the mountain that night under a nearly full moon. Exactly like the *good old days*.

Except in the *good old days*, Danny hadn't already been gone from a wife and two kids on a business trip for three days. One of whom had a stomach flu, then the other.

"Julie's tough," he said, "she can handle all that herself. She's psyched for us getting out there again."

Until she got the stomach flu herself, which he found out about while we were sitting down to a carbo-load lunch in a diner in Lone Pine.

"Dude, don't hate me," he said, coming back from the rest room, throwing his phone on the table, and collapsing into the booth. "Julie's got it now, and her sister had to come over and get the kids. I gotta go back, man . . ."

So we just said goodbye over a beer in the Mammoth-Yosemite airport, in — seriously? — the *John Muir Bar*. ("The mountains are calling, and I must grab a quick one.")

In the *good old days*, I would have turned around and gone straight back to Whitney Portal, scanned the wait-listers to make sure there wasn't some guy who looked both as reliable and fun to hang with as Danny. And if no one looked up to the task, I would have just headed up the mountain myself. Because, back in the *good old days*, I really did have a minor death wish.

Not so today. Today, lots of people are counting on me to show up in two days for a gig up north, so I'm driving. But it's a great drive, up the back side of the Sierra Nevada, two lanes and me past a wall of snow-draped granite and forest to my left, and folds of ruby and chocolate desert mountains to my right.

North to Reno, up over to Tahoe, back down into the shit, then over to Mendocino. For Earth Day, a gig with Johnny, some local festival about saving trees he went to war with Gordon over doing because it paid next to nothing after expenses.

After I dropped Danny off at the airport, I thought about circling back and finally visiting Manzanar, the historic ruin in the desert just north of Lone Pine where the US Government imprisoned Japanese-Americans during the Second World War. Manzanar was the perfect place for another government crime back then: it was newly empty, after Los Angeles stole the Owens Valley's water supply, making a mockery of Manzanar's name, which means "apple orchard," driving all of its farm families to sell out cheap or go straight to ruin, and creating a dust bowl that became the United States' biggest point source of toxic dust pollution. And all of it legal, just like the internment of all those Japanese-Americans.

Last year on a road trip out here with Radhe, just pulling into the parking lot and seeing the concentration camp rectangles in the sand, sent us both into boiling rages, and we couldn't face going in. And then, like now, there's a long drive and a lot of traffic ahead.

And I'm not feeling like confronting all that pain right now. Not after a fun night out with a good friend, after all this time.

It was like we'd only ever hit some friendship PAUSE button, and when I picked Danny up in Bishop yesterday, we just hit PLAY. We drove over the first big hill west of town, found the first campground, and set up at the camp site furthest away from everybody else. Just like the good old days, I put up the tent and he put up the kitchen, and we smoked a bowl and tossed a Frisbee. Then we read and snoozed and got up in time for more of the same, with the slow orange fade to pink-purple dusk, the sun early to slip past the wall of mountains just west of us.

The only thing different after all these years was how different the *other* guy looked: he'd lost half his long dirty brown hair — which always had a streak of pink or purple in it just because — or at least he's capitulated to half, and now it's just brown; while I've lost the rest of mine, or not really lost so much as watched it relocate. Danny is also a little bit thicker around the middle, like me and everybody else who doesn't kill themselves with exercise or get their primary care from their plastic surgeon.

Yes, Danny, the guy who ended up in Dudeville, with his outsized appetites for weed and meditation, his disdain for authority, and a flash of color through his long hair, once a Division I football player. I always got the athlete part: he was strong and fast, in great aerobic shape, as tall as Jill and me, and lion-hearted in the way he charged it up and down the mountain. And he had great body knowledge when he launched his snowboard into the air. But Danny? Who looked and sounded just like Kurt Cobain, if after a major rehab and few years at the gym?? D-1 football???

"Because I used to be really fast and could read guys," he told me, way back on one of our first trips. "So I played safety. But I didn't get a lot of playing time. Because every time I'd mow some guy down, I'd feel bad about it — apologize — help the guy up. That really used to piss off my coaches."

Which is exactly the kind of guy (or Betty) you want with you on the final push up some mountain. Danny and I had been up and down 40 or 50 of them, with Aaron or sometimes a whole rescue crew, but half the time just us. And I knew that for all the risk we took, we both knew how to manage them, and get back down in one piece. But still, when he came back and flopped into that booth in the diner and told me the news, I think I was weirdly, secretly relieved. Sure, I'm in OK shape from surfing two or three times a week, an intense yoga class or two at festival events with Amrita, a big bike ride every now and then; but my alpine and altitude chops were stashed away a long time ago in a trunk full of climbing gear back at Angel's Rest. I could also tell just by the sound of Danny's breath, chasing a Frisbee around while we were at only 5,300 feet, that he isn't be in any better shape either, especially with the two kids now. And what I most afraid of was that neither of us would want to call it, like a desperate game of middle-age chicken we'd never played before, and we'd push each other over the redline.

"Sorry for the situation up north," he said as we parted ways at the *John Muir Bar*. "It's a big succubus, and I gotta be there. Good catching up though."

And it was good catching up, just hanging out for a precious night. We fell right into our old camp routine without any chatter or confusion, a shared reverence for the small acts of improvising a life outside, if only for a night: mostly silent and ritualized long ago, the mundane business of boiling water and washing camp dishes, almost sacralized for their simplicity, durability and ease.

But there was one thing bizarrely unique to this particular camp. Danny stumbled onto it when he wandered off by himself — like he always used to wherever we were camped, mountaintop, river bottom, trailhead — to find just the right spot and meditate.

I watched him pick his way through the great heave of mounded sandstone spilling past our campsite, then pulled out my guitar to work on a new song Johnny had sent around.

"YEE-HAWWW!!!"

A piercing rebel yell, Danny's voice, from somewhere off in that maze of rock.

I looked over to see him pop up on top of the highest boulder, stomp his feet, and wave at me to follow, like he had an old cowboy hat in his hand.

"Injuns, Jack! Coming this way! Circle 'em wagons!" he yelled, and dropped back down behind the rock.

I put my guitar away and caught up with him on the other side of the rock, in a draw surrounded by rounded rock and spiked with cactus, and threaded with a little trail up to a plaque.

The plaque was a movie still from an old western, one that had been shot right there, with that tall stack of rock next to that squat round one. Some old matinee idol with dazzling teeth and pressed western shirt, dressed up as a cowboy; and some Italian-looking guys dressed and made up as "Indians."

And then another plaque, around the back side of the rock, except this one was a movie still of two perfectly clean-shaven guys dressed up like US Army soldiers and two "Indians," one with man-boobs and the other with a five o'clock shadow.

In a big dirt road cul-de-sac around the next bend, we found half a dozen other plaques from movies or TV shows: "Martians" in spacesuits; more clean-shaven cowboys and cavalry; "Mexicans," unkempt, with five-day shadows; a few more "Indians;" and a scene from the original *Star Trek* series.

Danny had stumbled into the reason for the campground, which we hadn't noticed while driving in because we were still trading catch-ups: L.A. had been out there to shoot all kinds of movies and TV shows, and why not? Up in those surreal hills, with great monolith boulders and craggy rock cliffs and spindly cactus, we could have been, depending on the camera angle, in the Sierra Madre of "Old Mexico," or out on a Texas cattle drive, or off on some other planet, waiting for the guy in the red shirt to get offed and the captain to fall under the spell of the alien planet's chieftainess, a Cold War-era Calafia.

We of course had to smoke another bowl — we were going to the movies, after all — then check out every last plaque and picture. We wandered in and out of each little park road cul-de-sac, looking at the still, standing back and looking at how, 50 and 60 years later, the cactus had changed, somewhat, but the rock seemed not to have changed at all. This was a living museum of all those false histories and bizarre fantasies, and they were hilarious.

Most of the old movie stars were perfectly coiffed, dressed in clean new buckskins over crisp versions of the western shirts you usually see on line-dancers in suburban bars. They sat astride gleaming horses, flashing big white teeth at the scowling, conniving "Indians" and Mexicans — one even playing a guitar he just so happened to have handy up there on his horse — amidst a harsh, stark, unforgiving landscape seemingly unchanged by time or the rumblings of the fault-line running right below us.

Texas, the Great Plains, Mexico, Mars — the area around this campground was none of those places, and now it's all of them, to people the world over. Because it was two hours from Los Angeles.

I first discovered the rich (and budget-friendly) diversity of California's geographic photo-genicity one afternoon while hiking out on Catalina Island, the rugged island 20 miles off the coast of Orange County. I was out there for a two-night gig with Johnny, in an old art deco casino and amphitheater from the Roaring Twenties on the waterfront.

Sam was pissed at Johnny and threatening to quit the band, again; and the best way I know to cool anybody off is a good walk in a great place, so we went to the park above the town, and ended up hiking back to ancient Greece. There were tall cypress trees, and classical building fronts covered in tile, courtyards with dry fountains, olive trees, and bougainvillea.

A minute after Sam was saying that somebody ought to be coming around the corner any minute in a toga, we heard a guy at the top of the grand staircase, reading to his wife from a brochure, that all the great Greek and Roman epics in the '50s and '60s were shot right there. Now, Catalina Island — admittedly, as Mediterranean a climate as you can imagine — is what people see when someone says they've been to Greece.

Later that day at the venue, we were talking with the stage manager during soundcheck and he said, "yeah, not just Greece and Ancient Rome, but the Wild West too. Still a herd of buffalo up there. Descendants from a herd they brought over for a couple westerns they shot, way up in the interior, back in the '50s."

And so too, rest of California, which is a stand-in for just about everywhere. Back on what the residents of Catalina Island call "the mainland," i.e., the smudge of brown hills and smog 20 miles to the east of their Greco-Roman-Great Plains paradise, you can check out Korea, half an hour west of Studio City. Korea looks exactly like Malibu Canyon, the north end of it anyway, because Malibu Creek State Park is where they shot the TV show, M*A*S*H. Those steep, dry, chaparral and juniper mountains surrounding the LZ where the helicopters would come in with the wounded? You can see them when you crest the Santa Monica Mountains, driving north to the 101 and the Valley: *Hey! I know those desert mountains — they're in South Korea, right outside the 4077th!*

But remaking the world's landscapes to look like whatever exotic place was within a few hours of L.A. might be the less remarkable trick that Hollywood has pulled off over the last century. Because it has also remade — or has tried to remake, and will never stop trying — our internal landscapes, our craving for the happy or just ending, for the lovers finding a way, the good guy always faster on the draw and saving the town (or the whole planet), the bad guy always getting what's coming to him. There will be a happy ending, the dream-makers tell us, regardless of plausibility, and no matter who gets trampled in the process.

*Don't worry, it will all turn out fine, things happen for a reason!* Fathers and sons reunite. Lovers find each other in the crowd at the last minute. And as the credits roll, over a reprise of the single from the soundtrack, the rugged rebel hero rides off into the sunset.

Then everybody goes home and takes care of the kids. Like Danny is doing right now . . .

No, that wasn't the big wild reunion out in the mountains I'd been expecting for the past few months. But it was good to see Danny, not just catch up on the phone one more time, good to see the way his eyes would wander and voice would trail off when he talked about his kids, and Julie, and the life they've made up in Portland.

I should go visit them sometime. I could take this very road, avoiding the grind of the 5 and just watch the Sierras rollercoaster by until they turn into the Cascades. But for now, more desert than mountains, a big desert canyon, and up ahead, Mono Lake.

Mono indeed. It's a ghostly lake, a great circle of mud brown on light brown, more salt than water, stretching through haze to the horizon. A lava dome island rises from its middle, a collapsed volcano, something that just happened on earth-time.

They should have shot those movies about life on another planet up here. Or maybe they did. And that lava dome island is where the alien version of Calafia ruled over her alien amazons, holding court, dispensing justice, bedding the occasional spaceship captain from planet earth.

Mono Lake is the belly button of this side of the continent: volcanoes to the north, mountains to the west, and all that desert rolling east. There was a time when I'd see desert like that, and my pulse would quicken, my feet twitch: *there's* reality, stripped not just of civilization but of nearly everything green, just sculptures of rock, salt, wind, and nothing. I'd head right out into the middle of it by myself and spend a few nights with the stars, the rock sculpture, and the Presence.

Today, no.

Today, after all that stoke for a great big mountain with Danny, I think I'll skip the glorious lonesomeness of the desert, and head up and over the mountains. Got the extra day to kill, and there it is — Tioga Pass — and it's open.

I turn west, and pass parking lot sized chain-up areas on both sides of the road, then slip past the ranger station and on through the open gate.

The van digs into the first climb up through the forest, and I switch over to bluegrass, music almost busy enough for the road ahead, with its climbs, dips, and dives, over and around ridges and peaks, and its harrowing swings out over empty space.

The *John Muir Bar*? Ha! The real *John Muir Bar* is just up ahead, 50 feet up an old growth tree.

For the pure joy of the sensation, John Muir would climb to the top of one of those trees, and strap himself in. And when the winds would gust, the tree would sway 20 feet, back and forth, and Muir would get a thrill-ride I can only imagine.

He was doing all that as far back as the 1860s, before there were words like *hiking* or *backpacking*. And he did it by himself, in his old woolen suits and plain leather shoes, for weeks on end. *The mountains are calling, and I must go*, he said. Because the Presence was up there, which he was perfectly OK just calling "God."

John Muir was the first white man to wander into the Yosemite Valley and wander back out to tell of it. And yes, he was indeed a white man. Because in his otherwise inspiring writings — and for all his originality of mind, enormity of heart, and depth of soul — he was also a classic, plain vanilla, nineteenth-century racist. Especially toward the Natives. And yet, and yet. He was fearless, and some say crazy, and wandered in his woolen suits and leather shoes down into that still unfathomable chasm, by himself, for weeks on end; built a cabin out of those trees with a hatchet and saw and hammer; and kept journals that would go on to be dog-eared paperbacks passed around climbing base camps all over the American West.

He'd come out of these mountains only long enough to tell the world about the glories of creation he'd found, how he'd seen the very face of God in the granite faces of these mountains and the splash of stars over the top of them when the sun sank into the mist a hundred miles west. He was first to come back from this place of otherworldly beauty, and say why all of it must be protected from the mining and logging chewing its way up the mountains from all directions. In the 1890s, he would co-found the Sierra Club, sparking the environmental movement; at the turn of the century, he would camp in the heart of Yosemite Valley with Teddy Roosevelt, describing what he'd seen out in these mountains, the unabashed religious feeling it gave him, and what a great desecration it would be not to protect all of it from the ravages of the human race. Roosevelt took all of that back to Washington, where he went on a preservation bender, establishing not just Yosemite National Park, but dozens of other parks and wilderness areas all around California and the west.

And what first inspired Muir is right over there, threading through the scream of geological time running north and west: the very spine of the Sierra Nevada.

I have to get out for a look, because how can you not?

Yes, that is Yosemite, way down and over there, a catacomb on earth-scale, excavated from beneath the roof of the world turned upside down, with its mammoth formations of rock and ice the size of cities pointing upward toward infinity.

*The mountains are calling, and I must go.*

Because if they did, how could you not? I couldn't not; I re-architected my whole life around that call. And so did tens of thousands of other people, with huge appetites and good intentions, and they keep coming.

I turn and see a truck rattling its way over the summit, and a bigger truck trying to get around him.

There's a whole long line of cars, trucks, camper vans, and minivans coming up the highway from the other side, bumper to bumper behind an RV groaning and rocking around that last switchback.

I climb back in the van and start down the other side.

What would the awestruck believer John Muir think of all this now? That we had all committed some terrible sin, and were committing it still, dragging hell up here to heaven with fire-breathing engines?

*The mountains are calling, and I must go.* Now, so many are "called," there are lines out the door in the permit office, hoping to pick up somebody's cancellation. And you really do have to make a reservation for a parking space in the John Muir Redwoods up in Marin. All for the misfortune of those trees sitting in a besieged grove half an hour north of San Francisco. Little do the hordes know that half an hour north of sleepy Santa Cruz, just down the road from Angel's Rest, there are ten times as many redwoods in Big Basin State Park, California's and the country's first state park, built in 1902: trees more than a thousand years old, marching down the from spine of the Santa Cruz Mountains to the ocean. No reservations required.

Up north of San Francisco, the ghost of John Muir — perhaps as punishment for his racism? — now haunts the exact thing Joni Mitchell sang about with such bitterness back in the 70s: a *tree museum*.

Which is funny, I suppose, because that's the gig the day after tomorrow: a fundraiser for another *tree museum*, way up in Mendocino . . .

But these mountains, with all that traffic crawling up and down their sides like ants, aren't calling. Rather, they're screaming: *Go away! Leave us alone!*

So I do.

I just keep driving, with bluegrass cranking, from the wind-swept, mind-bending roof of the world, all the way down to and across the wind-scorched, mind-numbing belly of the beast, the Central Valley.

When I get to the Valley, I switch over to an audiobook, John Steinbeck's weird *East of Eden*, because its desperate story is set in a natural and human landscape just as bleak, and I too can never scramble to get out of here fast enough . . .

And then, just like that, after a dozen or so miles of wide-open wine country and ranchland, there's the ocean again, wreathed in fog.

Mendocino, its name flowing like music, water, fog.

Breathing out.

When I get to the PCH, I have to pull over, scout the waves, see if anybody's out. A day I could have spent on Whitney could turn out to be an afternoon I spend on my surfboard. This is the living miracle of California, as a collision of impossibly beautiful places, long before it was scouted for movie and TV locations. This is what will last.

I breathe in the ocean, and breathe out all that traffic getting from there to here, breathe the chilly fog and tangy smell of cypress into the whole of my lungs, the whole of my body: ocean, trees, peace, home.

And why is this my home? How did that happen? I didn't grow up anywhere near the Pacific Ocean, near any ocean. Nutty as this sounds even to my own ear three and half decades later, I never even *saw* an ocean until I was 19 years old. No family vacations, no trips to the shore, no sandcastles or sunburns or saltwater taffy. And maybe this whole late-life surfing trip is just some massive overcompensation for childhood deprivation, me just making up for time lost so long ago that, no matter how much I hang around on the beach now, I'll never get it back.

The little town where I grew up was five hours from the nearest seashore, so it may as well have been on the moon. My parents had no money for things like vacations, and contempt for those around us who did. *For wasting all that time and money and gas to sit in traffic and stand in lines,* is what they grumbled.

When I was a kid, the only times we ever got in the car and went anywhere was to my grandmother's house, where my parents dropped me off before heading down to New York so my mother could see another new doctor who couldn't help her and my father could find new bars to get thrown out of.

I happened to mention that strange fact to Belinda, the slightly insane, mostly alkie bartender I was sleeping with in Baltimore — for no reason other than she and I worked in the same restaurant and kept the same late-night hours — while I was mopping the floor and she was counting out an especially full tip jar.

She sprang off her stool and said, "Well let's fix that right now!"

After three hours of hurtling over the nighttime void of the Chesapeake Bay and across the night-shuttered Maryland countryside, we were standing on a flat, empty beach in Ocean City, on the edge of the Atlantic, a blank wall of high-rise hotels at our back, half-drunk and half-hungover, shivering and starting to fade.

There was nothing to see and almost nothing to hear out there. No waves, just bumps of black glass rolling out of the void and lapping cold foam at our feet, and a handful of stars struggling to poke through the mist. It was cold and dark and lonely, no place I cared to be, a soul-chilling rather than soul-charging first impression of the ocean that might have been wholly different, had we passed out in her car and waited for first light and a little pre-dawn color, for the first inklings of the sun.

But she had to open the place at noon and I had class in the morning, three hours back the other way. So we found an all-night gas and coffee place and headed back. And the ocean, that first time, repelled rather than compelled me: it never seemed real, just another strange dream at the wrong end of the world, a place I'd heard was wonderful from other people, but I wasn't like other people. I was an orphan, and broke, and trying to figure out how to pay for another semester of college.

Six years later, I went back, with my wife this time, during my third attempt at a senior year of college, to the wide-open beaches of Assateague Island. We couldn't afford a hotel room and didn't have any camping gear, so we headed straight there and straight back from Baltimore. But not before I'd finally stood on my first real beach; and looked out at the infinity that is the ocean; and forgotten — if for just that one, crystalline moment of pure release — that I was broke, and 25 years old, and still trying to get through school, and married to someone for little reason other than she too was 25, and broke, and still trying to get through school.

When we split up six years later, I went back to Assateague with my brand-new camping stuff, and slept alone in the dunes, and felt that same glorious blankness in my body I now feel every time I stand here and look out at the ocean: that perfect release into the peace of infinite space and boundless time. I fell that first night into a dreamless sleep, the steady crashing of the waves onto that ribbon of dune and marsh, as if it all floated out there on the back of a turtle, held fast against the surging tides.

Here I am, three decades west of all that frustration, and sadness, and pain, on the other end of the continent, in the golden land of picture-postcard sunsets and happy endings. And all I can do is bitch about traffic, and begrudge the tourists and commuters their own moments at the beach with their kids, because they're clogging up the roads in and out of "my" beach town? Maybe the great blessing of getting what you want, like so many blessings, is also a curse. And maybe the things really worth wanting or having aren't on the picture side of the postcard.

I don't know. The ocean doesn't know either. It's just there, like the mountains are just there, utterly indifferent to my latest problem or my oldest pain. Maybe that's why my latest problem doesn't seem so big, or my oldest pain so sharp, when I'm just standing here, breathing in this infinity of water and all this boundless sky . . .

I climb back in the van and head up the PCH — though way up here, 150 miles north of the Bay Area, it's the Shoreline Highway — even as it cuts back from the ocean, climbing up into the hills.

After cresting a great grassy hump of a mountain with views out to a widening circle of ocean, I find the turnoff west for Cedar Crossing. The dirt road runs down a long draw through rolling hills like great slumbering giants cloaked in golden grass and spiked with oak and manzanita, then swings out onto a ridge looking down at the steel blue plate of the Pacific.

I'm a day early for the gig, and when the guy checking me in sees that I'm with Johnny's band, he perks up, shakes my hand again, and directs me around the back of the stage, to a wooded meadow for bands and exhibitors.

The meadow is empty but for an old barn down at one end, and one big tour bus, shut down for the night. I set up at the other end, under a massive oak tree, its lower limbs long and thick enough to be tree trunks themselves, but still waving out like limbs in a Van Gogh painting of a tree, dancing over the golden grass.

After I find my spot, I lock the van and poke around the place: it's a sprawling old coastal ranch gone mostly fallow. And the gig looks like any other festival — except for the smaller stage, only a couple feet off the ground and framed by enormous cedar trees instead of a lighting rig — just about perfect for a fundraiser to save this very ground.

"Save it from what?" I'd asked the guy when he was checking me in.

"The dang developers," he said, writing my license plate down on his clipboard.

"All the way up here? What kind of development?"

"Vacation homes," he said in a lilting southern accent. "Ranchettes. Hobbyist vineyards for folks down in the city."

To hold all that off, they're trying to raise enough money to buy this place, he told me in, and put it into the same trust as "the land running from that fence line over yonder, all the way down to the ocean. Purty, huh?"

"Yes it is," I said.

"Which is why we appreciate what Johnny and y'all are doing for us."

And which explains why Johnny and Gordon had such an ugly fight, in email with all of us copied, about why we would be doing this gig, instead of the Idaho State Fair which his manager had lined up for this weekend.

*To hell with the Idaho State Fair! And their fucking fireworks show!* is how Johnny ended the last email. *I don't give a shit how much money. Or about the damn fireworks. BTW isn't it wildfire season there too? Or don't those stupid rednecks care about burning down their own precious state?*

Gordon let us all know that we wouldn't be paid for this one, just our travel expenses and the tax write-off of what we would have been paid. But everyone in the band agreed to do this because, I assumed, no one wanted to be the one who didn't agree. And now I see why else. This place is special, and who wouldn't want to help?

When I get back to the van, which looks like a little blue toy under the upturned arms of that great oak, I spread out the same gear I'd packed up this morning with Danny to dry out and make myself some lunch.

Then I spread myself out on my tarp and look up into those arms.

I like this tree. I feel like it's aware of me, that it's been watching me cook and eat, and listening to me tune up and play the guitar. Through those enormous, flowing lower branches, I can see back down the draw toward the ocean, smothered now in a milky marine layer.

I play through two of Johnny's more obscure songs, good ones he wants to "dust off for this gig" he said in a separate email. Both were on his first album, the one before the one with "Sunset Road" came out and made him famous.

Back then, Johnny was known more for his songwriting than his records: "Three big major chords for the open road," he always grimaces when anyone asks him about his old work, "and one sad little minor for the girl you left behind."

I play through the last song again, and sing it out loud for the tree, a bittersweet ballad about a funeral for a long-lost friend who died young, and counting your blessings while you're still here. Which I can't help but do, as I play and sing and watch the sun drop into the marine layer, turning it creamsicle-orange . . .

The next morning, over a big breakfast in the suddenly bustling volunteers' tent, I pick up a tote bag with the event program and a bunch of brochures.

There's a map of this place, named Cedar Crossing when it was homesteaded 120 years ago apparently. Now, it's a tree museum, a precious, precarious 178 acres of what's left of a 10,000 acre stand of native trees: looming western red cedars and great dancing oaks; manzanitas red and wriggly like more Van Gogh paintings; and madrones, with their reddish chocolate bark peeling back from limbs smooth as human flesh, their arms like human arms. The historic photos in the brochures look like what's still here around the edges of Cedar Crossing, before it was logged off and ranched down to brown stubble. One brochure describe how they are trying to bring back what they can through the land trust: the watershed restoration they're doing; the wildlife corridor they're expanding; the planting of thousands of native trees exactly where they'd been logged off. Another shows the anatomy of a western red cedar, and explains how for millennia, the Natives along the coast — from here, all the way up to British Columbia — used it for shelter, clothing, tools, transportation, everything.

Interesting, I think, walking out of the volunteers' tent and looking over at the row of cedars, tall as a small city's skyline, lining the far end of the main meadow. I know from my reading that those trees used to support the 23 or so Native tribes up the coast, but I hadn't thought of them the way other books had taught me to think about the bison out on the Great Plains: that one species could define and sustain entire cultures.

But yes, these massive trees store such abundance, and such resilience, and if you brought one down, how could you *not* use every scrap?

I can well imagine doing exactly that, because I've seen it done.

Except it was a redwood tree. And a white guy.

*Michael's Magic House* down in Half Moon Bay, everybody calls it. It took him 21 years to turn every bit of that one redwood into a multi-level work of art he's been living in since he started framing it on the little lot he bought next to the ocean, and where he had been living in a tent for a year.

It's hard to miss it if you're biking or hiking along the coastal trail north of town: it's shaped like the prow of an old sailing ship, pointed straight out at the ocean, and finished with hand-cut fish-scale shingles and hand-carved gargoyles, the faces of sea gods and goddesses. And it's even harder not to hear about, if you're hanging around Angel's Rest when Brooke and Ike and Kenny are trading stories about jerry-rigging something, or arguing about who is the toughest person they know between Santa Cruz and San Francisco. Because Michael, an old salt who still comes down Angel's Rest to surf or sea-kayak by himself, always wins that one.

He's a ruddy, sun-blasted, wind-scoured carpenter and sculptor who must be pushing 70 now. But he sounds like he was an old salt even as a young hippie, when he was tough enough (and daring enough) to drag that old tree to his new lot, chop it up, and turn it into a giant sculpture of a house — along with the mushroom shaped potter's studio next to it, and the gingerbread surf shed next to that — all from a single giant redwood that had washed ashore right there at Angel's Rest.

The tree had come down one of the cliffs in a storm, or someone way north or south had logged it decades ago and lost control of it when it got to tidewater. Either way, it had been out to sea and back for no one knows how many years, only that its rings gave away its age: 986 years.

And there it was, washed up one day in the middle of the beach at Angel's Rest, and Kenny didn't know what to do with it. The lumber companies said they could never get the very odd permit they'd need for hauling it out of there and down the PCH on a giant flatbed to the Old Creek Mill, so Kenny was thinking of setting it on fire, which would also require a permit, but not one he'd bother getting. He'd just wait for a wet couple of days with a steady marine layer to cover the smoke and smell.

Which is when Michael happened to be down there surfing. He had just tapped himself out buying that lot; he was living there, in a tent, and trying to figure out how to find the money to build a house on it. And just like magic, 5,000 board feet of old growth redwood washed up on the beach.

If a timber company couldn't figure out how to wrangle a permit out of the county, the state, and the California Coastal Commission, then Michael sure as hell never would; so he didn't bother trying. He just waited until it was 3 A.M. one night, when he and a buddy with a huge flatbed and another buddy with an end-loader dragged it off the beach; chained and loaded it onto the truck in front of Neptune's; snuck it up the empty PCH at 15 mph; and dropped it on his lot and the empty meadow behind it.

For the next 21 years, he would mill the entire tree, with a chainsaw, right there on the lot, building and ornamenting as he went. And 21 years later, he didn't just have a house: he had a big, roomy, elaborate homestead, handcrafted from twice as much wood as necessary into what was more work of art than house, shaped like a mythic ship from a thing still living, a place worthy of that view and that tree.

People joke that it's Michael's "ark," with the ocean forever chewing away at the road out front. But the boat part is just for show, and Michael says if the ocean gets too close, he will just hoist the whole damn thing and move it down to Angel's Rest with us.

Oh well. So much for that plan.


HARRRUUUNA!

I'm jolted from standing on the coast trail in front of *Michael's Magic House* by that old-fashioned car horn and look up from the brochures spread out on the table.

It's Johnny's car — the enormous vintage 50's Cadillac he converted to biodiesel and painted pitch black — pulling up to the check-in over by the treeline, between a big camper van and small tour bus, sticking his head out the window, yelling at somebody. Classic rock star car: like something out of a movie, but politically correct, with that obnoxious old horn in case you hadn't noticed it.

I watch him pull in down in the camping area for bands and vendors, and don't feel like dealing with him yet; so I wander the other way, into the festival meadow, fast filling up with people, blankets, lawn chairs.

I drift past the vendors lined up along the back edge of the meadow, under that long line of towering cedars. People in denim, tie-dye, rainbow, hemp, and lots of hair scurry to set up stalls and tables in even brighter colors: veggie burritos, pottery, art, bumperstickers, *Save the Trees!*, hempy clothing, crystals, kombucha, *Oceankeepers*, hempy hats, veggie stir fry, weird woodwork, more pottery, more kombucha, *Restore our Salmon*, tarot card readings, henna tattoos, incense, *Save the Planet!* It's another bizarre bazaar, like the merch tables at Amrita's shows and the yoga festivals, but with all the *OMs* on the hats, t-shirts and tapestries swapped out for peace signs and green and blue earths.

Then that horn again, *HARRRUUUNA!* down the hill. That means it's time to punch in.

The rest of the band is probably here by now, or should be, and I should check in on Johnny's mood. We will need to get together not just for a soundcheck, but for a full rehearsal somewhere, before we dare go on tonight and close out the show without embarrassing ourselves. We've never done two of those three old songs as a group, and none of us have even heard some new song Johnny said he's just written, just for this festival.

Halfway down the hill, I can see Sam's van over near mine, in the shade of that massive oak tree, and he and Bill out front. Johnny's car is sitting off by itself, right in the middle of the sun-drenched field, and he's leaning against the front of it, yelling into his cell phone.

"Who's he yelling at?" I ask when I walk up to Sam and Bill.

"Take a wild guess," Sam says, another old denim shirt hanging off his rail-thin frame and acoustic guitar slung over his back.

"We rehearsing anytime soon?" I ask.

"We'd better," Bill says, scratching at something between the pearly buttons of his shirt, then going to light the cigarette in his mouth.

"Alright, boys," the voice barrels across the field.

We all turn to see Johnny storming straight over at us, black denim and black t-shirt and that old hat down over his aviator sunglasses.

"Rehearsal time. Mike's got our shit put together over in that old barn over there."

As much as "that old barn" looks like a movie prop from across the meadow of this tree museum, it's actually still a working barn. Chickens run in and out of its dusty shafts of light, and an old cow in a pen over in the corner stares at us as we plug in and warm up, mooing with the cacophony of amps, drums, fiddle strokes, and mike feedback.

"Good to have an audience, huh?" Ralphie jokes, pointing at her with a drumstick.

Bill laughs and bangs out on his keyboard the opening lines of the song about Mrs. O'Leary's cow, knocking over that lantern in her barn and starting the great Chicago fire.

"Hilarious," Johnny barks at him, but Bill keeps playing it.

Curtis tips his cowboy hat to cover his eyes, pushes his fiddle into his neck, and turns away to play the melody along with Bill.

"Knock it off!" Johnny growls.

The music stops, except for Ralphie, behind his drums in his usual tank top and sweatbands, testing each with a single beat.

I strap into my bass, cut the feed, check the tuning, then bring it up.

Johnny's phone rings, and he scowls at it, but walks out of the barn to take the call.

"Oh well," Curtis says, and launches into a fiddle tune off his mike.

Sam plays something to himself.

Ralphie and Bill check their own phones.

The cow gives me a baleful look, like she wants me to milk her, or make them stop making all this racket, or both.

*Sorry*, I say back with my eyes, and turn my bass on, just loud enough for me to hear, and run through the lines and phrases for the first of those the new-old songs. I slowly crank it up, knowing they will follow me, and one by one they do.

"Where'd you pick up that one? Used record store?" Sam jokes, as he steps over to Johnny's mike.

The next time around, he jumps in and sings it, almost exactly like Johnny did on that old record. Everybody opens up and the song fills the barn, worn and warm as these old timbers, mixing with the dust in the sunlight that spills down from the hayloft window.

We run through the other two new-old songs, Sam singing Johnny's parts, except when he's singing his harmony part to Johnny's melody, and they sound perfect in here: warm, cozy, and uncomplicated, like old photos of a life before it got messy, one you never had, but believe somebody once did.

When we're done, the whole barn is bathed in the lingering glow of the music, a sweet hum in the dust dancing upward into that light.

"So . . ."

I look down and they're all looking over at me, as if I were in charge.

"What?"

"What do you think, Jack?"

"I think we should just keep practicing. But I'm the new guy, and this is all new stuff to me."

"Cool," Ralphie says. "And speakin' of new stuff, you guys heard that new song of his yet?"

"Nope."

"Nope."

"Not me."

"Well to hell with it then," Ralphie says, "let's just play the set. 'Carolina Jane,'" he says and counts off the beat, "one, two, three . . ."

We play through the entire set, with Sam singing all of Johnny's parts, except for two songs with harmony all the way through, and Bill sings lead on those. Everything except "Sunset Road," which they've all come to despise, because it's the one song they've done at every single gig, as an encore, for the last thirty years.

When we're done, Sam pulls off his guitar and heads out to take a piss. Curtis is off on his own, playing a fiddle tune for the cow and chickens. Bill studies his phone, Ralphie's on the phone with someone back home, and Mike is re-stringing one of Johnny's guitars. Which reminds me of the real reason I got this job.

"Hey you guys," I say and pull my bass off. "We really ought to run through that new song and not just wing in front a crowd. Sit tight and I'll go find him."

Outside, Johnny is maybe 20 yards away, sitting cross-legged in the dust under an enormous red cedar, yelling into his phone at what I can hear from all the way over here is Gordon.

He waves me over, and I go sit next to him, Gordon still yelling back as Johnny hangs up.

"I hate that prick," Johnny blurts out, sighs, then turns to me, "I hate that he makes me give a shit about the money again."

"What's he doing?"

"Taking his cut for what woulda been the Idaho State Fair, out of what's coming from last quarter's gigs. It's not even five grand, but he's gotta make his fuckin' point."

"Well that sucks," I say because it's all about de-escalation right now. I'll check in with Gordon later.

"But don't worry," Johnny turns to me, trying to assure me with eyes I can't see because of his sunglasses. "I'll make you all whole. He's pulling the 15% back from you guys too."

"Huh," I say, rather than what I'm thinking, which is *Fuck you, Gordon, and good on you, Johnny.*

We sit there a minute, and I tip my head to look up at the cedar, its smoky sweet bark streaking red and brown up into long drapes of green.

He sighs and kicks his feet out in front of him.

"So," I finally say with a sigh. "The band sounds great. Ran through the whole set list, so we can just do a quick check-in. And run through that new song of yours — if we are, uh, really doing that."

"Aw, man! I can't sing that song right now," he says. "It's too real and raw. And I'm too pissed at that bastard for making me give a shit about money."

"Yeah, well. Money's funny that way."

He takes off his sunglasses and turns to study my face a minute. His wrinkled, sunken, darkened eyes show every last one of his 66 years and that last very tough rehab.

"Money'll destroy a man's soul, Jack. It's a false god, the Golden Calf, the thing that tears apart families, eats up the planet, sucks the life out of art. Money ruins everything."

"Yeah, but it can also protect a lot of things. Like these trees right here."

"Yeah," Johnny almost smiles, then leans back on the tree. "And it gives you a little breathing room to write a song because it's true, not because anyone's gonna buy it." He closes his eyes. "I'm just disappointed, Jack. Gordon used to know it was all about the music. Never ripped me off, always kept that shit at bay. But he's turned into just another fucking suit." He opens his eyes and almost smiles again, right at me. "At least he had the sense to hire you to babysit me."

We never do get to hear, let alone rehearse, that new song.

I have Johnny halfway to the barn when Gordon calls again about another thing, and that's the last anybody sees of Johnny until five minutes before we go on.

The green room is a canopy behind the stage, where Johnny finally warms up his voice as we sing through the first song with just the guitars.

Sam and Bill give me the look, so I blurt out, "So how about we do that new song?"

"Don't worry about that, you guys," Johnny says. "It's a raw thing, so why not keep it that way? Give it an old coffeehouse vibe, like a jam."

"Great," Sam mumbles and rolls his eyes. "A coffeehouse with a thousand people who paid 30 bucks to get in."

Johnny ignores him. "Couldn't be simpler, boys. It's in C, one part, ballad tempo, straight up one–four–five." Then he punches Sam on the arm. "Woody Guthrie, man. 'Three chords and the truth.' Like your old punk bands."

"Yeah, yeah," Sam mutters through what I can see is him trying his best not to smile.

Five minutes later, we're walking out onto the stage — a small one, maybe two feet off the ground and just wide enough to hold the five of us — and all of it, the stage, the crowd, all the trees, are bathed in a sea of sunset color.

There's no marine layer tonight, just high thin clouds coming in from over the ocean behind us, a riot of brushstrokes over the top of this whole meadow and draw, all the way to the wooded ridge past the audience. They're streaked with orange and rose, and bathe all the cedars at the other end of the meadow a burning magenta.

We plug in, Ralphie counts, and Sam kicks off the first one. We're nearly halfway through before Johnny makes his usual mid-song entrance. But he doesn't run or strut or bow or point or do any of his usual stuff; he just sort of ambles out, smiles, and waves. And the crowd doesn't roar; it applauds; and he tips his head.

Sam catches my eye and tips his head to say, *Huh. This is nice. Let's pull it back a little.*

He and I pull the tempo back a smidge, a little softer, a little quieter, the band follows, and everything flushes with that ghostly, fading color.

The stage is perfect for right here and right now, decorated with dozens of downed cedar boughs, and rainbow tapestries, the backdrop behind us a giant tree-of-life tapestry. I turn with the beat and take it in: forest-green and golden-brown and brick-red tree, and symmetrical top to bottom, with roots in heaven and branches on earth. Like what Rabbi Miriam used to say about *Etz Chayim*, the Tree of Life, the menorah, an upside down tree, with roots in heaven. Yes!

I turn back with the beat, and the crowd is beaming like they all do, sitting or sprawled out on blankets and singing along, dancers off to the sides, hula hoopers in the back. Lots of old hippies and young kids too; lots of tanned and smiling faces; lots of hair.

We play through the set list, and with almost no crowd noise and no back wall of the casino or convention center bouncing it back at us, we can hear just how warm and good and relaxed everything sounds.

When Sam plays the opening riff to the last song before the first walk-off, Johnny stops him mid-intro.

"Hold on a second there, fellas," he says, holding up his hands, his acoustic guitar dangling from his shoulders. "Just a minute."

He adjusts the mike, like he's about to launch into a story or, worse, a tirade. But his face is as relaxed as I've ever seen it onstage, and don't think he's going there.

He pulls off his sunglasses and sticks them up on his hat, then hoists his guitar into position.

The rest of the band is staring at him too, wondering.

Johnny closes his eyes and nods with his breaths, in and out, and starts picking out what sounds like a lullaby. It's in C, the slow, lilting tempo of a ballad.

Then he starts singing . . .

> *This old house*
> *Standing next to that tree*
> *Getting smaller and older and sweeter each and every day*
> *Waiting for the rain*
> *Waiting for the wind*
> *Another winter or two with these children away*
>
> *This old world*
> *Spinning round and round*
> *How many fires and how many floods till it's blown away?*
> *Cuz this old tree*
> *Was a friend of mine*
> *With birds that sing and leaves that bring*
> *Stories from the centuries*

Then the chorus, his head lifting and voice filling with a weary cry . . .

> *This old tree reaches for the sky, reaches for the light*
> *Wasn't he supposed to live?*
> *Wasn't he supposed to live?*

*Wasn't he supposed to live?*
*So much longer than you and me . . .*

The raw ache in his voice, without artifice or anger — just the resignation of an old man on the porch of an old house looking back on his life — shatters me as my fingers tip-toe the bass notes. Stay out of the way, Jack, make room for the old man to tell his story, let his tears flow.

Another verse, and that heartbreak of a chorus again. It's all I can do not to choke up and start crying, so I stare down at my fingers on the strings until the final hold.

The crowd slowly unfolds into applause, and I look over and see Sam and Curtis standing there, both of their mouths hanging open and eyes moist.

Sam finally turns to me and mouths *Wow.*

The next morning, after a long hard sleep in the van under *this* old tree, I wake up and the rest of the band is already gone.

An hour later, I'm thinking about packing up, but I'm still spread out on my camp table with coffee and my guitar and a book when this little kid walks up to me.

He's skinny, maybe eight, nine years old, with huge, unblinking brown eyes that make it hard to notice anything else about him. This kid can stare.

They usually do this only when I'm up on a smaller stage or the *bima*, before or after the show or service, while I'm futzing with something. Some kid or two would always do that at *Shir Hadash*: walk up, wide-eyed, watch me warming up or cooling down on the guitar, and try to piece together what they're seeing my hands do while hearing all this musical sound come out of this — shiny wooden *thing!*

But this kid is just staring at me, not at the guitar. And he's wearing a vendor's badge, down around his knees, which looks absurdly large next to his skinny legs.

Now I remember him. He was upfront last night, a bunch of kids dancing and jumping around him, just standing and staring up at us, especially Ralphie banging away on the drums.

"Hey," I say to him.

"Hi," he says and waves. "I saw you in the band last night."

"What d'you think?"

"What?"

I have no idea how to talk to children. "Um. Did you like the music?"

"I like music when there is the band there."

"We call that 'live music.'"

"Yes," he says. "I like live music. I can see how — I can feel when —"

"Do you play music?"

"At my school, and with my papaw. He has a big drum."

He claps his hands slowly — tiny brownish-red hands, lacquered with a weekend of camping in a dusty meadow — to a slow, steady one–two beat.

"Hold that thought," I say, and go into my van for a little hand djembe I keep around for just such campsite occasions.

And like maybe five times out of a couple dozen tries with kids on the *bima*, that little kid was right there on the drum. With my count, 1, 2, 3, a perfect steady drumbeat from those little hands.

I picked up the guitar and played a march and he was still right there following: *faster, slower, faster, faster, faster, and out!*

He puts the drum down, and turns to go, like he's late for something, or in trouble.

"I'm Jack," I go to shake his hand. "What's your name?"

"Tommy," he says. But just stares at my hand, then looks over his shoulder.

"Well, it's good to meet you, Tommy," I turn to put my guitar in the case. "You keep playing on that drum, and maybe —," and as I turn back around, and he's gone.

I pack slowly, no hurry to go anywhere today, and I like it here, as people all around me pack up their cars and vans and pull out of the meadow.

But no sign of that kid. Weird. Oh well.

I finish loading the van and start across the meadow to grab a coffee from one of the vendors still open.

"Jack!"

It's a little kid's voice.

I turn and there he is, his little hand half holding and half pulling a woman — denim shirt, black jeans, silver and turquoise beads, and boots — toward me. A beautiful woman, with long black hair and a very serious look on a cinnamon and chocolate colored face.

She looks mortified when they walk up, avoiding my eyes and shrugging a half smile. "I'm sorry about this," she says. "He said I had to meet the rock star from last night."

I remember her too, not from the show last night, but from the booths in the back yesterday. She was behind the table at the one for Salmon Restoration Project, explaining how they were lobbying to de-commission a dam to bring salmon back up their native river north of here.

I hung back, listening as she told a couple people about the salmon project for a solid ten minutes, because I was more than a little mesmerized by her. And not just because she's beautiful — dark, curvy, almond eyes, and all that long black hair down the back of her denim shirt — but because she reminded me of Jill and the other Bettys back in Colorado. She had that exact same physical intensity, rooted where she stood but poised to spring, a grounded, twitchy confidence that says *Don't even think about fucking with me.*

But I also noticed yesterday, and now really see why, she looks nothing like the Colorado Bettys, or anyone else I know or have known — since the girls from the Iroquois reservation who played basketball in the next town over and always beat the crap out of our high school girls' team. But all grown up now, into a woman who'd be coaching that team.

"Eve," she says, and thrusts her hand out to shake mine. "Tommy said I had to meet you."

"Jack," I say and shake her hand. It's warm and strong and feels good in my hand, and I can feel it buzzing in mine long after she's pulled it away.

"Mom!" he turns to her and pleads. "Not just *meet* him. For the hike! With everybody!"

"Oh, that's right," she says. "I'm also supposed to invite you for the walk, over in the preserve, with the caretakers. If you'd like to join us."

# 8 | ÚYTAAHKOO

"The Iroquois," I thought I knew to answer.

"You mean the *Haudenosaunee*," Eve corrected me, in the first five minutes of that odd, tentative, flirty but still deadly serious first phone call, the day after I get back to Angel's Rest. "The people who build a house."

She'd just asked me straight out, not *Where are you from?* or *Where did you grow up?* but "Whose land did you grow up on?"

My wrong answer was right enough though, because a few days later, I was meeting up with her and Tommy in a park over in Oakland. They were down from Humboldt visiting her sister, and why not? *Just to hang out*, she said and I said, though not sure which of us said it first. I had nothing else to do that weekend besides sit around Angel's Rest waiting for good waves and worrying about when we're getting kicked out.

But even after two more calls, which went on late into the evening — which made it feel like she was there with me, hanging out on the porch, watching the sun set over the ocean — the meet-up in the park over in Oakland "wasn't a date," I was informed.

"Because I don't date white guys," she explained, five minutes after I got to the park and Tommy asked me if I brought the drum before running off to play with his cousins.

"Fine with me," I told her as we sat and swayed on two swings, "because I don't really 'date' people, because it's too much like going on a job interview."

So it seemed settled. Until she looked over to see Tommy running around with the dogs and other kids at the far end of the park, then bumped me with her swing, and I bumped her back, and then she was spinning and bumping me with her foot, and we were swinging into each other and laughing like teenagers.

As she brushed right past me the first time, I caught the whiff of something like a scent from her hair, her skin, her breath, and it made something buried in my chest spring open. I timed my own swing past her, wanting more, taking a deep breath for more. But as she brushed past again, I realized it wasn't a scent at all; it was something that entered my body the same way and set it on fire. I was suddenly a 13-year-old boy and she was the most beautiful girl in school, the same age as me but way cooler.

And then she stopped my swing with her foot, and leaned in quickly to kiss me, furtively, smile, and kiss me again — then Tommy's voice shouting over there with the other kids — and she smiled again and kicked my swing away, and that was the end of it.

After that first not-a-date, our calls turned into a habit, almost every night. At first I chalked them up to mutual fascination: our lives could not be more different. Eve is a single parent and a schoolteacher, and lives in a house with Tommy — which they share with one of her cousins and her own daughter — in the same small town where their grandparents lived for decades. I'm single, and purposefully childless, and don't have a real job, and am living off the grid with a bunch of random people in a cottage falling into the ocean, and haven't seen anyone in my own family in more than a decade.

Except maybe our lives aren't completely different, as we found out during a marathon call, when I was stuck in a hotel room in Sedona for a gig with Amrita and she was stuck in a casino hotel up north for a tribal meeting. We'd both fled crazy parents in our teens and married in our early 20s for the exact same reason — because we were broke and alone in a strange city, and desperate to find a way to get the college degree that was the ticket out — and we both got divorced when most people were just settling down and having kids. We've each lost someone since: Leah to cancer; and Tommy's father to drunk driving. And we'd both run off by the age of 40, for solace and sanctuary from the once-strange city, to the mountains, trees, ocean. Her flight brought her full circle, to a big extended family up in Humboldt, while mine brought me west, to the end of the line, and a solar family of misfits at Angel's Rest.

I've never been much for the phone — it's too easy to pretend you're there when you're not — but with Eve I haven't been pretending. She could tell if I were, and I know she wouldn't hesitate to say so. But I've looked forward to those calls all day long — even if for just a few minutes because Tommy doesn't want to go to bed.

Every day for a couple weeks now, I'm driving or just staring out at the ocean, wondering what odd piece of my complicated life I might share with her next, and what piece of hers my story might shake loose. Because half of what she has to say is a surprise, and everything she has to say is interesting. Maybe that's just an occupational hazard: she teaches American history at the high school up in Fortuna; and I've been obsessed with the history of the American West since I was a little kid back East, reading all about it — the old authorized version, of course, back then — and conjuring what pieces of it I could in the woods all around our little town. Eve is also active in that salmon restoration project from the Cedar Crossing gig, and a couple other rights' reclamations with the Karuk tribe up north and the Ohlone tribe down in the Bay Area, not just conjuring but effecting real-time revisions to that old authorized version.

Or maybe I just like the sound of her voice.

Because there's music in the way she unfurls a sentence, something I noticed when we were walking through the preserve that morning: her voice is steady, insistent, direct, staccato almost, but then rises near the end of a sentence or story, like a Hebrew blessing, from the particulars of here and now to something like a rhetorical flourish at the end, an open question, an ellipsis . . .

"I do not know exactly," she said on that first call when I asked her the second question — after whose land *she* grew up on, the Ohlones, in Oakland — about her ethnicity. "Even with the DNA tests. As Native people, we are still lumped together as just that. Native. There were just a few California rancherias, or reservations, and so few people were left, and so many came back from somewhere else. They inter-married across the tribes, outside the tribes, with the whites, with whoever was just there."

Then a long pause on the phone.

It could have meant anything from *And you are white and single, and you are just there* to *It's past Tommy's bedtime and he's negotiating again* and I found myself holding my breath.

"But the family," she finally continued, "believes my mother's mother was Ohlone, and her father was Karuk. On my father's side, the tests cannot say who is *Californio* and who is just Mexican. They did not own land, only worked it, so there is no record."

"Like my grandparents on my mother's side," I told her, treading lightly, because my grandparents — as poor and desperate as they were — were white immigrants, so my family was shitted on for only the one generation before turning around and shitting on everybody of color.

"How is that?"

"They were teenagers in Italy, from really poor families during the war, and brought over to live and work on the big estates up the river from New York. Seven years to work off their passage."

Another long silence.

"Really," she finally said. "They were indentured servants. That is very interesting."

And it was interesting. But at that moment I'd just been whisked off the call and off my porch to maybe 50 feet out from the beach, watching the birds descend to mark the spot, and then the whale rise, a humpback, and another, rising to feed.

"Where did you go, Jack?" her voice cut through what always looks like a dream I'm having when I see whales rise.

"A pod of humpbacks. No more than 50 feet from the beach down here, breaching and feeding."

"Are there birds?"

"Yes, that's how I spotted them."

"So . . . anchovies then. That is too close in. And it is too early for humpbacks."

"I know."

"But it does sound beautiful down there," she said.

"It is."

Another long pause, then she said, "Will I get to see it someday?"

"I sure hope so."

Then the longest pause of all, awkward for not being awkward but for the sudden tease in the silence, the little tug in my chest — and the yearning I thought I could feel coming back from the other end.

"And so, all of that," she finally stammered, "all of it, is off the grid? All year around?"

"Yes," I said. And then felt a sudden panic: she and Tommy *must* get down here and see Angel's Rest before we all got kicked out.

"Self-sustaining. Very good. And you did not have to put up a casino," she joked. "Who knew."

I do like the sound of her voice.

Or maybe I just like her.

Or maybe it's just fascination.

But I suppose we are about to find out. Because after two weeks of those calls, and some unexpected and very steamy smooching on a park swing in Oakland, we are jumping right in: we're going on the mother of all non-dates, a whole weekend with Tommy and Eve's extended family, at a Native event up at Mt. Shasta, or *Úytaahkoo*, the "white mountain" as the Karuk call it. This will most certainly not be a date; this will be a major test.

I've rigged up a seat for Tommy in the back of the van, and he looks happy enough back there with *Musical Instruments of the World*, a big picture book I bought for him. Every now and then he leans up between our seats, and points to a page and asks Eve or me to say the name *glockenspiel* or *mandolin* or *zither*.

Eve is riding shotgun, and I can't help but steal glances at her. She's in all denim again, black jeans, jean jacket over black t-shirt, silver and turquoise and bone necklaces dangling from her neck, and the same dusty boots from Cedar Crossing. And all that black hair tussled in the wind, dancing around on that faded denim.

When we get onto I-5 and head north, she pulls off her boots, kicks back in her seat, and throws her bare feet up on the dashboard.

I try not to stare — we're hauling ass in traffic all of a sudden — but I can't help but steal glances. Her feet are a deep, warm brown, with dark blue toenails, and stained along the bottoms from going around barefoot all the time, like mine from surfing. They look strong and supple and soft, all at the same time, veined and solid but still the feet of a woman, with pretty little toes — like some of the more serious dancers or yoga teachers at one of Amrita's events — and the feet of a woman who got partway through college on a track scholarship. I have this weird, intense urge to touch them, to hold and caress and maybe even kiss them, and oh shit: she just caught me sneaking a peek and no doubt knows I'm thinking exactly that.

She gives me a little half-smile and slides her feet a little closer across the dashboard and scrunches and un-scrunches her toes.

Oh boy. Eyes on the road.

Strong and supple and soft, all at the same time indeed. That's how I describe all of her, and all of Jill, now that I think about it, and most of the other Bettys back in Colorado. But Eve has a darker, harder fire in her eyes, a steady, faraway stare. And yet, for all that intensity, there is still more patience than weariness in Eve's voice when she's answering what I know is a dumb or obvious question from me.

Which is encouraging. Because I have dozens of dumb and obvious questions about things I've always wondered from all my reading since moving west nearly two decades ago, and discovering that half of what I'd been taught about the American West was bullshit — more myth than history — and sometimes outright fiction or propaganda and not history at all.

Or maybe she really just wants to make sure I'm prepared for where we are headed right now: an annual inter-tribal gathering, in a place sacred to almost all the tribes of Northern California, a lake in the lap of *Úytaahkoo*, draped always in ice, snow, and what's left of its glaciers.

Many of these events, Eve says, are inter-tribal for the same reason she's not exactly sure about her ancestors. In California, there are only 109 federally recognized tribes left, out of some 500 tribes here before "contact" — before the Spanish came up from the south looking for gold and souls, the British from the north looking for beaver and timber, the Russians from the ocean looking for sea otter and slaves, and the Americans from back East looking for everything.

Because Eve is a history teacher, and all of this isn't just history but personal history, she's like one of those audiobooks about The West that Jill or Danny or Aaron and I would listen to on all those road trips around Colorado, the Northern Rockies, the Southwest. "The West," indeed, named by the ones who came last and took it all. I now know the histories behind so many of those false narratives about the "winning" of the west, i.e., the stealing of it, the horrific brutalities and deliberate or *de facto* exterminations by starvation, disease, predation. Many of the Native peoples, like the Cheyenne, Navajo, Lakota and Comanche, stood and fought as long as they could. Others, like the Nez Perce and Modoc, tried to run and hide as far away and for as long as they could. But they were all eventually broken, penned up, plowed under, their children kidnapped and sent away to "schools" where the "Indian" was beaten out of them.

"We were sitting ducks," Eve says, and turns to look out the window at the agri-industrial farmscape flying by at 80 mph. "Because we did not know war out here, not my people. We did not know hunger, or disease, because we had everything we needed and did not need to trade or raid or defend. The Ohlone lived all around the Bay Area, and down the coast to where you live now. The Costanoans were south of there, to Monterey Bay, and the Esselen south of there through Big Sur." She turns back to me, her eyes suddenly far away. "*That* was the California dream, Jack.

"Sitting ducks in the food-rich marshes of the San Francisco Bay," she turns back to the blur out her window. "A mild climate, oysters and clams and crabs for the taking. Acorns from all the oak trees they could mash into flour for everything else. Deer, rabbit, ducks and geese. Seals, sea lion, sea otter. Even whales washing up on the shore. The earth fed everybody who was here and they had no reason to fight."

"That why so many tribes, so close together, left each other alone?"

"Yes, exactly. Each with their own language. Tribes in the deserts and mountains, and out on the Plains, they had to spread out to find food, fight each other for it — especially after the Spanish brought horses and guns. My people did not have to go anywhere for what they needed."

Which sounds exactly like the California dream, except the part about everybody getting to speak their own language and not having to trade to eat.

"That does sound like the California dream," I say, because what else can I say. *Sorry? That sucks?*

"It *was* the California dream. Peace and plenty. But it is also why we were so easy to kill. We had bows and arrows for the deer, and spears for the fish, but we did not have war. Or immunity to anything, with no trade, and living in this easy climate."

Eve pulls her feet from the dashboard, and we drive on in silence.

"What is this one, Jack?" Tommy finally breaks it, pushing the book between us.

"Jack is driving, sweet pea. Let me see. That is a —," and she turns to me, "I don't what that is."

"That's a balalaika, a Russian instrument. Sort of like their guitar."

"Ba-la-laika," Tommy says. "That sounds funny."

I watch him in the rear-view, staring at it a moment, then going back to turning the pages We drive on in silence for minutes, Eve sitting upright and looking straight ahead. She finally kicks back in her seat, and puts her feet back on the dashboard, and I find myself oddly relieved.

I knew most of what she just said from *An American Genocide*, a grueling and detailed chronology I read when I moved out here last year. In 1769, at the point of first contact with whites, there were about 310,000 Native people in what is now California — speaking some 300 dialects of 100 different languages — and by 1846, there were 150,000, a more than 50% reduction. By 1880, just 54 years later, the census recorded only 16,277 Natives, a horrific near-95% reduction, an American genocide indeed.

Like everything else in California, the slaughter and suppression of its Natives had to be the first, the fastest, the most fantastically lied about, and then the most thoroughly forgotten. The Karuk, now with fewer than 5,000 registered members like Eve, is one of the largest to survive the genocidal onslaught of violence, disease, enslavement, and starvation from the four directions.

But that genocide was the outcome, the *after*. I hadn't ever really imagined the *before*, what all of this might have looked and felt like before that fateful first contact. But just imagine, in their pristine state: all these rugged mountains and rolling rivers, all those soaring stretches of coastline, and miles of grass-lined bayshore, and wave after wave of golden hills. Nothing here but dancing oaks and towering cedar and redwood, and birds and game and fish and shellfish for the taking, and no one here but small bands of people strung along the same margins — where water meets land and every sunset is a work of art — where everyone *still* wants to live. I can't imagine this idyllic *before* any more than I can imagine California even a generation or two ago, without 40 million people here tailgating each other in an angry rush for more money and a few selfies next to the ocean.

Back East, the *before* is most of what I knew about the Haudenosaunee, even though they were all around me. Our town was next to the Onondaga reservation; there was the big troubled kid from over there who worked at the gas station in town and everybody picked on; and lacrosse — their ancient game — was the status sport in my high school. And there was Little Ray, also from over on the rez; I worked with him washing dishes, my first restaurant job. He was still washing dishes two years later, when I finished high school and got out of there forever.

Little Ray, not to be confused with his father Big Ray, even though he'd died of a heroin overdose after coming back from Vietnam. I used to ask him if they ever dressed like that over on the rez, in the buckskins, with the long hair and war paint and feathers.

He just stared at me and said "All the Indians I know dress like me."

Which is to say they dressed like me too back then, in whatever jeans and t-shirts and flannel shirts were on sale at Sears or Penneys.

But their *before* was in the woods all around me, literally strewn through the woods outside the town where I grew up. The "Iroquois" — as the French had named them, everybody called them, and they called themselves back then — had been invaded from every direction, by the French, then the British, then the Americans. But they lived in a tough climate and had already known war, among themselves and with neighboring tribes before first contact. They had found a way to make peace among themselves, forming a confederacy of five (and eventually six) tribes to stand as one, while the French and British and Americans fought it out among themselves. And they learned early on to take whichever side promised them, in the decade and region at hand, the least destruction.

I knew the outlines of those stories from every book on the Iroquois I could find in our town library, devoured after a school field trip out to a longhouse excavation. They were the same woods I'd been playing in — hiding in, really — since I was old enough, seven or eight, I think, to run off for the day when things between my parents got ugly. In those woods, until I was twelve or thirteen and saved up enough for my first bike, I was surrounded by the Iroquois of my imagination, and I was safe.

The woods began where our street dead-ended, a couple hundred feet away. It was an easy sprint off into the sudden quiet of all those oaks, maples, sycamores, pines. Everything was green canopy and silence, with footpaths and deer trails I knew better than the streets of that town, the quiet giving way to birdsong and skitterings through fallen leaves. It was in those woods, when I was maybe nine or ten and pretending to run away from home — dreaming of when I'd be big enough to run away for real and somehow survive out there — that I first came across the Presence.

I could not see or hear the Presence — and back then I certainly had no name for it — but I knew it was there. And I knew it was aware of me, watching over me, wanting me to know in what sounded like my own voice but wasn't: *No, you cannot run away to these woods and survive, not just yet. But you will be alright. You will be. Just hang on.*

What I have since come to know as the Presence wanted me to know that it was not me who was stupid, or weak, or bad, no matter what they screamed at me every day; that my father was just a crazy, mean drunk who had made my frail, hobbled, helpless mother crazy and mean too; and that one day I would grow up and be able to run away forever, if only I could just hang on a few more years.

Twenty feet through that curtain of leaves it all just fell away, dropped along a quiet path through a break in the trees and into the woods. And then more and more woods, and a waterfall on the creek running through it all, always there, spilling into a little pool, all of it a million miles from the world. I would run off and scheme and dream in those woods, always about how I would one day run off for good.

But I was never out there alone. I was out there with all those Iroquois — I mean Haudenosaunee — along with Daniel Boone, Davy Crockett, Jim Bridger, the

Last of the Mohicans, Eagle Feather, Ishi "The Last of his Tribe," and all the cool kids I "met" in the pages of *Boys' Life* magazine, every issue devoured the first day it showed up in the school library. They showed me how to build shelters, start fires, dig pits for food, how to keep warm and dry and fed out there when the snow started falling. Huck Finn in particular helped me figure out how to survive on the run: how the next year, when I ran away for good, I could wander into town in the middle of the night for food and supplies, steal what I needed and sneak back out, and no one would ever know. I could live like a Haudenosaunee, the one who survived, like Ishi, and they'd never catch me.

Better still, I figured out after reading *Huck Finn* in ninth grade, that I could be just like him: the cleverest kid ever, the one who tricked his drunken father into thinking he was dead, and said *fuck you all, I'm outta here!*

In that very first conversation with Eve, I told Eve all about Little Ray and his father and my stupid questions and his funny answers. But what I really wanted to tell her about was that big kid from the rez who worked at the gas station. About how he never looked you in the eye, and always got picked on because he was big and slow and wouldn't fight back. Or about that stinking hot summer day, when I saw two bullies I hated from school — one of whom went on to be the big lacrosse star of our high school team, of course — corner him outside the dairy store, and slap him around to give up the big bag of candy he'd just bought. About how I stepped in and just stared them down, my eye-of-the-shitstorm mode in beta testing, all the way back in eighth grade.

That was the one thing I'd ever done right by any of the people on whose land I grew up, which wasn't much of anything. But I didn't tell Eve the story because I was certain she would think it was too preposterous to be true, that I'd made it up to impress her, to win a few Friend of the Indian points — a rez-cred bullshit story from just another appropriating spiritual tourist. No wonder she doesn't date white guys: they probably all have a story like mine, real or imagined.

So in that first conversation, I stuck to what I knew from the books — the data, the massacres, the epidemiology, all the genocides — and what I knew from the woods growing up: the longhouse excavation, the remnants of the fishing weirs in the creeks, the pieces of arrowheads and scraping tools I found. And about the lacrosse sticks the kids from the rez played with, hand-carved from ash by their grandfathers, baskets of rawhide and leather, fast as whips. They always crushed the snotty kids from my high school — with their shiny new plastic sticks, pricey cleats, summer lacrosse camps — running up and down the field in their converse knock-offs from Sears and unloading shot after deadly shot from those beautiful wooden sticks.

But beyond that, I dared not tell Eve that I *know* anything about what any Natives have ever been through because, compared to what she knows in her bones, in her genetics and epigenetics, I know absolutely nothing. Which is why, when she's telling me stories, I've just been listening and saying, *Yeah, I read about that . . . the slaughter at Sand Creek . . . at Wounded Knee . . . the Trail of Tears . . . the crushing of the Hopi . . . Chief Joseph almost making it to Canada . . .* knowing only from books those heart-shattering and horrific stories, written in the bright red blood of children, too young for the slave and sex trade, clubbed to death to save the bullets.

Because she really was testing me, at first anyway. And in the last few conversations this week, after she'd invited me to this gathering up north, I think she's been trying to condition me, for whatever stories of rage and pain I might hear this weekend, trying to scare me with the ugliest episodes in American history. Or maybe scare me off with how militant she can sound about all of it. Or both.

But yes, I've told her: I know. Or at least I *know* to the extent anyone can know from all those books I read or listened to on long drives, exactly how the West was "won": with starvation, alcohol, and disease; with humiliation, torture, and murder; with treaty pens filled with poisoned and/or powerless ink.

I also know that, because this is California, all of it happened out here in overdrive. What Eve just said about the climate, and how it made the Natives out here defenseless, is what accelerated their dispossession and destruction. Because unlike deer, or sea otter pelts, or old growth trees next to a waterway, or gold tumbling down a mountain stream, this soft, sweet, easy climate is — or was, back then — an inexhaustible resource. Unlike out on the Plains or up in the mountains, California's invaders wouldn't just steal all the beavers, bison, timber, gold, silver and copper and then move on from the pile of rotting corpses and toxic mining slag. They would come here, and covet the place itself, not just its resources, and seize all of it forever, just like people still covet this place today. *Because it's always so beautiful out here!*

How could the Natives stand up to any of that? To all those soldiers of fortune, greedy for instant wealth? To all those priests, greedy for untamed souls? To a European nation so drunk — half a world away — on the competitive power and mobilizing fantasies of imperialism, that it would dream up the goddess Calafia, all the way back at the beginning of the 1500s?

The "savages" they found out here were indeed "sitting ducks," as Eve says, living in peace in every sea cove, in every wooded draw up into the coastal mountains, in every Angel's Rest from San Diego to Oregon. And they could be taken in a season, by boat or boot, sword, cross, or pox.

"It's amazing any of your people lasted as long as they did," I said in that very first conversation, "given the circumstances."

"What choice did they have? What choice does anybody have? Up north, the Modoc and the Pit Rivers tried to fight back. Up into southern Oregon, they hid out in a maze of lava beds, in a desert that goes hundreds of miles in three directions. They held off for 185 days. Some 80 Modoc warriors, against 1,000 bluecoats. Because we tried to defend what was ours, and scare off those who would take it, and they called us the savages, the aggressors. The Spanish, and the Americans? They were just defending themselves, you know. By rounding us up, breaking us, killing us if they had to.

"Original sin, twice over," she said. "Slavery *and* genocide. They said they wanted our souls, and maybe they did. But what they really wanted was slaves. All those missions? Just another lie. In the 1930s, there were the Okies. Displaced, expendable, migrant labor, on ruined land. Now, there are wage-slaves from Mexico and Central America. Back then, the priests said they wanted to save our souls, even if it killed us in the process. But when the Spanish army caught up with the priests, and saw what they were doing, they took over, and turned us into slaves. There have always been slaves in California. We were just the first."

And the Catholic Church just made Junipero Serra a saint. The eighteenth-century priest who founded and designed every mission from San Diego to San Francisco around one thing: the whipping post. (Apparently, he had a special taste for the whip, which he liked to use on himself whenever he felt a tickle of savagery in his own loins.) The priest with a major road up and down the coast named after him, along the route of those old missions.

But it's easy for the millions of annual visitors to the missions to miss all that, as I discovered when I was checking out the one in the picturesque little college town of San Luis Obispo. A quick glance at a historic diorama of any mission, and it's easy to overlook or mistake the whipping post sitting out in front — where countless human beings were lashed, often to death, or lashed and left out to die and rot in the sun — because it looks like a cross.

Ugh.

And here I was, feeling all bulky because I stepped in, once, for a helpless Haudenosaunee kid getting picked on by a couple jocks from my middle school.

Now, I just feel like throwing up.

"How's it going back there, sweet pea?" Eve's voice jolts me from the horrible image of all those mission whipping posts, painted black with dried blood, that I've been carrying around since San Luis Obispo.

There's no answer.

We both turn to look, bump heads and laugh.

Tommy is asleep in his seat, the book slipped from his lap onto the floor of the van next to the little djembe I'd left out for him before I picked them up.

He looks so small and skinny and vulnerable, strapped by himself into that big seat. The sight of him like that flushes me with something I don't understand, something that feels like the adrenaline that comes with eye-of-the-shitstorm mode — except I don't know where the attack is coming from, and all I want to do is scoop up that little boy and shield him from all sides against it.

Eve gives me her biggest half-smile yet. But then she must be reading all of that on my face, because her smile crumbles into something like worry, and she turns quickly back to the road.

Ten minutes later, we are turning off I-5, heading down a highway south of Mount Shasta, I mean *Úytaahkoo*. In between breaks in the massive trees, the mountain explodes out of the earth, capped with gleaming ice, the sun screaming off what's left of its snowfields.

Eve tells me to turn left down a dirt road unmarked but for its forest service number, and we head up a long draw up forest service roads into the mountains. Then more forest service roads, but these ones are marked with hand-lettered signs saying *Antler Lake Gathering* in English and in what must be Native languages.

I feel my gut tighten a bit. I have no idea what to expect up here. Will this be a few dozen people, a few hundred, a few thousand? And how many white people? Half the crowd? A handful? Or just me? Will they be posers, hippie shamans, spiritual tourists like so many who wander through two or three of Amrita's events, ingratiate themselves with the Acoladies and Old Hempy Dudes, and are never seen again? And will Eve's friends think I'm another one of them, another white wanderer looking for a quick soul-trip?

"You OK?"

I look over and Eve is studying me.

So much for the poker-face that got me through years of corporate life, countless hours on the *bima* with Rabbi Miriam, and all those times onstage when Johnny melting down or Amrita was flying away. I don't know how Eve knows when I'm spinning — we met all of a month ago — but she does. Radhe, Leah, Jill, all the way back to my ex-wife? None of them could do that. And it made all of them a little crazy, especially when the next thing that came out of my mouth was exactly not what they wanted to hear.

Then another half-smile, this one seeming to say, *Don't worry. Just be who you are. This will be fine.*

It feels good to be seen like that. I think.

"I know," I say out loud. "I'm psyched."

"Psyched is good," she says. "But it is also OK to be nervous. This is a big deal. Most white people would not be comfortable doing this, even if they thought they were second coming of Kevin Costner in *Dance with Wolves*. Some people will pretend you are not there at all, and it won't matter when they see that you are with me. But you are with me, and with Tommy."

I don't know what to say so I don't say anything.

There is another sign, pointing down a rutted road through a massive stand of red cedar and blue spruce.

As we turn and go through the break in the trees, I hear the jangle of silver before I feel her hand, Eve reaching across the big gap between our seats, the bracelets dropping from her sleeve as her hand — warm, brown, female, and sexy-strong, like her feet — finds my knee.

"You have a good heart, Jack," she squeezes. "That is the only thing that matters up here. I see that, and they will too."

"Thanks," I say, because what else can I say?

"I also know that you are not afraid of a tough crowd."

"How do you know that?"

"I saw you on YouTube."

"Seriously? At some gig with Johnny melting down?"

"No," she says, "one of your old business presentations. When things were not going well with the Wall Street people. You and your boss, getting yelled at by those preppie jackasses."

"With Tom? You looked me up on YouTube?"

She gave me that half-smile. "I just wanted to see you one night."

"Back in that old world? That was not me at my best."

"Yes it was," she says. "Those people were vicious. Your boss rolled over, but you stood your ground. Made me feel proud. You'll be fine here. No Wall Street people."

I turn back to the road, and ease the van over the last little rise through the trees — and there it is, opening out in front of us: a sprawling meadow, stubbled with a riot of color. There are dozens of flags and hundreds of feathers flapping from long poles, big sticks painted with the names of tribes — *Winnemem Wintu, Yana, Klamath-Modoc-Yahooskin* . . . — all festooned with feathers, fluttering on the breeze; tents of every shape and size and color; and maybe 50 vans and trucks, sparkling metal in the blazing sunshine. It looks like an outdoor music festival, but with no stage, no fences, no focal point, just concentric circles of color and flags and feathers.

As I ease the van through the trees and out into open, the meadow opens down toward the lake, a shimmering pewter-blue disk, rippled with breeze.

I feel Eve pull her hand away and turns to look straight at me again.

I stop the van.

"You have a good, strong heart, Jack," she says again. "It will take some people a little time to see that like I do," she says. "Just be who you are. The man I saw on the stage at Cedar Crossing. The man who holds down the whole band, and does not get flustered, even when his crazy rock star boss starts to spin out."

"You noticed all that, huh?"

"I am a brown woman in America. I have to notice everything." Then, her half-smile again, as mischievous as I seen it yet, as she turns and nods at the meadow full of tents and flags and people. "Welcome to what that's like."

As we idle through the rings of tents and vehicles, Eve scans the flags flying over the campsites for a familiar one.

"There!" she says again and laughs.

She has to say it twice, because I don't hear the first time. I'd stopped the van to stare, because out here — in the middle of the meadow, clear of the trees, rising past the lake from the brown and green and stretching from one end of the horizon to the other — there it is, right there: the great upwelling mass of *Úytaahkoo*, hovering and vibrating in the midday sun.

We pull under the flag where she's pointing, into a cluster of vans and tents, the campsite for Eve's aunts and uncles and cousins.

Introductions all around, made lots easier by everybody — myself included — in sunglasses. I pull out my camp chairs, and we join their circle, Tommy already off with his cousins somewhere.

They are all dressed in bright colors and leather vests and faded denim, boots and cowboy hats and trucker caps and sunglasses, all with long dark hair, some salt and pepper, most in long braids. But beyond that, none of them look like each other. Some are dark as dark chocolate, others milky brown, others as white as me, but with high cheekbones, sculpted noses, penetrating eyes. They're all polite to me, especially the women, but stiff, like they don't want to be polite but don't have a choice.

The kids aren't polite at all. Tommy has run back with three of them after I've excused myself to pull gear from the van, and they stare at me like I've just arrived from the moon.

"These are my cousins!" he blurts out to me, as I'm trying to occupy myself with the important business of pitching my tent in the middle of the day. "Hey you guys, this is Jack! Mommy's new friend!"

"Hey there," I go to shake their little hands, but they all just look up at me, wide-eyed, mouths half open.

"Can I show them your drum, Jack?"

Which fixes everything with the kids. Tommy is in and out of the front of van with the djembe, and they're taking turns on it, so I can focus on pulling gear, setting up the tent for Eve and Tommy, and setting up my own spot in the back of the van.

Most of the kids beat on it randomly, like most kids do; but Tommy is right there, a steady one-two, one-two, showing them how it's done. He's really got it. I have no idea how to teach a kid to do anything, let alone play music, but it would be a cool thing to figure out how to do.

When I'm nearly done with all the make-camp futzing — the last thing I always do is pull out and tune up my guitar — I hear a very different drum, a big booming one, coming up the meadow from down by the lake. Tommy and his cousins are gone, and Eve is a few campsites over, talking with three women around her age, all with long black hair like hers, one holding a baby.

I wave to her and point down toward the lake, and she half-smiles and nods *Go check it out.*

As I walk down to the lake, the mountain beyond looming ever larger and more holographic in the fluttering heat, my pace quickens with the drumbeat, with that steady, insistent, one–two–three–four, like a heartbeat, or a march without beginning or end. It pulls on my body, and I can't help but follow, and want to hurry down there.

But I try not to hurry, just saunter down as casually as I can, like I've been to a million of these things — because I cannot help but notice that everyone I am walking by is stepping a little out of the way, or turning entirely away.

Down near the lake, there are 30 or 40 people, sitting in loose concentric circles of camp chairs around a tight circle of seven men, sitting shoulder to shoulder on stump-stools over a huge drum. I pull up to the loose, outermost circle of people standing and watching, and hover just past the last people, watching, listening.

The seven men, I can see from here, span as many generations. A skinny, pimply teenager with a bone choker and long braid down his black t-shirt. Guys in their 20s and 30s in leather vests and caps with tribal patches. A huge dude about my age, in sweats and a leather vest over a great brown hairless trunk. A skinny guy in his 60s, in a red vest covered with military service ribbons. And the oldest, sitting in one of those walkers, his hair all white and running out from under an ancient, sweat-brimmed hat ringed with feathers.

They beat on the drum in perfect unison, with long mallets made from hand-carved shafts and leather pouches stitched with rawhide, a rock-steady four/four beat, building slowly, barely perceptibly, to a climax of volume and tempo. Then, with no discernible signal or word or cue, right at the top when it feels like the drum is going to explode, all seven drummers cut to two/four and lay in harder still — *beat*-pause, *beat*-pause, *beat*-pause — and the bottom drops out, the volume suddenly halved and the tempo slowing up, back to that steady four/four again.

"Hey-yea-ah-wah!" the oldest guy lets loose with a piercing, wailing chant that shoots through me like an electric shock. I know they must be words, but I have no idea what they are.

"Hey-yea-ah-wah!" the others echo him, one after another, into a rising, rumbling chorus.

Two voices soar still higher than the leader, the rest coming in up and down the register: booming, growling, wailing, the whole range of male voices melding into one voice.

I have no idea what the song is — can't even tell if it's happy, sad, angry, scared, defiant — because it sounds like all of those things mixed together. Like crying and laughing at the same time, over heartache too big for words, or one voice, or one mood. Like a Hebrew chant, a *niggun*, a song without words, only a bittersweet tangle of sorrow and joy, loss and hope. Like an old blues song that goes back not a hundred years, but a thousand, the plaintive wail not just by the singer for his good or bad luck, but for the whole world.

They sing on like that for I don't know how long, and I finally feel my body — which has been on a strange high-alert since we got here — relax into the beat. I notice that I'm nodding with the beat and tapping my feet, left foot, right foot, and how could you not? And even as more and more people are coming down, and pushing past me to find a place in the circle or stand around me on the periphery, I finally stop trying to read everybody, and sink deeper into this transfixing rhythm and follow that singular, seven-layered voice.

In the middle of the next song, I cannot help but lift my eyes, from the blur of those seven mallets on that drum, across the perfect blue stretch of lake, and up to that great impossible glory of a mountain, hovering now in the heat and haze, its spiky summit exploding from its cloak of glacier ice, shining with such ferocity that it hurts to look right at it for too long.

My eyes drift back to the drummers, and the crowd, some of them out of their camp chairs and dancing in place to the beat now.

Two people split off from the circle, walking down to the edge of the lake, where I notice for the first time some sort of makeshift altar. I suppose I thought it was just a long flat stump or chunk of old driftwood; but when they bend down to put something on it, I can see that it's actually a knee-high wooden platform of small tree limbs lashed together, festooned with feathers, and covered with small objects.

I feel a bump from behind, and there's movement back toward the circle, flashes and whirl of color. Two dozen dancers have come together now to fill the meadow all around me, many in full buckskins, face paint, and feathers, bells jangling from arms and legs. I slip off to the side and watch them dance. Some move in small circles, shuffling their feet to the beat; others spin in wild gyrations, a blur of color and motion, feet pounding the earth with the drumbeat.

The drummers peak again, from straight four/four to one/two — *beat*-pause, *beat*-pause — and the dancers peak too, soaring dramatic stomps, spins, arms to the sky, back to the earth, up to the sky.

It reminds me of the ecstatic dancing I've watched from the stage with Amrita, or from the *bima* with Rabbi Miriam, the drums a heartbeat beneath sacred words sung over and over in unison, until they are just sounds, pulsing, a living creature conjured and held in the air over all our heads. Does it matter if it's Hebrew or Sanskrit, Latin or Greek or Arabic, or whatever language this is? It's where they all go: Sufi dancers, reggae rockers, the Grateful Yids at *Shir Hadash*, the Acoladies and Man Buns and Old Hempy Dudes at an Amrita *kirtan*, or the old hippies dancing along the front of the stage, arms outstretched, when Johnny is really on. When I watch them depart this world, loosening their bodies from their confines, dissolving into rapture, the ears within my ears can't help but hear: this is the same thing. This is where the human organism goes to dissolve itself, disappear, stop worrying, stop suffering, if only for a few minutes or hours.

It's time I stopped worrying too, standing out here in the middle of this meadow, noting every glance, icy stare, the occasional pointed finger, wondering what they're wondering about me. So I finally just set myself carefully down in the grass to watch the dancers like a few others have done — and in a rush of memory, I am reminded of the oddest thing, something I haven't thought about since it happened some 15 years or so ago: that festival up in Nederland, also next to a lake and surrounded by mountains.

I was with Danny and some of his friends from down in Boulder, my very first summer in Dudeville. Yonder Mountain String Band, Colorado's version of a bluegrass band on acid, was thundering out another fiddle tune for the dancers in front of the stage, a swirl of tie-dye, peasant skirts, and dreadlocks, and suddenly . . . *CRACK!* . . . the PA went out, and a big gasp from the crowd, but the band kept playing.

The dancers hesitated, wobbling in place, so the mandolin player waved them in tight to the stage, and the band moved to the edge and played on acoustically, faster still. With the music barely audible from back where I was sitting with Danny on his old Pendleton blanket, I noticed for the first time the manic cloud of dust rising from the dancers; and how it mixed with the joyous chaos of all those colors; and how quickly it dissipated against the mountains rimming the festival grounds.

Back then, I wanted to snicker, *Good for all you next-gen hippies in your moccasins, with your feathers and beads and face paint, communing with the old Natives.* But the snicker wouldn't come. Maybe it was all the weed, or the heat, or the music. But it struck me then how all those kids were dancing that furiously *not* because they were just a bunch of stoned kids — because sure, they were that too — but for the same spontaneous and genuine reason these people are dancing the exact same way, in front of me, 15 years later, and have been dancing this way since long before contact, since before recorded time.

I remembered thinking back then that those kids, most a time zone or two or three away from where they grew up, were dancing that way for the same reason the Native peoples of the West always have: the stomping of bare or buckskinned feet against a sprawl of earth — all in time to the same beat that gathered everyone into a collective heartbeat — was just another way of reaching out to feel the Presence, of finding the God who might be on top of that mountain most of the time, but who could be coaxed down here next to this lake by the music and dancing, by this wild *minyan* in a rainbow of color. It was a group way of doing what I always used to do alone, up above treeline or down in a desert canyon: part celebration and part prayer, a burst of energy sent upward into an infinity of sky that says simply: *Look at me, sky! I am alive, right here and right now! Me and my tribe and what else is there?*

But that's not it exactly, because something else is going on with these dancers. There is structure to what they are doing. This isn't one of Amrita's *kirtans*, with people swirling around, their bodies turning inside out, randomly. This isn't an ecstatic dance around the synagogue to a set of prayers. And it's not a bunch of stoned kids jumping around in a field somewhere because it's a sunny day and there's a great band.

I watch four of them dancing a circle, perfectly symmetical; another circle moving clockwise and spinning counterclockwise; and a third, stomping in a row, arms to the sky, back to the earth, back to the sky.

This is theater, ritual, clearly choreographed and deadly serious in execution. The dancers all have set moves and fixed gazes. And in the middle of them all, one dances solo, all white buckskins and black feathers, turning, squaring up, then dropping his shoulder nearly to the ground, then turning and squaring up the other way, and popping upright. I have no idea what they're doing, but it is exactly *not* like an ecstatic dancer's physical exploration of sacred music in some *shul* or at some *kirtan*: this dance itself is also the music, and looks as structured and charged with meaning as a text.

I don't know how much time has passed since I sat in the grass to listen and watch and nod to this mesmerizing music. And I never did go down by the lake to check out that altar. Because Tommy has other plans for me.

"Jack!" I hear him before I see him. "Time to eat!"

Back up near my van, Eve and her friends have set up long tables covered with cookstoves, bowls and platters piled high with food.

"Sit over here, Jack!" Tommy pulls me by the hand to the end of one table, where a bunch of kids are already eating. "Eat with us!"

"I think Jack wants to eat with the adults," Eve says.

She seats me next to her at the other table, and we fill plates with food I've seen all over — corn on the cob, pinto beans, grilled pieces of orange squash — and things that look they've come from another planet. When they go by, I do my best not to stare at it.

Eve leans in next to me and points at each one, "Salmon-on-a-stick, smoked eel, acorn griddle cakes, elk stew, tanoak mushroom stew, seaweed and acorn soup, huckleberry relish for the salmon, roasted peppernuts, *púufich* — that's deer — stew with vegetables, *axthah* — that's mussels — and hey Linda. What is this?"

"*Káaf*," Linda says.

"Of course," Eve says, "Indian Rhubarb, peeled. And that," she points at a big glass jar, "is manzanita berry cider."

"Cider?" I whisper.

"Not hard," she says out loud.

"Of course," I say. "Sorry."

I can feel all of them around the table, curious to see my reactions, and I try not to disappoint: surprise and delight at all the new food, most of which is really good, and all of which I say is wonderful.

For all this newness, it's no different than going to a wedding where you know only the date who brought you. I've passed the "I love your food" test and they moved on to sharing stories about people I don't know, laughing at old jokes I don't get. Like at those weddings, my date and the friendlier ones try to explain what they just said and the unfriendlier ones ignore me and go on to the next story, which I prefer.

While they talk, I eat and listen to the soft, steady, continuous drumbeats and echoes of song drifting up the meadow from the drummers and dancers down by the lake. The sun has just started to sink to the west behind us, and the icy glare of the mountain has softened to a creamy yellow-orange.

I hear my name again, and look up, and all eyes are on me.

"Haudenosaunee," Eve says.

"My goodness, from all the way back East," says her uncle, Pete I think. "You are a long way from home, Jack."

"I left a long time ago."

"Where is home now?"

"Between San Francisco and Santa Cruz."

"Ohlone land," he says, with an approving nod. "It is very beautiful down there."

"Yes it is."

"I have been to a sweat in San Gregorio. An old Chumash, up from L.A., Charlie Many Horses. Do you know him?"

"No, I don't think so."

"Have you done a sweat?"

"No."

"You should do a sweat," he says. "It is good for cleansing the heart. Especially a heart that has traveled so far from home."

They all nod and study me, and Eve's sister gives me the same half-smile that Eve always does, then does me the obvious favor of steering the talk away from me.

I half-smile back at her and breathe out.

I feel like I'm not just meeting family for the first time, which was always my final frontier with a new girlfriend — not that Eve is really even that — but going through a very delicate group job interview. I'm a white man, the most dangerous, lethal thing in the history of their whole people. And I can feel the tension — ranging from cautious curiosity to barely concealed contempt — from all of them.

And just as I'm musing that perhaps I'm imagining some or even most of all that, I hear a stern male voice cut through the laughter: "Who's the white guy?"

I look up and directly across from Eve and me, standing in the spot where one of her aunts had just gotten up to clear away dishes, there's an intense-looking guy glaring not at me, but at Eve. He's wearing a leather vest over a white t-shirt, with long hair down his back.

I nod at him, but he just stands there, making a show of not making eye contact with me.

"Good to see you, Eve. It's been a long time."

"Oh, Martin," one of Eve's aunts says. "Leave it alone."

"This is Martin," Eve turns to me. "My ex-brother-in-law."

"I'm still your brother-in-law. Even if your husband is with the ancients now."

I know better than to say anything, and even looking at him would be a provocation, so I study a scattering of cornbread crumbs across the red and white checked tablecloth.

"I'll be right back, Jack," Eve says as she wearily pulls herself to her feet and walks over and grabs Martin by the arm to pull him away.

But he doesn't want to be pulled away: he wants to stand there and glower, not at me, but all over me.

"Enough," Eve yanks his arm again.

He makes a show of reluctantly turning to follow her, and finally meets my eyes with a look of raw, bloody hatred.

I can feel that first little tickle of adrenaline, so I look down at my hands, close my eyes, breathe out.

"Don't worry about him, Jack," Eve's sister says to me. "That all has nothing to do with you."

I know that's true in particular, but not so true in general. "Thanks" is all I manage to say.

The silence around the table is suddenly suffocating, so everyone starts getting to their feet, gathering and carrying piles of dishes over to the wash tubs on the other table. I get up to help, but Tommy is there with the drum.

"Can we play now, Jack? You have your guitar, right? I want my cousins to hear you play!"

"That would be fun," I say, "but it's time to clean up."

He looks around at the others.

"Everybody has to pitch in, Tommy," Eve's uncle says. "Even our honored guest."

"OK," Tommy turns back to me. "But later?"

"OK, later," I say.

He runs off, and as I move around the other side of the table to clear dishes, I notice *Úytaahkoo*, its glaciers awash in rose alpenglow, the sun down behind us.

I help them clean up, listening to them share more stories, tell more jokes, stop to remember somebody. I can't follow any of it, or am too distracted to try. All I can see is that look in Martin's eyes. But that's how the afternoon went, down by the drummers and dancers, with the looks, the pointed fingers. I just didn't want to think about it, because I was too enraptured by what I was seeing and hearing.

But I am one of only four or five white people scattered in among the five hundred or so at this gathering, and I've been getting reactions all day that are hard to miss. The extremes run from people going out of their way to make sure I see their *Glad you're here* smiles to others like Martin who go out of their way to make sure I see their cold, harsh, accusatory eyes, hissing *Who the hell are*

*YOU? Why the hell are YOU here???* But it seems like most of these people, especially the older ones, are just looking right through or past me, like they want me to know that they know I'm here but couldn't care less, like I'm just a bad smell passing on the breeze.

By the time Eve comes back, she looks vexed and drained. She comes over to the last big washtub where I'm drying, stands across from me, and picks up a towel.

*Everything OK?* I ask her with my eyes.

"Everything is OK with *me*," she says out loud, in the sudden silence down the wash line. "Everything is never going to be OK with him."

"That poor boy needs to let his brother go," an aunt says. "It's been five years."

"It is hard to lose your big brother," another says. "Especially that way."

Then more silence, up and down the wash line, except for the clinking of dishes and utensils, and a sniffling sound.

I look up and notice Eve's face crumpling, her lower lip quivering, then tears. She puts down the towel and walks off.

I have no idea if I should go comfort her or leave her alone, and look over at the others. Her oldest aunt looks at me, nodding in Eve's direction, her eyes saying *Go comfort her.*

When I catch up with her, she's halfway down to the lake and the drummers and dancers, her arms crossed and head bowed.

"Hey," I say when I catch up with her.

"I'm sorry, Jack. It has been five years — since Joseph —," her voice trails off. "And seeing Martin, and how angry he still is —"

As we walk down the meadow, the drumming is intensifying — louder and faster — and I notice that it's all new drummers now, though I cannot remember the beat ever once pausing. There are also a couple dozen more dancers now, all dressed in buckskins dyed white, blue, dark brown, more feathers, face paint and headdresses, and more coming down the hill.

We wander down toward the lake, and Eve leads us away from the drummers and dancers, over toward the altar.

As we pull up, I can see that it's now piled up with rocks, carved figures, feathers, beads, pieces of paper. And next to it, something I hadn't noticed before: someone has dug a small pit, lined with rock, and stacked it in with firewood in an airy, three-foot-tall, triangular structure.

"Martin won't let him go," Eve says, nodding at the altar. "Five years, and I don't know how many of these ceremonies. This is another reason I came up here," she leans down and looks over the objects people have placed on the altar. "Because we all need to heal. Not move on, not forget. But to remember them, honor them, live on in their names, not stay in the in-between with them, burning. Tommy needs this too, even though he was too young to remember his father. But still, he asks."

She straightens up to stand next to me, and we both study the altar as the air around us darkens, picks up a chill.

I remember the story she told me on our third or fourth phone call, how her ex-husband Joseph died. He had been an activist, like Eve though "lots more militant," she said, which is why they'd moved back onto the reservation after college, to work in tribal government on land restoration, water rights, resource recovery.

He was also a binge alcoholic, like his father had been, and the reservation was a good place to keep that under control because you couldn't buy alcohol, except on the black market, which he would never do. But there was that long empty road east to the first town, and that liquor store just over the line, where he'd always buy two bottles: one to hide at the house, one for the drive home.

Eve said he did not die in a wreck, which is what I was expecting she'd say. He died of hypothermia, in his car, 15 feet out in an empty field, a mile south of their house . . .

There is a sudden warmth in my right hand, her fingers finding mine.

"I am glad you are here for this," Eve says, and looks up from the altar, her black eyes shiny with tears, alpenglow, and dusk. "This cannot be easy. But this is where I come from, who I am. Tommy too."

She squeezes my hand, and lets it go as we turn to go back up the hill.

An hour later, the last of the daylight is almost all gone and the temperature is dropping fast like it does in the mountains, but it's not dark. A full moon is rising to the east, just off the right flank of *Úytaahkoo*, and there are fires burning all over the campground, the biggest of all next to the drummers.

Eve has rounded up Tommy and his cousins, and there's a group of maybe 20 of us walking down toward the altar with our camp chairs. Everything and everyone is suddenly, intensely quiet. The drummers are still going, but it's a a slowed, softened, steady rhythm, no chanting, the pace of a processional. And no-one is talking for the first time since we got here. Not a sound from anyone, not even the kids, all of them clinging to somebody's hand, Tommy to Eve's.

When we get down to the lake to join the 50 or so people already spread out by the altar, I turn to see what looks like the entire encampment heading down to the lake with their chairs, all in silence. Eve's uncle keeps going, and sets his chair down right in the middle, near the front, and we all settle in.

I'm grateful for the failing light, the fire, the moon, its milky light on the mountain, the few stars strong enough to gleam in the half-lit sky, all the things to look at to keep me from staring at everyone around me, to think about that aren't about me, and what the hell I'm doing here.

The drumming stops suddenly, and the whole meadow is a deathly quiet. There is no breeze, and the lake is now a mirror, empty but for the watery, moonlit face of the mountain.

"Nem utel-yomi-n, hu'uni ka-li'ilaw ena."

It's a single voice, chanting more words I can't make out, coming from a group of seven men and three women, all in buckskins, walking from the drum circle toward the altar.

"Nem utel-yomi-n, hu'uni ka-li'ilaw ena," the others repeat the phrase, one of them with a hand drum, a beat on the first note of the three phrases.

Then, "Kani'i aye ka-li'ilaw miti kani'i aye," the single voice again, more cry than song.

The sound makes my throat tighten, then chest ache, then head swim, like I want to burst into tears, for no reason in particular and every reason in the world. It is filled with a kind of heartbreak I don't think, for whatever pain and losses I've endured over the decades, I will ever understand.

"Kani'i aye ka-li'ilaw miti kani'i aye," the others and the hand-drum respond as they approach the altar.

They circle behind the altar, right on the edge of the lake, and I notice for the first time that one of the women — the oldest by far, well into her 70s, her face a scrunch of wrinkles and crevices and covered in blue paint — is carrying a bundle the size of a small child, wrapped in a white blanket.

Ugh. That can't be what I think it is.

I turn and look at Eve, and she nods to me, *Yes. That's what you think it is.*

Then a piercing cry, "Ka-appi ka-ene'ene ka'unu ka-pa'apa!"

She steps back and chants, "ka-we'e'ama-kon she ma-t ka-ho'oye."

And then all of them together with the slow heartbeat of the hand-drum:

*Nem utel-yomi-n, hu'uni ka-li'ilaw ena.*
*Kani'i aye ka-li'ilaw miti kani'i aye,*
*Ka-appi ka-ene'ene ka'unu ka-pa'apa*
*ka-we'e'ama-kon she ma-t ka-ho'oye.*

And then utter silence, but for the crackling of the fire.

The man who'd led the chant steps out from behind the fire pit, stops to bow his head and say something to himself, then looks out at all of us.

"Brothers and sisters of the Shasta Nation, Karuk Tribe, the Klamath Tribes, the Coast Miwok, Plains Miwok and Wintu, the Pit River, Hoopa, Wiyot, Redding Rancheria, all good people of the Great Spirit who have come here to honor our ancestors. On this sacred day, when Sister Moon rises to dance with *Úytaahkoo*, we come to welcome the spirits of our grandmothers and grandfathers home. They are returned to their ancestral homeland, after their terrible journey through darkness, after more than a hundred years in the in-between, an awful wandering."

He stops, bows his head again, like he's praying — of course he's praying — for what has to be 30 seconds. And not a sound but for the fire over by the drum circle, hundreds of us sitting there in silence, watching, waiting.

He lifts his head and continues, "For one hundred and seven years, your bones sat unburied, without honor. For the white people to look at, and take pictures of, in their museum of living death. In that city of concrete, and money, and bad medicine, as far from your home as the stars, on land stolen from our brothers and sisters to the east, two hundred years ago."

He lifts his head higher, to the sky, and starts to murmur a chant I can't follow. On what sounds like his second time around, the hand-drum finds the rhythm of his song, then the other voices, and the voices all around me, Eve's too, and all her aunts and uncles and cousins, a sea of wailing that fills my chest like a fist clenching and releasing, clenching and releasing, a sound of anguish and fury and longing like nothing I've ever heard, and nothing I could ever reproduce.

While the chant goes round and round, building into an aural swirling of dark watery blue infused with yellow light, the leader turns and bends to squat in front of the fire pit, and lights it.

The chant grows louder, until it is midnight pitch shot through with streaks of that yellow light, and the flame flickers and catches in the paper, flaring up into the stack of wood. The woman places the bundle on the top of the wood, and her voice pierces all the others with the same chant, a death-wail.

The hand-drum comes in behind her, then the big drum again over in the other circle, the same chant.

Out of the crowd emerge four new dancers, dressed in white buckskins, holding feathered wands, their faces painted blue, who march-dance to the four corners of the fire pit, their gaze fixed on the bundle, now fully aflame, hovering in the middle of a suddenly raging fire. They turn with the beat, then square up, drop their shoulders nearly to the ground, turn and square up the other way, and pop upright. It's the same dance I saw earlier, and now I know why they looked so intent, why they were practicing for so many hours to get every footfall, every dip, every turn exactly right.

The fire flares up through the center of the wood, turning their dancing figures into a blur of white and blue and feathers and light, fluttering with the heat, a burst of sparks with each burst of their feathered hands from ground to sky.

As we wander back up the hill with the mostly silent crowd, a few talk in murmurs, whispers, and Eve turns to me and says, half under her breath, "I hope that was not too much all at once."

Back at the camp she tells me, in a still muted voice, what it took to get those remains back from a display case in a museum in Boston: ten years of lawsuits; an attempt at a federal law that never passed because some oil company didn't like it; and, finally, a public pressure campaign by the hundred or so Native American students enrolled in colleges all over New England.

"But those are just the bones anyone knows about," she says. "If you walk into any remote section of California that hasn't been dug for minerals or water, there will be bones."

"Like what they were digging up in the woods outside my town, the Haudenosaunee longhouse. Pots, tools, jewelry, weapons — and," I realize out loud, "bones. For a museum."

"Yes," she says. "This whole country is our graveyard. Our ancestors are buried everywhere. I know you had difficulties with your parents, that they were very bad parents, because they were so broken. But you do know where they are buried."

"Yes," I say. "I do know that."

Back at the campsite, dozens of people move soundlessly in and out of their vans, from car to tent, getting ready for bed in near silence. No laughter, no chatter, just a few quick words here and there, a kid complaining about something, a pan dropping on a rock. The only sound is the drumming and chanting down by the lake, that same rhythm and song, drifting up the meadow from the altar and funeral pyre. From up here, the four dancers, still going, look like apparitions against the flames.

Tommy is fast asleep before Eve and I can get him rolled into his little sleeping bag in the tent. But as I'm crawling out of the tent, he wakes up.

"Jack?"

"Right here, buddy."

"Are you going?"

"Just going to sleep."

"Where are you going?"

"To sleep in my van."

"You're not leaving?"

"No," I say. "Right over here in my van. I'll see you in the morning."

"Promise?"

"Yes, Sweet Pea," Eve says as she's getting her own sleeping bag ready. "He promises."

"Good night, buddy," I say, and try to back out of the tent as gently as I can.

I feel Eve backing out behind me, and hear her say, "I'll be right back, Sweet Pea. I have to go to the bathroom."

"Just a minute," she whispers to me, and I watch her slip off through a maze of tents and vehicles bathed in moonlight.

I go over to the van and pull my sleeping stuff out of the bin, set up for the night, and sit in the open doorway of the van.

The air is soft and cool, the breeze coming up from the lake in whiffs of dampness and music. The drummers and singers down by the lake are still going — an all-night vigil, maybe? — their chants still like sharp squiggles of that blue and white light against the blank wash of the moonlit sky.

I lean against the doorway frame and try to relax, but I am wide awake, my foot still tapping to the drumbeat, my eyes tracing those voices as the colors change from blue and white to green and yellow.

And there is Eve, slipping back through the tents, walking soundlessly up to me.

She sits down in the doorway next to me, and there are her fingers, five of them finding my left hand, and then five more, warm, supple, strong, entwining themselves in my guitar-roughened, surfboard-beaten hand.

"I very much appreciate that you are here for all this," she says to me in a voice so hushed I can barely hear her words. "This cannot be easy, all of this family and ritual at one time."

She leans her head against my shoulder, and my heart starts thumping in my ears, lots faster than the drumbeat down there.

"It's been fine," I whisper. "And some of it —," I nod toward the drumming and singing down the hill, "has been interesting. *Really* interesting. I'm glad I'm here."

She leans away from my shoulder, half turning toward me, her face lost in moon shadow. "Another religion to add to your collection?"

"Oh geez," I whisper. "Is that what you think?"

"I've seen those videos," she half-whispers. "You and the Hindus, you and the yoga goddess lady, you and the dancing Jews."

"Yes," I sigh. "All God, all the time. And all of it *is* interesting to me. For the music, the stories, the freakshow. But I found my own religion a long time ago. In places just like this," I whisper and nod toward the mountain, gleaming in the moonlight, like the beaming face of a great someone out on the town for the full moon. "In the woods back East, the mountains in Colorado, up on mountains on like *Úytaahkoo* over there."

"Don't you mean Mount Shasta?" she jokes. "You are a quick study, Mister Jack."

She squeezes my hand with all ten of those strong little fingers, and nestles back into my shoulder. I put my other arm around her, and she burrows a little deeper against my chest, under my chin. Something like a scent rises from her hair, her skin, her breath.

I take a deep breath for more. It isn't a scent, but it enters my body the same way, and I want her so badly I could explode.

Best to cool down a bit. This isn't going anywhere tonight, even if we both wanted it to. "But as religion goes," I sigh, if only to release the balling up in my chest, "the yoga people are fun, and it definitely lives somewhere in my body. And Judaism is where my head is, or where it's from anyway. But what happened down there tonight? That may be the most interesting and beautiful religious thing I've ever seen."

"And that's why you're glad you're here?"

"No. I'm glad I'm here for you. And for Tommy."

She turns to lift her face toward mine. "That's what I was waiting for you to say."

I cannot see anything but the outline of her face, sketched in moonlight.

"I'll see you in the morning," she whispers as she starts to pull away, slowly prying her fingers away from mine, one by one.

She stands to go, then turns and puts both of her hands on my thighs, and leans in to kiss me, all that hair showering down to enshroud us in that intoxicating scent, like rain, like an evergreen forest damp with it, like wet cedar and woodsmoke and sex.

Her mouth is hungry, and makes mine hungry, and I dissolve into her mouth, and everything dissolves.

She pulls herself away, sweeps her hair back, then goes to kiss me again — long, sweet, lingering — in center of the forehead.

"Good night, sweet man," she whispers, her words hovering like particles of light in the moonlit darkness all around me.


There is no way I am falling asleep right now.

I lean back against the doorway, listen to Eve crawl into their tent, and trace every sound with my ears: the tent zipper opening, then closing; then the rustle of nylon, and the zipper on her sleeping bag opening, the brushing sound of clothes and hair against nylon, and the zipper closing.

Tommy mumbles something to her, and her voice, as sweet and soft as I've heard it yet, whispers back.

A minute of silence, then the faint scratch of nylon, a tiny body rolling over in a little sleeping bag. Then the same sound but bigger, Eve rolling over in hers, filling it with those curves, and all that soft hair, and all that warmth.

I want her so badly I have to think of something else right now.

So . . . gear. A good time to sort it out, see what's missing or broken, see what I need to replace. But I can't do that without making noise. Especially with the doors open. I should shut them, but it's hot enough to sleep with just the screens down, like a big tent on wheels. And in case they need anything, they can just yell, like out on a mountain.

Which is a ridiculous thing to think, but I think it anyway, and leave the door open.

I want her so badly and I am wide awake and there is no way I am falling asleep right now.

Taking care of business is about what I got, so I do. But rather than fall asleep, now I'm just sweatier.

And vibrating. The drums are still going, way off on the aural horizon, and my ears are pegged to the sound of any movement in a tent 20 feet away.

All the things I wish I could say to her. And not the things I've been telling myself I should have said to Radhe, about losing Leah, or Freya fixing me, because none of those things seem to matter anymore. They just are. The pink and purple refrigerator magnet on Amrita's merch table is exactly wrong: things *don't* happen for a reason. They just happen, and you deal with them, on your own sweet time.

I wish I could tell Eve all that right now. And *"Hineni,"* the chant Rabbi Miriam would use to open her meditative service. "Here I am."

I also wish I could tell her that I wasn't exactly honest about one thing tonight: *yes, I do know where my parents are buried.* But I've never been to either grave, only heard about where they are from my sister, still back there, still dealing with them till the end. The last time we talked, now that I think about it, was her calling to say that he was dead from a heart attack. They were burying him that week in a churchyard in western Massachusetts, where he'd gone back at the end, and shacked up with another old, dying drunk right after our mother died.

Which was in — I'm not sure exactly what year. I was hiding out in Colorado, and hadn't seen either of them in 15, 16, 17 years maybe. She died in the hospital after she'd finally lost what was left of her mind — on suicide watch my sister said, choking on food she shouldn't have had — and was buried with her parents in the small town where she grew up north of New York. Going back for her funeral was the last thing I wanted to do because *he* would be there, and would make a drunken fool out of himself, because that's what he did. I haven't been back East to visit her grave because, well, I think if I did, I'd be too ashamed to cry. Or maybe I'd never stop crying, once I did.

As for his grave, there would be no shame, and no crying.

His grave in western Massachusetts.

And how's this for weird luck? We have a big Amrita gig at some retreat center back there, next month. Because "things happen for a reason," according to that refrigerator magnet, right?

I don't want to go see his grave. I don't need to go see his grave. But I could rent my own car, stay an extra day, and go find it anyway. Just to see what it feels like. I know one thing: there won't be any drumming or dancing.

I hear a big rustle of nylon over in the tent, Eve turning over, then a small rustle, Tommy turning over.

The drumbeat down by the lake. Crickets everywhere else.

Another big rustle of nylon, another small rustle.

I stare into the darkness, feel a breeze pass through the open van, and see that look of hatred on Martin's face: a dys-alchemy of rage, molten from generation upon generation of fear and pain and violence.

A small rustle of nylon, then a big rustle, drumbeat, crickets.

All I want to do is protect them, from all that came before, and all that might come still.

Drumbeat, crickets, here I am . . .

"You should try a sweat sometime," Eve's Uncle Pete says as he's coming out of his camper in sweatpants and a towel.

We are finishing up breakfast, and groups of men are going down to the sweat lodges down by the lake.

Uncle Pete comes over on his cane, looks at the pancakes still there, purses his lips, and turns to me as he's heading off. "You know, Jack. The Ohlone who lived where you live? They did a sweat just about every day. For them, God was on the inside. The lodge was the way in."

Eve comes back from the bathroom, and picks up one of the pancakes her uncle had been eyeing, and sits next to me. "He's right, Jack," she says. "The sweat lodge was their major religious practice. Perhaps another reason they did not go to war?"

"That is our Eve," one of her aunts says as she comes over, hands her a steaming mug. "She does not need a cup of coffee in the morning to start teaching. Even as a little girl."

Eve look like she can't decide between defending herself and being self-conscious, the first time I've ever seen her knocked off balance.

I bail her out with a subject change: "So where's Tommy?"

"The kids are all down at the lake," Eve says, "looking at tadpoles and frogs and other slimy little boy things. He gave up on you about an hour ago."

"I had a hard time falling asleep."

"Did you now," Eve half-smiles at me, then looks down quickly.

"The sweat lodge would not be a good place for you anyway then," she says. "It's very dehydrating. That is half of the hallucinations."

"What's the other half?"

"God," she says and picks up another pancake. "But you *should* do a sweat, Jack. It is like what your yoga people do, except —"

"Except on the inside."

"Yes," she says. "The Ohlone men did them every day. And maybe that *is* why they did not go to war, because they worked out their violence in the dark. But who is to say? History is not a controlled experiment."

"Hey Jack!"

Tommy is back, and his hands are slimy little boy hands, and Eve gets up to go help him wash. They're back a minute later, and Tommy wants to dig out the drum and play.

It's not that I don't want to teach him another little something about music. The kid has it, or so I remember from that festival last month. And he has been asking since the minute I picked them up yesterday. But I've been putting this off because I don't want even a few stray guitar notes of mine landing anywhere near this field, which isn't just some campground. It's sacred ground, *their* sacred ground, and I do not want to risk offending anyone. (Or draw any attention — any *more* attention — to myself.)

But kids can be persistent, I guess, and Tommy won't let it go.

"You may as well go ahead, Jack," Eve says. "Or neither of us will hear the end of it."

I go back into the van, and he's standing in the open doorway, watching me dig out the little djembe and pull my guitar from the case.

I sit him across from me, in the side doorway of the van, where no one but Eve and her aunt and sister — the only people in our camp not off somewhere — can hear us.

Tommy holds the drum in his lap, those big eyes fixed on my guitar, mesmerized as I check the tune and play a quick run.

Then he wedges the drum between his scraped and knobby little knees, and looks down at the drum with a kind of nervous wonder, as if it were a living creature that might leap away at any moment.

"OK, buddy," I say, nodding my head, "One–two, one–two," and we're off.

We play that same simple march in C major from back at Cedar Crossing, and wow! The kid really does have it. He stares intently at his hands as they pop-pop, pop-pop on the drum to my count; and half a minute in, those two little hands are already moving around on the drumhead, discovering how to make it pop on the downbeat and dampen it on the off-beat.

I speed it up and he follows; I slow it down and he follows.

But it sounds weird around here, like a drum and bugle thing, like — well — an invasion.

"O-K," I say with the beat, "and now we are going to stop, so get ready, one–two, one–two, stop!"

And he stops, right on the final beat, and looks up at me as wide-eyed as ever.

"Yeah, buddy. You did it!"

I turn to glance around at the camp, at the tents and meadow beyond. No one is paying any attention to us, except Eve, who is over washing dishes with her aunt and sister; but I can tell she is listening intently to us while they talk.

"Let's play another one, Jack!"

OK, maybe a minor key will not sound so strange. We play the same exact thing in A minor, a simple march.

His little drumbeats follow, right on time, and my fingers wander off the E7 to one of those old *Shabbat* kids' songs we did at *Shir Hadash* once a month. It's like in A minor, but with the flattened second as well as the seventh, that ancient Phrygian mode running through half of traditional Jewish liturgical music.

I slow it down a bit, to see if Tommy can hold the beat, maybe even spread out with a spontaneous finger roll. But he's only eight, after all, and hanging onto that drum like his life depends on it; so I bring it back to mid-tempo, and he relaxes into the one–two beat and even manages to look up at me for affirmation.

"You're doing great, buddy! You're really good!"

And he really is, so I see if he can shift to waltz time.

"OK, Tommy, now we count three," I say as I shift and nod ONE–two–three, ONE–two–three, and he's right there in waltz time.

And of all weird things that flow spontaneously out of my guitar when I'm just messing around with a few stray chords in Phrygian mode in waltz time, we're suddenly playing "Avinu Malkeinu," the musical refrain at the heart of *Yom Kippur*. It's an ancient, longing, bittersweet melody, and like everything in Phrygian, more primal than the formality of major or minor, a sound less for curious ears than for the whole hungering body.

And Tommy is right there on the beat, one–two–three, one–two–three, wow.

"All-right, and on-the-drum," I say, on the beat, slowing it down, "now we are going to stop–two–three, one–two–three, stop!"

He ends exactly on the final beat and looks up at me from the drum, like he cannot believe what he just saw his own hands do.

"Great job, buddy!"

"Did you hear that Mommy?"

"I did," Eve says.

I turn to see her drying her hands on a towel as she comes over and stands next to me.

"What was that, Jack?"

"Jewish music. A melody we do during the fall holidays."

"That was lovely," she says. "Like ocean waves coming in and going out."

Tommy stares up at us, then back at the drum, then back at us.

"But I think it might be time for the plant walk," she says.

"Yes, Jack — the plant walk! You should come! We learn about what berries we can eat, what ones make you sick, what plants are for medicine."

"Jack would like to do the plant walk, Sweet Pea," Eve says. "But Mommy needs him to stay here and help clean up, and put away the tent."

"OK," Tommy says, looking down at the djembe. "But can we play more later?"

A minute later, Tommy is off with a group of kids at the other end of the meadow, and our camp is empty, except Eve's aunt who has just settled heavily into her camp chair. Eve is still standing in the van doorway, watching me put my guitar away, but she doesn't move when I climb back out, just turns and stares at her aunt.

"Well," her aunt says. "No use in just sitting around. I can do that at home." She struggles to her feet, gives us a quick smile, and says, "I haven't had a good look at the dancers this whole weekend."

She walks down to join up with two older women making their way down toward the lake and the drumming.

I turn and Eve is sitting in the open doorway of the van, leaning back on her hands. Her flip-flops are sitting in the grass, her strong dark feet propped up on the jamb, her toes scrunching and un-scrunching. She gives me that half-smile, blushes again, shakes out that long black hair.

"So," I say.

"So," she says.

Her knees sway to the left, then to the right, then open slightly as they sway left again. My heart leaps into my throat.

She leans a little further back on her hands, looks up at the ceiling of the van, and shakes her hair again.

"Nice and cool in here," she says, "out of the sun."

"Well, yeah, it's always good for —"

"But I wouldn't know," she cuts me off. "Because somebody hasn't invited me in to see for myself."

And that's it. I go to step past her into the van, and she is rolling in right behind me and pulling the door shut with a heavy thud.

She sits back on her hands, her knees going back and forth like a pendulum, as she watches me scurry past my sleeping bag and camping mattress to shut the back doors and pull the screen down.

"Might be a good idea to lock it," she says.

"Yes," I say, and scurry past her to hit the lock and pull the curtain across the front, turning the van suddenly dark and cool and quiet.

Before I can turn back to her, four strong fingers are grabbing the top of the back of my jeans, and pulling me down onto the top of my sleeping bag. I feel like I'm falling through the floor of the van, freefalling into space, tethered to the earth only through Eve's mouth on my mouth, her lips and tongue as hungry as last night — no, hungrier, without the tentativeness, the furtiveness — and warm and sweet and giving and flowing into my own mouth.

I roll her over on top of me, and all that soft hair drops around us like a shroud, a prayer shawl, and there is that scent again, damp and spicy like summer woods after a quick rain. I want to drown in that smell, rising up out of her denim shirt like warm milk, I think, as her shirt is coming off, and mine is coming off, and then a bra is coming off. Her large, warm, soft breasts spill out across my quivering chest, two nipples hard as little fingertips skittering back and forth through my chest hair.

Our mouths are welded together, a dizzying kiss without bottom, as my hands run up and down all that warm, soft, glowing skin.

I feel her reach for my belt, and I pry my mouth away long enough to say, "I — hate to admit this — but I — brought a condom."

She props her chin up on my chest, her face inches from mine, and searches my face before bursting into a full smile.

"What? What's so funny?"

"You hate to admit that you came all the way up here, and dealt with all of these people and all the rest of my world, because you like me?"

"Well —"

"Besides," she rolls off me, onto her side, all that hair slipping off my chest and shoulders, leaving them feeling suddenly bare. "We don't need a condom."

"No?"

"No," she says, and finds my hand, and runs it down the middle of her smooth, warm belly until it bumps into something merging into where her navel should be. "I had a very hard time with Tommy's birth." Her fingers spread mine out across the high, hard ridge of what feels like a big scar, running from her navel down to the button on her jeans. "I had an emergency C-section, which did not go well, because we were living on the rez at the time."

Even in this shadowy light, I can feel her eyes searching my face for a reaction, and my only reaction is intense pain and sorrow for both of them.

"No more children for me. Which is fine. Tommy is a handful, and I am almost 40."

I say nothing because what can I possibly say?

"Is that OK with you? Aside from not having to get that condom, I mean? I'm healthy otherwise. And you too?"

"I'm healthy," I say. "I've been checked since the last time. Because she was a doctor, and — "

And I'm stalling for time because I get the two huge unspoken questions behind what she said about the condom and the question she did ask: *Is this monogamous, a commitment, more than just this right here and now? And if so, are you OK with no more babies?*

So I pretend to think about the answer longer than I need to, because I want her to know that *Yes, this is not just about here and now,* and (whew!) *Yes, no more babies for you.*

"That's even better," I say. "You know how old I am. And Tommy is a handful. A good handful."

"Oh, Jack," she sighs and starts to say something else, but her voice cracks, and she lifts her face to kiss me. Then her hand is around the back of my neck, pulling me down on top of her.

We roll back and forth, out of our jeans, and find each other, and keep rolling back and forth and stroking. Then I feel her leg, fiercely strong, encircle my hips and pull me over on top of her.

"Please be gentle," she whispers. "It has been a very long time."

I stop, and prop up on my elbows and search the shadow of her face, wet with kisses and what look like they might be tears.

"How about *you* be gentle," I say, and gather her in my arms, and roll her over onto me.

Another shower of hair enshrouding our faces, inches from each other, forehead to forehead and nose to nose as she brings her knees forward, and then unfurls her body down the length of mine, and everything is suddenly wet and hot and bottomless as my penis disappears into her.

I do not move a muscle, just my hands back and forth over her butt, clenching and unclenching as she glides back and forth along my body.

She moans softly, as her hips slowly and steadily release, and waves of that same intoxicating scent rise from between those big, soft, sweet breasts and big dark brown nipples slipping up and down my chest. Then she pushes herself up to sit, and rocks back and forth and rotates her hips, as I push all the way into her, all the flexing muscles and ropey scars and drenched pubic hair of our two pelvises dissolving into gyrating, liquid fire, blinding light, and a sudden intense upwelling of pleasure, a thundering, shuddering explosion . . .

"Wow," she says, as we float back and she settles under my arm.

"Wow, yes," I say. "That about sums it up."

I feel her whole body shudder alongside with an aftershock of pleasure.

"Wow," she says again, and sinks in a little deeper, burrowing her face into the side of my chest. She kisses her way back up, and sinks in, her leg curling up and wrapping itself around mine, entwining it all the way down to our feet and toes.

"I like the way you smell," she says, burying her nose in the side of my neck.

"I like the way you smell."

"Is it that simple? This?"

"No," I say. "Not at my age, anyway. Nothing is simple."

She chuckles. "And nothing is simple when you are a single mother, with all this family around you watching everything you do, and you live in two different worlds at the same time."

"I don't know about the family part, but I do know about living in two different worlds. For a while, I was living in three."

"I know," she says. "That is one of the many interesting things about you." She lets out a long sweet sigh, her normally insistent teacher's voice as peaceful as I've ever heard it. "I had a feeling it might be this good, Jack, you and me. I do not know exactly why, but I do know how much I wanted you."

"You did? And you knew how much I wanted you?"

"Yes. I could tell on those phone calls. I could tell that you do not like talking on the phone, but you never wanted to hang up."

I don't feel like talking now either, actually. I want nothing less than for this moment to last forever, to hold her close to me, her skin now slick with sweat and mixed with the sweat of my own skin, my arm never feeling as strong as it does right now, draped in her hair, clutching her to me.

"I thought that maybe Jack is just another white voyeur, another lost hippie-dippie who wants to go Native. Or maybe he really just likes Tommy, because he never had kids. And being a dad to a wonderful little boy is what he is really after."

Ha! Ike!

"I know a guy who's after exactly that," I say, thinking back on all those sad, wistful conversations with him down at Angel's Rest. "But that's not my trip at all. I came up here because I couldn't wait for those phone calls. Because I couldn't stop thinking about you from the minute I drove away from Cedar Crossing that afternoon."

"I know that now," she says. "It just all seems so improbable, so random."

"That, and everything else in life."

"Yes," she chuckles. "But most luck is bad, not good. Most of what is good in life comes from hard work. The bad stuff, well . . ."

We lay in silence, and I cannot tell where her body ends and mine begins, until she lets out a long, weary sigh and then, as she settles back in, her body seems to melt even further into mine.

"But then I saw it on the drive up yesterday, and I knew."

"Saw what?"

"The way you were looking at my feet, up on your dashboard."

"You noticed that, huh? Sorry about that."

"Don't be sorry, silly," she says as runs her hand down my chest and across my belly, a little flicker of desire bursting out of all that sweet calm. "I liked it. It made me feel good. Made me feel wanted. And all of me, not just me for somebody's trick with an Indian girl. You make me feel *seen*, Jack. Even after I tried to scare you with all the horror stories, with all that sadness about Tommy's dad. You still wanted me. You still showed up. I have not felt that way in a very long time."

"Not showing up wasn't an option."

"Not until you have had your squaw anyway," she says, and pokes me in the ribs.

"What? Had what? Are you kidding?"

"Yes, silly," she nestles back up under my arm. "Of course I am kidding." She lets out a long sigh. "But you are right. That is nothing to joke about."

"No."

"That's how it was, you know. It's why so many more Native women than men survived. We were like everything else the trappers, hunters, miners, whoever, just took for themselves, because they could. The women were no different. To them, we were trade goods."

"Well that's just goddamn awful," I say, even though I knew about all that. If anything, it was another reason I was unsure about all this. "I don't even know what to do with that."

"You don't have to do anything," she says.

Her leg tightens up around mine, and her toes scrunches up into the bottom of my foot. I slip my foot around behind her foot, and thread my toes through hers, and they squeeze each other. Then her leg pulls tighter around me, rocking me back and forth as her finger whisks across my belly. There is another flicker of desire down there, but it feels icky now, forbidden, so I take a deep breath and close my eyes.

"But you know, Jack," she says and props her face up to look me in the eye, her eyes black and steady and warm and full of as much light as I've ever seen in anyone's eyes. "It's very different, when the squaw gets to say 'no.'"

"I would imagine."

Her hand circles my belly, then slips down and gathers me gently in her hand. And in one motion, her leg rolls me over on top of her and her legs are opening, all of her is opening, and she guides me inside her again and says, "And it is very, very different, when she gets to say 'yes.'"

# 9 | THE GODDESS OF NEVER NOT BROKEN

I'm sitting in Neptune's with Ike and Brooke on this fine morning, drinking coffee and watching squadrons of brown pelicans dive out of the pink mist to strafe the waves for breakfast. They're teasing me about Eve, because I haven't really said much about her. But a certain look comes over my face when I say her name, apparently; because every time I do, they grin at me, Brooke with a gossip-buddy mischievousness, Ike with a little wincing around the edges, like the bro who just came in second in some competition, but he's happy for me.

I'm just about finished telling them about my big plan to drive up to Humboldt later today to hang with Eve and Tommy this weekend, when I get a text from David: *Call me. Important. Kind of an emergency.*

"Amrita's in the hospital," he says, from some hospital over in San Jose, when I call. "Not too far from you, right?"

"Why me? We're not really close."

"She doesn't have any family up here, and she doesn't want any of the Acoladies to see her this way."

"This way?"

He lowers his voice. "Major bad reaction to some plastic surgery. Some kind of immune reaction, or infection, or something. Her neck is all swollen up and looks really nasty, and her face is kinda fucked up. She's bombed on something, and all she does is cry and sleep and wake up crying."

Which explains why we didn't do that gig down in Ojai last weekend. The big annual retreat with all of her yoga teacher training graduates, postponed the Wednesday before.

*Amrita a little under the weather. Needs a little time to recover. Will be fine by Bhaktifest next month,* was the text from Gordon to the band and crew.

That's all Gordon said, and I didn't think about it again, because the cancellation meant that I could head north to the gathering up at *Úytaahkoo* with Eve and her family.

Now I feel like a little bit of a selfish jerk. I've been floating around on this Eve cloud since then, and it didn't once cross my mind that something might be seriously wrong with Amrita. There were back-to-back casino gigs with Johnny last week, and long, languorous, lusty phone calls every night with Eve; and I haven't really noticed, until now, that Amrita's steady stream of email dried up. First, the ones to David and Jenna and me about new songs, upcoming gigs, links to videos we should check out or *Just a quick hello to say I love you!* Then, her daily "affirmation" blast emails to us and her hundred or so Acoladies. And finally, the gussied-up versions of the same emails that always come a day or two later — revised, shortened, and dusted with sparkles and sugar, like the sayings on her refrigerator magnets — to the 100,000 fans on some listserv Gordon says they've been compiling for ten years. All finally stopped, about a week ago.

I'm just about to hang up — and thinking I should leave now for the hospital so I can go straight north and be up there, if not on time for the early picnic dinner we've been planning, then to see Tommy before he goes to bed — when I hear David say the oddest thing: "Make sure you bring your guitar."

"Really?"

"I know it sounds weird, Jack. She's a mess, and mostly out of it. But she can still sort of chant. It's more like a hum, actually. But it's the only thing that seems to cheer her up. She asked me to bring my harmonium, and Jenna and I did some mantras with her, and it seemed to comfort her. A little. Stopped her crying for a little bit anyway."

We hang up and I watch the row of pelicans make another low pass over a perfect glassy curl of a wave.

Shit.

Humboldt is a long haul, six hours north, so I should go pack and head out now. If Amrita is really that sick, she won't want me around for long anyway; and someone else will surely show up to relieve me. She does have those 100,000 fans, not to mention those hundred or so ferocious Acoladies — climbers, cougars, and tiger moms all — and word will get out soon enough.

Speaking of those 100,000 fans: before I put my phone away, I take a quick look at Amrita's Facebook page. There is nothing, just a notice about the "postponement" of the Ojai event posted maybe a few hours after I got the text from Gordon, followed the next day by one of her usual affirmations — but I think those are posted by the Acolady who does all that for her for free.

Before I can get up to go, Brooke is off to a morning in her welding studio, and Ike is studying me as I put my phone away.

"Something wrong?"

"Amrita's in the hospital over San Jose," I say, heading out in the sudden blast of sunshine over the hill. "The guys in my band are with her now, but they have to take off, so I'm going to keep her company."

He struggles to his feet. "What happened?"

Not sure how much I should share, so I just say "not sure."

"Let me know if I can help," he says through the open window, propped up on his good leg.

The hospital over near San Jose sits like the glittering flagship in a flotilla of shiny glass buildings, docked next to the concrete spaghetti of a massive cloverleaf where an old freeway crosses a new one.

I find a place to park, figure out the room — Nancy Smith's of course, because Amrita doesn't have a last name because she isn't really Amrita — and make my way to the right floor with my guitar. By the time I get there, Jenna is already gone, back to her place up in Berkeley, and David is antsy to hit the road for his own place down in Ventura.

"Thanks for coming, brother," he says. "She didn't want me to leave until you were here."

He leads me to her room down the hall, and goes to push the closed door open.

"Shouldn't you knock? She might be — you know —"

"She wants it closed all the time," he says under his breath. "She does her you-know in the bathroom." Then he pushes the door open and announces into the room, "Hey, dear one — it's me again. And Jack's here too. You awake?"

I tiptoe behind him into the room, darkened but for the afternoon light coming in through an enormous window with a view of the freeways below.

Amrita is turned toward the window, a skinny lumpen shadow under the white linen of the big hospital bed. She seems tethered from disappearing altogether into the bed by three tubes suspended from IV bags.

I can't see her face, even with her hair pulled back and tucked into a surgical cap to make room for a bulky dressing encircling her neck.

"Amrita?" David says, a little louder, then turns to me. "She's like this about half the time. Drugs, sleep, both, I guess. We've just been hanging around in here," he points at the two chairs, "instead of the waiting room."

He picks up his harmonium and hoodie, and is gone a minute later.

I turn and notice that there are no flowers or cards anywhere in the room, just a dog-eared copy of the *Bhagavad Gita* and a set of mala beads on the table by the window.

I put my guitar down, and tiptoe over to catch a glimpse of Amrita's face, scrunched up on the pillow. The right half looks mostly like her, though ten years older with no make-up and no sun in who-knows-how-long; the left half is an amorphous, cherry-red bulge, from behind her ear to around the corner of her jaw, swelling to swallow half her neckline in an angry, grotesque ballooning that looks fiery, painful, ready to explode.

I have no idea what to do, so I sit in the chair by the window and text Eve.

*Amrita in the hospital in San Jose. Really sick. Here with her now & no one around. Kinda weird. Talk?*

*Picking up T. Talk in 1 hr?*

*OK.*

I open my guitar case and stare at it a minute, look over and see that she hasn't moved, and close it with my foot.

I pick up the beat-up copy of the *Gita* and remember reading it after that very first rehearsal, when she was riffing on the story. She could imagine herself most like Shakti, she said, happy to be Shiva's consort while he was busy regenerating the universe. It was important work after all, like being the model girlfriend for the divine rock star who was busy creating the Hindus, setting them up to dominate India, Sri Lanka, and the rest of South Asia, at least for a time. Within that larger creation story, the *Gita* is the Hindu master parable about maintaining your poise — keeping your shit together — when your world is falling apart and you have no choice but to deal with something that sucks.

"By whose authority?" Arjuna asks his charioteer.

The charioteer reveals that he is Krishna, which means he's God embodied in the world, at least until this particular song ends.

"What is your name?" Arjuna asks.

*I am the beginning, middle, and end of all beings,* Krishna answers.

More or less the same answer God is said to have given Moses on the mountain, when Moses was arguing — more than asking — why he, like Arjuna, should have to deal with these foolish people and all their bullshit. (Because Moses was a good Jew after all, and Arjuna would have made a good one too.)

*I was what was, I am what is, I will be what will be*, God answered.

Which was apparently good enough for Moses, as it was good enough for Arjuna. Not that it mattered; either way, they were left to clean up the mess. Or, when in Rome, make like Marcus Aurelius and just deal.

I put the book down and look over at Amrita, and she hasn't moved. It's odd that for all the people who adore her — no, who worship her — for those 100,000+ on the listserv and those 110,862 Facebook followers, there is no one here. No one has figured it out, no one has come crashing into this cold and lonely hospital room to rub her pretty feet, read to her, sing with her. Just Jenna and David, and now me. Her band.

But maybe it's not so odd. None of those people are family, and family is who shows up, or is supposed to show up, right? If you have one, I mean. And where is Amrita's? I've never heard her mention anybody. And she's never had a boyfriend, just whichever Man Bun was her consort of the moment and all the rest of the Man Buns buzzing around her like horny bees waiting for their turn. Is she an orphan? Is she like me, someone long ago severed from her parents, siblings, and everybody she grew up with? Because that could just as easily be me over there in that bed, by myself, with no one coming.

That cold, stoic, heroic aloneness used to work for me just fine, was something I actually took some sort of bitter pride in — if in what now seems like a pathetic, martyr-like way that only a Marcus Aurelius might find ennobling.

I remember trying to explain that to Jill one time. And not only did she *not* get it, but it may have been the thing that finally drove her away from me, after all the other things I did and said that should have driven her away years earlier. It was our last night in camp, on that long road trip when I drove her from my old house in Colorado to her new grad school apartment in Sacramento.

"I don't want this to sound weird," she blurted out. "But what would you do if you were suddenly sick? Like really sick? And you're all by yourself? You have no family, or anybody really close to you. And I know you're all down with your climbing bros. But that's just Dudeville, everybody's just passing through, and you are too."

I remember having no good answer, just staring at our campfire and drinking more whiskey instead of answering.

"I know if I got really injured out here," she went on, "or sick — like with cancer or something — I could count on my mom. Or my aunt. Or my sister. What would you do?"

I finished my whiskey in a swallow and swished it around in my mouth, my head swimming with the weed and the long drive that day around the backroads of the Sierras.

Then the words just spilled out of me before I could stop them: "I would just die," I said. "Period. End of story. Lights out. And I'd find a way to do so without anyone's help."

Even though we were shrouded in near darkness, I could see her hard stare, her mouth suddenly agape.

"You would just die. Just like that."

"Yes."

I could feel her breath catch, stop, start again. "You're serious."

"I am."

"That makes me so sad," her voice cracked, as if she were trying to choke back tears.

"I'm sorry," I said. And I was sorry, not for what I'd said, but for saying it to her, out loud, the thing I thought I'd never say to anybody. "But you asked."

"Yes," she cleared her throat. "I did."

"I know it's harsh," I said. "But I'm all alone in the world. Always have been."

"Except for the nine years you were married."

"Yes, except then. And maybe that's why I stayed married so long. My wife was an orphan too, and we were all we had."

She didn't say anything, instead picking up the bowl, lighting it, taking a long hit, and handing it to me.

"And independent of all that —," I said, then took a long hit of the weed even though I remember being plenty stoned, because I was feeling suddenly defensive and expansive at the same time, and as far away from her as I'd ever felt, and knowing I'd have to talk my way back, "which is really just a matter of practicalities and logistics — the truth is I'm not at all afraid of the physical act of dying. Seriously. My life was total shit for 20 years. And then it was a total grind for 15. And for the last five years it's been great — heaven on earth. So why not go out on top?"

What a self-aggrandizing jackass I used to be. *Just a matter of practicalities and logistics.* I actually said that. Wow. What a difference a couple heartbreaks and turning 50 makes.

"Jack?"

I look up and see Amrita, lifting her head from the bed.

"That you?"

I walk over as she tries to push herself up out of the bed, while also trying to look away to avoid my eyes in shame, as if she could disguise the angry red swelling gripping her neck and half her face.

"Hey there," I say, and find her hand in the bedding. "It's me. I'm here. And I brought my guitar. David said a little music makes you feel better?"

She finally looks up at me and her eyes, already glassy with drugs and sleep, flood with tears. "Oh, Jack," she says. "I knew I could count on you."

"Of course."

She's openly weeping now, like a sloppy drunk. Except the booze is running down one or two of those three tubes into an arm — normally suntanned, rippled with taut little yoga muscles, and jangling with mala beads and bracelets — suddenly gray, pale and thin, barely large enough to hold the IV.

"That's what Gordon told me about you, Jack," she sniffles. "You're the man that shows up. No matter what." Her voice starts to drift, like she's talking in her sleep. "When things are blowing up. There you are. Just like Gordon said. The strong one."

I suppose this counts as a shitstorm too, and here I am in the eye of it again, though there's hardly an adrenaline rush.

"I'm right here," I say. "Do you feel up for a little music?"

"That would be sweet," she mumbles.

I pull out my guitar, and check the tuning. And with just my fingers — no flatpick, no fingerpicks — I take a long slow breath, and coax out the quietest guitar voicing of the softest mantra we do, her version of the *moola* prayer, a pure warm bath of a melody.

I'm barely through it the first time when I hear her weeping. I look up from my guitar to see her crying, openly this time, the whole skinny ridgeline of her body shaking beneath the covers. I'm not sure if she wants me to stop, or go on, or if she might even try to whisper out the chant herself. But I press on anyway, singing the Sanskrit myself, and think of what the words have come to me over the years.

> *Om* (Please! Whoever's out there!)
> *Sat Chit Ananda* (You, the formless, conscious bliss, love and joy . . . )
> *Parabrahma* (who created everything . . . )
> *Purushothama Paramatma* (and shows up inside us to give us strength)

> *Sri Bhagavati Sametha* (in your divine, creative feminine form)
> *Sri Bhagavate* (in your divine, unchanging masculine form)
> *Namaha* (Thank you now and always)

I can just barely hear, over my own voice and the soft, harp-like twinkle of my guitar, her voice humming along, a low, papery moan, a lament from far away.

I play and sing on, softly enough to hear her and let her hear herself, round and round the *moola* prayer . . . until after I don't know how many times through, she's stopped humming and weeping, and from what I can see of her face, she's more passed out than asleep . . .

The crappy part is having to break the news to Eve, which is also breaking it to myself: I'd better stick around until somebody else gets here, which could be today, tonight, who knows? I haven't seen a doctor or nurse since I got here, and somebody should be looking after her. She looks completely defenseless over there in that big cold bed: sick, vulnerable, wasting away, and alone.

I'll call Gordon and ask him what I should do, and maybe David again tomorrow. There has to be somebody else we can call, like Diane — I'm sure she'd love to hear from me, yay — or maybe Amy/Amie/Aimée from up in the city? But David did say she doesn't want any of the Acoladies to see her this way, so it'll have to be Gordon.

As I'm digging out my phone, it rings: Eve calling back almost exactly an hour after I'd texted her.

She says she's completely cool about the situation and my not making it up there tonight, because that's exactly who and how she is: a rock, immovable, imperturbable. Which just makes me want to see her more. So Moses, Arjuna and Marcus Aurelius be damned, I bitch and moan about it. I also want Eve to know I was really psyched to head up there; but she's more concerned about what could wrong in the hospital, why there aren't any nurses around, and if I'm going to be here all night, would there be food for me?

I tell her I have stuff out in the van, was ready for the trip up to see them, and I'll call her later.

An hour later, Amrita is still fast asleep, and I'm sitting and paging through the *Gita* when a nurse about my age wanders in and sighs dramatically — for my benefit? to say she's overworked? so I don't pester her? — while checking Amrita's IV tubes.

"She OK?"

"You'd have to ask the doctor about that."

"Alright. When's the doctor coming around?"

"He's busy. He'll be around when he can."

"Great," I sigh.

"I can tell you that she's as OK as anyone could be. With this severe an infection, and the immune reaction," she says without turning to look at me. "Most people her age would have died. But she's extremely strong, as you probably know." She goes to enter something in the computer over in the corner, and when she's finished, she looks up at me for the first time since she walked in. "Are you a member of her family, finally?"

"Not really. I'm in her band."

"Her band," she snorts, looks at my open guitar case on the floor, and sighs, "Weird."

*Yeah, fuck you*, I think, and pick up the *Gita*, not to read it but to make sure she caught my *fuck you*.

I am definitely spending the night right here. I'll figure it out tomorrow, and get up to Humboldt later, or even on Sunday. Eve and Tommy both have Monday off from school, so I still won't have to leave until Tuesday morning.

After the nurse wanders back out, I check on Amrita, who is more bombed than ever, sunken further down into the huge bed, with only her sweaty forehead and one clenched eye showing above the covers.

I head out to my van to get the book I was taking on this trip — the *Gita* is great but I've read it and I don't consider it holy, so I don't need to read it 108 times, like the yoga crowd says you should. At this point, I'm more interested in finding the hospital cafeteria, because this is going to be a bit of a haul . . .


In the cafeteria, thanks to some shitty salad and more caffeine I don't need, I start to get pissy. Why do I have to deal with this? She's my boss, and only my part-time boss, not my girlfriend, or my sister, or my mother. I was looking forward to a picnic dinner on the beach tonight with Eve and Tommy; and now I'm stuck down here, waiting for the Valley and the rest of the Bay Area to flood with holiday traffic tomorrow.

Then I hear a voice, way in the back of my head, Leah's voice, talking about Billy Jacobson.

*I know it sucks, Jack,* she says. *When it's been a long week, and you're tired, and you don't have it to give. Just don't forget — you're doing it for Billy Jacobson.*

That's what she told me one Friday night when we were grabbing an early dinner before *Erev Shabbat* service. I was exhausted from a grueling week at work; and as much as I loved playing the music and running the band most of the time, I really didn't feel like dragging into *Shir Hadash* for yet another Friday night circus.

But all Leah had to do was say my own words back to me.

I had barely been aware of Billy Jacobson, the self-conscious, almost pathologically shy gay man who would come alone every Friday night and Saturday morning. He would sit in the center of the front pew, but rather than sing or clap or get up and dance, he would just tip his head back on the pew, his eyes closed and face blank, and disappear into the music.

It wasn't until we were meeting in a bar and going through the usual congregational chit-chat that Rabbi Miriam spilled the news to me, thinking I already knew: "Billy Jacobson went into hospice yesterday."

"Huh?"

"You didn't know? He has inoperable brain cancer. We should get a *minyan* together and go in and do a *Shacharit* or *Ma'ariv* with him as soon as we can."

"Won't that be a little much, all of us in a hospice room?"

"Maybe, and maybe we can dispense with the *minyan*. But not with you," she said. "He told me he never got much out of services, until you showed up and revved up the music. He said he loves music, and hearing you play and sing has been one of the few things that's helped him find any peace these last few months."

*You're doing it for Billy Jacobson,* I hear Leah's voice again, and can almost feel her squeezing my elbow across the restaurant table. *For whoever that might be in the congregation now. Someone is hurting, and your music will help them.*

And right now, that someone is Amrita, the yoga rock star with 110,862 followers and no actual friends.

I finish my crappy cafeteria coffee, check my phone, and text Eve: *Just hanging around the H. Call if you're bored. I am!*

She doesn't text back, which is strange, so I lose myself in my phone, looking at Amrita's Facebook and Instagram and Twitter and all that crap, wondering what to do next, whom to call. Yes, Leah — Amrita is Billy Jacobson right now, and he also had a rabbi and whole congregation looking after him. Amrita has all of me right now, and I'm not enough.

So I give in and text Gordon. I've been holding off on asking him for help for the same reason, I think, that David and Jenna did: he is hardly Amrita's friend. On top of that, I've watched him turn out to be an even bigger asshole toward Johnny than Johnny is toward anyone. Sure, the guy found me, lined me up with these two gigs, and even set me up at Angel's Rest. But that's his job; he's everybody's manager, and rakes 15% off the top of everything, so let him manage this too.

He calls me right back.

"Thanks for being there, man," he says over the roar of L.A. traffic into his open convertible, not stopping to listen as usual. "Amrita's got a real friend in you, Jack. I've got some feelers out for some help tomorrow, but can you hold down the fort until then? I'd be up there myself, but Chloe's got a big opening down here tonight, and we're the hosts."

"But —"

"Oh, and while I got you, Johnny's gig at Coyote Mountain Casino —," he says, his voice drowned out by a horn blast. "— which should be fine, because it looks like we're gonna have to cancel AnandaFest that week anyway. Oh, and her workshop in Kripalu — you know, that place in Massachusetts — the week after. Cool? Gotta go, man!"

Which at least gives me something to do on my phone: clean up my calendar. Which includes deleting that trip back to Massachusetts. Along with the extra day I'd set aside to go visit my father's grave back there, something Eve was pushing me — in her quiet, imperturbable way — to do.

I hover over the calendar entries for the event, the flights, the rental car, ready to delete them. In those four found days, I can go surf somewhere out of the way, or figure out a place to live when we get booted out of Angel's Rest, or best of all, go back up to Humboldt to hang out with Eve and Tommy.

Easy to chalk up the miss to an act of God, *force majeure, deus ex machina.* Because if I were the type of true believer who thinks God is actually sitting around "up there" — you know, waiting to see which football team prayed harder for victory before granting it — then why wouldn't He decide to strike down Amrita with a life-threatening surgical complication for the sole purpose of sparing me what I know will be an awful reckoning?

I'm heading back up to Amrita's room, and notice that the sun is setting already and the hospital an unearthly quiet, when I realize Eve hasn't texted me back. I haven't heard from her in several hours now, actually, which is odd. She's usually right there.

Back up in the room, Amrita's doing a little better. She's sitting up in bed, and there's a tray of food, full but for an apple core and dessert crumbs.

When I come in, she forces a smile at me, and we chat about the weather, the hospital, the food, but I can see her fading, sliding back down under the covers.

I settle into the chair with *Cadillac Desert*, the book I'd stashed in my guitar case, and get up only to turn on a light when the sun is finally down and the room dark.

The book is fascinating and bitterly funny, so I don't know how many hours have gone by when I look up for some reason, and a moment later, there's a knock on the door. Who can that be? An Acolady, finally?

I walk over and open it quietly, just enough to see who's out there.

And it's Eve! Standing there with a big bunch of wildflowers!

"Hey! What are you doing here?"

"What it says in my calendar. I'm seeing you."

After a long walk around the hospital, and a visit down a dark, empty corridor for a little smooching that only makes it harder to separate for the night, we decide that it's better if I stay in Amrita's room tonight. It'll be yet another goodbye full of sweet longing, but Eve will drive back to her sister's place in Oakland for the night, rather than all the way over to Angel's Rest.

I'm in high alert mode anyway, so after we kiss goodbye and she drives off, I go to the window and look down at the frozen sea of headlights and taillights down on the freeways, and imagine everything terrible that could happen on her way up there. She will be inching her way along the same freeway that collapsed during the '89 World Series, and wouldn't now be the perfect time for it to come down again, with all that holiday weekend traffic sitting at a dead stop inside its stack of concrete.

But no: she texts me two and a half hours later that she made it the 45 miles back to Lily's in Oakland.

I sink further into the chair, and fall asleep somewhere out there in the middle of the dry, dusty, ruined Cadillac desert . . .

Eve is back in the morning, surviving once again the latest earthquake that never comes, if not the traffic that never stops, because this is the first time I've seen her rattled about anything.

"Geez, Jack," she says. "I forgot how friendly everyone is down here, especially at eight-thirty in the morning. Uncle Pete was covering his eyes every time we had to merge on and off the freeway."

"Uncle Pete?"

"Yes," she sighs, "he came down with me and I dropped him at Lily's before I saw you last night. He says he wanted to come down, because you got him thinking about his friend. Remember? A Chumash, who he says lives south of Angel's Rest?"

Down the hallway, Uncle Pete is at the far, empty end of the waiting room — leather vest, western shirt, jeans, boots, and hat — walking around in circles and humming to himself.

He stops when he sees us. "Jack — hello," he says. "I am giving the traditional prayer of thanks for surviving a near death."

He waits for my reaction, then cracks a smile, closes his eyes and goes back to his humming and circling.

"We will meet you in the cafeteria on the first floor when you are done," Eve says to him.

"He thinks that's funny," I say to Eve on our way down the elevator, "but the Jews actually have a prayer for that."

"He was not kidding," she says. "That was that prayer."

After breakfast, Eve and Uncle Pete leave for his friend's place on the coast. They will be driving right past Angel's Rest on the way, I note, which is a little frustrating: I wanted to show her my world, or mine for now anyway: that spectacular stretch of road, golden hills and rolling meadows and cliffs spiked with wind-shaped trees, hawks and eagles soaring over all of it, and all those views out to the endless ocean.

But no.

Back up in Amrita's room, she is awake and sitting halfway up in bed, eating most of the breakfast someone brought her. She looks to be doing a little better this morning. But, according to the younger, much friendlier nurse who is checking her IV tubes, she will need to be here for three more days, until she's done with the heaviest of the antibiotics.

"But it is going to be a long haul," she turns and leans close to me and says under her breath.

I sigh as I sit back down in the chair that now hurts for my having slept in it, sort of, last night, and force out a smile at Amrita.

She's still awake but looks like she wants to drift off to sleep again.

It's time to text Gordon, and rather than listen to his bullshit, just tell him flat out that, as her manager, he needs to "manage" this. Which may or may not be true, but what do I know about show business?

The nurse forgets to shut the door on her way out for some reason, so I go to shut it and there's a familiar voice saying hi to her and — Ike? Really?

He limps in with a big bouquet of flowers, and a card.

Amrita slips down under the covers, trying to hide her red and swollen jaw and neck, and whimpers, "Ike!" and bursts into tears.

I know they know each other through Kenny and Gordon, but is that it, or is there something more? And how did I not know?

"Hey man," I say and move between him and her bed.

But he goes to limp around me, and Amrita looks up at me and nods, *It's OK, I'm glad he's here.*

Well, huh, I think, and sit back in the chair, and watch him move carefully around to the side of her bed, and lower his great frame and shoulders to hug her.

Definitely something more between them. Was he ever a Man Bun? One of the breastfeeders? It never would have occurred to me in five more years of working for one and living with the other, but they would actually be perfect for each other: lost, lonely, hungry 25-year-olds stuck in 55-year-old bodies and lives.

"I'll give you guys a break," I say, and go to leave.

I wander the halls of the hospital for another hour, look at the stuff on the walls, try to meditate in the chapel — which nearly puts me to sleep — so I get another coffee and head back up.

Amrita is sitting up in bed and Ike is telling her one of his old war stories from the pro tour. They both look up at me like I've interrupted them.

"Hey braw," he says. "If you want a break, I'm good here for a while. We're just catching up on old times."

Then he actually winks at me — this 55-year-old former professional surf-crusher dude — like we're in eighth grade, and he wants me to go back to study hall so he can make out with his new crush.

"Yes, Jack," Amrita says, her voice still frail and strained, but much stronger than even a day ago. "You must be exhausted."

HORN!!!

This holiday weekend traffic is insane, every lane stopped in every direction, cars lunging into gaps with horns and middle fingers. Uncle Pete has probably had a complete nervous breakdown by now.

I'm so tired from the last 24 hours that all these people in all these cars don't even seem real. Like her over there, in the passenger seat in that red Porsche, a giant puff of blonde hair with a giant puff of blonde dog in her lap. Not sure where she ends and the dog begins. Always with the damn hair out here, like Jason's Golden Fleece.

But who am I kidding? I love Eve's hair, long, black, and beautiful . . . and she's waiting for me on the other end of this parking lot stuck half up the mountain to the coast.

I can't make this traffic go any faster, so I just submit to it, let my weary mind drift . . . from Eve's beautiful hair . . . to Amrita in that hospital bed . . . back to Eve . . . back to Amrita . . . and . . . Ike? How weird is that? Those two?

Amrita, runner-up for Ms. Wisconsin turned yoga rock star for the ages — and Ike? Former surf pro and one of the pioneers of kitesurfing, limping around in the body of a wounded old prizefighter, with the big, desperate heart of a lonely teenager.

He still talks like a teenager, anyway: surprised and hurt that the world is going his way, full of magical thinking that it might, if he pleads his case hard enough. He's still pleading his case it seems, when he's telling me the story. Like to his father, when Ike announced that he was quitting baseball to surf every day after school.

*To surf?* his father screamed at him. *Over my dead body!*

*But there's a contest, Dad!*

*Contest?*

Ike won that contest, and Ike's father found other contests for him, all leading up to the junior pro tour. Ike came in fourth on that tour, the first year he entered, and won it the next year. Ike's father even learned to surf himself, so he could coach Ike, and manage the contests, gear, prize money, and those first Quiksilver and board shop sponsorships.

Then the Hawaii guys took over, the Kelly Slaters and Rob Machados, and solid fourths and fifths turned tens of thousands in sponsorship money into a couple thousand and some free gear. And Ike's father, as the fathers of many young athletes tend to be, was better at his day-job than managing a sports star. As an engineer, he could also build cool shit with surfboards and sails and whatever else was at hand, and was one of a group of tinkerers who designed those first creaky windsurfing rigs that Ike would take out on the ocean. That's how his son became a pioneer in windsurfing, which was blowing up everywhere from the Columbia River Gorge to the north shore of Maui, with Orange County right in the middle.

But, apparently, the big airs Ike and those early windsurfers were getting weren't big enough, so his father started messing around with the next wave in wave-riding: kite-boarding. Ike was one of the first to harness himself into one of those huge kites, wedging his feet into the straps mounted on a modified surfboard, and fly across the waves. And he might have been the world champion at it, when a tour finally coalesced around the sport. But one day, he was out when the wind was too big for anybody else, himself included; and he lost control of the kite when the wind shifted, suddenly, to onshore. It brought him in way too close, and he went down, hard, right where and when a wave was pulling out, and shattered his pelvis, and his career was over. Despite two surgeries and six months of intensive PT — which is how he got to know Freya so well — he would never be able to surf again, never be able to get around without that pronounced limp, left only to sit on his perch at Angel's Rest, and stare out to sea, and see all that he had lost . . .

And there it is, the top of the hill and that very ocean.

Two hours after leaving the hospital, I've made it the 40 miles over to Angel's Rest.

A hundred feet north, I catch two red flashes out by the gate: big red pennants now, flying from the poles holding the resort developer's signs.

And there is Eve's little old pickup truck, parked out by the road, looking like a rusty red toy in the shadow of a half dozen oversized surfer vans and trucks.

Shit. I forgot to give her the key to the gate, when I gave her the key to my house.

When I get down there, she's sitting out on the porch, watching the ocean.

Before I can get out of the van, she comes over and is pulling the door open, and I'm climbing down into her arms . . .

Ten minutes later, we are a sweaty, spicy tangle of hair and sex, flecked with grains of the stray sand in every bed at a beach.

"I will say Jack," she sighs as she slips down alongside me, "I was not this hot and bothered, until I saw that van of yours."

I've got nothing for that except a groan and a sigh.

"Isn't that the cliché?" she asks. "About vans and guys on the make? I think I have seen bumper stickers about that."

"Yes," I groan. "Lots of bumperstickers. 'If the van's a rocking, don't come knocking.' That's one of the classics."

She slides down the length of me, wet skin on wet skin, our bodies melting together.

"There are worse clichés to have in life."

"Ha," I snort. "I'd settle for just the cliché."

"What do you mean?"

"I mean that particular cliché just happens to be the subject of Johnny's best-selling song ever."

"Really?"

"Oh yes. 'Sunset Road.' The van, the small-town girl, the end of the —," I catch myself.

"The end of the trail," she says. "Oh. Wonderful."

"Yeah."

She lets out a long sigh, "I don't think I needed to know that, Jack," and nuzzles up under my chin. "Let's just pretend that our very first time ever was in my family's sacred teepee, OK? We were not in some silly old pop song. We were in a ground-breaking, revisionist western. Is that better?"

She pushes herself up onto an elbow, her hair slipping like a curtain across her other shoulder and my shoulder, and gives me that half-smile. "I can be Sacagawea, and you can be Kevin Costner."

An hour later, we're playing house.

I'm cooking, and she's sweeping the sand off the old floor, then studying and rearranging the rocks and shells on the shelves of my bookcase.

We eat out on the porch, watching seagulls dive-bombing the beach in front of Neptune's and a couple surfers out at the point. Brooke buzzes back and forth on her dirt bike down on Beach Road, scattering the seagulls, stopping to tinker with the engine.

Eve calls to check in with Tommy, back in Mendocino with her cousin. And right before she hands the phone to me she says, "we wish you could be down here with us too, sweet pea," then catches my eye and looks away.

That was odd, feeling the old familiar tickle deep down in my body to run away, but the rest of me staying right here anyway, the same sensation of an itch I had that first morning with Leah's parents, an itch I could just call an itch and didn't need to scratch.

"This is a special place," Eve finally says, "just like you have been telling me. Beautiful. But it feels a little strange too. Because it is falling apart maybe? Or because we know the awful thing that is about to happen to it?"

I give her a tour of Angel's Rest: the shell of Neptune's, the ruins of the old campground half buried in sand dune, Ike's perch up at the north end, with its view opening all the way south to Monterey Bay and the mountains of Big Sur in the smoky haze beyond. The last of that fire from June is *still* not out.

It feels strange sitting up here on Ike's perch without him. I should text and see if he needs us to come relieve him. But if he did need us, he'd text me back.

"Yeah, man!" one of the surfers hollers and we look over to see his buddy catching a perfect wave, shooting straight out of the pocket at the beach.

Then another scattering of seagulls as Brooke flashes through them on her dirt bike and up the hill and gone, and they settle back down in the empty lane.

Eve's fingers find mine, her hand filling mine, her head against my shoulder. I know Angel's Rest will soon be another thing I've lost and found, that it's going to end sooner than later. But right now, I'm glad only that Eve got to see it, to see what brought me here because right now, the world is just about perfect.

Eve and I are sitting out on my porch reading when the breeze picks up and sun starts to set.

I text Ike to let him know that I'll be heading back over to relieve him for the night.

*Dont bother. All good here.* He texts back. *Have fun with Eve!* Then another text: the *winky-wink* emoji.

Which means that Eve and I get to spend our first night together in the same bed . . .

Seagulls squawk inside the void of sound left behind each wave going out.

A pair of them cry to each other over their breakfast, lifting from water to sky in my mind's eye as I lay here motionless, Eve curled up around me, the room filling with the peach and periwinkle of sea light at dawn.

Before we can roll out of bed and make coffee, Eve's phone rings: her sister Lily is out by the gate, down from Oakland for the day with her daughter.

I run up to unlock the gate, while Eve looks through my mostly empty kitchen for something to cook. And it's not just Lily and her daughter, but Uncle Pete too, and an older man in a black t-shirt, leather vest, jeans, dusty old cowboy hat.

"Sorry not to warn you ahead of time," Lily says to me, when I jump out to unlock the gate. "You know Indians don't go anywhere without relatives."

Back down at the house, Eve has managed to dig out, thaw out, and put together enough food for a big breakfast for more than two of us, but not quite enough for all six of us. But her sister has food and I run over to Brooke's to borrow some eggs; and half an hour later there are seven of us, crammed onto the deck, eating and watching the tide go out.

When we are done, we all go out for a walk along the beach, wide and flat with the tide all the way out now.

Eve and her sister head north toward the point — which makes Ike's perch look empty as ever and reminds me I need to get back to the hospital soon — Lily's daughter behind them combing the beach for shells.

I start to follow them, but Eve gives me that half-smile, then nods toward Uncle Pete and his friend, who have started down the beach in the other direction.

I catch up with them as they make their way past the riprap holding in Beach Road and the ruins of the old state park beach. Uncle Pete's friend, Charlie Many Horses — who lives and works on a ranch just down the road, in the hills above Pescadero — has stopped suddenly, in the exact middle of the tide-emptied cove. He stands there and surveys the cliffs looming over everything and dropping straight to the sea. This cove is usually a chaos of cross-waves; but with the tide this low, it's a maze of standing pools, iridescent in the morning sun, black spines of rock spiked with mussels, stretches of dark sand streaked with sea foam.

Charlie stands there, his eyes still scanning the clifftops, then the break in the rocks where the ocean comes in.

"Right here," he says, closing his eyes.

He turns to face the ocean and closes his eyes too, wisps of silver and black hair under his hat blowing in the breeze. He closes his eyes, takes in a big breath, and his long, lined, coffee-colored face starts to quiver, almost like he wants to sneeze. Suddenly, it is flushed with pain and worry, like he's watching something terrible happen and is powerless to stop it.

"Oh my," Uncle Pete says.

"Yes," Charlie says, then opens his eyes and turns to me. "Do you feel that?"

But I feel only what I ever feel on an empty beach — the Presence, abiding, aware, eternally patient — the same thing I've felt on top of mountains, down in desert canyons, next to great rivers, deep in the woods all the way back East. And sometimes a voice.

But no voice right now, only a long weary sigh from Charlie.

"It was right here," he finally says. "Something very bad happened. And not that long ago."

"Not long ago, people-time?" Uncle Pete asks. "Or earth-time?"

"Just yesterday, earth-time. A hundred years maybe. Wasn't us. White people, and white people. Not even a hundred years ago."

I turn to face the ocean again, close my eyes, and try to imagine whatever it is he just saw, or thinks he saw. But I see only what I hear: the lull of the ocean at low tide and cry of the gulls; a little wind in my ears; and then, finally, that still, small voice, somewhere in the swim of energy between the back of my head and the back of my chest, the Presence.

*Listen*, it says.

And that's it.

*Listen.*

I reach out across the waves with my ears, the way I would always reach out in the mountains, or down in one of those canyons, but all I can hear is ocean.

And Uncle Pete saying something, from far away.

When I catch up to them, Charlie turns to me and says, "Pete says you have not done a sweat?"

"Me? No."

"You should come do one, Jack. We have a good lodge on the ranch, back in the forest. Far from the road, far from everything."

"Yes, Jack," Uncle Pete says. "A very good lodge. And it is good to sweat, to cleanse and strengthen the heart. Good, especially," he waves toward the old cottages up ahead — tumbling down from the cliff to what's left of Beach Road, the rip rap, the beach, blanching like old bones in the suddenly hot morning sun — "with all of this change coming."

"Sure, why not," I say so they'll change the subject. "That would be interesting."

We walk the rest of the way back in silence.

"Good," Charlie says as he picks our way over the riprap onto Beach Road. "You will come sweat tomorrow then?"

I haven't said a word about it either way; but back at the house, when Uncle Pete tells Eve and her sister about Charlie's suggestion, a sweat lodge on some ranch down in Pescadero is suddenly my plan for tomorrow.

This morning, though, I have to get back to the hospital to relieve Ike.

Eve was going to come with me. But Lily and her daughter came all the way over here to see her and the ocean, and Uncle Pete and all of them want to check out Half Moon Bay, so they'll drop Eve off at the hospital on their way back to Oakland. Lots of moving parts, lots of improvisation. Family, I suppose.

The late morning traffic is still pointing at the beach, so I'm back at the hospital in an hour.

Amrita is sitting halfway up in bed, looking at her phone, and Ike's great frame is sprawled out over the chair by the window, fast asleep.

"Hey there!" I say as cheerfully as I can when I walk in with my guitar.

She looks up at me and smiles weakly, like she is going to start crying. "Oh, Jack. There you are again."

She still has that big bandage all the way around her neck like a whiplash collar; but the swelling has gone down, and her face is less puffy and red.

"And our friend," she whispers, nodding over at Ike in his surf shorts, flip flops, and Hawaiian shirt, like he just got off a cruise ship at the wrong port of call. "Such a sweet man. I can't thank you both enough."

I set my guitar down as quietly as I can next to the other chair, but Ike clambers awake.

"Hey, man," he yawns. "Back already? What time is it?"

"Time to go get a proper night's sleep," I say. "Traffic sucks, so you might want to grab some coffee for the ride."

He lets out a huge lion's yawn. "Traffic. Awesome." But he doesn't get up to leave, only smiles over at Amrita and she tries to smile back, one of her big beaming stage smiles, even with all that bandage swimming around her jaw.

Something is going on with those two.

"Think I'll go grab myself a cup right now," I say.

When I get back to Amrita's room with a big coffee, Ike is gone and Jenna is there, standing over Amrita and holding both of her hands, and there's a harmonium sitting next to my guitar.

"How blessed am I?" Amrita says. "Two-thirds of the best *kirtan* band in the business."

"Do you feel up for a little chant?" Jenna asks her.

"Always!"

Jenna looks over at me, *Want to play?*

I nod *Why not* and go close the door, and five minutes later, we have our instruments out, and are finding our groove as quietly as we can, trading phrases in C major, a hushed version of our usual invocation.

Amrita has pushed herself up as far as she can in the bed and closed her eyes, her hands in prayer position in front of the opening of her hospital gown.

"What do you say, Jack," Jenna says as she pumps the harmonium, weaving that big, lulling organ chord into a plaintive A minor. "We sing to the god of healing."

I can't remember which one that might be. "Seems like the right time and place," I say, tuning my bottom E string.

"Yes," Amrita says, "I could channel a little — Dhanvantari — today." She tries to squeeze out a big, heavy, grateful smile, which makes her look like she's about to burst into tears again.

Jenna starts in on a chant we've done many times, always to Saraswati, the goddess of music and the arts, and I see why two bars in: the chants scan the exact same way, four even beats.

I follow Jenna with the guitar, playing and singing the response line as quietly as I can. Amrita is swaying as best she can over in the bed, trying to sing along, her voice weak, frail, cracked, but she's eking out the melody. . .

> *Om shri Dhanvantari namaha!*
> *Jai jai Dhanvantari om!*
> *Om shri Dhanvantari namaha!*
> *Jai jai Dhanvantari om!*

A couple rounds through, and Jenna and I are locked in on the rhythm; and just like any gig with hundreds of people in front of us, the room starts to soften and melt, the music flowing out of us like a fountain of orange, pink and purple water.

I'm jolted back by burst of weeping: Amrita, over in the bed, tears streaming down her face, her whole body shaking.

Jenna notices too, and we nod to each other and dig in a little harder, a smidge more tempo and volume, and put our heads down and keep singing.

It's too bad Dhanvantari is a god and not a goddess: if there were ever a time for Amrita to take on a deity's persona for the sake of the performance, now would be it. She always likes to say that she is the goddess of plenty, or wisdom, or devotion; and as elliptical as it seems when she launches into the story, the goddess *du jour* does make sense, the music fits, and the crowd eats it all up.

I glance over at Amrita, and she's still weeping and her body still swaying, but softly, quietly, with the rhythm of the music.

Which goddess is she really? And if she can be all of them as suits the mood, is she really ever any of them? Or maybe, as Radhe once quipped to me after a *kirtan* — my Radhe, not Radhe the goddess! — Amrita is really Akhilandeshvari.

"That's a mouthful to say," I told her. "Who's that?"

"The Goddess of Never Not Broken," Radhe said.

Jenna and I play and sing on, and I watch Amrita over in the bed, sobbing and singing to herself.

Yes, that's exactly who she is, without the glitter and disco ball lights, without Jenna and David and me playing at full tilt into a boomy sound system. The Goddess of Never Not Broken. And how perfect for the Acoladies, the Man Buns, the Old Hempy Dudes, and all those Lost Girls of Yoga. But "Akhilandeshvari" is a hard name to say back to her, let alone sing, especially when you're trying to dance at the same time.

Jenna starts to bring the chant down, and I'm right behind her.

We sit in the looming silence left behind for a good 15 or 20 seconds, and let the echoes of the music circle the room before crumbling to the floor.

Amrita beams at us from over in the bed and says, "let's do another, please."

We start in on a rowdier chant we always do to Ganesha, quiet as we can.

Thirty seconds in, the door flies open, and a nurse with a perfectly trimmed brown beard storms in. He puts his hand on his hip and frowns at us, like he's going to yell at us for the noise.

We cut the volume to a whisper, but keep playing, Jenna staring at him, defiantly, challenging him to yell at us.

He stands there glowering, but there's something off about it; then he catches my eye and bursts into a big grin, goes to shut the door and comes back singing along.

We pick it back up, and a tiny blonde nurse comes in, and tries to make herself even smaller, scrunching herself up behind the IV thing.

She puts her hands in *Anjali Mudra*, and chants along: Jenna leading, and Amrita, the two nurses and me singing the response. An actual *kirtan*. In a hospital room.

Amrita sits up in her bed, her face dried of tears and calm as the horizon of the ocean, breathing in and singing out. She *is* Akhilandeshvari, bathing in a rare moment of respite and peace for nothing more than having survived the worst medical consequences of her own brokenness.

Jenna volunteers to spend the night, even before I tell her I have "some people" visiting back at Angel's Rest, so I sneak out after Amrita falls asleep.

I claw my way through the Sunday afternoon rush hour back to Angel's Rest, just as the sun is going down and a big spontaneous party is getting under way down in Neptune's, with Eve the guest of honor.

The stereo Brooke has rigged up behind the bar is blasting some old jam, and everyone has come down with beer, wine, something to eat: Ike, Ryan and Brittany, Chuck the Hippie Mailman, and Brooke still in her welding stuff with a black streak across her cheek.

I bail her out of the stream of questions about her life up north — not that she needs it, or seems to mind, but it does feel a little rude — by changing the subject, ever so slightly, to Uncle Pete, with a question on my mind since this morning out on the beach with him and Charlie.

"So Chuck," I ask him, because he's been living at Angel's Rest for 20 years and is resident historian, "did anything violent go down on the beach, maybe a hundred years ago or so?"

"Why do you ask?"

"Because her uncle Pete and his buddy were picking up something heavy down in the cove, at the south end."

"Don't know of anything," Chuck says. "But that doesn't mean something didn't happen. The bootleggers who ran in and out of here used to land down there. The south cove was deepest water in close, with no rocks, and they came in with heavy loads. When they think it was?"

"A hundred years ago."

"That woulda been right in the middle of Prohibition. And it was all gangsters, and no law. Coulda been a shoot-out or who know what."

We all sit and think about that for a long minute.

Eve finally breaks the silence, "I should call Tommy," and stands to go.

She heads north up Beach Road with her phone, and all eyes turn to me.

"So," Brittany says and nudges my foot. "We like your new girlfriend, Jack."

"I like her too," I say. I know where this is going, so I flip it around to Ike. "And speaking of new girlfriends," I say to him. "You and Amrita?"

"Oh come on, man," he waves me off.

"What? I saw the way you were looking at each other."

"Dude, please. She's way too old for me."

Eve and I are finally alone again, up on my porch watching the sun set, when she calls Tommy to say good night.

He wants to talk to me more than her — about his day, about some kid he saw with a guitar, and could I show him how to play sometime? — until Eve finally grabs the phone from me and tells him goodnight.

We go to bed early, and sleep in late, and I don't want any of this ever to end, even though I know it will.

She will head north tomorrow. And I will head south for a gig with Johnny the day after that. And for all we know, Angel's Rest will be gone the day after that, and with it everything Brooke has built to keep all of this running.

I lay here in the morning light, Eve under my arm, listening to cry of the gulls over the crash of a big tide. This *will* all end, like all things do. And where I used to find a bitter comfort in that, a pyrrhic freedom in knowing that, ultimately, none of this matters, I am filled only with sadness, a strange longing for a thing I haven't even lost yet.

I pull her in tighter.

She stirs, and runs her finger down the centerline of my face, pausing on my lips.

I go to say something.

"Shh," she says. "I know. Let's not worry about that right now."

I was planning to go back to the hospital in the morning, with Eve to keep me company while I keep Amrita company; but Ike is out on the porch, knocking, and grinning past me into the house when I answer, to let me know that he'll take a turn today.

He's doing me a huge favor, of course, but maybe it's because she's not too old for him after all? Which of course I know. In fact, they're perfect for each other. Maybe another day alone with her in the hospital, especially now that she's perked up a bit, and he'll see that.

When I go back inside, Eve is saying goodbye to someone on the phone.

"That was Uncle Pete," she says. "He and Charlie are doing a sweat this afternoon, before we leave. And they want you to join."

"A sweat lodge? Today?"

"Yes. They always do that near the end of a visit. A big tradition for the men. Charlie says you look like you could use one."

"So you've never done one?"

"Of course I have, with women. It is very powerful, and you will feel altered afterwards."

There must be a strange look on my face.

"But you do not have to if you don't want to. A sweat is very powerful, and if you say no it will not hurt my uncle's feelings."

Half an hour later, we're pulling into a dusty horse ranch tucked into the hills outside Pescadero, where Charlie lives and works as a caretaker for the absentee owner.

The place is almost too perfect. A long drive in from the road, on a dusty lane down a canopied corridor of old oaks, past pastures with white fences and a dozen horses. A big pond with ducks and geese and a little fishing dock. Windmill, red barn, gingerbread house, chickens everywhere, an old dog on the porch.

Uncle Pete and Charlie are sitting on stumps in front of what looks like an old carriage house, converted into a living space, and wave as we pull up.

"Somebody looks like he's ready to sweat," Uncle Pete says to Charlie.

Charlie studies me for far too long. "Maybe," he finally says.

"Mabel is in the big house canning," Charlie says to Eve.

"I will say Hi," she says, then points at her running shoes. "Then go for a run on these hilly roads you are always telling me about. I could use it."

"Good," he says. "Maybe Jenny could too. Maybe see if she'll join you. She's over in the barn."

And then nobody says anything.

It's a thing I've come to notice about them. They stand there, visibly musing, like they are all replaying everything we just said, not jumping to the next thing. It's like meditating in any other group setting, without saying as much, no words, just standing there, musing. Or like Danny and Aaron and me, back at the trailhead after a hard climb.

It's the same thing up the trail: Charlie, Uncle Pete, and a chunky young brown cowboy — as much *vaquero* as Native — who pulled up in a pickup a few minutes after us. We're walking up a wooded draw, a high canopy of eucalyptus towering and creaking overhead, towels around necks, not talking, just walking.

Eve is off running the backroads of the ranch with Charlie's daughter, which all of a sudden sounds like a better plan.

Because this is kind of freaking me out, and I don't get freaked out. Bullies don't scare me; big mountains and big waves don't scare me. Floodlit stages, and crowds of upturned faces, and people writhing on the floor all around me in a spiritual frenzy don't scare me. But nope, this is definitely freaking me out, the steady silence and utter seriousness of these men, the deliberateness of this pace up the trail. I feel like I am going to marching up this hillside to some kind of reckoning.

We break from the trees, and start across a rounded meadow of grass shimmering gold with the sun. And there it is: a black mound at the edge of the forest, a trace of smoke rising out front, a man standing over the fire. A sweat lodge. And it looks terrifying, like the portal to a place I suddenly realize: I do not want to go.

The only thing I can imagine seeing in there is the abyss; the only I can imagine thing hearing is a cacophony of music genres, and maybe the voice of the Presence, which I've only ever heard in the wide open spaces, and know would deafen in an enclosed space.

But I cannot turn back. Because this is another test, if not from Eve then from whatever trajectory I've been on that flung me, from alone next to the ocean with my sorrows, into the middle of her life.

Then it all happens in a blur of auto-commit: my body starts to go and I have no choice but to follow, like dropping off a mountain face or climbing onto an ocean wave. Just hold on. Because that's the only option.

"This is Nathan," Charlie says as we gather around the fire in front of the lodge, a bulging half dome of old wool blankets.

"He is our fire-tender for today. We owe great gratitude to Nathan, for assisting us on our journey today."

I watch what they do, then do it myself: drop trow, down to the full monty but for a water bottle and towel around my waist.

"We always say there is no honor in making your body sick," Charlie says to each of us, then turns to me. "Because this is your first time, you should stay by the door. You will see things, and they will feel good or bad. Listen to what your body says first. Go out if you feel sick."

He turns and disappears through a flap in the blankets, and Uncle Pete and the *vaquero* follow.

I wait to go in last, and take my place by the door.

The light is smothered. Absolute darkness.

I work my way onto what feels like a stiff wool blanket, and hear Uncle Pete sigh a few feet to my right.

Then the heat, like an ocean wave, knocks into me.

And out of the darkness, hovering in the pitch, a pulsing orange: a hot rock in the center of the circle.

Flash of light, and Nathan comes in with another rock — a bright orange glow — and I can see shadows around the circle, the others sitting cross-legged, Nathan crouching.

*HISS!*

A rush of steam off the rocks, billowing up into my face, and a wave of intense heat, and a flash of light as Nathan slips out.

And absolute darkness again.

My mind jumps around, looking for somewhere to land: Eve's face, the view from Ike's perch of the last wildfire smoke over Big Sur, the tide way out this morning, bootleggers gunning each other down under a full moon, all that traffic back to the Valley, Amrita in that hospital bed, the nurses chanting with us this morning. Perfect. Just ride that.

I play and sing the chant in my head, and go from face to face in the hospital room, Amrita, Jenna, the nurses, back to Amrita, and my lungs fill with heat and wet, and everything starts to ooze, the words and music running together like red and purple and pink watercolors on paper turning to tracing paper turning to glass, then like rain on a window filled with moving red and white lights from the street beyond.

I go back to the chant, but words are turning to sounds, and filling with orange sunlight, the chords turning from minor to major, and it's morphing into "Sunset Road" of all damn things, sprinkled with colored light — now red and blue and yellow and green flying around in front of my blacked out eyes, and I'm out on a dance floor with the song as it color-swirls into an extended jam, and I'm playing and dancing to it at the same time.

"Wee-no-way, mah-oh-way," a voice from across the circle.

It's Charlie's voice, those two words again, drenched in all those colors, and now something about blessings, and giving thanks.

*Pop-Pop-Pop!*

It's a hand drum, and Charlie's voice melting into a quiet wailing chant, words like colors and light, dancing around to the steady beat of that drum.

Uncle Pete's voice joins the chant, and another voice, and then voices within those voices, and more voices within those, but they are colors not words, dripping like more rain down black glass, lit up red and blue and purple and green from behind.

A flash of light, the tent flap open again — blinding, white-hot, searing light — and I close my eyes, and there's the sizzle of water on hot rock and another rush of steam and heat and darkness again.

Silence, for second, minutes, ten minutes?

*Pop-Pop, Pop-Pop!*

The drum and Charlie's voice again, sounds I can't decipher because I can't spell them out in my mind's eye. They're muted, even, insistent, like my heartbeat in my ears.

More colors, flashes of light, pulsing with the drum, and then *POP!*

And silence, welling up all around me. No words, no drum, just a tiny hiss of water bubbling in the pores of the hot rocks, and an enveloping silence.

In the vacuum of sound, music, way down at the bottom of my hearing, another jam like "Sunset Road," slowly coming up with the turning of a giant volume knob. I reach for it, but can't turn it up any faster than it wants to come, and as it gets louder, there's a neon purple squiggle through it, a jazzy guitar line. It's an Allman Brothers thing: long, loose, plaintive lines, and the slow gathering of rhythm, a train rolling out of town. I can't switch tracks so I just let it feel good, this rambling boogie of a pace, good for an open stretch of road, or a long, loping run, like Eve out there somewhere, running up a forest trail to the same tune, maybe right past here, maybe all the way up the ridge to the redwoods.

The colors start exploding all around her, like fireworks gone wrong, setting the fields all around her on fire, and she's running faster, with tears streaming down her face lit up by the fire, trying to outrun it, and what if I can't catch her?

I try to shake away the image, force in a breath, reach out with my ears for any sound at all. But it is quiet as a tomb in here, the eternal quiet of the ocean after sunset from far away. Even the last hiss of the rocks is gone, only that faint orange glow, and the sound of my own heart, throbbing in my ears, drowning out everything.

*Don't be an idiot!*

Words, barely audible beneath the drumbeat of my heart, from way back in my head. The Presence?

The drumbeat slows, quiets.

*Don't blow this one!*

It doesn't sound like the Presence, or my own voice.

*How many more second chances do you think you'll get? Don't blow it! Just allow it. Because you are allowed.*

Then my own voice: *Allowed? To what?*

*To be loved.*

It's Leah's voice.

*Is that all? Is it really that sim —*

Before she can say anything, the drum again, *Pop-Pop-Pop!* and Charlie's voice, and Uncle Pete's.

More colors in front of my face, like fireworks again, but this time where they're supposed to be — high overhead.

I tilt my head to watch them fill the sky, and I can feel the tickle of grass all around me, laying back in that field and watching them with Leah two summers ago. They're lighting up her face, the headscarf, the splash of freckles across her nose and forehead and where her eyebrows used to be, flashing in her tired, lashless, blue-gray eyes.

But she's not blinking with each burst of fireworks this time. She's looking right back at me, right through me then, to me right now.

*It's OK, Jack.*

*But —*

*I died, Jack. Shit happens. Give yourself a break. And don't blow this one.*

Back at Angel's Rest, Eve and Uncle Pete have to leave soon if she wants to get back up to Humboldt in time to put Tommy to bed. And I need to get back over to the hospital.

But I can't seem to want to move, or do anything, or even talk. I'm still altered, well beyond words, long after we get back to pack her up for the drive north.

It doesn't seem to bother Eve one bit: she asks me something, and I just stare at her.

She gives me that half-smile and says, "It's OK," and goes about the rest of her packing.

This must be how everybody is after a sweat. And maybe she'd be *more* worried about me if I were my usual self, bouncing around trying to fix and arrange everything for their journey, talking routes, traffic, water, food.

Instead, I'm just sitting here watching her arrange her things and floating, empty and elated, my mind blank and body as peaceful — all the way down to the bottom of my stomach — as it's ever been. It's the same sweet, full-body wooze that would rush in the moment I'd get back to the trailhead after climbing a huge mountain and skiing off. The freedom of having nothing left to give, do, say, or prove.

The spell finally breaks when everything is loaded into her truck, including Uncle Pete, and I'm driving up to the gate to let them out. Suddenly alone in my van, I feel a strange, quiet yearning — for what? to go with them? — like I miss her already and she hasn't even left.

"I will see you soon?" she says, getting out at the gate to say goodbye.

"Of course."

"Good."

One more long, wet, luxurious kiss, and I'm watching her truck turn left up the PCH and disappear into the tunnel of wind-sculpted cypress to the north.

An hour later, I'm heading up the same road — off to the hospital for another night with my guitar and *Cadillac Desert* — when I run smack into the Sunday afternoon beach traffic heading back over the hill.

But it doesn't bother me because I'm still floating: from Eve; the party last night; the sweat lodge; her hands on my face when she pulled me in for the best goodbye kiss I've ever had and could ever imagine anyone ever having. I am *gone* on her.

But how to make sense of it? Where does all of this work? Because I am clear on one thing: I *will* make it work.

Sitting here stopped in traffic halfway up the hill, my thoughts run together across time, mixing and matching people, and how odd all of this has been, with all this extended *family* suddenly flooded through my carefully constructed sandcastle of a life, like the first big wave on an incoming tide.

Back in Dudeville, I once completely checked out on Jill for the dumbest reason of all. Her mother was a little weird, and she'd said something to me that was supposed to be funny but wasn't. I can't even remember what it was; but I took it the wrong way, made bigger than it was, used as an excuse to disappear one night. I tried to fix all that with Leah's parents a couple years later. They were warm, friendly, and welcoming — a little too much, a huge lift for me, but I hung in there. And now there isn't just Eve, but her huge extended family, way in my face, and a little boy too.

Eve first warned me, way back at *Úytaahkoo* when we surrounded by her aunts and uncles, "Indians don't go anywhere without relatives." And she wasn't kidding about that. She also told me, "most Native tribes were matrilineal, and so were we, so I hope you like my relatives, because you're stuck with them."

Maybe that's the trick to making it work: not having much of a choice not to. Because where has this great freedom of mine, this infinity of choice, gotten me all these years? Alone. Maybe the most profound choice of all is the choice just to sit with what you have, in the place and time where you were born, and worship its god, and leave the rest to the realm of fantasy, daydream, myth.

But I'm an American orphan; I'm not really from anywhere. What choice did I have but to chase fantasy, daydream, myth?

I came of age on the land of the Haudenosaunee and found the Presence out in their woods. But they were not my people, and everything else I knew growing up pointed west.

Or did it? Maybe everything really is just a circle?

The Haudenosaunee were matrilineal. I remember reading about that way back then in the school library and thinking: wouldn't that be great. My mother could kick my father out, and we'd both be free of him.

It was a fantasy that got me through most of sixth grade, now that I think about it.

A matrilineal society, with the women in charge, how interesting. Maybe organizing everything through the mother's clan is the origin of the whole goddess trip: the mermaid, the Amazons, the Hindu goddesses, Calafia. Maybe we were all supposed to be matrilineal from the start. But it was a primordial power men couldn't bear not having; and so that power was snuffed out; and now we are all dying for the divine feminine, for the spiritual thing erroneously entangled with sex that Amrita gives everyone.

Maybe that was the real source of my father's rage: at his mother for her immigrant's shame, self-denial, and flashes of rage; and at his wife for being so sick, for growing only sicker under his crazy, drunken rule, and for falling apart a little more every year . . .

Back over at the hospital, Amrita looks much better.

She has a smaller bandage around her neck, exposing a red and angry jawline. But the swelling is down, and her face is almost back to its normal shape — princess-thin, aquiline, feminine — and the rest of her color is coming back.

When I settle in to the other chair, I can tell that she has been trying to stay awake to keep Jenna company. But Jenna's harmonium is closed up and ready to go, and I can tell by the way she brightened up when I walked in that she's been itching to leave.

Jenna is gone five minutes later, and Amrita is still fighting off sleep — like she thinks she needs to keep me company now — with talk about all the great gigs coming up.

"It's OK," I say, over and over. "We'll sort all that out when you're on your feet."

"But Gordon," she mumbles, "he'll reschedule the events from this month. In between next month's . . ." She keeps repeating herself, and finally drifts off, mid-sentence.

I pull the blanket up over her, and settle into the big chair for the evening with my book, a bagful of trail food, and a canteen of coffee.

But my thoughts keep drifting off the page: to Eve's face, and all those colors in the sweat lodge; then Eve running through the redwoods, and everybody down in Neptune's kidding me about her; then Eve lying alongside me in bed yesterday morning . . .

I awaken from my sprawl in the chair to a knock on the door. Early light floods in the window and my book is sitting on the floor at my feet.

It can't be another nurse — they were coming and going all night without knocking — so I'm bolted awake.

Amrita is already awake, trying to sit up and blink away sleep.

There's another knock, a little louder this time, before I can get all the way over there.

"Hey Jack!"

A half-hushed, half-excited greeting through the crack in door, and a thrust of flowers, and it's Diane, the Acolady.

Uh-oh. Amrita does *not* want any of these people to see her.

"Hey," I half-whisper back, and stand in the gap in the doorway.

"Hey yourself," Diane says, loud enough to be heard into the room.

"Um," I'm not sure how to handle this. "What are you doing here?"

"Oh, Jack! Don't be silly. I'm doing the same thing *you* are," she announces past me into the room. "I'm here to take care of our amazing friend."

She looks like she wants to bulldoze right past me. But for all the forcefulness of her persona, I can see her take in over my shoulder what we've been dealing with for the past three days — the smell in the room, the quiet sadness hanging over all of it — along with the eye-of-the-shitstorm look I must be giving her, with Amrita ten feet away, probably hiding under the covers when she heard Diane's voice.

She moves up close to me and says under her breath. "Gordon called me last night and asked me to come. I just drove up from L.A."

"Just now?" I whisper. "All the way from L.A.?"

"Yes," she whispers. "I left as soon as I heard. Exactly like she did for me, when she heard I had breast cancer." Then, past me into the room, she says, "So where is that amazing woman?"

"Is that my soul-sister, Diane?" Amrita's calls out from behind me, full of sudden energy and forced cheer.

"Yes it is, honey!" Diane says and pushes past me.

And that's that. At least I can go get some coffee and breakfast.

When I wander back up to the room, Diane has pulled the chair over next to the bed and Amrita is awake and animated; and I feel like I've just stumbled into a private conversation. They've stopped talking, and are both staring at me.

"So," I say.

"So, Jack," Diane says. "Our friend here tells me you have been in here this whole time?"

"Well, not the whole time. Jenna has been here, and we did some *kirtan*."

"That's right," Amrita says. "It was beautiful. We chanted to Dhanvantari for healing, and the nurses came in, and sang along."

"That sounds so beautiful, honey. I wish I could have been here." Then she turns to me, her face suddenly hard, and says "but it sounds like you were under heavy guard."

"I know," Amrita says, and gathers Diane's hands in her own. "It's been so scary and hard. But you're here now."

"I am," Diane says to her, then turns to stare at me again. "And I will be staying until they let you out of here." Then her face softens, just around the edges, the first time I've ever seen it do that, and she says, "Jack and Jenna are good friends, honey, and they've done enough. Now it's my turn."

"Wasn't just me," I say. "Ike was in here helping out too."

"Oh, that's right, Diane," Amrita says to her. "Jack's friend Ike. He is *such* a nice man. He was once a famous surfer, you know. And," she teases Diane, "I think he's single. Right, Jack?"

"He is in fact single," I say, and try to turn it into a joke. "But after spending the night in here with you, I was thinking, you know — maybe you two?"

"Oh Jack, please," Amrita waves me off. "He's a very sweet man. But he's much too old for me!"

## 10 | FATHERS & SONS

I never had kids, never wanted them, so I have no idea how to do this whole Dad-at-the-beach thing. And yet, here we are, and all I can think is *SNEAKER WAVE!*

The rest is weird, if only because it doesn't feel weird at all. But Tommy is an exceptional kid: thoughtful, sensitive, kind of a little adult. Maybe because he has half a dozen people looking after him, not just Eve? He takes everything in, and remembers everything — like Eve, I would imagine, at that age.

I watch him play in the sand, squat down and just start digging, and it makes me smile. Then . . .

*SNEAKER WAVE!*

My mind's eye sees the ocean rushing in to grab him, sweep him away, and do I yell for Eve and her sister, way down the beach now? Or just go straight in after him?

I shouldn't be so keyed up about it, but this is my first time on this beach. Never seen that break, never hiked those cliffs. This is their beach, way up north in Humboldt — my turn for the big weekend drive — and it is big and wild.

It just reopened after last winter's storms blew the creek out to sea, which was a river of mud and trees by the time it got down here. The cliffs have been stripped of everything green and brown, leaving the hillsides a raw, gleaming gold in the last of the sun.

There are only two surfers out there: 13- or maybe 14-year-old girls, fighting hard for overheads, making half or more.

Eve and her cousin are walking the other way, flip-flops in hand, heads bowed in what looks like a serious conversation, slowly shrinking into flecks of color below the cliffs.

I sit back on this long black rock, smoothed by a million waves with the tide out, breaching from the wet sand like the top of a whale, and watch Tommy play, and study the incoming sets even more intently that if I were paddling out there myself.

Nope, no sneaker waves today. Not that kind of day. Not that this place isn't capable of it: whatever storms at king tide tore off half that cliffside over there was that kind of day times three.

But *SNEAKER WAVE!* is the first thing you learn — or should learn — when you hike down to a beach like this. Along with *NEVER turn your back on the ocean.* (It's the *ROCK!* you learn your first day out rock climbing, and the *AVALANCHE!* the first time you cross into backcountry snow.)

I watch Tommy move down the beach, where the sand flows into a swirl of tumbled cobbles, gray, white, black, brown, some as big as softballs and round as eggs.

He's not going to turn his back, is he?

No.

Whew.

I have no idea how to be a father. But does anybody? Aaron and Danny seem to have figured it out, but I have a good excuse compared to them: I have no idea how to be a son either, because I never really was one.

Though I did go act like one, sort of, finally. Not that I thought it would change any of that, but I did go back.

At first I thought it was because Eve was testing me about that too. "Never been to your parents' graves? Really?"

But that's not why I went.

I went all the way back to western Massachusetts last week because — well — it was finally time. Amrita's event at Kripalu, originally timed by Divine Intervention to put me 45 minutes away from my father's grave, was canceled by a Divine Surgical Complication. And the actual momentum for getting on the airplane may have been a point of pride: I didn't want Eve to think I was afraid to.

I know now — on the other end of the journey — that she was testing me for all the right reasons. "Never been to your parents' graves?"

I didn't know how to tell Eve that it was only because of the persistence of my sister to stay in touch, despite my active resistance since moving west, that I even knew where those graves were. She'd called me last year to let me know that he'd dropped dead from a heart attack, just in case I wanted to go to the funeral, at some churchyard back in North Adams.

"North Adams," was all I had for my sister after a year or two of no contact. "Huh."

After cursing the place for as long I can remember, and making it all of 200 miles west in 70 years, our father had ended up back in "Goddamn North Adams."

"That's right," she said. "Goddamn North Adams. Found himself another old, dying drunk. A real bitch on wheels. You don't want to know what it was like dealing with her."

"Sorry about that."

"Don't be sorry," she said. "You made your choice. I made mine."

North Adams was a sooty, hollowed out New England mill town when I'd last seen it, back in the '80s. My ex-wife and I had gone up that way for her best friend's wedding, and I'd always been curious about the place where my father grew up and his father still lived, the grandfather I never met because they hated each other that much.

The North Adams I revisited last week has been fully re-made. It's now buzzing with art galleries and fancy food, with a smidge of Dudeville at one end, thanks to the whitewater running through town. It's also just 45 minutes of postcard-pretty rolling farm country and white steeple towns away from Kripalu, the big yoga retreat center where Amrita does a major event every year.

Except this year, of course, because she was in the hospital.

But I went anyway, because I had no decent answer for Eve's perplexity and dismay. *Never been to my own parents' graves? What the hell is wrong with me?*

I hear a wave crash and look up to see Tommy dragging a big piece of driftwood onto the mound of cobbles and other two pieces he's dragged over there, framing some kind of shelter.

Such a kid thing to do, I suppose. Like the shelters I built in the woods when I was his age, and something I'm sure I would have done if I'd been anywhere near a beach as a kid.

I look out at the ocean, the tide most of the way out, quiet but not brooding, just lulling. Even its colors are muted: slate, jade, shadow. And Tommy's mound of cobbles is way past the tide line, so he'll be OK even as he turns his back to the ocean.

I sit back on my elbows on the rock, one eye on Tommy and the other looking up at that dancing Shiva, two feet taller than me, bathed in orange and purple light on the altar at Kripalu.

That vast, silent, empty room — like that whole campus of churchy, brick and white stone buildings, looking out over a great green grassy bowl and lake and mountains beyond — turned out to be the best and worst place for last week's strange journey backwards, a soft landing after a long, hard, screeching halt.

It was a mad rush getting there: the cross-country flight out of San Francisco, the rental car through Boston traffic. I wasn't really thinking through what I was doing; I was just traveling, like to any other faraway Amrita gig with my suitcase and guitar. Except there'd be no band or crowd waiting when I got there. No one at all. Just me. And all that quiet and empty space, and the dancing Shiva, and the ghosts of Goddamn North Adams.

It came crashing down on me after checking in and going into the big empty room — the "Great Hall" they call it — where we were going to have the event: a soaring, cathedral-like space in the center of the main building. It was carpeted from end-to-end for yoga and dance and meditation, and bathed in half light from tall skinny stained glass windows to a ceiling so high it may as well have been the sky.

I was sitting by myself on the floor with my guitar, in a space big enough for a couple hundred people spread out on yoga mats, Shiva dancing up on the altar. And then that impossible thing again, in the overtones of my guitar. I hadn't heard them since all the way back in Utah, in those days without light or end after Leah died, and all I could do was play, sleep, and play some more: the hum of faraway voices, deep down in the box of my guitar, still there when I'd stop, fading slowly to black. They were there in the Great Hall at Kripalu, in the long sustain of the last few notes, rising from the sound hole of my guitar, up to that ceiling like wisps of smoke.

What were they? The rational part of me knew they were just sound waves; but the other part of me knew they weren't always there when I played the exact same things, so why now? And why there? Were they echoes of all the chanting, praying, dancing and singing that had gone on in that enormous space over the decades? From events like Amrita's, and those held by a hundred other yoga gurus, *kirtan* musicians, teachers, scholars, mystics? From the hundreds of Jesuit monks who lived, worked and prayed in that same building and room in the decades before it became an ashram? From all the way back to the Mahicans in the 1700s?

"I looked it up," Eve had told me on the phone the night before I left. "They were the Mahicans, the real name for the Mohicans, but they were driven out very early, in the 1780s."

But it wasn't a chant I heard, and it wasn't in Mahican, or Latin, or Sanskrit. It was that same old voice, in English.

*You don't really need to go, not if you don't want to. You are safe and fine right here.*

*Safe?* I stopped playing and almost laughed out loud. *Of course I'm safe!*

But that was it. Not another word.

And it wasn't Leah's voice, like in the sweat lodge last month. It was the voice from all the way back — the still, small voice of the Presence — the one that would rise from the center of my chest to the crown of my head when I was climbing a big mountain, or working my way down to the bottom of the canyon, or standing next to the ocean on an empty beach.

No, I thought; I don't have to go at all. But I wanted to — even if thinking about it did make my gut tighten — if only so I'd never have to wonder about it again, never have to answer that sharp, serrated question about my parents' graves in a way that begged all the other questions I don't want to answer.

I laid back on the floor of the Great Hall, and looked up into the shadows of where the ceiling must have been. The voice of the Presence was gone, but not the echoes of all those other voices, the footfalls of all those dancers, the oceanic breathing of all the yogis and yoginis who'd sat where I was sitting, diving to the depths of their consciousness, all consciousness. And I don't think I've ever felt less alone than I did in that exact moment. *You are safe and fine right here.*

Or maybe it had nothing to do with any of that. Maybe it was knowing that Eve and Tommy were safe and fine, way out west, on the other end of the continent.

"Perhaps landscape is your actual religion, Jack, like it is mine," Eve told me, way back in our first phone call.

So maybe it was that: the landscape, the very ground beneath Kripalu that had drawn the Mahicans there, and then the monks, and then the ashram people. Those Jesuit monks had found ready access to their god right there in the Stockbridge Bowl — in that same enormous sweep of meadow down to the lake and the mountains beyond — because so too had the Mahicans.

But the monks' religion had come from far away. And so, on that sacred ground, ringed by those ancient, rounded New England hills, they built right over the top of it, with a soaring room to resemble a cathedral from somewhere else. Then came the ashram people, who pulled out the pews, carpeted it over, and replaced the cross with a dancing Shiva.

The Mahicans may have been kicked out centuries ago, but they exacted some kind of belated karmic revenge when the old ashram went the way of so many Americanized Vedic movements. The followers fell for a charismatic guru, who came along in the wave of grief when Swami Kripalu died, and who preached celibacy while bedding half the place, nearly destroying Kripalu in the process. But he'd been banished to Florida, I heard murmured in the dining hall.

And now, as far as I could tell, Kripalu isn't beholden to any guru, even as hundreds of them pass through, like Amrita, for an *à la carte* weekend workshop. It is beholden only to space and place and the echoes of all those prayers and songs — to all those voices rising from the sound hole of my guitar. That great empty hall was centered over what would emerge through time as a great collective heart: a heart that felt, last week, like it was still beating through the floor of the Great Hall and into my own; a heart kept beating by people who will always seek refuge from crowded cities and unholy ground to meditate, pray, practice yoga, dance, sing, draw, write, play music, and — I found out that first morning — grieve.

I poked around and looked in half a dozen classrooms and studios, all full of people in workshops, yoga teachers in training, a small group doing something with paints and paper, and the largest, a group of a hundred or so older-looking people in a room labeled *Grief is a Tunnel: Meditations on Moving through Loss.*

After two days of wandering the place and its grounds, a dozen hours on my guitar in the Great Hall, and lots of yoga and sleep, I was ready for the cemetery in Goddamn North Adams.

I'd brought a couple prayers to read — one from the *siddur* we used at *Shir Hadash*, and one Eve gave me — and a small rock to place on the headstone. I'd brought my old tallit, my Jewish prayer shawl, if I felt the need to say Mourner's *Kaddish, minyan* or no, which is what a normal son would do. I also brought a bottle of his favorite cheap whiskey, because that's what the angry son does at the grave of a drunken father, in a movie anyway, pouring it out in a showy flourish of bitter triumph or infinite sadness.

Which is better than what I could have done, what I'd fantasized about doing for years: gone back to his fresh-cut grave and taken a piss on it. To hell with his favorite whiskey. He'd tried for decades, but only in death was he finally sober, and who was I to screw that up? Just a cold beer for me, and maybe some weed; and when I was done, I'd stand over that fresh swath of green grass, and take a good, long steaming piss.

But no. My oldest friend, my childhood rage, didn't show up for the graveside service. Just me, my tallit, that stupid bottle of whiskey, and a shrinking emptiness where my old rage used to live.

When I got there and finally found his grave — way over in a section with no monuments and not many stones — I couldn't do any of it. Not *Kaddish*, or the readings, or the whiskey. I just stood there, staring at his name chiseled by itself into that cold new stone, and felt — nothing. I even made myself sit cross-legged on the ground next to that rectangle of newly sunken grass, closing my eyes, trying to remember or feel something, anything. But nothing came. Just blankness.

It was the exact opposite of what was percolating up through the ground over at Kripalu; and all I wanted to do was hurry back there, and sit out front in the meadow, watching people wandering around inside themselves, play my guitar in the Great Hall, and feel something again. Which made me wonder, as I sat there —

feeling more and more nothing and fidgeting to leave — if the land itself wasn't punishing my father with its horrible silence, the way he punished himself his whole life with cheap whiskey and sour grapes for everyone and everything.

Was my father, in his mean, carping, drunken bitterness, just an extreme version of the worst impulses of a whole nation of people who would see a place like the Stockbridge Bowl — and the first thing they'd do would be to drive out, at gunpoint, the people who were living there? And was this raging emptiness and frustration in someone like my father just one tiny, unseen, unsung expression of why there is so much violence and hatred and stupidity in America? Is it why so many people want to punish complete strangers, like the redneck waving his gun around in Radhe's face, for all they don't have, all they think they're entitled to, all they think would make them happy, if only "they" hadn't taken it from them, when it was never theirs in the first place?

The Mahicans learned that lesson centuries ago: people will steal it, or shoot you for it, and turn around and make it your fault. Radhe learned that same exact lesson last year in San Jose: they will threaten to shoot you for something as stupid as a parking space. My father, I realized as I sat next to his grave, could have been that guy . . .

CAW!!!

A gull screams by my head

SNEAKER WAVE COMING???

I look past Tommy at the ocean. Nothing coming at all, just those two girls out there working the point.

He's dragged two more long chunks of driftwood onto the mound of cobbles, and has assembled a good little structure.

The tide is well out from him now, the waves organizing as far out as the point.

I stand and stretch, and look down the long end of the beach.

Eve and her cousin are walking back this way, no longer in some heavy talk, just walking along looking out at the ocean. Eve catches me looking at them and waves.

I wave back and sit down on the rock and go back to watching Tommy. He's trying to square up the driftwood, and I cannot help but smile: I would be doing the exact same thing if I were his age. Always trying to build something out in those woods: a fort, a lean-to, a treehouse, an igloo. No wonder I ended up in engineering when I made it to school.

How lucky for Tommy that he has this beach and all this ready driftwood. At his age, I was still ten years from my first glimpse of the ocean. And not only was

I *not* surrounded by aunts and uncles and cousins, but I never did meet that grandfather in North Adams.

I nearly did, and was reminded of that just last week, on the drive back from the cemetery. It was the first little town south of North Adams, on my way back to Kripalu. I was a little spooked — not by the cemetery but by the emptiness it elicited inside me — and was pushing it to get back: to my guitar, a good meal, maybe a good long cry in the Great Hall, the one I couldn't find anywhere near that grave.

It was one of those towns so perfectly quaint — all white clapboard and black shutters, with the old stone church and white steeple, the statue in the town square and the little babbling brook — that it looked too perfectly New England even for Hollywood's version of New England.

But when the road crossed a little creek at the other end of town, I noticed a red clapboard building with brown shutters, a tavern, with an empty parking lot next to it, and remembered all of it in a rush: the terrifying hour my sister and I spent in the family station wagon in that parking lot.

I was halfway up the hill when the whole of it hit me, so I turned around, went back and parked next to that old tavern, and remembered the whole thing.

We had driven all the way back to Goddamn North Adams that day with just our father — our mother was too sick to travel in those days — for some reason he never explained. We thought we might be meeting our grandfather for the first time. But, to our great disappointment, even for childhoods defined by nothing but disappointments, we never did. We waited in the car outside our grandfather's house, eyes fixed on that grubby little door, more mud streaks than weathered white paint, for what felt like an hour — I was about Tommy's age then, and as full of energy — so it was probably only a few minutes.

When the door finally flew open, my father came storming out and slammed it behind him, and got in the car.

We knew not to say a word.

Five minutes later, we pulled into that tavern with the red clapboard. He barked at us to stay in the car in that parking lot or else. And we did, terrified to get out for fear that he'd come out right when we stepped out of the car to play, knowing that whatever slapping around we'd be getting later would be that much worse because he'd have a reason to give it.

What felt like an hour passed, then part of another hour, and my sister fell asleep and I braced for the worst.

But the worst did not come. He was as drunk as I expected when he came out and got behind the wheel — nothing new there — but he didn't yell, or hit either of us. He just hunkered down over the wheel.

My sister woke up, forgot what was going on, and started crying, and that's when he finally started yelling. When she wouldn't stop, he pulled the car over, and I braced for it again — the slap or punch that would land wherever it happened to land in the back seat — but then, nothing.

He turned and looked at my sister, then at me, then hunched back over the wheel and burst into tears.

It was shocking: I'd seen him crying and howling with self-pity when he was drunk or hungover and my mother was screaming at him. But that one day, by the side of the same road I was on just last week, he just sat there, as sad and helpless as I'd ever seen him, clutching the steering wheel and sobbing.

"Are you OK?"

I look up and see Eve and her cousin standing over me.

"Sure," I say, sniffing in hard, and wondering what jumble of sadness and pain she must have seen written all over me. "Just another day at the beach."

"If you say so," she says, studying my face. She looks past me, up toward the road.

"No sign of Uncle Pete yet?" her cousin asks.

"No," Eve says. "Not yet."

"Uncle Pete's coming?"

Eve points to her phone and shrugs, *Yes, more relatives coming.*

"My daughter changed her mind," Eve's cousin says. "She wants to go to the beach now. Kids."

*Yes*, I think. *Kids.*

Then, suddenly, this strange thought: *I should call my sister. I will call my sister. Tonight.*

I watch Eve and her cousin pull blankets from the big canvas bag we brought, and spread them out on the sand next to my rock. Food, water, books.

They get settled in on the blanket, Eve with her book, her cousin with her phone.

I can't decide if I want to join them on the sand, or go play with Tommy, or take a good long walk myself the other way.

Eve looks up at me from the blanket, studying my face and asking again with her eyes, *Are you OK?*

"Just been thinking about the trip last week," I say.

"Oh. Of course." She glances at her sister, who is engrossed in her phone. "Do you want to talk about it?"

"Not really. Not right now."

"Alright," she says. "Let me know if you do."

She goes back to her book, and I go back to the ocean.

She *was* testing me, as it turns out, and she was exactly right. I had to figure all that out — or at least figure out that it was something I'm never going to figure out, that it was something I'm just going to have to live with for the rest of my life, the way people eventually learn to live with a missing limb.

"Hey! Jack!"

I look over and Tommy is coming back.

"The tide is out now, like you said! We can walk the other way!"

Eve looks up from her book, glances at me, *You OK going with him?*

"Yeah, let's check it out," I call back to him and pull myself to my feet.

Eve gives me that sweet half-smile, and all the sadness and sorrow that had been gathering and tightening in my chest runs down through me and out the bottom of my bare feet into the sand.

Tommy and I walk across the wide glassy sheen of sand left behind by the outgoing tide.

I chuckle to myself when I see that look of Eve's again: *yes*, I could have said to her, *I'd better be OK going with Tommy.* Because I know there will be a lot of that when I move up here next month.

A little beige apartment in a little beige building in town, three minutes from them — the thing I always feared — and now can't move into fast enough.

Sure, I'd be right there toughing it out with Brooke and Ike: squatting until the bitter end, going NIMBY-nuclear at permit hearings, rooting for the white-hat lawyers as they root around in the bowels of three bureaucracies for regulatory *obscuranta* to torment the black-hat lawyers.

But no; it's time to go. Which is so much better than saying *it's time to leave.* Because you hate this town. Or your friends have all left. Or your girlfriend just died.

Because I was always leaving for someplace west, I always thought the California coast was the end of the trail, and not just for me but for everyone. It *was* the sunset road, the long goodbye kiss at the end of the movie, the golden gate to God-knows-where. And for me, Angel's Rest would be the perfect last stop.

But now, there is them. Not just her, but *them.* Who knew?

Johnny, maybe. He didn't sell all those copies of "Sunset Road" because it was just another silly hippie/country fantasy. People bought them because it was a fantasy at the edge of their own town, not the edge of the continent; and they could cast themselves and whoever they wanted — for a night, for the summer, for the rest of their lives — at the end of that road. And it was a fantasy that might actually come true: some day, you might just find somebody, and it might just be that simple and sweet.

So while this whole stinking mess of a country goes south, I think I'll just follow the trees and go north, and be with them, all of them.

Tommy sprints ahead, across the last of the wet sand, over toward the rocky outcropping where the waves bend around the point. Then he turns to wait on me, his back to the coean.

I hear *SNEAKER WAVE!* and jog over to catch up with him.

We walk along the water's edge and watch the two surfers out there coming off the point. They've worked their way up here with the tide out, catching quick rights off an emerging seastack, looking ragged and about done.

Tommy bounces up onto the smooth flat rock where the point hits the beach.

I climb up next to him, and as we stand there side by side, I feel his little hand finding mine.

His eyes are fixed on the surfers, as big as I've seen them yet, his mouth hanging open.

One surfer catches a last wave and rides it in, straight toward us. She has flaming red hair and freckles, and can't be more than 14 years old.

"Hey," I call over to her. "Nice work."

"Thanks!" she says, flashing a huge smile full of braces.

She gathers her board and leash, and heads in.

Tommy lets go of my hand as she walks by.

He waits until she is halfway up the beach before jumping off the rock, into a little tide pool lit up with the colors of living creatures and tumbling stones. The remnants of waves push in and out, water moving through the rock like breath.

Tommy scrabbles along the foamy edge of the little pool, bending down for something.

He stands and shows me a rock in little hand, streaked with red and gray and round as a planet, then turns to look out at the ocean.

"You gonna throw it?"

He looks down at it. "Not this one. This one's for you," he says, and hands me the stone.

# REFERENCES & INSPIRATION

## MYTHOLOGY

*The Bible: The Book of Jonah, for the character of Johnny*

*Greek Mythology: Daedalus & Icarus, for the character of Ike*

*Norse Mythology: Brokr, the Blacksmith Dwarf, for the character of Brooke*

*Hindu Goddesses: Visions of the Divine Feminine in the Hindu Religious Tradition,* David Kinsley

*Surviving through the Days: A California Indian Reader; Translations of Native California Stories and Songs,* Herbert Luthin, editor

*The Origin and the Meaning of the Name California: Calafia the Queen of the Island of California,* George Davidson

## NON-FICTION — NATIVE AMERICA

*An Indigenous People's History of the United States,* Roxanne Dunbar-Ortiz

*The Indians of the Berkshires and the Hudson River Valley,* David C King

*The Heartbeat of Wounded Knee: Native America from 1890 to the Present,* David Treuer

*Recovering the Sacred: The Power of Naming and Claiming,* Wynonna LaDuke

*Braiding Sweetgrass,* Robin Wall Kimmerer

## NON-FICTION — NATIVE CALIFORNIA

*An Island Called Calfornia: An Ecological Introduction to Its Natural Communities,* Elna Bakker

*The Ohlone Way: Indian Life in the San Francisco-Monterey Bay Area,* Malcolm Margolin

*Indian Tales,* Jaime de Angulo

*An American Genocide: The United States and the California Indian Catastrophe,* Benjamin Madley

## NON-FICTION — COLONIZED CALIFORNIA

*Tracks Along the Left Coast: Jaime de Angulo & Pacific Coast Culture*, Andrew Schelling

*Cadillac Desert*, Marc Reisner

*The Bakersfield Sound: How a Generation of Displaced Okies Revolutionized American Music*, Robert E. Price

*Ecology of Fear: Los Angeles and the Imagination of Disaster*, Gary Davis

*The Edge: The Pressured Past and Precarious Future of California's Coast*, Kim Steinhardt and Gary Griggs

## FICTION

*The Adventures of Huckleberry Finn*, Mark Twain

*The Grapes of Wrath*, John Steinbeck

*East of Eden*, John Steinbeck

*Big Sur*, Jack Kerouac

*Tapping the Source*, Ken Nunn

## POETRY

*Selected Poetry*, Robinson Jeffers

## MEMOIR

*The Mountains of California*, John Muir

*The Jew and the Lotus*, Rodger Kamenetz

*Caught Inside: A Surfer's Year on the California Coast*, Daniel Duane

*All Our Waves Are Water: Stumbling Toward Enlightenment and the Perfect Ride*, Jaimal Yogis

## FILM

*Momentum Generation*, a documentary directed by Jeff and Michael Zimbalist

*Laurel Canyon*, the documentary, directed by Allison Elwood

*Laurel Canyon*, the feature, directed by Lisa Cholodenko

# ACKNOWLEDGMENTS

*That Golden Shore* was informed and inspired by everyone I've made music with over the years, from the punks in Pittsburgh in the '80s and bluegrass crew in Maryland in the '90s, to the heavenly choir at the Bhaktishop, Monday night jam at the long lost Caldera Public House, and the railriders at the Laurelthirst in Portland.

Special shout-outs for teaching and inspiration, listed in order of appearance, to Sam Matthews, Craig Havighurst, Archie Warnock, Kathy Kallick, Annie Robertson, Rabbi Aryeh Hirschfield of blessed memory, Rabbi Ariel Stone, Melanie Hall, Fred Coates, the late, great Jimmy Boyer, Lewi Longmire, Paul Baczuk, Tasha Danner, Diana Hulet, Alicia Jo Rabins, Camilla Lombard, Rabbi Benjamin Barnett, and Michelle Alany.

Heartfelt thanks for close reads and unvarnished feedback from my dear friends Benjamin Barnett, Karen Blauer, Rob Bodner, Steve Cohen, Tasha Danner, Joe Howton, Gabrielle Glaser, Kathy Goodman, Diana Hulet, Sarah Krakauer, Claire Levine, Camilla Lombard, Sarah Loughran, Jon Norling, George Pillari, Julie Poust, Khris Tabaknek, Larry Ullman, and Erica Zelfand. And extra special thanks to Matt Snook for a second time through, and going easy on me with the astronomy lesson.

Thanks to the great team at Bayamet Books, and to Heidi Roux for the perfect cover and crisp interior design.

And finally, the last word goes to my beloved wife and best friend, Sara. She sifted through multiple drafts, sat patiently through countless rants, and endured much of the pandemic with a husband in zombie-author mode. Her incisive mind, soaring heart, and sweet grace inspired and sustained this book from conception to completion, as they do me, every day.

# ABOUT THE AUTHOR

J.D. Kleinke wrote *That Golden Shore* while living, surfing, teaching yoga, and playing music in Half Moon Bay and Encinitas, California. *That Golden Shore* is the sequel to *Dudeville*, J.D.'s coming-of-middle-age adventure story about a late-30s corporate dropout turned backcountry snowboarder and mountaineer.

J.D. is also the author of *Catching Babies*, a medical novel currently in development as a television series, as well as *Bleeding Edge* and *Oxymorons*, two works of non-fiction about the American health care system. His work has appeared in *The New York Times*, *The Wall Street Journal*, *Freeskier*, *The Surfer's Journal*, *The Inertia*, and numerous other publications.

He currently lives with his wife in Portland, Oregon.

CPSIA information can be obtained
at www.ICGtesting.com
Printed in the USA
JSHW020506210521
14956JS00004B/19